MIDSUMMER ROSE

Catherine Lyndell

POCKET BOOKS

New York   London   Toronto   Sydney   Tokyo   Singapore

This book is a work of fiction. Names, characters, places, and incidents are either products of the author's imagination or are used fictitiously. Any resemblance to actual events or locales or persons, living or dead, is entirely coincidental.

An *Original* Publication of POCKET BOOKS

POCKET BOOKS, a division of Simon & Schuster Inc.
1230 Avenue of the Americas, New York, NY 10020

ISBN: 1-4165-0698-5

This Pocket Books paperback printing September 2004

10 9 8 7 6 5 4 3 2 1

POCKET and colophon are registered trademarks
of Simon & Schuster Inc.

Cover art by Ken Otsuka

Printed in the U.S.A.

A MIDSUMMER NIGHT

"Don't worry. I understand perfectly." Cressida slipped her fingers out of Robert's hand and walked quickly ahead of him down the lane. Just a few more steps and they would see the gates of Hayvenhurst Hall before them. Just a few more steps and this whole mistake of an evening would be over.

"Just *what* do you understand?" Robert demanded, catching up with her.

She would not look at him.

"Oh . . . that tonight is best forgotten. That tomorrow you'll be wanting to dance attendance on Mrs. Whitworth again, and that it would be embarrassing to you to be reminded that you spent a summer's night dancing with her maid. *That's* what I understand."

"*Do* you, by God!" Robert's curse was all of this earth, and so were the strong hands that closed on her shoulders to swing her around until, startled, her magical mood of resignation broken, she looked up into the real and living, furiously angry face she loved best in all the world. . . .

Praise for Catherine Lyndell's *Stolen Dreams*

Books by Catherine Lyndell

Ariane
Border Fires
Journey to Desire
Midsummer Rose
Stolen Dreams
Tapestry of Pride

Published by POCKET BOOKS

MIDSUMMER ROSE

Chapter

1

Cressida was running down the back stairs with an arm-load of stained and crumpled sheets when she heard her father calling from the hall. His voice boomed up the wide front stairs and echoed off empty walls where paintings had once hung, coming to her as a cracked, irritable call. "Cressida! Blast you, girl. Where the devil are you now?"

Cressida dropped the sheets into an empty washtub in the scullery and darted through the kitchen. She paused momentarily at the sight of Betty leaning over a steaming basin of hot water and soda, scrubbing away at something with a vigor that made her gray topknot vibrate and her spectacles shake on her thin nose.

"What—*more* washing up?" Cressida asked. "I thought I'd cleared away all the dinner things last night." And it hadn't been an easy task. She'd been up until past midnight with her hands red from the soda in the washing water— but she'd been determined that old Betty shouldn't find the mess the gentlemen had left behind waiting to greet her this morning.

"They had the best wineglasses out in the library," Betty informed her. "Your mother's crystal. And not for port,

1

which at least is a gentleman's drink, but some of that nasty foreign stuff. Sinthy or whatever they calls it."

"Absinthe," Cressida said bemusedly. "Oh, dear, Papa *promised*. . . . It made poor George Fotheringhay-Shaw blind, you know. Can there be a worse drink for an artist to indulge in? I can't think why they *will* do it."

"Mad, blind, weak of mind, the lot of 'em," Betty said. "Not to mention as how it leaves nasty greenish stains on the carpet, which I've got the wet tea leaves on right now, Miss Cressy, an' we'll have to hope for the best—*and* they'd left two of the glasses in the fireplace. When I found 'em there was ashes caked dry on the rims."

"At least they didn't throw them into the fireplace, like the last group." Cressida grinned and won a slight answering twitch from Betty's tight-pressed lips. "Look, Betty, just leave the glasses to soak—I'll do them later."

"That you will not," Betty said. "Ruin your pretty 'ands, you would."

Cressida laughed ruefully and buried her reddened, cracked fingers in the folds of her skirt before Betty could see and lecture her about a Young Lady's Rightful Position. They both knew that Cressida could not act the young lady of leisure and keep Riversedge in any kind of order with only Betty left out of all the servants they'd once kept; but if Cressida said so, Betty would take it as a slur on her abilities and would work herself into another fit of rheumatism to keep Cressida out of the kitchen and the scullery and the laundry.

"*Cress-i-daaaa!*" The howl echoed through the stone-floored kitchen.

"Goodness, he *is* angry. I'd better run," Cressida gasped, and she picked up her skirts and bolted through the green baize door that separated the servants' quarters from the rest of the house. The old hall carpet was more of a hazard than a help to her running feet; she swerved around the two worst torn spots with the ease of long practice. What tripped her up was the new hole where Trevor Bayne-Fleetworth had put his cigar out two nights earlier. She fell forward, putting out her arms to stop herself, and fell right against Trevor Bayne-Fleetworth in person. He was still in evening dress; the starched white shirtfront he'd worn for dinner the night before smelled of sweat and cigar smoke now.

"My, my, such enthusiasm!" Strong hands gripped Cressida's arms and set her upright while she was still rubbing her nose where it had come into contact with Bayne-Fleetworth's hard chest. "Don't be in such a desperate hurry, sweetheart. I'm not that hard to get." He dipped his head and brushed full pink lips across hers before Cressida guessed his intention.

"Don't," she protested vainly.

"When you threw yourself into my arms? I'd be no gentleman were I to resist such a fetching lure, sweet Cressy." Bayne-Fleetworth bent to kiss her again, more leisurely this time, and Cressida turned her head away. He nibbled the tip of one ear gently. "Of course," he breathed, "now that we mention it, I'm not a gentleman. Not when a lady wishes it otherwise. . . ."

Cressida stamped the heel of her serviceable, much-mended boot down on Trevor Bayne-Fleetworth's elegant instep. He fell back with a howl of pain and released her.

"What's the matter with you?" he called after Cressida's back as she marched on down the hall at a more sober pace. "Damn it, girl, I wasn't expecting such airs from Isolde Parris's little sister! You ought to lighten up and enjoy life like your sister!"

And that, if Cressida had needed it, was all the impetus she needed to present her plan to Papa.

Augustine Parris had gone beyond anger to plaintive despair by the time she reached him at the foot of the front staircase. "Ah, finally you arrive, Cressida *mía,* and too late by half! Where *were* you? I looked everywhere."

Cressida reflected briefly that Augustine Parris's "everywhere" evidently did not embrace the servants' stairs, the scullery, or the kitchen.

"I thought you would want to say good-bye to our guests," Augustine went on. "But Aubrey and Witherspoon had to leave, and there's only young Trevor left."

"I shall be only too happy to say good-bye to Mr. Bayne-Fleetwood," Cressida said crisply. She nodded to Trevor, who was limping down the long dark hall toward them with a nasty smile on his face. At least, she thought, he wouldn't try to kiss her now—not when her father was standing right beside her.

He did worse; he took her hand and nibbled up and down from knuckles to elbow with his full, wet mouth, in a parody of polite leave-taking that made Cressida feel physically ill. It was all she could do to keep from jerking her hand away and slapping him. But her father was standing there, smiling benignly, and if she took offense at Trevor's behavior he would be annoyed with her. She didn't know quite why, but he'd reacted that way before.

Finally Trevor released her hand. Cressida resisted the urge to wipe it on her apron. "My most sincere thanks for a delightful weekend, Parris," Trevor said to her father. "We'll be seeing you in town again soon, I trust?"

"Oh, aye, directly, directly," her father agreed. "Would take this train up, in fact, but I've a few chores to see to here first. The cares of a country estate, my friend. . . ." He sighed gustily. "You young men are lucky, able to devote yourselves entirely to your art. As a family man with responsibilities, I envy you sometimes."

Trevor Bayne-Fleetworth's entire artistic production, to Cressida's knowledge, consisted of two pen-and-ink drawings that he claimed had been highly praised by Aubrey Beardsley. Cressida also knew what Beardsley had actually said: "Bayne-Fleetworth lacks some of my eye for line and proportion, but I envy his gift for unblushing obscenity."

On the other hand, Cressida's father had not even produced two drawings in the last five years. So perhaps he had a point about the difficulties of combining art with family life.

"As a—er—family man with responsibilities, you really ought to bring this little country flower up to London with you, Parris." Trevor smiled at Cressida; she might have thought the smile was genuine if she hadn't been warned by the evil light in his eyes. "She deserves a chance to

4

acquire the—er—polish and sophistication and other charms so delightfully *displayed* by her sister.''

"You will miss your train, Mr. Bayne-Fleetworth," Cressida said when at last it became evident that Papa was not going to hit him for this comment.

"Ah, yes. My train." Trevor sighed and shrugged massive shoulders. "Such a wearisome distance to the station. I can't think why you do not keep a dog cart at least, Parris. I grow quite faint thinking of the effort before me."

The train station, like everything else in the village, was just three minutes from the front door of Riversedge. Cressida raised one dark brow fractionally and waited, trying to conceal her impatience at Trevor's blathering. She could not keep from tapping her foot as the train whistle sounded in the distance. Did the man mean to miss his train on purpose and inflict himself on them another night?

"And just how badly," Trevor inquired, "do you want me to catch the train? I don't suppose you'd care to carry this bag for me, pretty Cressy?" Trevor smiled down at her, brown eyes wrinkling in his bronzed face, as certain of his charm as if she hadn't just that minute rebuffed him. "We could say another—and sweeter—farewell at the station."

"If you miss your train, we'll be happy to put you up for another night," Cressida told him, "but I feel I should warn you that there's nothing in the house but cold shepherd's pie for dinner, and as I've just this minute stripped the last clean sheets off the beds and dropped them in the wash, you'll have to lie on a bare mattress or a damp sheet tonight."

Trevor's confident smile wavered at the edges. "What desperate housekeeping! You'll have to manage better in London, sweet Cressy—and I can wait till then to enjoy the pleasure of your company again." He tipped his hat to Augustine and set off down the overgrown drive, swinging his traveling bag with an ease that belied his protestations of faintness.

Usually Cressida felt nothing but joyful relief when one of Papa's weekend parties ended, but Trevor's parting words had thrown her into a confusion that slightly clouded her pleasure at seeing the back of him. A slight frown creased the creamy skin between her dark, even brows, and she tugged absently at one shining brown ringlet that had trickled loose from the knot at the back of her head. London? Why should Trevor be so confident of meeting her there? He must know by now that she never left Riversedge.

"Papa?" She glanced questioningly at the tall man beside her. She felt a familiar twinge of guilt at the sight of his stooped shoulders and pale face, the gray streaks in his curly red beard, and the dark circles under his eyes. "Take care of Augustine, girls," her mother had said. "He's not fit to manage himself. I'm glad I leave two good girls to look after him."

Cressida blinked away the small tears that sprang to her eyes. This was no time to be indulging in guilt about her past failures—she would simply have to manage better in the future. And the time to begin was right now.

"Papa, come inside," she said. "I need to talk to you."

"And I to you, Cressida. We've some plans to make."

Cressida led the way into the library, the one well-furnished room on the ground floor, without troubling herself too much about the nature of Papa's plans. No doubt he'd thought of something else they could sell—but what on earth could that be? The old house had already been stripped of all the good furniture, the vases, the silverware, and the oil paintings of a bygone era. Oh, well, no doubt she'd find out in due course—and whatever it was, Cressida promised herself, she wouldn't protest too much. They would need some money if her plan was to succeed—at least enough to fix the roof and make a couple more bedrooms habitable.

She wrinkled her nose at the stale smells of liquor and smoke that pervaded the library. Going to the tall French windows that overlooked the river, she pulled the drapes open with a single vigorous yank that sent clouds of dust and rotting tapestry fibers to tickle her nose. Behind her, Augustine whimpered plaintively at the bright light invading the room. Cressida pushed the double windows open and leaned out into the garden, taking a long strengthening breath of fresh air scented with flowers and earth and river water, before she turned to face her father.

"Now, Papa," she said. "I've been thinking. This life isn't good for you—you know it isn't—and I'm worried about Isolde. It's not right for her to be staying alone with you in London, with all those—" She paused. The only words she could think of to describe her father's set of determinedly decadent fin-de-siècle artists would be decidedly rude, coming from a girl of twenty to her father. "Well, with all your artistic friends." If she herself was exhausted with the effort of fighting off Trevor Bayne-Fleetworth and Aubrey George and Witherspoon Tracy for just one weekend, what must it be for Isolde, living in a London flat where all these men and others like him were constant visitors? But that wasn't what worried her most—it was Trevor's comment and others like it that she had heard. Apparently Isolde *wasn't* fighting them off.

"And your work is suffering," she went on, as tactfully as possible alluding to the fact that Augustine Parris had produced not one single completed painting in the last five years. Surely he would see for himself that he would be much better off in the calm and peace of Riversedge than in that noisy, crowded London flat with people interrupting him at all hours? She and Betty could take care of her father—feed him good nourishing meals and see that he kept regular hours—and with his health and nerves restored maybe he would also recover his dazzling dexterity with the brush.

"And finally"—she produced her clinching argument—"we can't afford the expense of two establishments." Not on the small income her mother's trust fund had left them, anyway. The London flat dated from the happy days when Augustine Parris had dashed off wall-sized oil paintings every three months and collectors had vied for the latest installment of his work.

"Cressida *mía*, I could not agree with you more," her father said, sinking into a leather-covered armchair that

7

puffed up clouds of ancient smoke and ashes under his weight. "I am delighted that you've finally come to your senses."

"I?" Cressida wanted to laugh with delight. How *could* Papa pretend that it was by her choice that he and Isolde spent most of their time in the London flat, leaving her to struggle alone with the impossible task of keeping Riversedge together? But that was Papa for you, she thought fondly—never able to admit he'd made a mistake, always claiming it was somebody else who'd lost his shirt studs or left paint-stained rags in the laundry tub.

"You're quite right," her father went on, fumbling on the table beside him for his beloved pipe, "and I should have seen it for myself long ago. Criminal to leave you here alone for so long!"

Cressida opened her mouth to assure him that she didn't mind, hadn't minded, that she'd never wanted anything more than to live at Riversedge and tend the gardens her mother had created, but before she could speak his next words took her breath away.

"It's high time you joined us in London. Give you a chance to meet some more nice young fellows like Bayne-Fleetworth—"

"Papa," Cressida said in a vain attempt to stop what she sensed was coming next, to make it somehow not be true, "I abominate and despise Trevor Bayne-Fleetworth!"

Her father only gave a tolerant chuckle. "Quarreled, have you? Ah, youth, youth! Never mind, *cara,* there are plenty more like him in London."

That was exactly what Cressida disliked about the city.

"Anyway, you'll have your pick of the fellows once we get you out of those ratty brown dresses—I think I'll have Isolde help you pick out something different. Striking. *Aesthetic,*" her father said with satisfaction, apparently remembering the flowing draperies of silver-spangled blue and turquoise that Isolde considered appropriate day attire for the city. "Can't think why you dress like that, anyway," he grumbled, returning his myopic gaze to Cressida. "Bad enough you had to turn out such a little brown mouse of a

8

girl—at least you could try to do something about the way you look."

"Papa," Cressida said, "we haven't enough money to buy me a complete new wardrobe. And I don't want new dresses anyway—I'd rather have a new roof over the kitchen. And I don't wish to go to London!"

"Nonsense! You're my daughter, you'll do what you're told. I want you in London. Isolde never did learn to cook, and there's dust an inch thick under my bed, and the cost of sending my shirts out to the laundry—it's ridiculous that an artist should have to be troubled with these petty details! Besides," Augustine added, remembering his ostensible reason for bringing Cressida to London, "it's time you had a chance to get out and have some fun and meet some nice young men. I'm not doing my duty by you, Cressida, and that's a fact. But everything will be different now. Some new clothes, we'll give dinner parties again—you do remember how to do that tipsy cake your mother used to make?—and maybe the occasional jaunt to the Continent. Paris. Rome. Milano." Her father sighed. "Napoli, *bella* Capri. . . ."

"And just where," Cressida asked with a sinking feeling, "do you think we'll find the money for all this?"

Her father regarded her with a benign smile, still in his imagination floating beneath the blue skies of Italy, in a place where the creative artist was properly appreciated. "Very simple, Cressida *mía*. I'm going to sell Riversedge. We'll close the house and let old Betty go today. And tomorrow you'll come to London with me, to be at your father's side where you belong."

During this season the western side of the garden, a rocky bank leading down to the very edge of the river, was a fairyland of white bellflowers and tiny blue Siberian iris, planted years ago by Cressida's mother and now growing wild in every crevice between the rocks. Above the white-and-blue carpet, the silvery-green leaves of the weeping willows swayed downward in long graceful festoons until they were reflected, dancing and shivering with watery light, in the rippling currents of the river.

One large boulder just by the water's edge had been Cressida's favorite spot since childhood, and there she betook herself a few minutes after her father's startling pronouncement.

What a reversal of her own hopes and plans! She had been an idiot, spinning fantasies of a happy rural life in which Papa painted while she and Isolde kept the house and garden and they all lived within their income. Papa had shattered that idyllic dream with a few brutal words, asking if Cressida really thought an artist like himself or a poet like Isolde could survive among country yokels, with no more intellectual stimulation than a weekly visit from the vicar or a game of cards with the village schoolmaster? The very thought was laughable. A life that crept along at a country pace might do for Cressida, but his and Isolde's souls were meant for finer things—and it was high time Cressida took her place with them.

At most she'd been able to win a week's delay and a partial reprieve for Betty. Papa truly didn't understand that she could not just shut up a country house on a day's notice; she'd had to do some strenuous arguing to convince him that the value of the property would not be enhanced by abandoning the house to wind and weather. As for Betty, Papa had grudgingly agreed that she might stay on as caretaker until the place was sold—"but at a greatly reduced salary, mind you," he warned Cressida.

Since they had not paid Betty's nominal wages for over a year, Cressida didn't think she would mind a theoretical reduction in her nonexistent pay. At least Betty would have her meals and a roof over her head until the house was sold, and then—

Cressida's mind blankly refused to carry her beyond that point. As long as Riversedge remained unsold, she could pretend that her move to London was temporary. She would pass a season in Papa's noisy, smoke-filled flat, she would evade Trevor Bayne-Fleetworth and the other young artists trying to impress her with their decadence, she would ignore their sly jabs at her lack of style, and perhaps, by autumn, Papa's mercurial nature would have lighted on some other whim and she would be able to persuade him back to Riversedge.

And perhaps not. Soberly, arms locked around her drawn-up knees, Cressida stared at the water running past the battered toes of her serviceable boots and faced the alternative. By autumn Riversedge might be sold. She might have no other home than the London flat, and this water garden—her last link with Mama and with other, sweeter memories—might be hers no longer.

"He hates it here now," Cressida whispered to the running river, "but we were happy once—we *were!*"

That seemed like a dream or like a story in a book, the memory of those golden years when Mama had sweetly balanced Augustine Parris's artistic temperament against the needs of her two girls, the decaying house that had been her own childhood home, and the garden that was her dearest love. Cressida had grown up in the sunshine of Mama's gentle laughter, kneeling beside her as she weeded and dug in the damp earth and sang a quiet hymn of praise to the Creator of all growing things. Papa had painted Mama's golden beauty as a Madonna, as Dido on the shores of Carthage, as Elaine, the lily maid of Astolat. Isolde, as she grew and showed signs of coming into the same ripe beauty, had been by turns a cherub, a Carthaginian virgin, a lady of King Arthur's court. Even Cressida had had her turn in the sun: that last summer, when she was fifteen and they were all pretending that Mama's persistent cough was nothing serious, Papa had painted her with a basket of violets echoing the purple tones in her eyes and the sun giving some light to her fine mousy hair.

Critics had said that *Girl with a Basket of Violets* was Parris's finest creation. What they didn't know was that it had not been Augustine Parris's art that gave the otherworldly light to Cressida's eyes, the promise of happiness beyond anything known to mortal men to her tremulous smile. Augustine Parris had simply recorded what was there

11

for all the world to see, a young girl on the brink of woman-hood and trembling with the ecstasy of her first love.

Had she even known it was love she felt? Cressida smiled, a little sadly, and shook her head at the happy ignorance of that long-lost summer. She had been young for her age then, sheltered, and content to work in the garden with Mama or play long imaginative games based on the stories she had read. And that summer had been brightened by the presence of a new friend, a lanky American boy whose guardian had sent him to study with the vicar for the summer. Whenever he could, Robert escaped his Greek declensions and Latin conjugations for the quiet pleasures of Cressida's world of flowers and fantasy. With him by her side, the acted-out stories of pirates exploring the island in the center of the river, of Elaine floating in her barge down to Camelot, of knights and castles and fair damsels had taken on a new sweetness. Cressida had been too innocent then to know that what she felt was love; she only knew that when Robert was with her, the stories were real and the river was magic and the whole world seemed hushed and expectant with the promise of some unknown joy waiting just around the next bend of the water.

Robert had not touched that innocence. Probably, Cressida now realized, he had not been even tempted to do so. There must have been a dozen times that summer when he could have kissed her upturned face, turned the romantic tales into a reality that would have burned in her blood forever. But he had never made a move toward her, and she had been too shy to hint at her dreams. Now she thought she had been a fool. Robert had been mature for his age—orphaned young, raised up by a remote guardian whose only interest was in training the boy to take over the business empire he'd inherited in childhood. At seventeen he had been almost a man—and Cressida, at fifteen, had lagged behind her older sister, not ready to give up childhood dreams. It had been kind of him—nothing more—to amuse her by entering into her games. Probably he had wanted to distract her from the sad reality that underlay that summer, to keep her from realizing that Mama's cough would never go away.

That fall an early frost blackened the flowers in the water garden. Cressida, running indoors to bring Mama the sad news, had found her mother coughing her life away in one last gush of blood that stained the carpet in that room forever.

Isolde and Papa had mourned Mama wildly and passionately, as was their natures. Cressida had felt something inside her frozen on that cold October day; she'd been still and quiet and unable to speak of her grief to anyone, even when Robert came to call and awkwardly tried to condole with her. No doubt he had thought her unfeeling. She would never know now. As soon as the funeral was over, Papa had shut down the house and taken them on an extended tour of Italy, where he drowned his own grief in wine and light and long hours in fellow artists' studios. They had been gone for nearly a year, and when they returned at last Robert was no longer residing with the vicar. It seemed that on his eighteenth birthday, his guardian had come to take him back to America, where he was to begin taking over the control of his great inheritance.

The vicar said that Robert had wished to be remembered fondly to all the family; but he mentioned no special messages for Cressida, and she was too shy to ask if Robert had mentioned her personally. If he had, she thought—and thought again and again, in the lonely years that followed—he could always have written. She had no idea where he lived in America, but he could always have found her easily enough. It must be that he didn't wish to.

Papa always referred to her as his little mouse of a daughter. In Italy he would introduce Isolde, taking pride in the way the Italians were stunned by her glowing blonde loveliness, going into lengthy discussions of how and in what particulars Isolde resembled his beloved dead wife. "And this is my other daughter, Cressida," he would say eventually, and the Italian artists would give a polite nod in her direction.

She couldn't blame Papa. Her mirror showed her a quiet,

pale girl with eyes deep-shadowed by grief and mousy brown hair strained back tightly from a thin face. A girl no one would notice in company; a girl who would hardly be remembered by a rich young American. Long before they returned from Italy, long before the strain of her long quiet mourning ceased to show, Cressida stopped looking in her mirror for anything except to make sure that her hair was smooth and her collar straight. When she did look, she was usually in a hurry, a little tired, a little worried, and so the mirror never showed her the smooth white forehead; the infrequent, enchanting, flashing smile; the dancing light in the eyes that had caught Trevor Bayne-Fleetworth's attention.

Now Cressida sighed once, remembering how quickly she had had to grow up in Italy and since their return. Where Mama had easily laughed away Papa's artistic extravagances, Cressida could only timidly remonstrate in a manner that was sure to annoy him. She had trailed behind him through Italy, recovering dropped brushes and mislaid sketchpads and correcting his misreadings of the railroad timetables, and it had all been very good training for the thankless task she returned home to—running Riversedge on a tenth of the money there had been during Mama's lifetime and trying to placate Papa when he wondered aloud why she couldn't manage to keep the house in good order and serve decent wine with their meals.

Gradually, over the last few years, he had taken to spending more and more time in their London flat. He'd moved his painting gear up there, saying the light was better and the constant flow of visitors inspired him, but Cressida suspected the real reason was so that she wouldn't know how seldom he touched a brush these days. Isolde seemed to like staying in London with him, mixing with his friends, whom she considered modern and stimulating; she had decided to be a poetess this year, after an unsuccessful brush with the theater last year and a brief infatuation with Japanese painting the year before. And Cressida had remained in Riversedge, patching and painting and cleaning to keep the old house from falling to pieces, and not nearly as bored as Augustine and Isolde supposed she must be. She'd had Mama's garden to tend, and her memories of Mama and Robert, and—well—Papa was probably right; she would grow into a desiccated old maid with nothing but memories if something wasn't done.

But must that *something* mean the loss of Riversedge? Cressida felt as if she had lived these last five years by drawing on the stock of happiness stored up in her childhood; and now that source was to be closed to her. Without the shabby old house, the river, and the constant succession of flowers, she would hardly know who she was.

"I can't bear it!" she exclaimed aloud, and then, soberly: "I *must* bear it."

She picked up her skirts and made her way back toward the house. Halfway back she stooped to pick a bunch of slender blue iris, and while she was on her knees she absently pulled out a few weeds that had crept in between the rocks, and what with one thing and another the sun was high in the sky by the time she returned to her duties.

"Look at you, Miss Cressy," Betty scolded when she crept into the scullery in search of a vase for the iris. "Your fingernails are a disgrace to the family! And you've got mud on your skirt again—it'll have to be brushed out, and you'd best pray it doesn't leave a stain, for we daren't turn the material again!"

"No," Cressida agreed with a faint smile, "I think the seams would collapse entirely if we unpicked them one more time. Isn't it fortunate that the print is already dark brown? Maybe the stain won't show." She sank into the comfortable old overstuffed chair that she'd moved into the kitchen before Papa could sell it and held out the irises to Betty.

Betty had her own opinions about letting a young girl like Cressida spend her days in serviceable dark dresses that didn't show the dirt. But she looked at the blue shadows under Cressida's eyes and wisely held her peace. The child was exhausted with dancing attendance on her father and his selfish friends all weekend. Perhaps the spell in the garden had done her some good. She had few enough amusements.

"You go on upstairs and take a rest," she urged Cressida now. "I can get Mr. Parris's meal, and—"

"Oh, my!" Cressida sat bolt upright. In the pleasure of sun and earth and growing things she had quite forgotten the doom hanging over their heads. "Oh, Betty, I forgot. I have terrible news!"

"Mr. Parris is moving back here?" Betty hazarded. "With all his friends?"

"Worse!" Haltingly, Cressida explained her father's decision to Betty. She emphasized that Betty was to stay on until the house was sold, so that she wouldn't be out of a position right away. "And maybe it never will sell," Cressida finished, beginning to feel better since Betty was taking the news so calmly, "for only a—oh, a stockbroker, or something like that, somebody who works in the city and makes lots of money, could possibly afford to fix all that's been allowed to go wrong around here. And a rich stockbroker would want a showplace, something modern and more convenient to London. Papa is forever complaining about having to change trains to get here. He says that's why he doesn't visit more often."

And a good thing, too, Betty thought, but again she held her peace. Shameful it was, the way Augustine Parris had taken advantage of Cressida's sweet nature all these years, leaving her to slave away at keeping this big house in good condition while he and that selfish little madam, Isolde, had their pleasure in London. If he were any kind of a father he'd be making a push to get Cressida established in country society where she belonged, seeing that she met the nice young men a girl her age ought to know. Instead he let Isolde run wild with his artistic crowd and ignored Cressida except when he wanted to show off his country house retreat to his artist friends.

"It may be all for the best," Betty told Cressida. "It's time you made some young friends, and surely *all* the men in London can't be like your father's set! You've been too much alone here, my dear—'t'isn't right, and you know it!

16

It's no kind of a life for a young girl, tending my rheumatism and reading to the vicar and crocheting for the church bazaar. You ought to be—oh—going to grand balls in lovely gowns!''

Cressida giggled. "Oh, Betty. Do I *look* like somebody who belongs in silk and satin, dancing the night away?" She spread her hands with their broken fingernails and patted the muddy spots on her much-mended skirt. Brown hair, brown eyes, brown skirt—Papa was right when he called her a little brown mouse of a girl, and she had no business to feel hurt, for it was only natural an artist would be offended at having such an undecorative daughter. Cressida swallowed the lingering sting of pain and forced herself to laugh merrily at Betty's fancy.

"Dressed the part, you'd look as fine as any of those great ladies," Betty insisted loyally, "and your sweet nature—"

Cressida shook her head. "Somehow, Betty, I doubt the young men who go to these affairs are interested in dancing with a *sweet nature*. Anyway, we haven't decided where I'm to make this great debut, have we? Who's going to give the ball? Reverend Thornapple?" she teased. "Or will old Mrs. Creevy come out of her perpetual mourning and open the post office for the occasion? There must be room for two couples at a time to dance in the hall there."

"There's Lady Hayvenhurst," Betty suggested.

"With whom I am *so* well acquainted," Cressida responded dryly. "Let's see—in the last five years she has opened the church bazaar three times and I think she has said a total of five sentences to me, including last year when she commented that Mr. Paxton's vegetable marrow was quite the largest she had ever seen! And considering Hayvenhurst Manor is twenty miles from here, my chances of futhering the acquaintance in between church bazaars are of the slightest!''

Chapter

2

*A*ugustine Parris returned to London by the afternoon train with the distinct feeling that fortune was smiling on him once again. His hangover had abated, allowing him to enjoy the brightness of the sunny day; he was already anticipating a string of warm days in Italy this winter, when he had disposed of that tiresome house and its sad memories; and his hands were hardly trembling at all. Even the slovenly disorder of his studio, with empty bottles and filled ashtrays, empty canvases and untouched tubes of oils, could not disturb his cheerful mood. He did not even curse his older daughter, Isolde, for her failure to clean house while he was gone and to prepare a tempting dinner against his unheralded return. This absence of mind at first rather shocked Isolde, who had already prepared her customary defiant speech about The Life of the Mind and a Poet's Need for Total Concentration; but she understood when Augustine informed her that Cressida would be joining them at the end of the week.

"And high time," Isolde said. "She can deal with these little domestic details—she likes to do that sort of thing." She drew on a pair of blue silk gloves and paused at the mirror to admire their effect against the sweep of mauve and blue silk that draped her uncorseted form in aesthetic style. "Well, I'm off, Papa. It's almost time for Jenny Long-hampton's poetry recital, and afterward Trevor and I may go on someplace interesting."

Augustine saw her off the premises and sat down in his littered studio to enjoy a cigar and a glass of wine. He was still savoring the last of the bottle when his agent, John Shackelford, called on him.

"Good news, Parris," Shackelford began without preamble, stripping off his gloves and hat and looking round for somewhere to lay them. His nose wrinkled at the dusty disorder of the studio; after a moment's thought, he replaced the hat on his head and tucked the gloves under his arm. "I think you're about to come into fashion again."

"I," said Augustine Parris grandiloquently, "have never been out of fashion. There have been seasons when the world has failed to appreciate my genius—what of that? The true artist, Shackelford, rises above these things. Eternity shall be my judge."

"Very well, very well," said the pacific Shackelford, "but eternity's a long time coming, and rent comes due more punctually. There's interest in your *Girl with a Basket of Violets*. A rich collector—American, I suspect, but at the moment he prefers to remain anonymous."

"A lot of good that does me," Augustine grumbled. "You talked me into selling *Girl with a Basket* four years ago—I suppose those jumped-up nobodies who purchased it for a song shall now reap the benefit of the rich American's interest."

"And you as well. So this collector wants to know if you've painted other pictures with the same subject."

"Other pictures!" Augustine guffawed. "If you'd seen my little Cressy, Shackelford, you'd know better than to ask. A little country mouse of a girl—nothing to inspire the artist's eye there."

Shackelford remembered the luminous, violet-tinged eyes of the girl in the painting; eyes too large and brilliant for the young face, eyes that looked with joy upon life and lit

19

a spark of that joy in the hearts of all who gazed upon the painting. Had Augustine Parris done those eyes out of his imagination? Hard to believe; the man's other paintings were earthy, pedestrian representations of ripe feminine beauty. He thought that he would like to meet this "little Cressy," to see for himself if she was such a nonentity as her father seemed to believe.

"Well, no matter," he said. "I don't suppose you'd care to do another portrait now? This man seems willing to pay well for it."

Augustine Parris hid his right hand behind the bottle to conceal the slight but definite trembling in the fingers. "Inspiration fails me," he growled. "You don't understand the artistic temperament, Shackelford. All depends on creating the mood first—the inspiration, the *sentiment*. The actual brushstrokes on canvas are the least part of the work." And what if he failed? It had been some little time since he attempted a serious painting—months, maybe. His imagination refused to allow the horrid possibility that he had not painted for five full years. Impossible! Surely he must have done *something* since *Girl with a Basket of Violets,* something else to show this rich collector—for it must be the Parris style that attracted him, not Cressida's undistinguished little face. It was just that he couldn't, right this minute, call to mind any more recent works that might be languishing in the back of the studio. All he had to offer—

"Wait a minute!" He jumped to his feet, dashed to the pile of boxes and baskets that had occupied the drawing room, still untouched, since the day of his return from Italy four years previously. "Somewhere in here—damn, I'm sure I packed them—ah, here!" Augustine cried in triumph. His rootings among the anonymous straw-packed parcels had produced a yellowing sketchbook, which he held aloft for Shackelford's admiration. "Original pencil sketches for *Girl with a Basket.* Maybe your rich American would buy those? I'd offer him some of my later work," Augustine Parris said, and it wasn't quite a lie, for he certainly would have given Shackelford any more recent paintings if he'd had them, "but since you think he's particularly interested in this subject—"

"I'll see what I can do," Shackelford said without much enthusiasm.

After the agent's departure, Augustine found himself restless, unable to settle back into the mood of quiet satisfied contemplation from which Shackelford had roused him. Besides, the bottle was empty. A quick search of the grease-coated kitchen revealed nothing else to drink. Doubtless Isolde's raffish friends had descended over the weekend, Augustine thought with annoyance, drinking up his stores of wine and emptying the larder. And the inconsiderate girl had failed to replenish the supplies. It was a good thing little Cressy was coming up—she could free both of them from these tedious domestic details.

Little Cressy. Imagine someone really wanting that picture of her, which Augustine remembered as having been painted in a dull conventional style quite unlike his usual work. He'd done it to please his wife, and she'd had the monumental inconsideration to die before the oils were dry on the canvas. Well, if this collector wanted more pictures of Cressida, he couldn't have come at a better time. She'd be here on Friday, and after she cleaned up the flat and stocked the larder, she could pose for him in between her other chores. He might even make some preliminary studies now.

Augustine dashed into his studio, kicked the semicircle of chairs that occupied the center of the room out of the way, hauled out his largest easel, and set up a piece of canvas that had been primed and ready to paint on for— hmm—must be some time now; there was dust on the top edges. Well, no matter. Inspiration mustn't be blocked by trivial details like that. Let's see—this would be the first Parris painting to go before the public in—well, quite some time. It would have to be striking. Bold, unconventional, sizzling with colors almost too brilliant for the eye to bear— recognizably in the Parris style, yet a major advance in theme and design from his previous work. It would prove to the waiting public that he hadn't been wasting the last few years, that he hadn't lost his touch. He had been assimilating his own work and the masterpieces he saw on his Italian tour, growing internally as an artist, and now he would dazzle the world with his new style.

Augustine squeezed out some viridian green onto his palette and regarded it with a jaundiced eye. Such a brilliant shade of green in the background would quite overpower Cressy's delicate features and subtle coloring. A pity it wasn't Isolde, with her high-colored blond beauty, who'd caught the collector's eye! Perhaps he should start by lining out the main proportions of the picture in charcoal. Ah, here was a stick—wet on one end from being dropped into a not-quite-empty absinthe glass, but the other end would do well enough.

He raised his arm, ready to bring the charcoal across the canvas in a grand sweeping gesture, then paused and frowned. What *should* be the theme of this painting? The Rape of the Sabines, with Cressy, half naked, thrown over the shoulder of a brawny Roman modeled after, say, Trevor Bayne-Fleetworth with all his unnecessary bulging muscles? No, Cressy would never consent to pose in the nude or even the half nude; besides, she didn't have enough up top to make it worthwhile. She'd be better as a slender classical nymph—Diana bathing, spied upon by Actaeon. No, Cressy would insist on being Diana modestly draped in a tunic, which would spoil the whole point of the scene.

Augustine cursed under his breath and threw the charcoal stick down. It rolled across the uneven floor, leaving a sticky black streak. The devil with it! A man couldn't paint in the grand manner when constrained by some collector's whims. For that matter, he couldn't paint at all now; it was nearly four o'clock, time for his blasted pupils. It was indecent, a man of his talent frittering away his genius on instructing a group of dilettantes. The world didn't appreciate the needs of a true artist. At a minimum, he should have privacy and freedom to paint. Freedom from monetary worries, too. And someone to take care of domestic details. And an audience capable of appreciating his creative genius.

He had barely gotten the semicircle of chairs arranged again when his students began arriving. Within minutes the untidy studio was full of giggles and gossip, flowery scents and big flowered hats cast down anywhere. Augustine regarded his ladies with a kindly smile, softened as always by the presence of so much sweet femininity gathered together. Not a brushstroke's worth of true talent in any one of them, he thought as always; they were rich bored ladies who were paying more for the amusement of going to an artist's studio than for any serious instruction.

The fleeting thought crossed his mind that those young artists who did want serious instruction weren't coming to Parris; could it be that after only five years' seclusion they had forgotten him or considered him a has-been? Impossible! Augustine shook his head vigorously to drive away the thought and bent to kiss pretty Lily Whitworth's white hand.

"Ladies, ladies, your presence graces my humble studio like a nosegay of sweet-smelling flowers on a deal table." A nicely turned phrase, that; perhaps he should have turned his talents to literature, Augustine thought. Later, when his ladies were settled before their easels and mutilating the subject he set them as an exercise, he would have to discuss with them the tragedy of being a Renaissance man in a workaday world that left him no time to exercise all his talents. He could count on sympathy and languishing glances, and perhaps one of them would even be inspired to revive the fine old custom of patronage of the arts. Their husbands were rich enough, weren't they?

As the ladies settled to their work, Augustine strolled among them, dispensing a jocular comment here, a tenderly veiled critique there. Some of them were pettish at the lack of a subject to draw; Augustine had meant to set them to a still life of three pears and a bottle of wine, but somebody had eaten the pears over the weekend and he had carelessly stuck the butt of his cigar into the empty wine bottle, lending it a raffish air quite unsuitable for a ladies' painting class. Besides, none of them had the technique to render an object distorted behind curved and colored glass; after seeing what they could do to a vase of daisies, Augustine really did not think he could bear to watch them attempting to draw a cigar inside a bottle.

"There is no subject this week, ladies," he announced, "because . . . because . . ."

Lily Whitworth tittered behind her coquettishly tipped half veil of beaded black net, and Augustine allowed his fancy to toy with the notion of dropping the minx into a vat of Prussian blue. By God, he had a rich imagination. A pity these dull women couldn't follow him into the empyrean world of his fantasies—and that thought saved him.

"There is no subject because this week, my dear ladies, I wish you to exercise the most important organ of the painter's anatomy—one which our previous exercises have left untouched. No, no, dear Mrs. Langley," he assured a blushing society matron, "I intend nothing which shall bring a blush to the cheek of Innocence."

Mrs. Langley looked rather disappointed.

"The organ to which I refer, my ladies, is the imagination!" Augustine put one hand on his breast and strolled around the room, gratified to see how all these pretty women craned and twisted in their seats to keep their eyes fixed on him. "Ah, Imagination, sublime Fantasy, thou should'st have been named the muse of all the arts. What but Imagination—"

He broke off, annoyed. They weren't looking at him anymore; they were craning their necks to see *around* him. "Imagination, what else—" Augustine began again, broke off again. What *could* they find so fascinating in the back wall and the studio door? "You are to paint," he concluded abruptly, more than a little peeved, "you are to paint, today, whatever you fancy." And let the silly bitches make what they might of *that!* he thought as he stalked back toward his comfortable chair at the front of the room.

"Excuse me," said a new, unfamiliar, and distinctly masculine voice from the general region of the door, "but I am new to this class. Could you, perhaps, give me a little more guidance?"

Augustine whirled with a most grievous lapse of dignity

24

and finally understood what had lost him the attention of the class. Standing in the door, clad in a gray suit, hat in hand, a diffident smile on his lips, was the most perfect specimen of young manhood Augustine had ever seen. Tall, broad-shouldered, with close-cropped black hair curling around a forehead that Praxiteles might have sculptured, with blue eyes and a firm nose that might have been stolen from Michelangelo's *David*.

"I forgive you," Augustine exclaimed enthusiastically, "I forgive everything, my young friend, if you will be the Actaeon for my Diana!" His artist's eye was stripping the gray suit and the hat and all the trappings of civilization from the caller, and he felt secure that under the suit was a body as perfectly proportioned as the face—totally masculine in a way that would have made Bayne-Fleetworth's bulging muscles seem like a parody of manhood. No wonder he could not visualize his painting of Diana and Actaeon; it wasn't Cressy who was at fault, but the absence of a male figure suitable to set opposite her. With this young man as a model of youth and manly desire, with Cressy as the very semblance of shrinking maidenhood, he would be able to paint the masterpiece that should announce his return to the world of art.

"You mean me to play the model for the class?" the vision of perfection demurred. "I fear there must be some mistake. I came to take lessons, not to give them."

Augustine's jaw dropped. Never, in all the years since he had sunk to giving lessons, had anybody appeared but the frivolous society ladies who came to flirt and be flattered. Could it be that this young man was a serious artist?

"Is it all right?" the young man asked as Augustine's silence outlasted his patience. "I know I should have spoken to you beforehand, sir, but your agent, Mr. Shackelford, seemed to think it would be all right if I just came straight on—"

It all fell into place, and explained the young man's slight, barely perceptible accent. "The rich American collector!" Augustine exclaimed, forgetting to be tactful as he

mentally doubled his usual lesson fee. No, triple the fee—
any less and the boy wouldn't value his instruction.

"American, I own, but hardly rich, nor a collector of
anything save dunning notices," the boy said ruefully, and
he held out his hand. Mechanically, Augustine shook it
while a whole collection of fantasy castles came crashing
down around his head. "May I introduce myself? Robert
Glenford—"

"The boy who came to study with the vicar," Augustine
said instantly. "How could I not have known you?" The
sense of familiarity that had been nagging him was now
explained.

"I've grown a little," said Robert dryly.

"You have indeed. Filled out, too." The boy who'd
spent that summer playing with Cressy had been a weedy,
leggy young thing, awkward with his new height and still
shooting up at a pace that kept him and everybody else off
balance. Now, at well over six feet, he seemed to have
grown into his length of arm and leg and developed muscles
to clothe what had been a lanky frame. "But the line from
nose to brow is a sure indicator," Augustine mused, "and
the ears. . . . Look, ladies!" He began lecturing with true
enthusiasm. "By these features you may know your man,
no matter how he may age, change, or even seek willfully
to disguise himself. Learn to see these proportions, and
you will be on your way to success as a portraitist. First,
the space between the eyes . . ."

He twisted Robert Glenford's head this way and that,
pointing and measuring with his calipers, while the ladies
whispered and giggled and took full advantage of the invitation to stare at this strikingly handsome young man.

Robert felt his much-measured and discussed ears growing bright red. He fixed his gaze on the front wall of the
studio, looking over the ladies' heads, and tried to think of
something else until Augustine Parris should tire of his lecture. This was horribly embarrassing, but it would never
do to offend the man now, after he'd gone to all the trouble
of tracking him down and inventing this excuse to get to
meet him again.

It had been five years since he sailed for America to take up his inheritance, and if anybody had asked he would have said firmly that he had quite forgotten the little English girl with whom he had spent the last enchanted summer of his boyhood. Certainly she had forgotten him; she'd never replied to the note he scrawled and left with the vicar, giving her his address in America, nor had she answered the two long letters he sent to Riversedge that winter. It had been a hard and lonely time for Robert, struggling to take the reins of a vast business empire while his guardian stood aloof and refused to give advice on the grounds that Robert must learn to stand alone. It had been worse yet when he realized that his guardian meant him to fail—that he'd been kept in England, away from any training in business, for a reason. He was too unversed in the business world to understand then how the man might gain if Robert wrecked the empire, but over the winter he set himself to learn and understand and manage the inheritance his father had left him. And twice, when the task seemed too hard and the loneliness had all but overcome him, he'd poured out his heart to Cressida in those long letters, saying things he hated to remember now. Confessing all his weakness, begging her to wait for him, telling her just how much their summer together had meant to him and how deep a place she had made for herself in his heart.

He'd been a fool, writing such things to a schoolgirl, leaning on her as if she were everything his lovesick heart had wanted her to be. Probably she'd scorned him for his weakness; even more likely, she'd been alarmed at his words of love, herself too young for such strong feelings. Now, five years older and wiser, Robert could see that he'd mishandled the matter badly. And until he caught sight of Cressida's portrait in a friend's house, he'd thought that it was all over—a boyhood fantasy, not a grown man's obsession.

Even then, with all his longing for Cressida revived by the picture, he wasn't willing to call on the family at Riversedge; the way he'd poured out his heart in those letters, written to a girl who never cared enough to scribble an answer, made him writhe with deep embarrassment whenever he remembered his words. No, it would be much better to come across them casually, almost accidentally, to exclaim with surprise over the coincidence while making it perfectly clear to Cressida that he had quite outgrown his boyish fancy for her.

It had been easy enough to disguise his interest in the portrait as an interest in the painter's style. When John Shackelford mentioned that Parris gave lessons to a selected few, Robert had been truly delighted to hear the news. What better way to reenter the family circle?

It had all worked out perfectly—with one slight hitch. Cressida was not there.

Oh, he hadn't really expected to see her among the circle of wealthy dilettantes who played with their paints and brushes in Augustine Parris's painting class. Or so he told himself, fighting down his instant and unreasoning disappointment when he saw that none of the pretty faces turned toward him belonged to Cressida. She would be somewhere in the background, slipping in and out like a slender, quiet shadow, unobtrusively seeing to everybody's comfort until she could escape to her own private world.

But it was worse than that. She could not possibly be living in this crowded, untidy flat. It was impossible to imagine his Cressida in a place that smelled of cigar smoke and stale liquor, with dust on every flat surface and sticky anonymous stains on the floor. If Cressida were here, there would be open windows, clean shining floors, and a faint scent of lavender in the air.

Perhaps after class he could chat with Augustine and find out what had happened to her. Probably, he thought with a mental jeer at his own lovesick foolishness, probably she was married by now, with a couple of fat little babies tumbling round her feet and no time to remember a lanky schoolboy who'd fallen in love with her when she was too young to return his feelings.

There was no chance for casual conversation now, not while Parris had such an audience. When he finally stopped measuring Robert's head and lecturing on the proportions of his features, he began strolling about the half circle of chairs, commenting on the ladies' work. He held pretty Mrs. Langley's hand to correct her brushstrokes, flattered a plump young matron outrageously while hinting that she might find it useful to sketch a figure in correct proportion before starting to lay on the oils, and delivered a short speech on the trials of the artistic life while standing behind a slender young widow whose black half veil and bent head concealed her features from Robert. He supposed she was pretty, or Augustine wouldn't have absently laid his hand on her slender shoulder while he gave his speech. The man was clearly in his element, basking in all this feminine attention; Shackelford had said he complained about being reduced to giving classes, but Robert—faintly amused despite his own deep depression—thought Augustine Parris was happy enough with the situation.

The hour of the class was soon over, but the ladies weren't so easily dispensed with. It seemed that all of them took an outrageously long time to clean their brushes and draw on their gloves and settle their enormous flowered hats on their pretty heads. This one had a problem with her drawing that she felt needed Augustine's attention in a private lesson, that one had to wave her white hands in the air while exclaiming loudly about nonexistent paint stains, and every last one of them found some excuse to linger and chat with Robert on her way to the door. He was embarrassed all over again to find that Augustine's directions to the ladies to paint their fantasies had resulted in twelve figures of a tall, dark-haired young man vaguely resembling himself. It was a good thing, he thought cynically, that he'd pretended poverty when Augustine first spoke to him! At the time he'd meant only to dissociate himself from the "rich collector" because he didn't want Cressida to hear that he'd been offering ridiculous sums for any drawing of her. Now he thought that there might be some freedom in being a poor American artist instead of a rich American businessman. The ladies might cast languishing glances at him, but they didn't invite him to dinner to meet their daughters—and Robert, made old for his years by the constant necessity to evade marriage lures at home, was heartily glad to be spared the same problem in English society.

Only the young widow—she *must* be young to have such a slender, erect back, such smooth white arms peeping out beneath her enormous crepe sleeves—only the young widow didn't show any interest in him. She lingered longer than any of the others, in earnest and low-voiced consultation with Augustine about some faults in her drawing, but never glanced his way. Just because it was so long unsatisfied, Robert's curiosity increased. Doubtless she'd looked at him when he first came in, but he'd been too taken aback by the sea of staring female faces to notice which one she was. Now he tried to place her from memory and had just decided that she must be the freckled one with the slight squint when she turned away from Augustine, drawing on her long gloves and saying in a soft voice, "Very well, Mr. Parris, I shall endeavor to correct my faults by next week— but you must promise not to be too impatient with me if I fail, for I vow I'm quite afraid of the great man's anger!"

She had a very pretty little tinkling laugh, like a shower of silver bells; cold and hard as silver, too, but Robert didn't think of that just then. All he was aware of, as she finally turned toward the door and raised her eyes to his face, was that he had been wrong.

Quite, quite wrong. She wasn't the freckled one and there was no trace of a squint on the wide blue eyes that looked up at him through her veil. Her tiny, porcelain features were all in perfect proportion and there was no mar at all on the perfect skin. And she was looking at him with slightly parted lips, as though she wanted to speak but had been suddenly overcome by shyness, and Robert couldn't think of a thing to say to put her at her ease.

"Until next week, Mr. Glenford," she said, offering him one delicate white hand while she tried to hold her bundle of easel and brushes and paints with the other. Her little fingers were too small to grasp such a load; everything cascaded to the floor at once, she gave a horrified gasp, and Robert was able to move again. He was down on his knees before the last brush hit the floor, collecting everything and assuring her that it didn't matter, nothing was broken or spilled.

He couldn't let her struggle down the stairs with that impossible load of equipment—although he did wonder somewhat how she had managed to make her way up the stairs in the first place. On the way down he learned that her name was Lily. Lily Whitworth. And although she wore deep mourning, he somehow got the impression that she was not all that grief-stricken in her widowhood; she didn't exactly say so, but one could gather that her husband had been an older man, the marriage something pressed on her by her family when she was too young to resist. "I was not unhappy," Lily said firmly in a voice that somehow conveyed exactly the opposite and "He was very kind" in colorless tones that told Robert about the complete absence of love in the marriage.

She had a carriage waiting in the street; the groom had obviously been walking the horses up and down for some time. Lily gave a little shriek of dismay, apologized for keeping the horses waiting, jumped into the carriage, and was off before Robert could even say a polite farewell. Not that it mattered, he supposed; he would see her next week. . . .

Somehow, it seemed, he had decided to continue with this farce of painting lessons. He would have to buy an easel and brushes. He went back upstairs to ask Augustine about the best place to go in London. Augustine was only too happy to advise him, and in the course of the conversation he mentioned casually that the studio should look considerably neater by next week—his second daughter was coming up from Riversedge to live with him and keep house here.

Robert had forgotten, for all of ten minutes, that he was there to find out what had happened to Cressida. Now he felt absurdly pleased to hear that she was still unmarried and quite unable to wait a week to see her.

"But I'd like you to come back before the next lesson," Augustine went on. "Having a little party here on Friday—

31

welcome my little girl to London—besides, I want you two young people to get to know each other.''

"We have met," Robert pointed out.

"Oh—as children! That's different. This," said Augustine, "is *important*. I meant it about you posing for me. I'm commissioned to do a big oil painting for the next Academy show—Actaeon spying on Diana. I want you for Actaeon and Cressy for Diana. You'll do it?" He peered anxiously up at Robert. "I—I could remit part of the fee for your lessons in consideration of the modeling."

And he would be spending hours with Cressida. Robert swallowed his embarrassment at the concept and agreed.

Five days later, Cressida surveyed the crowded disorder of her father's flat and told herself firmly that she did *not* have a headache. Papa had invited all these people here to meet her; it would be very rude and ungrateful on her part to plead a headache and flee into the narrow bedroom she was to share with Isolde, especially now, when the party had barely begun. Anyway, she wouldn't be so tired if she hadn't been too stupid to ask Papa what time he'd invited his friends for. She could see now that it had been foolish to assume they'd keep such early hours as country people.

When she'd arrived that noon, lugging the two heavy suitcases that held all she could take away from Riversedge, she'd been a little dismayed to learn that her father proposed giving a party that very evening.

"But, Papa," she'd protested, surveying the tumbled flat, the empty bottles and dirty plates, and the glasses that had been used as ashtrays, "Papa, you can't possibly entertain in this—this—" Not for the first time, words failed her.

"Tush," her father said. "A little picking up and washing, that's all that's required. We'll sort it out in no time."

Cressida was not deceived by her father's words into thinking that he meant to offer any help more practical than a few words of advice. And Isolde was nowhere to be seen; Papa didn't even seem to know where she had gone, or to care! A little wearily, she unpinned her hat and set it carefully on top of her largest suitcase, the only clean surface in the house. It was her only hat, and she had just trimmed it with a brown velvet ribbon, hardly worn at all, taken from one of Mama's old dresses; it wouldn't do to ruin the ribbon with a grease stain. "Just let me change into an old dress," she said, "and perhaps you could find a bucket? And a mop?"

"Thought that *was* an old dress," Augustine muttered, looking in displeasure at Cressida's practical traveling costume of dark brown foulard, "and I'll have to go all the way down to the supervisor's room in the basement to borrow a mop—oh, all right, all right!"

He disappeared shortly after delivering the cleaning supplies, and Cressida worked frantically all afternoon to bring the flat into some sort of order before the guests arrived. At five o'clock Augustine reappeared with two bottles of wine and asked plaintively if Cressida meant him to starve while she did all that unnecessary scrubbing. She prepared a quick dinner for him, then washed up the dishes and hurried to put on her best dress.

At seven Isolde appeared, announcing that she was exhausted from the trials of the afternoon; she had read three poems to her study group and had delivered a slashing critique of somebody else's effort, most of which she insisted on repeating to Cressida.

At nine o'clock Trevor Bayne-Fleetworth and George Witherspoon banged on the door and announced that they had come to keep these two pretty girls company while they waited for the party to begin.

Now, at midnight, Cressida stood alone in a room full of strangers. No one had troubled to speak to her since she slapped George Witherspoon's face for trying to put his hand down her bodice, and she was just as happy to be left alone—only, she did feel so very awkward, the target of sidelong glances and little laughs and with no idea how to talk to any of these people! The air was thick with smoke and fragments of laughter and conversation jangled upon Cressida's ears from every side. "A young Frenchman, my dear, and *deliciously* decadent—Aubrey should illustrate his works. . . ."

Cressida tried not to understand the French poem that followed. Fortunately there was enough going on elsewhere in the sitting room to keep her distracted. In one corner of the room, Aubrey Beardsley had commandeered a stick of his host's charcoal and was sketching—on the wall!—the outlines of the drawings he proposed to make for a new play of Mr. Wilde's on the subject of Salome dancing before Herod. In another, three wispy, languid young men were intent on the ritual preparation of their absinthe. One held three glasses of jewel-green liqueur on a tray; another dropped a cube of sugar onto a small sieve and held it over one of the glasses, while a third slowly poured cold water over the sugar cube. The sugary, icy water dripped from the sieve into the glass and changed the clear green liqueur to an opalescent yellow fluid in which, to Cressida's imagination, evil lights danced and beckoned the users. The magic of the transformation attracted other watchers; by the time the third glass was being prepared, Cressida's view of the entertainment was blocked by a pair of slender, laughing girls who cuddled up to a broad-shouldered young man, his back to the room as he watched the transformation of the absinthe.

"Fools," drawled Trevor Bayne-Fleetworth beside Cressida.

She looked up, startled. "I thought you were among them." She gestured toward the young man whose back was still presented to them. Most of her father's artistic friends were rather pale, weedy types; their determined pursuit of decadent sophistication didn't leave much time for the hobbies of rowing and boxing with which Trevor kept himself fit.

He misunderstood her, or pretended to. "Sweet Cressida, I have as many vices as any other man." He leered at her. "But stupidity is not among them. I don't intend to go mad or blind from poisoning myself with wormwood. It would defeat my plans to live a sinful life until extreme old age."

"At which point?"

"I shall repent," said Trevor solemnly. "Preferably with

my dying breath—any earlier would be such a waste, don't you think?"

In spite of herself, Cressida smiled.

"In the meantime," he said with another leer, "we have to begin giving ourselves something to repent of, haven't we? Plans are useless if one doesn't act on them."

Cressida removed the hand that was gliding around her waist. "Your plans, Mr. Bayne-Fleetworth, not mine."

He sighed. "It's a woman's place to inspire and guide me. But if you refuse, I shall seek out Isolde."

He had not far to look; Isolde had abandoned her discussion of French poets to watch them. Trevor slipped an arm about her waist and spoke low, coaxing words into Isolde's ear. She laughed brightly, tossed back her loose golden locks, and disappeared with him in the general direction of the front door.

At least, Cressida thought, Trevor wouldn't be introducing Isolde to absinthe or inviting her to visit an opium den in Limehouse—something she'd heard two of the other guests laughing about earlier. Trevor Bayne-Fleetworth's interest in sport would keep him from the more ruinous forms of dissipation.

On that thought, she glanced back toward the corner where the absinthe drinkers were doing their best to ruin their eyesight. The broad-shouldered young man whom she'd taken for Trevor had moved slightly. Cressida caught just a glimpse of his face. He was bending down to catch the words being whispered into his ear by the pretty girl in black who hung on his arm, and as he moved he looked directly into Cressida's eyes for one heart-stopping moment.

A glimpse was enough—more than enough. She moved back instinctively, seeking the shadows, and trod on a recumbent poet who yelped in protest. Cressida made her apologies mechanically, glancing about the room for some avenue of escape. She felt sick and her head was spinning. How could she not have known Robert the instant he walked in the room? He had grown, filled out from the lanky youth she remembered. His face showed the maturity of a man's thoughts and feelings, but there was not room for a moment's doubt in her mind. Robert—here, and Papa had not warned her! Robert, whom she'd dreamed of so long before she accepted that he had forgotten her, now flirting with a pretty girl in a black dress and oblivious to her presence. Robert, who'd stood in her mind for everything that was good and true and clean, in the middle of this dirty, disorganized party, hovering over a glass of poison like the rest of these—

"Fools," Cressida whispered. "Fool!" and she did not know whether she meant herself or Robert. She stared unseeing at the stained wall opposite, willing herself not to turn her head and look at the absinthe drinkers again. She must not, *could* not face Robert until she had gathered her wits, until she could be as cool and polite as any lady greeting a long-lost and almost forgotten acquaintance.

Robert had quickly become bored with the transformation of colors that so fascinated the absinthe drinkers; he was only standing there to persuade Lily Whitworth, who did not understand these things, that it would be quite inappropriate for her to join the young men who were bent on poisoning themselves in the name of artistic inspiration. Lily was so innocent, so sheltered, despite her brief unhappy marriage. She thought it would be harmless to try a sip of the stuff—a dashing, daring thing to do; she pouted when Robert refused to encourage her, hung on his sleeve, and teased him about being too sober to make a true artist.

"If you hadn't told me yourself that you were a poor artist," she teased, "I'd take you for one of those stodgy businessmen in the city, with your well-cut coat and your sober manners! Why did you bring me to Augustine's party if you didn't mean us to have a good time?"

Robert forbore to mention that he hadn't exactly brought her to the party; they had encountered one another on the stairs and it had been sheer coincidence that they entered together. He had been taught that it was rude to contradict a lady—even one who was being a little silly and asking for trouble. And just now he was too distracted to pay much attention to Lily's teasing.

Cressida was here! On entering the party he'd given up
hope at once; this crowd of languid, artistically decadent
young men and women would have been so repellent to
her, he couldn't believe she'd put up with them. But she
was here, after all. He'd seen her for a moment only, a
pale, serious face framed in the clouds of smoke being
puffed up from the poets who had commandeered Augustine's sofa cushions for a smoking party on the floor.
She might have been a vision conjured up by his imagination, staring straight at him from the smoke with wide,
long-lashed eyes that silently asked, *What are you doing
here?* But now, while he absently tried to detach his sleeve
from Lily Whitworth's clinging fingers, the people between
him moved slightly and he saw her again. As Augustine
had promised, his daughter Cressida had come up from the
country to attend the party.

And he wasn't imagining her, for the Cressida of his
dreams was young, carefree, her face alight with laughter
or glowing with the dreams she spun for the two of them.
He had never imagined her like this—pale and careworn,
with dark circles like bruises under her eyes, with thin
shoulders braced against some invisible assault. Only the
eyes were the same—luminous, framed by silky dark
lashes, carrying her whole soul in one glance and offering
it to him forever.

He wanted her to look at him again instead of staring off
into space like that. He wanted to take her hands and comfort her for whatever hurt she was suffering and make everything all right. He wanted Lily Whitworth to go away and
give him space to think.

And he had not the faintest idea how to accomplish any
of these things.

After an agonizing period of inching forward through the
crowd and enduring the inane babble that passed for wit in
this group, Robert found himself within shouting distance
of Cressida. Lily Whitworth was still tenaciously with him,
but that didn't matter.

She turned toward him and spoke as soon as he reached

her side. He could almost have imagined that she'd been aware of his progress through the crowded room. But she showed no other sign of interest in him, just the barest civility that she would have accorded to any of her father's guests.

"Good evening, Mr.—Glenford, is it?" Cressida nodded to him as if they'd just met yesterday.

"You recognized me."

"Of course."

Of course. Had she some slight fondness for him? She seemed to be smiling slightly. Probably she was remembering the love-struck fool who'd poured out his lonely soul in his letters. Probably she was trying not to laugh at the memory. Robert felt eight feet tall and as clumsy as he'd ever been in his awkward youth. "It's been a long time— I wasn't sure you'd know me." His collar was too tight.

"Six years?" There was the faintest shadow of doubt in her voice.

"Five," Robert corrected her. Could he really have meant so little to her? But of course. She hadn't even bothered to answer his letters. It was amazing she'd even recognized him.

"Oh, yes. I remember now," Cressida said. "It was the summer before my mother died."

Robert mentally cursed himself. How could he have been such a clumsy clod? Naturally that tragic year was the last thing in her life that she'd wish to remember now.

"A sad time for you. I hope—" What could he say he hoped? That she'd forgotten her mother? That her life was happy now? Either seemed an incredibly foolish remark when he looked at the dark shadows under her eyes. Robert ran a finger around the inside of his collar, slightly easing the intolerable constriction, and to his inexpressible horror found himself babbling like a drunk or a madman. "You're not happy, are you? I can tell. Neither am I, but I can take care of you. You need to eat more. You should rest. You're too thin, and you don't belong here. Let me—"

Lily Whitworth's tinkling silvery laugh interrupted his insane flow of words. Bless the woman, she'd seen what a fool he was making of himself—she was going to save him from himself by interposing a screen of light social conversation. "Robert, *dear,* whatever are you going on about? It's hardly good manners to tell a lady that she's as thin as a sack of bones or to laugh at her poor little dress for being out of fashion."

Was *that* what Cressida had thought he meant? He'd only wanted to take care of her. Instead he'd insulted her; he could see the bewildered pain in her eyes now. Robert briefly considered drowning himself at her feet, but there wasn't a lake handy.

"I didn't mean—"

"Come, Robert," Lily interrupted him, "I've promised to let my dear friend Jillis Peyrefitte meet you—as long as she promises not to get any ideas!" She laughed her tinkling little laugh and fastened her fingers like claws on his arm. Robert felt as though he were being attacked by a small buzzing insect. One couldn't swat a lady away, but he wished very much that Lily would stop talking about people he'd never met and did not care to know. He couldn't think. Didn't she understand that it was *Cressida* standing before him, his love, with a little bewildered frown between her eyes as though she still couldn't quite place him?

"Pray excuse me," Cressida said now, before he could speak again, "I really must be going now. My, um, my friends are waiting for me."

She turned with a bright smile and waved at a bronzed young giant who was just shrugging into his coat. Robert watched her follow the muscular booby out of the flat. He wanted to go after her and get her back, but Lily was hanging on his arm, and Cressida had made it quite clear that she had no use for him. So he turned back into the hubbub of the party and didn't see Cressida running down the stairs to make an unwelcome third between Trevor Bayne-Fleetworth and her sister Isolde.

"Forgive me for intruding," Cressida pleaded when she caught up with them. "I—I really could not bear it a moment longer in there."

39

"Two lovely ladies," said Trevor Bayne-Fleetworth with ponderous gallantry, "are always better than one."

And Isolde looked thoughtfully at her sister's white, strained face and decided, for once in her life, not to point out to Cressida that she was very much in the way. It looked as though Cressida knew it anyway.

Chapter
3

Someone was banging on the front door of the flat. Cressida sighed, got up from her knees, and dropped the soapy rag with which she was endeavoring to remove the sticky-sweet splashes of absinthe that had puddled and dried on the baseboards overnight. In two hours of sweeping and scrubbing, with all the windows open to the cool morning breeze, she had almost managed to rid the flat of the lingering odors and stains of last night's party.

Unfortunately, her burst of furious activity hadn't done quite as much to cleanse and calm her soul as it had done for her physical surroundings. While Cressida had sponged away the charcoal traces of Aubrey Beardsley's Salome on the parlor wall, she wondered if Robert had looked at those wickedly sensual lines just before he told her how thin and plain she'd become. While she had swept up the crumbs on the studio floor, she wondered just who had arranged all the cushions and draperies on the floor for the impromptu "Roman feast" that a last departing guest had enthusiastically described to her. And had Robert been one of the participants—Robert, bleary-eyed with absinthe, his firm mouth loosened in lines of dissipation, looking down with

41

desire at the laughing blond widow who leaned against his knee?

Cressida could imagine the scene as clearly as if she had been there. She strove to convince herself that all she felt was disgust with Robert for wasting himself in such a fashion.

But she couldn't help slipping into a daydream in which she had stayed at the party after all; in which she, not Lily Whitworth, could have sat on the cushion at Robert's side; in which Robert looked down at her and saw . . . what?

At that point in the daydream she got a fresh cloth soaked in hot water and soda and attacked the absinthe stains with renewed vigor. She was hot and splashed with water and her arms ached from scrubbing when the knocking on the door roused her from her furious burst of activity.

All Cressida's clanking with buckets and brooms hadn't roused Papa and Isolde from their morning sleep, but the pounding just outside the flat was another matter. It must be a bill collector, she thought as she rose to her feet and wrung out her damp cloth over the bucket. Nobody else would sound quite so determined. Not that she'd had much experience with the breed herself—the village tradesmen who supplied Riversedge had learned long since not to give Augustine Parris anything on credit—but Isolde had often regaled her with stories of her and Papa's adventures in evading irate London tradesmen.

Cressida dallied, squeezing out the cloth yet again and hoping that Papa *would* be awakened in time to deal with this caller. She really did not feel equal to putting a white apron over her dress and pretending to be the maid, as Isolde claimed to have done once. Still less could she imagine roaring at the man like a mad bull until he ran away in fear for his life, as Isolde said was Papa's favorite trick.

"I don't suppose you ever tried *paying* them," Cressida had suggested.

"With what?" Isolde's sleepy laugh turned into a yawn. "There's never any money. And when there is, we can't waste it on paying old bills—not when we need, oh, decent clothes for me, and wine and food for Papa's friends, and any number of quite practical things, Cressy! No, it's much easier to go on as we do. Eventually the men give up, and then—well, there's always somebody else willing to supply us on tick. For a while. . . ."

Now Cressida remembered that conversation and shook her head ruefully. She had better go and see what this man wanted. Perhaps she'd be able to pay him out of the contents of her slender purse; Betty had refused at the last moment to take her month's pay, saying that Cressida should have the money by her in case of an emergency. "You might need to come home suddenly and your papa not have the train fare," she'd suggested.

Dear Betty! She could hardly have imagined that an emergency would come up so suddenly. Cressida investigated her purse on the way to the front door and flung it open with her speech already prepared.

"I don't know what you've come about, but if it's more than two pounds seven and threepence, you'll just have to . . ."

She stopped, scarlet with embarrassment, and gazed up into Robert Glenford's piercing blue eyes without the faintest idea how she was going to finish the sentence she'd so unluckily started.

"It may," said Robert gravely, regarding her with a slight smile, "it may come to just slightly more than two pounds seven and threepence. Indeed, I suspect it will cost me quite a lot more to buy gifts for all my female relatives. However, the charges should be laid to my account, not yours. All I want from you is advice."

"Me?" Cressida gasped. "Advice?"

"Shopping," Robert clarified. "I want to buy something for my aunt in America. And my cousins. All girls. I really don't know where to begin. Thought you might be kind enough to help me out?"

Cressida glanced down at her water-spotted dress with the threadbare cuffs.

"If you're not otherwise occupied?"

Now, she thought, was the time to send him away—

43

quickly, thoroughly, with dignity. After all, she had her pride. Robert had forgotten her existence as soon as he left England five years ago; at last night's party he'd been too involved with his absinthe and his pretty blond widow to say more than a few words to Cressida. Why should she now run to do his errands for him? She had more self-respect than to jump every time Robert lifted his little finger, didn't she?

Didn't she?

It was just, Cressida told herself, that she couldn't *think* of any good excuses why she couldn't accompany him. He knew she was just arrived in London and had no acquaintances in the city to lay claim to her time. If she said she was promised to Isolde for the day, Isolde would very likely wake up just in time to deny the story.

And it would be rude to refuse this simple, ordinary request without even giving a reason.

Wouldn't it?

"I'm not dressed for shopping," Cressida managed at last.

"I can wait while you change."

And somehow, without exactly having agreed to the plan, Cressida found herself back in her bedroom, slipping out of her working dress and into her good brown foulard so that she could spend the morning with the one man she had sworn, for her peace of mind, to avoid at all costs while he was in London.

Oh, well, it was only one morning. What harm could that do?

"Wake *up,* Izzy!" Cressida heartlessly ripped the bedclothes from her slumbering sister. "You've got to help me do up the buttons on the back of this dress—I can't manage without."

"Mmph? Don't call me Izzy. Detestable nickname." Isolde sat up, rubbed her eyes, and dexterously fastened the long row of buttons on the back of the brown foulard. "Ugly dress. Where y' going?" Even as Isolde mumbled the question she was slithering back down among the crumpled bedclothes, a sleepy golden mermaid diving into a warm sea of linen sheets.

Cressida colored. "Shopping. With . . . Robert. To buy presents for his family."

"No!" Isolde sat up and the sheets fell to her waist. She had not troubled to put on a nightdress.

"You think it's not proper?" Such scruples in Isolde rather surprised Cressida. "But we've known him forever. . . ."

"Didn't think he'd have an eye for you," Isolde murmured. "Turn 'round. That *is* a ghastly dress. Wouldn't you like something of mine instead? No, you're right, all my clothes are too big." She was all awake now, vibrant with energy. "Let me fix your hair, anyway—that knot makes you look like everybody's maiden aunt. And pinch your cheeks to get some color in them. And at least take my Japanese sash. That's right—it sets off your little waist. You've got quite a nice figure, Cressy. You ought to do more with yourself."

"Robert thinks I'm too thin." She couldn't help blurting out that humiliating reminder of last night's brief conversation.

"Robert," Isolde mumbled through a mouth full of hairpins, "is a fool. Either that or he hasn't looked at you properly. Raise your arms. Look over one shoulder. That's it. *Somebody* should rescue the boy from Lily Whitworth. I wish I'd answered the door," she sighed, "but fair's fair, you got there first, and I won't have you wasting your chances. Smile. Better. But perhaps a little rouge . . ."

"No!"

"Scent?"

"Absolutely not."

Already Cressida hardly felt like herself. With her hair hanging around her face in soft curls, a tortoiseshell comb of Isolde's holding up the back in a high loop of brown swirls, a brown-and-gold Japanese obi making her old foulard sparkle like a dance dress—why, she might have been going to a masquerade! She fled Isolde's offers of rice powder and a little something to darken her lashes, and bumped into Robert waiting in the hallway.

"Ah. Ready to explore the wilds of darkest Harrods?"

"Um—no—I don't think—that is—"

"Wrong answer. You're my trusty native guide, remember?" Robert looked her over with a mischievous glint in his eyes. "Hmm, fetching costume the natives are wearing this year. Come on. I'll wager we can discover the sources of the Nile before tiffin—*and* find something for Aunt Adelaide into the bargain."

"What counter, please, madam?"

The impressive gentleman in morning coat and silky black mustachios waited deferentially for Cressida to express an opinion. The slight bend of his back and the upward tilt of his eyebrows indicated his readiness to spring into action as soon as she spoke, having no desire but to see that this unimpressive young lady was served with the best of Messrs. Harrods' drapery goods.

"Toiletries first," Cressida told him. "Then we'll look at your silks, and perhaps the lace department?" She looked up at Robert, who was doing his best to disappear into the woodwork behind her. He nodded and the floorwalker bowed.

"This way, madam."

"This," Robert whispered into her ear, "is why I wanted you to come with me. This bloke terrifies me."

"He's only a floorwalker," Cressida whispered back. "He's just here to help you find the right department."

Robert looked through the vast, high-ceilinged room and shook his head. Already, at eleven o'clock in the morning, the room echoed with the rustle of ladies' long gowns and the clatter of their high-pitched laughs. One whole end of the room was piled high with bolts of precious shimmering silk in rainbow hues. The other end was taken up with an array of glittering polished glass cabinets displaying every feminine frippery imaginable—lace collars and silver-backed mirrors and pearl buttons.

"I wouldn't have the faintest idea where to begin," Robert said firmly. "It's a blessing you agreed to come with me, Cressida. I'd be lost without you. Where shall we start?"

"Something for your aunt?" Cressida suggested. "Perhaps a dresser set?"

The assistant brought out combs and brushes and mirrors seemingly without end, each set more elaborate than the last.

"Which do *you* like?" Robert asked. "They all seem so ornate. Too heavy for your hands." He lifted Cressida's slender hand and the brush she was holding. The brush was too heavy—he'd been right about that—but he found that he'd been deceived by Cressida's appearance of fragility. The hand he held was thin and tense and the skin was roughened by work she shouldn't have had to do. But it wasn't weak and soft like Lily Whitworth's dainty little hand. Cressida's slender body was vibrant with strength and energy. He could feel the current flowing through her and him, a single pulsating wave of energy that filled them both.

And he had to say something casual. She'd made it clear enough last night that he was the merest of casual acquaintances to her, somebody who merited only a brief greeting before she went off. A few minutes later Lily Whitworth had casually mentioned that Trevor Bayne-Fleetworth had also disappeared. What could the man's attraction be that she would desert the party her own father was giving for her to go off with him? And what kind of father would let her do it?

If he asked, she would say it was none of his business. If he let her see that he cared, she would probably laugh at him. She might even mention those idiotic letters, and Robert thought that he might just possibly die right there on the floor of Harrods if Cressida began laughing at the lovesick boy who'd written such extravagant letters to her.

And if he held her hand a moment longer, he would have to kiss her; his resistance was crumbling with each breath he took.

"What do you think of this set?" He pointed at random.

At least the gesture forced him to release Cressida's slim fingers.

Fortunately, he'd picked something reasonable to point out, a carved tortoiseshell comb and brush set that was quite the loveliest thing on display—if you didn't count Cressida's dark-fringed eyes and gentle smile among the displayed items. The amber and gold tones of the tortoiseshell swirled into a fantasy of seafoam and shells on the back of the comb; the back of the brush was a smiling mermaid discreetly draped in carved locks of amber hair, while her scaled tail formed the handle.

Cressida studied the carved set for a long time while she concentrated on steadying her breathing and calming her racing pulse. She was supposed to be helping Robert pick out presents for his American relatives, not—God help her!—not falling in love with him all over again. She should be thinking about lace-trimmed handkerchiefs, not about the warm strength of his fingers enclosing hers. She should be remembering how disgusted she'd felt last night, seeing him among the absinthe set, sinking to the level of the rest of Papa's "artistic" friends with their frantic pursuit of every kind of depravity.

The fact was, she should be anywhere and doing anything rather than spending an entire morning in his company. This was madness. Only last night she'd recognized the strength of her feelings and had promised herself that she'd keep well out of Robert Glenford's path until he returned to America. And this morning, he'd only had to present himself at the door and request her company for her to break that promise immediately.

True, Isolde and Papa had still been asleep, so she'd *had* to answer the door. True, all he'd asked was her help on a little shopping expedition, to pick out a few trinkets for his female relatives. There should have been no danger to her peace of mind in such a simple, public little outing.

Just being near Robert was all the danger anybody could want. And if she didn't say something about this tortoiseshell set, he would probably think she had lost her mind. "It's very pretty," Cressida said, "and I like the colors."

Best of all, it was not dear—far less expensive than the silver and ivory set the shop assistant had first shown them. Still, she looked at Robert for confirmation. "It's not too expensive?" Papa had said something about bad investments, an incompetent guardian. When Robert asked her to come shopping at Harrods with him, he might not have known how expensive London shops could be. She didn't want him to be spending more than he could afford because she picked out the wrong items.

"Not in the least," Robert said firmly, and the shop assistant carried the comb and brush set away to another table for wrapping. Cressida felt relieved. He didn't seem in the least worried about the price; he couldn't be that badly off. Still, he had indicated he had quite a number of gifts to buy; perhaps she'd better steer him to a less expensive shop.

"You never did tell me exactly how many cousins you had?" Her rising inflection made a polite question of the statement.

"Six," Robert said firmly.

"Six girls in the family!" It seemed strange he'd never mentioned this plethora of female relatives in all the summer when they'd played together at Riversedge. Cressida wondered if any of them were pretty. Probably all of them were. Her imagination gave Robert a family populated entirely by dainty blond girls with porcelain profiles and tinkling silvery laughs—American replicas of Lily Whitworth.

"We'd better go to Liberty's Oriental Bazaar," Cressida decided, telling herself that it was none of her business how many pretty girls Robert Glenford shopped for. "They have quite a variety of—oh, silk scarves, and sandalwood soaps, and lacquerwork hairpins. . . ." If he had six more presents to buy and not that much money to spend, Harrods was no place for him.

Liberty's Oriental Bazaar was less formal in atmosphere than Harrods. Here, instead of a gentleman in morning dress, they were greeted by a lady in a long-trained velvet dress who smiled and chatted easily, almost flirting with Robert, as she showed them to the long counter of imported trinkets at the side of the store. Cressida was easily able to pick out six different little gifts for Robert's unknown cousins. She thought that he would be relieved to have the shopping over with, but instead he seemed disposed to linger. He wanted a dress length of Liberty silk for his aunt, he said firmly, and Cressida should help him pick it. He steered her over to the silks department and held up the end of a shimmering blue-violet silk to her face. Cressida knew without looking in the mirror that the violet shades in the silk would match her eyes and that the soft blue shadows where the material fell into folds would make her hair seem brighter by contrast. And it was so smooth! She touched her fingertips to the surface. The roughened skin of her hand caught on the smooth glide of silk and Cressida jerked her hand away before she could pull a thread and destroy the shining perfection of the fabric. Reality weighed heavily upon her. What was she doing here? Robert wanted to pick something for his aunt, not for her. She couldn't even afford to *look* at this stuff.

"It's . . . lovely," she said, reluctantly turning away from the violet shadows and blue shimmer of flowers, "but you should pick something that suits your aunt's coloring, not mine."

"I thought I might get you something too," Robert said. "In thanks for your help with the shopping."

Cressida shook her head, smiling. "No, Robert. You mustn't be so extravagant, not when you're—I mean, Papa told me that your circumstances had changed—" Her cheeks burned and she stared at the toes of her shoes. How gauche of her, to remind Robert of his poverty! Isolde would have laughed and turned the offer aside without embarrassing her escort. "In any case," she said, recollecting what she should have said in the first place, "it would not be proper for me to accept such a gift from a young man."

"Then you'll have to tell me when you find something that *is* proper," Robert laughed.

"Meanwhile, what about your aunt?"

"Oh. Well. Her coloring is very like yours. She's tall like you, too, and slim. So anything that becomes you would do well for her. I'd be very grateful if you would let me see how all these silks look beside you."

"Oh, well, if that's the best way to pick something for your aunt. . . ." Cressida murmured, quietly giving up on reality. She couldn't actually let Robert buy her such a costly gift, but as long as she was here she might as well enjoy the day. She had to get through this shopping expedition somehow; she had to smile and laugh and act as though Robert's presence did not disturb her in the slightest. She would pretend that she and Robert were engaged to be married—secretly, of course, so they mustn't give any hint of their feelings to the shop assistants—and that he was buying all these pretty trinkets for her. Her imagination rather failed at explaining why a secretly engaged couple would go on such a public shopping trip, so she decided to skip over that part of the story and work it out later, in the privacy of her room. For now, all she had to do was sparkle at Robert, act as though she didn't have a care in the world, and play with the most beautiful Japanese and Indian printed silks in London.

Once Cressida had the fantasy firmly established in her mind, the morning passed quickly—all too quickly. While Robert held up lengths of fabric printed with flower gardens or Oriental carvings, she smiled and imagined that they were choosing lengths of cretonne to replace the faded curtains in the morning room at Riversedge. When he called on her to admire the countertop covered with elegant fripperies for a lady's dressing table, she was able to make all the requisite sounds of delight while she pretended that he was trying to guess which dresser set she would want for a wedding present. They wandered from Liberty's to Debenhams' and back to Harrods, and Robert kept purchasing little trinkets and having them sent back to his hotel, and after the third or fourth token protest Cressida stopped trying to protect him from spending too much. After all, she had no right to criticize how he spent his money or what extravagant gifts he wanted to send to his female relations in America. And if she kept trying to interfere, he would politely point out that it was none of her business—and such a reminder would be very hard to fit into the gossamer strands of the dream she was weaving about the day.

It wasn't a difficult dream to maintain. Being with Robert again, even after all these years, was so pleasant and natural that it was easy to pretend they'd never been separated—that their childhood friendship had ripened naturally into love, that today was just one on a long strand of shining wonderful days. Certainly Cressida didn't imagine that any man, no matter how much in love, could be kinder and more attentive than Robert was being today. He took her arm when they crossed a street, instinctively stood between her and an oncoming carriage, opened doors for her and saw that she had a comfortable chair when they wanted to browse at one counter for any length of time. And Cressida, used to the casual ways of her father's friends, to young men who had thrown off the shackles of conventional courtesy as part of their artistic freedom, flushed prettily under the spell of these minor attentions.

Once or twice she had to remind herself that she was simply benefiting from Robert's impeccable manners. She had no doubt that he would have treated a duchess or a charwoman with exactly the same courtesy. No, perhaps not; part of good manners was making people feel comfortable, surely, and Cressida could not imagine old Betty, for instance, allowing Robert to bow to her as he opened a door or to whisk a chair behind her when her legs grew tired.

She gave an involuntary gurgle of laughter at the thought, and Robert set down the pearl-buttoned gloves he'd been toying with and looked down at her with a smile that made her breath catch in her throat. How many times she had imagined him coming back from America to take her in his arms and look down at her just like that, with a smiling face but with serious eyes that told her without words just how much she meant to him!

And, of course, his look didn't mean that at all; she was getting too involved in her fantasy, that was all.

"Dare I ask what the joke is?" Robert inquired.

"I was just wondering if you are so polite to everybody

you know," Cressida confessed, "and imagining what Betty would say if you held her chair for her or took her arm."

Robert grinned. "She would probably call me an impertinent young jackanapes and accuse me of trying to embarrass an old woman with my coming ways. And then, with any luck, she'd sit me down in the kitchen next to the old iron stove and give me a biscuit. Does she still make those little molasses cakes with the peppermint chips on top?"

He remembered Betty without any helpful reminder, he could even imitate her voice and turn of speech; he could remember the kitchen where he and Cressida had come for snacks. *How could you remember so much, and forget me for so long?* Cressida wanted to demand.

But, of course, one couldn't say such a thing; it would be most impolite, and anyway there was no need to ask Robert to explain how utterly, drearily forgettable she had been. Cressida gave a sharp sigh as the fragments of her dream shattered around her.

"What's the matter?" Robert asked at once.

As Cressida stammered some excuse, he studied her face and announced that she was pale, probably tired and hungry. Cressida seized on the excuse he offered and then wished she hadn't done so.

"And I," Robert said, "am a thoughtless brute, to keep you standing and walking all morning on my trivial errands. We'll lunch at the Carlton."

"No!" Cressida protested at once. It was one thing to watch Robert spending his money on ivory dresser sets and beaded purses and Liberty silks for his family, quite another to let him treat her to lunch at the most expensive and exclusive hotel in London.

"What, don't you care for the decor? Maybe you're right," Robert agreed at once. "All that red plush has a decidedly depressing effect on a lovely spring day like this. Besides, your complexion deserves to be set off by the palest pastels. You see, I *do* have an artistic temperament," he interjected, "even if your papa does think I'm good for nothing but to serve as his model. Oh, hadn't he told you that? I don't know how I came to agree to such a thing—deuced embarrassing—here, spare my blushes!" he begged as Cressida began to smile.

"You will probably," she told him, "catch your death of cold. Papa has been talking of doing something with a classical theme—and his studio is *not* very well heated!"

"Classical," Robert murmured. "Scanty draperies? *Oh, dear*, what have I got myself in for? Oh, well—" He looked down at Cressida, and this time there was a distinctly wicked gleam in his eye. Now she felt like blushing, though she did not quite know why. "I suppose," Robert said, "there will be compensations. Well, that settles it; we're not lunching at the Ritz either. I'd wanted to order Escoffier's salmon timbale for you, but all those imitation Corinthian columns around the dining room would put me right off my feed, now I've remembered your papa's intentions. It will have to be the Berkeley, I suppose—"

"Oh, *please*, no!" Cressida protested.

"Don't you care for Francatelli's style? The entrees *are* rather heavy," Robert said with an air of sweet agreeableness, "but he does an excellent *tarte meringue*. You used to love sweets."

"There's a very nice tearoom upstairs here," Cressida said faintly. She had never been there, but Isolde had made slighting mention of Harrods' new tearoom as a place where desiccated dowagers munched cream cakes and destroyed the reputations of any girls who violated their antiquated notions of propriety. A tearoom, Cressida thought, could not be so expensive as the fashionable hotel restaurants Robert was suggesting, and it had the added attraction that they were unlikely to encounter Isolde or any of her bohemian friends there.

"I will not," Robert said firmly, "I absolutely refuse to allow you to spoil your digestion on tea and cakes when you should be sitting down and eating a proper meal in comfort."

"But it's such a lovely day," Cressida pointed out. "Perhaps we could buy some bread and cheese and have a picnic lunch in the park."

Robert began to demur, then looked more closely at Cressida and suddenly became very enthusiastic about the notion of an alfresco lunch. She understood the meaning of his searching glance well enough. He had finally noticed the faded lines along the seams of her dress and the telltale crease at the hem that showed where it had been turned and lengthened so that she could get another year's wear out of the dress she'd outgrown three years previously. Cressida felt her cheeks grow hot with shame. It was true, she might be neat and clean, but she was hardly dressed in a style suitable for the Carlton or the Ritz.

"The champagne is acceptable," Robert allowed some time later, "but we didn't pack enough ice around it."

"We needed all the ice for the frozen cream meringues," Cressida pointed out. She lay back on the grass and gave a little sigh of contentment and repletion. Her vision of bread and cheese in the park had never materialized; instead Robert had left her looking at jewelry boxes while he consulted with two grave gentlemen from the catering department of Harrods. A few minutes later, just as he hailed a hackney cab, a wicker picnic basket the size of a small steamer trunk had materialized; and ever since they reached the park, Robert had been pulling out luxurious trifles with the air of a conjuror producing silk handkerchiefs from the air.

By now Cressida was full of good food and a little dizzy from the champagne and from laughing at Robert's ability to talk nonsense with a straight face, and she had ceased to care about the world outside the enchanted grassy circle where they sat, almost surrounded by flowering bushes and looking out over a miniature lake. If Betty could see her now she would say that Cressida was too old to be lounging on the grass like a hoyden, and if Isolde could see the remains of their picnic lunch she would give a little scream and start lecturing Cressida on the need to keep her figure. And none of that mattered—or did it?

"There's one cream meringue left," Robert told her.

"I suppose I'd better not," Cressida said regretfully. "Isolde says—"

"Well, of course Isolde can't feast on pastries," Robert agreed. "She's already in danger of becoming more blowsy than voluptuous. But you need building up. As your medical adviser—"

"And just when did *you* become a physician?"

"My understanding of your condition is not based on textbook study," Robert said. "Don't interrupt! As your medical adviser, I prescribe a strict diet of partridge pie, meringues, and champagne, with liberal doses of sunlight, spring flowers, and laughter. Overindulgence in London smoke is strictly forbidden, as are late nights and parties with too many weedy, absinthe-swilling young fools."

From his tone, it sounded as though Robert had not, after all, been among the absinthe-drinking set last night. Perhaps he had just been watching. Cressida felt irrationally relieved. After all, Robert was a grown man now, and his life had little to do with hers, and it shouldn't concern her what minor vices he indulged in. All the same, last night she had felt as though something had been taken away from her—something infinitely precious, that she hadn't even known she possessed—when she thought that Robert had grown up to become just as silly and jaded and vicious as the young men she most detested in Papa's set. And now she felt as though the world had been given back to her on a silver platter. Riversedge was all but lost, Robert was only passing through her life, but for that moment Cressida had no interest in acknowledging dull reality. The present moment was just as real as anything else—and in this present, she was lying back on a grassy bank under an overhanging arch of lilac, with Robert sitting beside her and talking nonsense in a very grave tone of voice. And just at the corner of her vision was an arching wooden bridge whose Japanese style made Cressida feel as if she were living inside one of Mr. Sullivan's musical comedies.

"The flowers that bloom in the spring, tra-la," she sang.

Robert's voice harmonized with hers.

"The flowers that bloom in the spring, tra-la,
  Breathe promise of merry sunshine,
  As we merrily dance and we sing, tra-la
  We welcome the hope that they bring, tra-la,
  Of a summer of roses and wine,
  Of a summer of roses and wine."

On the last line Cressida's voice died away to a wistful thread of song, as she remembered the last time she and Robert had sung together. It had been that golden summer before Mama died, when they played at pirates and recited the best bits of Shakespeare's plays in the wisteria arbor and sometimes sat down together at Mama's old piano to play four-hand adaptations of popular songs.

"It *was* a 'summer of roses and wine,' wasn't it, Cressida?" Robert murmured, and she knew he was lost in the same memories. "Do you suppose we can go back there?"

There was a tinge of sadness in Cressida's answering smile. Overhead the sun and the lilacs were a glory of gold and lavender, and Robert's face was in shadow, but his head was bending closer to her. She felt on the verge of some momentous discovery. Any minute now his lips would brush hers and the world would change, the world would be made new around her. . . .

And tomorrow, or next week, or next month he would go away again and forget her, just like last time. But she wasn't a child now; she was a woman—and her heart would break if she gave it into his keeping and he forgot her as easily as he had before. . . .

"No," Cressida said, sitting up and brushing the meringue crumbs off her skirt in one swift motion. "No, we can never go back. Mama is dead, and Riversedge is to be sold, and you—"

"What about me?" Robert pressed.

It had been a mistake to sit up, perhaps; their faces were very close together now, and the overarching branches of lilac and wisteria shielded them from the sunny park where children played and clerks from the shops ate lunch out of greased paper packets.

You will forget me again, Cressida had been about to say, but of course she couldn't say that; she would rather die than let him know how hurt she'd been when they never heard from him again, how much of her girl's heart had already been given to him without a word said on either side.

"Oh, I don't know about you," Cressida said with an attempt at a careless laugh. "You will have to define yourself to me again!"

"I can think of nothing I'd like better. But you'll find that I haven't changed, Cressida."

She did not answer that, just surveyed his broad shoulders and tall, well-filled-out frame with a good imitation of the lazy, sarcastic smile Isolde gave to her admirers.

"All right—I've grown up. But I haven't changed. Not," Robert said, flushing, "not in anything that matters. Have you?"

No, Cressida thought, looking away. He hadn't changed—and neither had she. He was still able to make her feel, when he looked at her, that she was the center of his universe. And presumably he'd been able to make Lily Whitworth feel the same way when he was flirting with her last night. And just as he'd now forgotten Lily, he would forget Cressida again when the next girl took his interest.

And she hadn't changed either. For years Cressida had been telling herself that she was a different person now, that her memories of Robert were a child's memories, that if she ever did happen to meet him again his smile would have no power to light her heart and his voice would no longer give her a secret thrill of pleasure.

It wasn't true. Right this minute, sitting beside him in the heart of London, knowing perfectly well that he had forgotten her the minute he left England and would forget her again as soon as he stopped visiting Papa's studio— right now, if he bent his head toward hers, she would kiss him in broad daylight with nothing but a few branches of flowering shrubs to conceal them from the entire city of London. No, Cressida thought, she hadn't changed. She had been a fool five years ago and she was an idiot now. Not much improvement!

But at least now she might be clever enough to keep her feelings to herself.

"Everyone changes as they grow up," she said finally, looking away from Robert's searching eyes. "I'm a different person. So are you. That summer ended long ago."

"But a new one is just beginning."

It was really rather an idiotic comment, but for some reason the low-voiced words made Cressida's heart beat faster. She looked down at her hands. One hand rested in her lap; the other lay on the new green grass. Robert's fingers were very close to hers. His hand moved closer; one broad fingertip stroked the inside of her wrist. A sweet, dizzy breathlessness seized Cressida. She felt as if the champagne bubbles were dancing in her blood.

If this brief casual touch could do so much to her, what would happen when he kissed her? It mustn't happen—she would be lost, utterly lost, quite unable to conceal her feelings any longer.

She wanted to lose herself. The singing in her blood was too strong to resist. She swayed toward Robert. Somewhere in the distance people were talking in loud Cockney voices. Cressida waited, lips parted, for the irritating noise to cease.

Instead it got louder.

" 'Ere's a good spot, luv. Come ahn then, be a sport," urged a young man's voice.

"Ooh, Mortie, ye're such a tease!" A shrill giggle burst upon Cressida's ears. Large, work-reddened hands pushed the branches of lilac aside, carelessly breaking the slender stems and bruising the blossoms. Cressida looked up into the staring eyes of "Mortie," and the girl peeped over his shoulder.

"Coo! All the good spots is already taken!" the girl complained.

"Come ahn, Vi!"

The would-be courting couple retreated. Cressida sat

with her face burning, afraid to look at Robert, until a muffled choking sound alarmed her.

His face was as red as hers felt, and he had one hand clapped over his mouth to stifle his laughter while his broad shoulders shook. "You should have let me take you to the Savoy," he said when he regained his composure. "This sort of thing *never* happens at the best hotels."

All too true, Cressida thought. Her embarrassment wore off and she was conscious of a fierce, unreasoning disappointment. It seemed she had no choice but to be sensible. Even if she decided to be as wild as Isolde, fate was against her!

"What's wrong?"

Robert was too sensitive to her moods. She would surely betray herself if she had to be around him much more. Cressida told herself firmly that it was a very good thing they'd been interrupted. "Nothing," she said, too quickly. "Nothing at all. This was a lovely spot for a picnic. I'd much rather have come here than to some fancy hotel restaurant. Besides, you mustn't be so extravagant. Papa told me how your wicked guardian had squandered your inheritance."

Robert was slowly turning red again. Cressida put one hand to her lips. In trying to talk about anything but her feelings, she had managed to be supremely tactless. Of course Robert didn't want to be reminded of his financial problems. She began to stammer an apology, but Robert interrupted her.

"Er—that's all right, Cressida. Really. You see . . . well . . . oh, the deuce with it!" he burst out, pulling up and crushing a handful of grass in his agitation. "If I'd known what a confounded *nuisance* being poor would be, I'd have been rich from the start—but it's too late now. . . ."

Cressida wondered if a streak of insanity ran in Robert's family. Or perhaps it was trying to live with those six female cousins—or was it eight? She couldn't remember now—that had turned his wits.

"I certainly agree that poverty can be a 'confounded

nuisance,' " she said, "but I haven't yet got the trick of being rich instead."

"Yes. Well. What I meant . . ." Robert tugged at his collar and reduced the starched linen to a crumpled rag. "Actually, my guardian didn't dissipate my inheritance."

"Oh. Then . . . you mean you lost it yourself?"

"No."

"Then what happened?" It was terribly vulgar to keep asking somebody about his fortune like this, but Robert did seem to want to talk about the subject, and he was having a very hard time saying whatever he wanted to say. Cressida felt it was only her Christian duty to assist him.

"Nothing happened. I'm rich! I'm disgustingly, obscenely, vulgarly rich! *Now* do you understand?"

"No," Cressida said honestly. "Not in the least. Oh, well, I suppose poor Papa got the story mixed up. I shall have to explain to him that he got everything hind end foremost, as usual."

"No. No, don't do that. He didn't exactly get it wrong. I mean, I *told* him I'd lost all my money."

Cressida decided that there must definitely be insanity in Robert's family. Perhaps the tale about his parents having drowned in a boating accident was a canard, put about to conceal the dreadful scandalous truth. Probably they'd gone completely insane years ago and had been locked up for their own good. Probably somewhere in America there was a gloomy old mansion house, set in the middle of a forest, with barred windows from which bloodcurdling shrieks sounded. . . .

"You see," Robert said, "it can be rather a nuisance being rich. At least in America. I couldn't go *anywhere* without some mother introducing her spotty daughters to me and trying to get me into a compromising situation with them."

"Did they *all* have spots?"

"Those that didn't," Robert said gloomily, "giggled. Which was, on the whole, worse. Anyway, when I came to England I thought it would be pleasant to go about as an ordinary fellow. So if a girl seemed to like me, I'd know it was *me* she liked and not the money. So when I looked up your father again it seemed like a good idea to try that out . . . I don't quite know why I thought of it just then. Terribly unmannerly of me to lie to him, of course. Be very embarrassing to explain now. Rather just let matters go on as they are—if you don't mind?"

Cressida thought she could understand perfectly why Robert had been inspired to lie to her father. One look at Augustine's studio and he'd probably noticed the air of real poverty, the shabbiness and the lack of furniture. He had realized that if Augustine knew he was rich, there'd be an endless series of requests for small loans and attempts to sell him unfinished paintings.

And Isolde would probably have tried to talk Robert into paying for the publication of her poems.

Cressida blushed for her family. "Of course," she said quickly. Then she blushed again for herself. "I suppose it must have seemed very funny to you—this morning, I mean—watching me try to find inexpensive little gifts for your aunt and cousins." A sudden thought struck her and she looked at him with new suspicion. "Seven girls in the family, was it? Or six? Or eight?" She couldn't quite re- member what Robert had said—and from the way he was avoiding her eyes, neither could he.

"Or none at all," Cressida concluded. "Robert, what *was* all that about?"

Robert looked at the shadowed violet eyes of the only girl he'd ever loved and found himself absolutely incapable of confessing the truth. How could he tell her that he'd invented the whole shopping expedition just for an excuse to spend the morning with her? How could he confess that every pretty trinket he'd bought was intended for her? After he'd just been complaining about girls following him for his fortune, she'd be bound to assume he was trying to buy her interest. She would think him the greatest egotist alive.

Unless, of course, she returned his feelings just a little bit. There'd been moments, especially that magic moment just before Vi and Mortie interrupted them, when Robert had felt quite sure that Cressida did remember him and could learn to love him. But then, he'd felt even more certain of the bond between them when his guardian took him back to America. He'd been so sure of her affection that he never thought to censor the wild, lonely, unhappy letters he sent her. And look what had happened then! If she *had* been learning to care for that gawky boy, his passionate letters must have scared her into a retreat so profound that she couldn't even acknowledge them.

If he scared her away the same way this time, he'd never forgive himself.

And she was still looking up at him with those wide, faintly doubtful eyes, clearly wondering whether he could explain all those lies he'd told her or whether he was mentally unbalanced.

Perhaps he could work his way round to the explanation gently.

"I—er—it wasn't *exactly* all lies," he said. "I mean, I don't have an aunt."

"*Or* cousins," Cressida prompted, ever so sweetly.

"Or cousins," he agreed. "But I did want to buy a—a rather special present for a rather special girl, and I thought you could help me pick it out."

"Someone you've known for a long time?"

If he said, "Five years," would that be too unromantically obvious?

"In some ways," Robert said carefully, "I feel as if I have known her all my life. I feel as if we have lived and loved in past ages, as though our souls were destined always to meet in life after life."

"And does the lady know about your previous acquaintance?"

The little minx was laughing at him.

"I don't know," Robert said honestly. "I was hoping you could help me find out." He took both of Cressida's hands in his, and was encouraged by the fact that she didn't draw back. "You see, in another way I feel as if I had only met her this week—since I came to London, in fact."

Cressida snatched her hands from his grasp as though he

had pinched her. "Well, I don't know if I can help you, then, for the only ladies *I* know of whom you've just met this week are the ones in Papa's art class—and I don't know them very well. But if it's that Lily Whitworth you brought to the party last night—"

Jealousy, Robert thought, was very revealing. If Cressida could leap so quickly to the wrong conclusion about his lady love, she wasn't as bright as he had thought—or else she was blinded by her own feelings. He smiled broadly. "If I asked you to help me pick out a gift for Lily Whitworth, do you think you could make any useful suggestions?"

"It all depends," Cressida said frostily, "on whether you dare entrust her with the information that you're still disgustingly rich. From what Isolde tells me, I should think Mrs. Whitworth would like nothing so well as a vulgarly large diamond. But if you want to playact with her as you did with me, why don't you invite her on a romantic picnic in the park and see what kind of results you get?"

"Ah," said Robert, "but I still don't know what results I got *this* time. How did it work with you?"

Did he expect her to confess just how close she'd come to falling in love with him all over again? Did he think it funny to try and break her heart again—just for practice—just so he'd know how to do it when he had Lily Whitworth's company instead of hers? Cressida stood up. "You are rude," she informed him in clear, ringing tones that carried out far beyond their secluded grassy nook. "And impertinent. And I don't ever want to have anything to do with you again!"

"You don't understand," Robert protested.

"Oh, I think I understand quite enough."

"Let me explain! Please? Come on—let's walk around the lake and I'll . . ."

"I wouldn't walk to the end of the street with you!" Cressida flashed. "Save your explanations—they're not needed. Go and buy your Mrs. Whitworth diamonds. It's nothing to me. I'll be perfectly happy if I never see you again!"

Robert felt his own temper boiling over. "Then," he

said, gritting his teeth and trying to produce a pleasant smile, "you'll have to keep your eyes closed for the next three months, won't you?"

"Certainly not," Cressida said loftily. "I have no intention of intruding on Papa's art classes. You may take as many classes as you like without ever being in the same room with me again!"

"Fortunately," Robert said, "fortunately for our future relationship, the picture can't be painted on those terms."

Cressida bit her lip. "Picture?" she repeated.

"You must have heard your father discussing his new picture. The one he means to exhibit at the Academy. The great work that's going to get his career started again. The inspiration of a lifetime," Robert prompted gently. "The one we're to model for."

"You mean—the one *you* are modeling for," Cressida corrected him.

"He hasn't mentioned the theme to you? Actaeon," Robert said gently, "spying on Diana. Bathing. You're to be Diana; he says Isolde doesn't look pure and spiritual enough."

"It's too much," Cressida cried out before she could stop herself. "I really cannot bear it!"

She fled, and before Robert could catch up with her she had been intercepted by the shop girl Vi.

"Couldn't 'elp 'earin' your quarrel, ducks," Vi said in a loud whining voice that grated on Robert's ear. She cast a venomous glance back at Robert. "Thought 'e'd get yer off in the bushes fer a bit o' slap an' tickle, did 'e? I 'ad ter send me Mortie off wiv a flea in 'is ear fer the sime reason. Men! Who needs them, I ask yer?"

"You're right," Cressida said gratefully. "Men! Who needs them!"

The two girls went off arm in arm like old friends, and Robert lacked the courage to interrupt them.

Chapter

4

*S*ince Papa's decision to sell Riversedge, Cressida had awakened each morning with a sense of doom hanging over her. She had almost gotten used to the sensation. But the morning after her picnic with Robert was ten times worse then her usual awakening. She didn't just feel doom hanging over her; she felt crushed beneath its weight, utterly incapable of rising and facing the new day. Oh, why had she lost her temper and betrayed herself so thoroughly? She had been doing so well, enjoying her harmless dreams of Robert's love and acting perfectly calm on the surface. If only they had parted on those terms, he might have gone back to America never guessing that she still loved him; and she, in time—fifty or a hundred years, say—might have been able to forget him again.

Cressida felt quite sick at the memory of her jealous outburst. Now Robert would remember her as a spiteful, petty cat who clawed at any other woman within range. Worse, he was probably laughing to himself to think that she, mousy little Cressy, had ever imagined herself capable of competing with a fashionable beauty like Lily Whitworth. *That* was the memory of her he would take back to America.

Then she remembered the worst part of all. He wasn't going back to America. Not yet. Not only would he be in the studio every week for his art lessons, he would probably be there *every day* to pose for Papa's picture. And she would have to be in the same room with him, pretending composure while he talked about Lily Whitworth. Pretending not to care. Pretending not to notice that he would probably be laughing at her all the time. Pretending not to mind that she had to stand up on the stage at the far end of Papa's studio, wrapped in some flimsy drapery that would allow Robert every opportunity of comparing her awkward thin figure with Lily Whitworth's perfect curves.

Two large tears trickled out of Cressida's eyes and she tried, not very successfully, to stifle a sob. The bed she shared with Isolde shook under her and Isolde flopped over with a muttered curse.

"Try to keep still, will you?" she requested of her sister. "*Some* of us were up rather late last night."

Cressida swallowed another sob and Isolde rose up on her elbow to peer at her sister's tear-streaked face in the dim light. "What's the matter, Cressy?"

"I can't bear it," Cressida said. "I don't think I can even face getting out of bed this morning."

"Oh, if *that's* all—" Isolde laughed. "Out late yourself, were you, Miss Propriety? Don't worry, I won't tell Papa— and he won't care if you sleep till noon; we all do. Go back to sleep. If you let me get some rest I'll ask Trevor to take you with us again tonight; Aubrey's going to have a crowd in to look at his illustrations for *Salome*. I understand they're quite wickedly decadent."

Sheer horror at the prospect of the promised treat drove Cressida out of bed. She pulled on the first clothes she could find and vacated the crowded, untidy bedroom where Isolde's aesthetic dresses and Oriental scarves were draped over every surface including the floor.

The rest of the flat was not much better. Resounding snores behind the closed door of the studio indicated that Papa was still abed. The sitting room and kitchen were cluttered with dirty saucepans, half-empty glasses, ashtrays with puddles of wine in them, wine bottles with cigar ashes in them, half-eaten apples, orange peelings, cheese rinds, and bread crumbs.

Cressida felt almost too weak to stand and look at the mess. Who would have believed that she'd scrubbed the flat from top to bottom on Friday before the party and again Saturday morning before she went out with Robert? After she'd gone to bed last night Papa must have brought a few of his friends home.

She would have sat down, but there wasn't a chair in the room that was free of sticky wine splashes. She rested one hand against the wall and leaned there wearily, trying to summon up the strength to do what had to be done—collect trash for the dustbin first, then put away Papa's books and brushes, air out the rooms, scrub all the surfaces. . . . With any luck she could be done by noon. By that time Papa and Isolde would be stirring and looking for food. And in the afternoon, since it was a Sunday and he had no classes, Papa would probably want her and Robert to pose for figure studies for the new picture.

"I can't bear it," Cressida said aloud, and then, "Well, then, I *won't* bear it. Not today, anyway." With sudden new resolution, she put on her worn traveling cloak, scribbled a few words on the back of an unpaid bill to let Papa and Isolde know where she was going, and let herself out of the flat before anyone awoke to stop and question her.

From Papa's Soho flat to the railway station was a long walk in city terms, a short one to a girl who had been used to the freedom of country lanes until two days previously. It had never occurred to Cressida that she might employ a hackney cab to transport her and her suitcases from the railway station to Papa's flat, and she never thought of hailing one now. She walked briskly and steadily on the sensible, well-worn shoes that Isolde had described as "not worth giving to the charwoman, always supposing we employed one," and the exercise brought a little becoming pink to her cheeks. The fine drizzle of morning rain made her think about the dew on the grass at Riversedge, the prospect of a day's escape from the city made her eyes sparkle, and more than one passer-by stopped to stare at the shabby young girl who marched so happily through the streets of Soho.

The railway carriage was crammed full of brightly dressed ladies on their way out of town for some sort of excursion, flushed and bright-eyed and chattering at high speed all the way out of London. Cressida had been somewhat dismayed to find the train so crowded on a Sunday morning, even more dismayed to discover that to reach Riversedge on a Sunday she would have to change at Little-Muchton-on-the-Marsh and again at Wold Willoughby; but she was in a mood to overlook these minor inconveniences. As the train gathered speed she leaned her head back on the padded plush seat and closed her eyes. She felt like a very minor heroine of a Sunday magazine story, escaping from some of those perils that were never fully described but that made one's spine tingle delightfully nevertheless: just what *had* the Wicked Viscount in *A Maiden's Blush* intended to do to Angelina Darcy? Cressida mused.

This intriguing question occupied her until the train was well out of London. After a while, when the delighted exclamations of the ladies with whom she shared the carriage told her that they were safely in the country, she opened her eyes and reveled in the sight of green lanes, blooming hedgerows, and gently rolling hills with newly plowed fields.

If only she were leaving London for good instead of only for the day! With very little effort, Cressida mentally transposed a few chapters of *A Maiden's Blush* and revised the story so that the Wicked Viscount—who now bore an amazing resemblance to Robert Glenford—was proved in the final chapter to be brave and true and pure of heart and entirely worthy of the maiden's love. He carried her off to his house in the country, where Angelina occupied herself with redesigning his gardens and raising a flock of blue-eyed children who for some unaccountable reason all had slight American accents.

Lost in her fantasy, Cressida managed for some time not to hear the happy chatter of the ladies of St. Withburga's on their annual church outing. Unfortunately, a familiar name caught her ear, and after that she couldn't *not* listen. As the ladies chattered on about the vicar's embroidered slippers and the idiocy of that Low Church curate who wanted to take the candles off the altar and the difficulties of managing the flower-arranging schedule, Cressida tried to become happily deaf to their conversation once again. But it was no use. No matter how firmly she told herself that the name was a common one and probably had nothing to do with anyone she knew, she was now tense and unhappy and unable to sink back into her happy dream.

Eventually, after a long aside on the topic of certain people who never took their turn at polishing the monumental brasses, the two ladies directly in front of Cressida returned to the subject that had first caught her attention.

"Mrs. Whitworth won't be there today, will she?" asked the one in the flowered hat.

"I shouldn't think so," replied her somewhat older companion, a woman with a beaky nose protruding from a nest of brown net veiling and with an air of authority about her decisive nods and gestures. "She spends most of her time in London, you know."

"But the dear vicar assured me that the family was still in residence!" wailed Flowered Hat.

"Lady Hayvenhurst will be there, but we shouldn't expect to speak with her," Brown Net Veiling replied briskly. "It's very generous of her to open her gardens for the church excursion and I, for one, don't intend to presume on her good nature by reminding her of our acquaintance. As for Lily Whitworth, she's not *really* part of the family, you know. . . ."

Cressida gathered from the rest of her speech that the Lily Whitworth who had ensnared Robert was connected by marriage with Lady Hayvenhurst of Hayvenhurst, the matriarch of the county. Quite closely connected, in fact; she was the widow of Lady Hayvenhurst's young brother Julian.

"There's a child, too," went on Brown Net Veiling, "a little boy. *Not* Lily Whitworth's son, though; young Whit-

70

worth had some sort of involvement with a Brazilian girl he met on one of his exploring trips. He *said* they'd been married, but . . ." Her voice dropped a little and Cressida heard no more, somewhat to her relief. She was beginning to feel like an eavesdropper. Common sense told her it would have been very hard to avoid Brown Net Veiling's penetrating voice even if she had wanted to; conscience replied that she hadn't wanted to close her ears, that she had been avidly listening to casual gossip about a young woman she barely knew, and that it served her right if she couldn't forget about Lily and Robert for the rest of this trip!

Isolde had complained that young Mrs. Whitworth was always going on about "her" country estate. But she hadn't known—or hadn't mentioned—that the estate in question was Hayvenhurst, barely twenty miles from Riversedge. Cressida mulled over the bits of gossip she had heard and concluded that Lady Hayvenhurst must mean to leave the estate to her nephew, Julian's son. Lily's stepson.

In which case, the little boy would be expected to live there, and Lily would probably live there too, to look after him.

With Robert.

Cressida's overactive imagination immediately produced a revised version of *The Maiden's Blush,* in which Viscount Glenford and the Wicked Widow moved into Hayvenhurst Hall and Cressida Darcy, her heart broken by the viscount's callous toying with her affections, expired of consumption and poverty in the gatekeeper's lodge. Just before her death the viscount discovered that the girl he had abandoned was living there on his own property. Overcome by remorse, he rushed to her bedside, but it was too late; there was time only for some lengthy and quite beautiful speeches of farewell, which Cressida composed with tears in her eyes while the train steamed into Little-Muchton-on-the-Marsh and out again. She didn't come out of her trance until the train stopped with a jerk five stations down the line and the church ladies began to gather themselves and their hats and umbrellas.

"Oh, my goodness!" Cressida gasped, sitting bolt upright in her seat. "Where *are* we?"

"Hayvenhurst, dear, and the hired brake is waiting to take us all to the estate," Brown Net Veiling answered without quite looking at Cressida. "Hurry up, now, we don't want to be late!"

"Wold Willoughby?" Cressida murmured. "Little-Muchton-on-the-Marsh?"

"No, we passed Little Muchton five stations back, dear. We're already at Hayvenhurst. Come along, now." Brown Net Veiling took hold of Cressida's arm and propelled her briskly through the emptying carriage. "I don't believe we've met, have we, dear? Are you a new member of our little group? This way, mind the step, and don't catch your skirt. I do try to keep up with everybody, but my responsibilities are so great. . . ."

Cressida listened, half dazed, to a detailed explanation of the problems involved in managing the Committee to Save St. Withburga's Roof, the St. Withburga's Rummage Sale, the St. Withburga's Choir, and, of course, the St. Withburga's Ladies Garden Club. The energy and efficiency of Brown Net Veiling had Cressida seated in the hired brake that was to convey the ladies to Hayvenhurst Hall before she had a chance to explain that she was not one of their group. By then a morbid fascination with the site of her latest fantasy kept Cressida silent. Why not go along on the garden tour? She'd seen Lady Hayvenhurst at numerous fetes and church bazaars but had never been introduced to her. There was no reason why she should be recognized in this group—and come to that, Cressida thought, no reason why Lady Hayvenhurst should find it strange to see one of Augustine Parris's daughters on a garden tour. She could look over the grounds of Hayvenhurst Hall with no real danger of any social encounter.

And she really had no business at Riversedge today; her unannounced return would only upset Betty. Her hastily scribbled note to Papa, telling him that she'd remembered some instructions she had to give Betty about the airing of the upstairs bedrooms, had only been an excuse to get her away from London for the day.

Away from Robert.

Well, she could stay away from Robert just as well in the gardens of Hayvenhurst Hall as moping around Riversedge, Cressida thought; and perhaps seeing something new would take her mind off things.

"Besides," she announced defiantly, rather to the confusion of the plump middle-aged woman squeezed in beside her, "I've never seen the Hayvenhurst gardens, and I should rather like to!" Cressida could hardly imagine anything lovelier than Riversedge, but Mama had created that small paradise with little money and only one hired boy from the village to help her with the heavy work. It would be interesting to see what somebody with unlimited money and an army of gardeners could achieve on land that wasn't so different, in soil and weather conditions, from that around Riversedge.

"Well, yes, of course, dear," Flowered Hat agreed, "that's why we're going there. The Flower Clock is famous, and so is the topiary garden. And look, we're nearly there—that must be the gate up ahead."

"Mind the lion's paw, dear," Flowered Hat advised Cressida sometime later.

Cressida ducked under the raised paw and found herself staring at a giraffe whose long neck rose up straight in front of her.

"Oh, dear," mourned Flowered Hat, "I've caught my skirt in the peacock! I *do* hope I haven't damaged its tail!"

"Let me help you." Cressida knelt down by the sweeping fan of branches clipped to the shape of a peacock's tail and carefully disentangled a ruffled pink crepe flounce from the thorny branches. The pruned head of the peacock hovered just above her, giving her an uneasy feeling that she might be pecked at any moment. Really, apart from being green and rooted in the ground, this poor unfortunate bush had the most amazing resemblance to the bird it had been trained and clipped to imitate.

73

Catherine Lyndell

"Looks ever so natural, doesn't it?" Flowered Hat said, admiring the "peacock" after Cressida released her.

"Indeed it does," Cressida agreed. They had said the same thing, with slight variations, about the giraffe, the swan, the hippopotamus, and the other animal shapes Lady Hayvenhurst's gardeners had created by rigorous pruning and training of box and privet shrubs. The Hayvenhurst topiary garden was famous in the county; it was called "the green zoo."

Cressida thought she had never seen anything so hideous in all her life.

"Come along, ladies, do come along!" Brown Net Veiling called back to them. "We're to tour the bedding gardens next, with their famous clock—I'm sure you don't want to miss that!"

Obediently, Cressida and her companion trailed the rest of the group down a flight of marble stairs to a shallow parterre where solidly packed beds of scarlet geraniums and yellow alyssum assaulted her eyes. In the midst of this display there was indeed a round shape like a clock face. Cressida blinked, rubbed her eyes, and saw that an arrangement of close-packed pink alpine phlox made a circle of Roman numerals round the edge of the circle of white moss phlox, while two long "hands" composed of brilliant blue lobelia pointed to the hour and minute. The lobelias were planted in long thin arrow-shaped boxes that swung on a central pivot, and Brown Net Veiling was intent on getting everyone close enough to hear the head gardener's explanation of how the clockwork mechanism underneath was ingeniously protected from dirt and water by a glass box.

Cressida decided she had been too critical of the topiary garden.

"Oh, isn't that too clever!" Flowered Hat gushed. "And imagine getting lobelias to bloom so early in the summer! Don't you just love it, Mrs. . . . Mrs. . . ." She glanced uncertainly at Cressida. "Oh, we haven't been properly introduced, have we? But I'm *sure* I've seen you at church. Didn't you help with the choir boys' picnic? I'm Genevra Witherspoon. You must know my husband."

"Must I?" Cressida murmured.

"Of course. He's on *all* the church board committees, and he reads the lessons," Mrs. Witherspoon said with an air of finality that suggested the matter was completely settled.

"Then I must know him," Cressida agreed. "Er—would you excuse me? There's something at the other end of the terrace I want to look at."

She sidled away from the group, ignoring Mrs. Witherspoon's squawks of protest that Cressida would miss the explanation of the flowered clock mechanism.

At the end of the terrace of bedding plants another flight of steps led downward, toward a lake that Mrs. Brown Net Veiling had dismissed as "unimproved, not really part of the formal gardens at all." The misty view of soft green trees and water, with a hint of some gentle color half hidden behind the trees, attracted Cressida far more than the stiff Italianate gardens through which the church group had been guided. From this distance the vista almost reminded her of Mama's garden at Riversedge.

As she went down the curving steps Cressida felt as if she were walking into another world. A series of low walls enclosed little private gardens, each one leading into the next, while at the end of the long mossy path the lake glimmered faintly blue. Walls of old bricks in soft earth tones were all but covered with Virginia creepers and clematis; the long garden beds on each side spilled over with a profusion of hardy country flowers, and every once in a while an opening in the beds led to an inviting shady seat underneath a wisteria-covered arch. Wandering through this gentle, natural garden, she lost track of time, forgot that the damp moss underfoot would stain the hem of her dress, forgot completely that she was supposed to be following the prescribed path laid out for the ladies of St. Withburga's Garden Club.

The sun broke through the clouds for a moment and Cressida blinked, startled by the dazzle of light flashing off glass somewhere beneath the trees that encircled the lake. What could that be? She started forward to investigate, then stopped as she heard an apologetic cough behind her.

"I'd no' go that way if I was you, missus," said the soft Scots burr of Lady Hayvenhurst's head gardener. "Leddy Hayvenhurst will be in her glass house now, tending to young Master Julian's plants, and she'll no' take kindly to being disturbed at the task."

"Oh!" Cressida turned and saw the gardener's eyes twinkling at her from under his ancient checked cap. "I'm sorry—I didn't realize I had strayed so far. This garden is so lovely, after—" She bit her tongue. It would be extremely tactless of her to criticize the formal bedding arrangements and tortured topiary of the gardens nearer the house; very likely they were this man's pride and joy. "I'm sorry, Mr. . . ."

"Craigie. Alexander Craigie. Leddy Hayvenhurst's head gardener," the man introduced himself. "And no offense taken. It's a treat for me to see a pretty young leddy enjoying my gardens, especially one wi' the good taste to like the Lang Walk better than that trash up by the Hall." He made a face so expressive of his own disgust that Cressida smiled in relief, recognizing a kindred soul. Of course, she knew better than to take his flattering words at face value. If this garden—the one he called the Long Walk—represented the gardener's own taste, and the stiff formal gardens nearer the Hall were only what his employer forced him to make, naturally he would find anyone who shared his opinion beautiful and clever and possessed of all the virtues. Mama had felt the same way about anybody with the good taste to prefer her water garden to the clipped and trained hedges around the vicarage.

"Mind you," the gardener added, "the Lang Walk's no' what it'll be come high summer. You should see it when the daylilies come out. . . ."

This, too, was familiar to Cressida. There couldn't be a gardener alive who was not eager to explain that the garden was not at its peak just now; you really should see it next month, when such-and-such a flower was in bloom, or next year, when the new perennials had their growth, or in ten years, when the newly planted wisteria had grown to cover the porch. She sat down happily on a damp stone bench and listened to Lady Hayvenhurst's head gardener expound his plans for the Long Walk. They discovered a mutual admiration for Mr. William Robinson's book, *The Wild Garden,* which had been a direct inspiration for much of Cressida's mother's work.

"I used the second one more, ma'sel'," Mr. Craigie told Cressida. *"The English Flower-Garden.* You'll mind what he says in there about using the hardy herbaceous flowers in perennial beds. . . . No? You've not seen that book? Aweel, that's a pity, lass. I'd be glad to lend it to you, but I suppose you'll be going back to London with the rest o' the leddies. . . ."

"Oh, my goodness," Cressida gasped at this reminder of her position, "not if I don't get back to the group, I won't! They hired a brake to bring us here from the station . . . and it's ever such a long way. . . ."

"Aye," the gardener agreed. "Best go through Marble Arch, that'll bring you around tae the front of the house." He chuckled at Cressida's confusion and pointed down a path she hadn't explored. "That way, right across the front lawn. You'll see why I call it Marble Arch when you get there."

Cressida picked up her skirts and ran in the direction the gardener had indicated, feeling her mud-stained hems flapping against her ankles and uneasily aware that the sensation of dampness she'd felt on sitting down on that bench had not departed when she got up. She wondered, without pausing to check, just how much of the greenish stuff on the stone bench had transferred itself to her skirt and whether she could get back to London without ever turning her back on anyone.

"Oh, bother!" she thought, and then, emerging into the sunlight at the end of a long shaded path, "Marble Arch. Yes, I see." The front lawn of Hayvenhurst Hall was dotted with statues of all vintages, some classically nude, others draped in stone renderings of modern bustles and frills. Cressida dodged around a one-armed Venus, ducked under

77

the raised hands of three dancing Graces, skidded around a little girl petting her stone dog, and came to a halt before the black bombazine dress and clanking keys of a woman whose face was as stony as the statues around her.

"You're late," the woman announced in tones that brooked no argument—not that Cressida was inclined to give any.

"I know," she said humbly. "I ran all the way—"

"That," said her interlocutor, "is only too obvious. You must learn not to run, or at least not to *pant* when you do so."

Cressida was so used to hearing this sort of criticism of her habits from Isolde and her father that she was hardly surprised to find a total stranger taking on the same role. She looked around an empty drive.

"Have the ladies from St. Withburga's left already?"

"The garden club? Yes, they're long gone—not that it's any of your business!"

Cressida wondered how this stern woman had recognized her for an imposter. Perhaps some of the ladies in the church group had compared notes and realized that none of them knew the mousy little girl in the brown dress. Still, it did seem hard-hearted of them to have abandoned her here with never a word. She wondered even more how she would get back to the railway station. She tried to tell herself that she'd made longer walks many a time, but there was a certain difference between a morning ramble through the fields around her own village and a seven-mile walk along a paved road, in thin city shoes, when she was already tired from running.

"You'd better come in," the woman who had intercepted her announced, and Cressida felt a wave of relief. Presumably Lady Hayvenhurst had been informed of her plight and would order a dog cart or a gig out to take her to the station—she certainly wouldn't want Cressida left sitting on her doorstep!

"I am Lady Hayvenhurst's housekeeper. You call me Mrs. Simpson."

There seemed to be no useful reply to this. Cressida followed the housekeeper through the long wet grass that clustered around the statues, noting rather sadly that her shoes squelched and oozed water at every step. They were the only respectably thin shoes she owned, and she'd been wearing them every day to please Papa, but there was no help for it now; she'd have to go back to her boots.

The housekeeper veered off at an angle before they reached the dry gravel of the front drive. Cressida plodded on until a sharp yank on her arm jerked her back.

"Whatever do you think you are doing, my girl? The front door's not for the likes of you!"

Cressida was shocked out of her silence. "Well, really," she declared, "I didn't expect to meet Lady Hayvenhurst *personally,* but surely—"

"Meet Lady Hayvenhurst!" Mrs. Simpson sounded positively shocked. "I should say not! Whatever put such a notion into your head, my girl?" Her fat red hand again restrained Cressida as she turned toward the front door. "Now you listen, my girl, and listen good, for I'll not expect to be telling you this again. Front door's for gentry. Servants and tradesmen go round the back—I should've thought you'd know that much, at least, for all I'd been warned you'd not been trained in the orphanage! Very good of Lady Hayvenhurst it is to be offering you a home and a good start in service, and I don't want to see you insulting her ladyship with your up-and-coming ways again! Come along o' me, now—this way!" Like a ship with billowing black sails, Mrs. Simpson towed Cressida along by one arm toward the back of Hayvenhurst Hall, talking so continuously as she did so that Cressida could not get a word in edgewise.

"What's your name? Cressida? Heathen nonsense! I don't hold with my housemaids putting on fancy names as belongs more to the gentry. And made-up names at that. The letter from the orphanage said your given name was Jane, and Jane you'll be as long as you work under my direction. Here's where we go, through the stable yard. You don't look the sort as would be loitering and casting eyes at the stable boys, I'll say that for you anyway."

"I should think not!" Cressida burst out indignantly. "And, Mrs. Simpson, there's been a mistake. I'm not—"

"Yes, yes, my girl, anybody can see you're not properly trained for the position. You don't need to explain that to me! Never you mind. I'll have you work with one of the other girls until you know your duties. Now don't interrupt again when I'm speaking! Had that dress from the orphanage, did you? Hmmph! They didn't turn you out in much style, did they?"

They had reached the back door by now. Mrs. Simpson led Cressida through a damp, stone-floored scullery into a cavernous kitchen where two iron cookstoves stood side by side in the arch of what once must have been an enormous fireplace. She spun Cressida around with one meaty hand while she continued talking, thinking out loud as she mentally measured Cressida for a housemaid's uniform. "Two print dresses and one black one for afternoons, aprons, caps— you're a little bit of a thing, aren't you? Never mind, we can take up one of Abby's dresses to do until you have time to make your own. You can't show yourself downstairs until you've got the black dress made, but it'll take me that long to teach you proper manners anyway."

Cressida's cheeks burned pink as Mrs. Simpson went on with her breathless monologue. She had known her dress was shabby, but never in her wildest fantasies had she imagined that someone would take her for an orphanage girl going out to service—or that her sturdy old brown foulard dress would be scorned as unfit wear for an underhousemaid!

The embarrassments of her situation seemed to be multiplying faster than she could reckon them up. Oh, how could she have been such an idiot! If only she'd made it back in time to catch the brake back to the station with the rest of St. Withburga's Garden Club! It would have been bad enough having to explain her plight to Lady Hayvenhurst and begging a ride back to the railway station. Now she would first have to explain to Mrs. Simpson that she was really a lady and not the new underhousemaid from the orphanage—a task that so staggered Cressida, she hardly knew where to begin.

"You'll have one afternoon a week for your free time, to begin with and, of course, Sunday morning for church." Mrs. Simpson shot her a sharp glance. "You are Church of England? Of course you are—what am I thinking of? A good church orphanage wouldn't be bringing up girls as Dissenters. You can sleep with Abby. Come on upstairs. I'll show you your room and you can put your things down . . ." A frown creased the housekeeper's plump white forehead and she looked closely at Cressida for the first time since they'd met. "Don't you *have* anything but that reticule? Lord help us, I don't know what the world is coming to; I'd think even the orphanage wouldn't send a girl out into the world without so much as a hairbrush to call her own. Never mind, I'll see you're fitted out, and we can stop the cost out of your first month's wages. Come along, now."

Mrs. Simpson led the way up endless flights of narrow back stairs without even pausing for breath, lifting her black bombazine skirts and keeping up a running commentary on the dust and black beetles and other signs of failings on the part of the current housemaids. In between complaining about the laziness of the absent "Abby" she threw out questions to Cressida and answered them herself. By the time they reached the topmost landing Cressida was out of breath herself and quite impressed with the housekeeper's boundless energy.

She was also favorably impressed with the room Mrs. Simpson showed her. True, it was narrow, set right under the eaves of the house with a sloping roof so that one couldn't stand up in most of the room. But it was bright and pretty, with fresh flowered curtains at the window and matching coverlets on the two narrow little beds, and the casement window opened onto a view of the Long Walk and the lake at the bottom of the garden. Cressida gave an involuntary sigh. For a moment she almost wished she were the orphan girl for whom this bright, neat little room was destined. She imagined what it would mean to wake in the mornings to a view of the Long Walk, to be paid for cleaning up the messes left by other people, to have a definite free day in each week. To the Cressida who'd left Riversedge this would have seemed a very cramped, mean existence. To the Cressida who felt choked on London smog after two days in the city, who had nothing to return to except waiting on Papa and Isolde and trying to conceal her feelings from a man who loved somebody else—to this Cressida the housemaid's room at the top of the stairs looked very much like a refuge.

"You're to be downstairs by six thirty sharp every morning," Mrs. Simpson informed her. "First off you sweep the carpets—I don't suppose you know how to lay the dust first?"

"Damp tea leaves," Cressida answered promptly, "or wet sand. Sprinkle over the carpet, let stand five minutes, then sweep off." She'd done the same chore many a morning at Riversedge.

"Hmmph!" Mrs. Simpson snorted, but not disapprovingly. "You may do at that. Now, you and Abby will do the breakfast room and the front hall—clean, dust, and tidy—lay the breakfast by eight fifteen. Then you can clear off upstairs to make your beds. I expect always to see this room exactly as neat and clean as it is now, you understand me? Breakfast in the servants' hall at eight thirty then at nine thirty you'll help Abby with the work of the day. Tomorrow's Monday, so you'll trim the lamps and clean the lamp chimneys; Tuesdays you clean the silver in the dining room; first and third Wednesdays you clean the front hall and polish the brasses, second and fourth you clean the dining room and polish the oak table; Thursdays . . . well, never mind, Abby will tell you each day what the task is. You're to be through with the downstairs work before lunch; from then until tea I expect to see you usefully employed on some improving task. In your case, you can begin with sewing your new uniforms."

"Is that all?" Cressida felt that Mrs. Simpson must have left something out of the list of chores. What she'd mentioned sounded like a light morning's work, far less than Cressida did at home, and here she wouldn't even have to cook meals for herself—or anybody else.

Cressida Parris, are you seriously thinking of being an underhousemaid at Hayvenhurst?

Mrs. Simpson puffed her chest out and said in a lofty answer to Cressida's question, "Lady Hayvenhurst can well afford an adequate complement of servants. We're not one of your nip-farthing establishments that tries to put a good face on things by having one underfed tweeny to do three girls' work. It was your lucky day you came here, Jane!"

Cressida was beginning to think it might be indeed. *Why not stay here?* she demanded of her censorious conscience. Why not indeed? It didn't have to be a lifetime commitment. This post would give her someplace to eat and sleep for a few months, a safe place where Papa couldn't find her—as he would if she retreated to Riversedge—and bully her into coming back to London. She would just stay here until Papa got started on his Academy picture using some other model—just until he got far enough along that he couldn't change his plans and make Cressida model again. Maybe, Cressida calculated quickly, it would be safer to wait until he had quite finished the picture. Until Robert had gone away again. . . .

The bubble of mad humor that had sustained her thus far suddenly deflated. Robert. Yes. Of course, it would be wise to stay away from London until Robert had married his Lily and gone back to America with her. After what she'd overheard from the ladies on the church tour, she didn't have much fear that Lily would come down to Hayvenhurst with Robert; from what they'd said and what Cressida had seen, the young widow much preferred the gaiety of London to this quiet, rather staid establishment in the country.

If she took this position, Cressida reflected rather sadly, there was very little danger that she would have to face Robert ever again in her life.

Which was a very good thing. Wasn't it?

Mrs. Simpson observed Cressida's sudden pallor, the droop of her shoulders, and the mournful look in her eyes, and misinterpreted these signs in a very natural way.

"You look ready to drop, dear," she observed. "Such a

skinny little thing as you are, I'll wager they didn't feed you properly at the orphanage—and then walking all that way here. Come along downstairs. It's not time for a meal, but I'll have Cook find something for you.''

As she was hustled back down to the kitchen, Cressida reflected that she had better find out exactly where this orphanage was and what had happened to the girl who was supposed to be interviewing for the housemaid's job this morning. But she had no chance to pose tactful questions; Mrs. Simpson talked all the way down the stairs, talked her into the kitchen, and issued her instructions to the cook in between another series of questions that she answered herself before Cressida had a chance to do so.

"Ready to start today, are you? That's good. I like to see a willing spirit in a girl. Give her some of that veal pie from last night, Mrs. Leonard. You can see the child was half starved at the orphanage. It's too late in the day for you to be showing yourself belowstairs, of course, but I'll have Abby help you cut out the material and you can begin sewing your new uniforms after lunch. You *can* do plain sewing, I trust? Straight seams and hems? Let's have a pot of tea, Mrs. Leonard. Nothing to pick you up like a nice cup of tea with plenty of sugar. At least you've a nice speaking voice—not like the last charity girl we took on— I'll say that for you. Where'd you learn to talk so proper ladylike, Jane?"

It took Cressida a moment to realize that she was being addressed; the housekeeper's rather cavalier rechristening of her hadn't quite sunk in yet.

"I . . . ah . . ." she stammered at last.

"Don't talk with your mouth full, child!" Mrs. Simpson admonished Cressida before she'd even thought of an explanation for her upper-class accent.

"And don't *you* go terrifying the girl, Simpson," an even more aristocratic voice admonished the housekeeper from the doorway.

"Your ladyship!"

Mrs. Leonard and Mrs. Simpson jumped up from the worn kitchen table and stood one on either side of Cressida.

"Just giving the new housemaid a bite to eat, your lady-ship," the housekeeper informed Lady Hayvenhurst.

"She's that peaked, you'd think a strong wind 'ud blow her away," the cook added.

"So I see." Lady Hayvenhurst slowly looked over the table. A broken veal pie and a plate of chocolate biscuits were set before Mrs. Simpson; Mrs. Leonard had a slice of rum cake and a pot of tea before her place. Cressida, on whom these luxuries were supposed to be lavished, kept her eyes modestly lowered and tried to think herself into the skin of an orphanage girl in her first job. Surely Lady Hayvenhurst wouldn't recognize her? Cressida was familiar enough with Lady Hayvenhurst's iron-gray hair and tall, angular figure from having seen her opening any number of garden shows, village fetes, and church rummage sales. But Cressida herself had never taken any part in these country affairs; she'd always been "the mousy little Parris girl—you know, the younger sister" trailing behind Papa and Isolde, all but eclipsed by their bohemian brilliance.

"Stand up, girl, when her ladyship does you the honor to come into the room," Mrs. Simpson hissed into Cressi-da's ear, reinforcing the command with a pinch that made Cressida squeak in surprise. She got to her feet as awk-wardly as any country girl, ducked her head and muttered, "Yes'm," when Lady Hayvenhurst asked her something—what, she scarcely knew.

"You call *me* ma'am," Mrs. Simpson corrected her with another tweak. "Lady Hayvenhurst is 'your ladyship.' I'm that sorry about her manners, your ladyship," the house-keeper apologized in the next breath. "She's really a bright, taking little thing, but of course she's had no training to speak of and she's shy of your ladyship, as is only proper."

"Very likely," Lady Hayvenhurst agreed in a voice so dry that Cressida felt sure her masquerade had been discov-ered. A tide of warmth began creeping up her neck, only to be dispelled by Lady Hayvenhurst's next words. "Well, no need to frighten the child still more, Simpson. I'm sure she'll do very well."

As she left the kitchen, Lady Hayvenhurst reflected that

her eyes were still as good as ever. It *had* been the younger Parris girl she'd seen being towed around to the kitchen door by her officious housekeeper. What the child was doing there and why she was trying to take service as a housemaid were mysteries that remained to be solved—but not today, not in front of Simpson; she would wait until she could question the girl in private. Or maybe—Lady Hayvenhurst's lips curved upward at the thought—maybe she wouldn't question her at all, not quite yet. She wasn't socially acquainted with the Parris family, but county gossip had long declared it to be a crying shame, the way that rackety Augustine Parris exploited his younger daughter. For years, it was said, she'd been little more than a maid-of-all-work to keep Riversedge open for him and his bohemian friends, giving her no chance to meet eligible young men. If the girl was so desperate that she'd rather work as a paid servant than slave for her father without wages, Lady Hayvenhurst saw no reason to spoil her game at the outset. Something would have to be done, of course, but not immediately; she was impressed by the girl's spirit in taking this chance, and it would be a pity to ruin the masquerade for her by letting her know she'd been recognized before she'd even started.

Lady Hayvenhurst went back to the small sitting room where she kept up with her correspondence and extracted from one gilt drawer in her elegant desk the note from the mistress of the Farthingdonshire Christian Orphanage regretting that the girl who was to have been sent as an underhousemaid had run away to marry a cowman and would no longer be available for the post. It had been careless of her not to notify Simpson that the new housemaid was not coming—careless but, as it turned out, providential too. Humming tunelessly to herself, Lady Hayvenhurst tore the letter into shreds and dropped the fragments of paper into the fireplace.

Chapter 5

"*B*last that girl!"

An empty bottle flew through Augustine Parris's studio and splintered against the far wall, leaving a pile of sparkling glass shards in a puddle of red wine dregs. "Damn and blast," said Parris mildly, "it wasn't entirely empty after all. Waste of good wine—and who's to clean it up now?"

This reminded him of his grievance. He snarled at the empty canvas on his easel, dramatically picked up one of the sticks of charcoal and snapped it in two.

"I cannot work," he announced to the empty room. "My inspiration is gone. An artist must be shielded from the difficulties of life, not thrown into the raging maelstrom of emotional torment. My eye for color, my instinct for design, my unerring hand—what are all these without—"

"Your model?" suggested Isolde. As it was scarcely noon on Monday morning, she had not troubled to dress yet; her magnificent curves were loosely wrapped in a black-and-white garment that suffered from the illusion that it was an authentic Japanese kimono, and her yellow hair streamed in a mass of careless curls (and a few careless tangles) halfway down her back.

"I was going to say," Augustine corrected her, "without my peace of mind." He glowered at the naked canvas. "But a model would also be useful. I don't know what Cressida is thinking of! Bad enough that I had to cancel yesterday's session because she took it into her head to go down to Riversedge, but I did think she'd have the common decency to come back by the evening train so that we could start work today. Now it's too late. I have to start setting up for my blasted ladies' painting class. Even if Cressida walked in the door this minute it would be too late to send for young Glenford and start a really productive work session. Even if she were here right now," Augustine Parris elaborated with a slight whine creeping into his voice, "even if she were already artistically draped as Diana, it would be too late. And after class the light will be too bad to start. Really, you'd think the girl didn't care anything at all for my career."

"You might get that impression," Isolde agreed with a lazy smile, "especially since she's not going to walk in the door right this minute—or tonight—or next week, for that matter."

"What?" For once Isolde had her father's full attention.

"The afternoon post just arrived." With a tantalizing motion, Isolde waved a sheet of closely written white stationery at Augustine, then tucked it somewhere inside the folds of her black-and-white wrapper. "Cressida has met some friends in the country. She's going to stay with them for a few months."

"Oh, no, she isn't," Augustine contradicted his elder daughter. He breathed heavily through his nose. "She knows I want her here to model for *Actaeon and Diana,* and by God, she's coming home if I have to take the train down and drag her back bodily! Where did she say she's visiting?"

Isolde shook her head with an appearance of regret. "I don't think she wanted you to know."

"She didn't say?"

"If she *wants* you to drag her back to London," Isolde pointed out, "she can always write again and let us know where she's staying, can't she? Maybe she'll do that—or maybe you'd better find yourself another model. Do tell me what you decide on—later. I must dress now; I'm reading my new poem at Constantia's salon this afternoon." Just before turning to leave, Isolde let her lazy glance drift down to the floor at the far end of the studio, where a red wine stain was set off by a halo of sparkling glass shards. "Perhaps somebody should clean that up before your artistic ladies come," she observed. "It seems you can't expect Cressida to do it—not this season, anyway."

With a mocking laugh she flitted out the studio door, already pulling at the ties that held her wrapper in place. Just outside the door she stopped short, gasped, and snatched frantically at her loosened belt.

"I wouldn't breathe so deeply," Robert Glenford advised her. "It's undoing the good work of your fingers." He took the belt from Isolde's lax hands, pulled it tight about her waist, and tied it in a neat bow. She looked up at him, breathing deeply in and out, on purpose now rather than from shock. He was only the second man she'd met in London to whom she could look up without bending her knees; something about either the city air or the artistic life seemed to stunt men's growth.

Robert Glenford differed from Papa's artistic crowd in a number of other ways that puzzled and intrigued Isolde. His behavior just now was a case in point. Most men never looked farther than Isolde's magnificent bosom; most of them wanted to remove her wrappers rather than tie them back on, and they babbled about painting and the beauty of nature while they worked on her.

Even Trevor Bayne-Fleetworth, whose initial attraction for Isolde had simply been the fact that he topped her by six inches and made her feel delicate and tiny, usually didn't gaze into her eyes; once he looked that far down, his eyes naturally kept traveling.

Robert Glenford seemed provokingly immune to her charms; and Isolde, who was used to complaining bitterly about the difficulties of carrying on an intellectual conversation with men whose eyes never left her bosom, now thought with regret that at least she was having *some* effect on those other men. Glenford was looking at her as though she were some inconvenient piece of furniture that needed to be politely set aside.

"If you'll excuse me," Robert said at last, "I had some business with your father." He tried to sidle around her, but Isolde was quite large enough to block the studio door.

"If you mean the modeling," Isolde said, not moving, "didn't you have his note? It's off. Cressida's disappeared."

"Yes, I know. Your belt is coming loose again," Robert said. "Wouldn't you like to go and get dressed? That's what I came about. It's not right for an innocent young girl like her to be traveling around alone. I want to escort her back from Riversedge."

If anybody had called Isolde an "innocent young girl," she would have been insulted at the implication that she lacked worldly knowledge, and if they had tried to force her into going chaperoned like a polite society miss, she would have subjected them to a fierce lecture on the Rights of Women. All the same, she felt one pang of something very like jealousy. It might be very restful, just once in a while, to be protected from the world by a man like Robert Glenford.

Who was still not looking below her chin, although he was clearly aware of the inadequacy of her morning wrapper.

This time Isolde tied the belt herself, twitching the loose ends of the bow with an irritable little jerk that all but undid her good work. "Then it'll do you no good to talk to Papa," she said with a laugh that sounded very affected even in her own ears, "for he has no idea where she's gone, and cares less, save for being angry that she's not back to be his model!"

"I . . . see," said Robert, looking deep into her eyes, and Isolde had the uncanny feeling that he understood much more than she'd said. "I thought Cressida had gone to Riversedge. I take it that's not true? How do you know?"

Isolde shrugged. The artless gesture tightened the wrapper revealingly about her upper body. "Well, she's certainly not there now," she replied obliquely.

"You mean she's been missing for a day and a half, nobody knows where she is, and Parris isn't even *worried?*" Robert demanded.

Isolde shrugged again. "I didn't say that *nobody* knows where she is—only that Papa doesn't know." She saw no point in giving away any more information than she had to. At least Robert Glenford wasn't looking through her like a piece of unwanted furniture now! It was rather gratifying to have his attention.

"Well, where is she," Robert demanded, "and what's she doing? Why did she . . ." He paused and his face slowly turned dark red.

"You think she ran away from *you!*" Isolde gave a little crow of laughter. "No such thing. She didn't say a word about you in her letter—only that she was tired of our way of life and meant to stay with friends for a while." That was almost true; at any rate, Cressida had begged Isolde not to tell Robert how she felt about him, so Isolde felt that her little lie was only a means of keeping faith with her sister. "It was really quite rude of her," Isolde went on, forgetting about Robert for a moment in her own annoyance with Cressida. "I'm sure I did all I could to make her feel welcome here. I told her she could sleep as late as she wanted and that she should ignore Papa's fussing about the mess in the flat just as I did. She could perfectly well have picked up our bedroom and cooked an occasional meal for us and let him fend for himself if he didn't want to be there at mealtimes, but no, she had to turn herself into his slave and clean the whole flat and run herself ragged trying to keep him eating healthy meals! And I even put myself out to introduce her to all my friends, or I would have done if she'd stayed around. Just yesterday morning I told her she could come to Aubrey's party with Trevor and me, but then when I got up she'd already slipped away!"

"Amazing," said Robert. He placed Isolde's hand on his arm and led her into the sitting room, where drawn shades and artistically placed draperies somewhat disguised the squalor of the room. "Do sit down and tell me all about it. I can't imagine why she would run away from such a pleasant life."

Isolde gave him a flat, weary, utterly bored look. "Oh, yes, you can," she contradicted him. "I saw how you looked at the party Friday night. You're a nice, pure-minded, clean-souled American boy, and you despise my set and all we stand for, and you think the better of Cressida for running away."

"It's not my way of life," Robert conceded, "and I don't think it's Cressida's, but that doesn't necessarily mean I despise you, Isolde."

"Don't you?" Isolde leaned back on the soft settee, raised her arms above her head, and pretended to yawn. "God, sometimes *I* despise this life! It's all so weary and boring and utterly pointless. But then, what isn't?"

"You don't mean that." Robert reached forward and gently twitched the folds of Isolde's wrapper shut. His hand lingered for a moment and Isolde looked up through her lashes with a little three-cornered smile that usually drove men wild trying to guess what she meant by it.

Robert didn't even seem to notice. He tugged at the front of Isolde's wrapper again and listened to something—what? The sharp corners of the folded letter scraped against Isolde's skin. She grimaced slightly and tried to wriggle into a more comfortable position, but the letter wouldn't cooperate; one corner was insistently digging into a very tender place. Isolde wriggled again and this time she heard it too: the very faint crackle of paper whenever she moved.

She flung herself backward across the length of the settee, one hand clasped protectively over her bosom. Robert did not move. Leaning forward like that, with one hand outstretched, he should have seemed ridiculous. But he looked as if he did not know or care how he appeared.

"I wasn't going to ravish you, you know," he said. "I only wanted—"

"Cressida's letter." Isolde tilted her chin and gave Robert her most provocative smile. "Come and take it, then—

or aren't you man enough to take a letter from one poor weak girl?''

"Let's say, rather, that I'm too much a gentleman to try to take the letter from where you've hidden it," Robert suggested. A dull tide of red rose up his neck and washed about his ears, but his voice remained perfectly steady. "And if that doesn't satisfy you—I'm also too intelligent to try ripping your clothes off with your father in the next room preparing for a class."

"Oh, Papa doesn't care what I do!" Isolde laughed. She stopped in midbreath, feeling oddly desolate. What she'd said was perfectly true, but suddenly it struck her as no laughing matter.

"Well, I do," Robert told her. "Your family was very good to me when I was in England before, and I would like to think of you as my sister and my good friend. A man doesn't like to see his sister flopping about on the settee and almost falling out of her dressing gown."

His flat tone and unromantic choice of words made Isolde feel like a hoyden just out of the schoolroom being admonished to sit up straight. She did sit up, and gazed resentfully at Robert. He'd taken all the fun out of her little game.

"Oh, all right," she said ungraciously. She held out the letter so that Robert could just see Cressida's neat handwriting crossing the coarse sheet, then snatched it back before he could take the paper from her hand. He could just make out the one tear-splotched line, ". . . cannot bear to see him again, so. . . ."

"I won't give you the letter, but I'll tell you where it came from: Hayvenhurst Hall."

Robert nodded slightly. "I understand that it would be quite improper of me to read what your sister has written in a private letter to you, but could you tell me what else she said?"

"Nothing about *you*," said Isolde, lying unblushingly. "Just that—she doesn't like living with us—and she won't model for Papa—and she's visiting friends and doesn't know exactly when she'll be back. I was going to tell you where she was anyway, even if you hadn't bullied me," she added. "I think you two prim-and-proper types will get on very well together—you're much more her sort than Trevor is!"

"Bayne-Fleetworth? Is that why she's left? Did he . . ." Robert's ears began to turn red again.

"Make improper advances to her?" Isolde caroled with an artificial laugh. "Of course not—he hardly knows she's alive." But he'd begun to notice. Isolde considered Trevor her property, even if he didn't know it yet, and he had paid altogether too much attention to Cressida when she joined them on Friday night to get away from Papa's party. She was quite content to have Cressida down at Hayvenhurst Hall instead of moping about the London flat with those big mournful eyes of hers that lured men to try and cheer her up. Besides, the little mouse *did* deserve a bit of fun for once, instead of being left to molder away at Riversedge or becoming Papa's maid-of-all-work in London. Isolde had done her best to show the kid some fun, but since she didn't have the joie de vivre to enjoy a good time in London—Isolde shrugged her shoulders again and made a face like a disappointed kitten.

"I hope she's having fun at Lady H.'s house party," Isolde said. "And she'd probably think *you're* fun, too, and she's welcome to you. And if you can keep her mind off Trevor Bayne-Fleetworth, I'll dance at your wedding." She slipped off the settee and went to her room to dress, feeling mildly complacent at the way things had turned out. Robert Glenford was a dry stick of a fellow and no fun whatsoever, but he'd do remarkably well for Cressida; her little sister was a fool not to recognize that, and an idiot not to see that Robert was mad for her, and running away to Hayvenhurst instead of staying in London and gently encouraging Robert's advances had been the height of folly. With all those hours of modeling in Papa's studios, swathed in a few wisps of filmy drapery, even Cressida should have been able to bring the boy to the point of proposing!

Well, Isolde had done her little bit to straighten things out for her sister—true, not until she'd established that Robert would be absolutely no use to her. She'd thought it might be fun to get him interested in her; it might make Trevor jealous, might provoke him into giving her the kind of passionate attentions she'd missed of late. But Robert was too dull and proper to be any fun. Very well, let him go down to Hayvenhurst Hall and surprise Cressida. Isolde spared not a thought for Cressida's anguished plea for her to keep Robert, of all people, unaware of her hiding place. The girl didn't know what was good for her, and she was lucky she had an older sister with some knowledge of the world to straighten her life out.

Isolde might have felt slightly less complacent if she'd remembered who else had connections at Hayvenhurst Hall or where Robert might turn for an invitation.

Lily Whitworth had awakened that Monday with a shiver of pleasurable anticipation that rather surprised her. Lately everything and everyone she knew had seemed extremely dull. Ever since Julian's death, in fact, she'd been feeling peevish and out of sorts. She'd tried all the crazes of the moment, looking without success for some amusement. First, she'd tried Sports. That had been a serious mistake. Lawn tennis made her hot and sweaty, archery was for female Amazons with great ugly muscular arms, and bicycling was absolutely out of the question.

This year, it had been Art. The china-painting class was full of boring old ladies and taught by a mousy young man with barely three strands of hair on his receding chin. The music lessons had seemed to show rather more promise—the violin teacher was French, and although he looked rather weedy, there might have been interesting developments from their hours alone. One never knew about Frenchmen, Lily thought. But they *were* too emotional. This one had broken down in tears after only the second lesson, begging her not to study music any longer because he could not bear it. He said no more than that, but Lily was perceptive enough to read between the lines. Naturally she could never marry a man so far below her socially, and a foreigner at that; poor Monsieur Jean must have been in despair when he thought about the gulf that separated them.

No wonder he said that every note that came from her violin was a torment to him! Lily dropped the lessons at once—one could in decency do no less—and found afterward that the thought of music made her too sad to search out lessons with another teacher.

Augustine Parris's painting class was to have been her last foray into Art; Lily firmly believed that nothing was worth more than three tries. If things didn't work out after that, it was time to move on to something else. She would give up Art and try Good Works as a source of entertainment and social life.

The prospect was so dispiriting that she had actually gone back to Augustine's studio for a fourth class after the boredom of the first three. And behold, her perseverance was rewarded! Lily considered the appearance of a handsome, personable, and wealthy young American as a direct sign from heaven that she was meant to continue in her artistic career. Or course, there was that nonsense he'd talked on Friday about having lost all his money—ridiculous! Lily studied the society sections of the daily papers avidly. She might be slightly unclear about why Captain Dreyfus was in such trouble with the French government or why Mr. Keir Hardie had formed the new Independent Labour Party, but she could have recited the guest list at the Duchess of Binghampton's ball from memory and she knew exactly what Highly Placed Personage had been seen (in disguise, of course, and absolutely not to be recognized as the Prince of Wales) at the Canterbury music hall.

And she knew that the American millionaire, Mr. Robert Glenford, had lately been visiting London as the guest of Mr. and Mrs. Oswald Farquharson (of the Sussex Farquharsons, naturally, not the inferior Northumberland branch).

So if Robert Glenford claimed to have lost his money through unfortunate speculations, he must be joking—mustn't he?

A slight frown marred the porcelain perfection of Lily's features as she sipped her morning cocoa (it was after two o'clock, but she had slept until past noon) and considered the question. She already regarded Robert Glenford as her personal property; he'd appeared in the drawing class like a direct message of heaven's approval; he'd carried her things to the carriage afterward and had escorted her to the party that night. Clearly he was smitten with her charms. And it was *most* inconsiderate of him to leave her in doubt as to whether he was really the sort of man she could afford to marry. The pittance she received from Julian's estate hardly paid for this minuscule flat, a maidservant, and a miserly dress allowance; for theater tickets, flowers, dinners at the Savoy, and all the other details of a truly satisfactory life Lily was dependent upon the good wishes of the gentlemen she met. Fortunately, most gentlemen wished her well and were only too happy to provide some little treat for her. But if she remarried, her admirers would drift off to pay court to some more eligible lady. It was therefore absolutely necessary that Lily's future husband be financially able to replace the covey of admirers who vied with one another to make her life rich and full. Couldn't Robert see that?

Lily considered this question, still frowning ever so slightly, until the afternoon post brought news so shocking that it temporarily put everything else out of her mind. She could hardly concentrate on the important task of dressing for the Monday drawing class to which she'd looked forward with such excitement, and when her fool of a maid brought the black crepe veil instead of the half-mourning hat and scarf of deep lilac that Lily had decided to begin wearing that day, she didn't even slap the woman.

"Such terrible news!" she announced that afternoon when, ravishingly attired in the lilac hat and scarf that framed her fragile blonde beauty so enticingly, she swept into Augustine Parris's studio and sank down like one about to faint.

The cheap straight-backed chairs that Augustine Parris provided for his students rigidly repulsed Lily's attempt to assume a gracefully languid pose. She sat back up, from necessity, and adopted a different but no less charming position. Perched on the very edge of the seat, with her back as straight as any well-brought-up schoolgirl's, she clasped her hands under her pretty little chin, let two large tears well to the surface of her blue eyes, and told her tale of woe in a voice that quavered ever so little.

"It's my stepson, Gregor," she told the artistic ladies, who had dropped their charcoal sticks and pencils to cluster around her—a necessity if they wanted to hear the story, since Lily had dropped her voice to a near whisper to demonstrate her extreme agitation. Augustine Parris, Lily noted with irritation, remained leaning against the studio wall, arms folded, looking quite detached from her troubles. He was even rude enough to carry on his whispered argument with Robert Glenford. Lily had heard a few words between them as she entered the room and got the impression that Robert wanted to leave without attending the class, pleading some urgent business that he was reluctant to specify. Augustine was most insistent that he stay and model for the ladies again—which, Lily thought with a flicker of amusement, probably accounted for the shy American's pretense that he was urgently wanted elsewhere! But it was none of her concern; her own problems were far more important.

"Is your little boy ill?" Mrs. Langley asked.

"Heavens, no, nothing like that." Lily managed a quavering laugh. "And he's not *my* boy—a great child of nearly eight. Didn't you hear me say he was my stepson? But he's all I have left of my darling Julian, so naturally I treasure him, even though it is difficult at times. What do *I* know of raising boys? Of course the loss of his father disturbed him—one must make allowances for that—and the headmaster of his school assured me that some of his . . . less pleasant . . . actions were merely a reaction to grief. I felt sure the child would straighten out in time. I put a *great* deal of effort into finding the right school for him—one that specializes in these difficult situations."

Sydenham Manor was in fact a very popular school with parents who were in the Indian Civil Service, or addicted to mountaineering in Switzerland, or otherwise too far away or too busy to interfere in the running of the school. And Jerrold Jessop, the headmaster and owner, displayed his understanding of these difficult situations by not troubling the parents with excessive reports on the progress of their sons; a quarterly bill, with extra charges for keeping boys at the school over holidays, had been the full extent of his correspondence with Lily in the two years since Julian had died and she had put Gregor into the school. Until today.

"He's being sent away from school," Lily announced. "Even dear Mr. Jessop can't do anything with him. He didn't say *exactly* what the problem was, but it seems to have been very bad."

The listeners were left with the impression that Gregor had been sent away from school for something really nasty, like torturing small animals.

"So you see," Lily concluded, letting the tears drop to her cheeks, "I shall have to give up my art lessons at once."

She noted that Augustine Parris's noble countenance remained unmoved at this devastating news. Doubtless, as an artist and a man of deep sensibility, he had learned to conceal his finer feelings. Lily entertained no doubt that the loss of such a promising pupil—and one, moreover, to whom he had given such close personal attention—was breaking Parris's heart, both as man and as artist. But what could she do? There could be nothing between them; he was too old and, worse, too poor for Lily. And her artistic career, she announced with gloomy satisfaction, was finished now.

"Naturally the little boy will need your attention at first," Mrs. Langley agreed with a sympathetic sniff, "but surely your maid could look after him for the hour or two that you spend at lessons?"

There was a chorus of rather limp approval from the other students. If Lily hadn't known how much everybody adored her pretty face and sweet nature, she might even have suspected that the artistic ladies felt they would survive her disappearance. But that did seem too improbable to imagine—and besides, the other women in the class weren't her concern; Robert Glenford was of far more interest. Lily peeped through her damp lashes at Robert and was gratified to see that his attention increased as she explained the exact details of her sad plight.

"Alas, I cannot even remain in London, so there is no question of my continuing to attend Mr. Parris's class," Lily said. "How could I keep that great boy in my flat? There's barely room for me—a bedroom, a dressing room, a tiny parlor, and a closet for my maid. I shall have to take him down to Hayvenhurst. And that woman—I mean, my dear sister-in-law—will expect—I mean, naturally I'll *want* to stay with Gregor to see how he goes on. Until I can find another school for him. And that," Lily said, drooping prettily, "may take some time, considering the circumstances."

Since the principal circumstance of Gregor's departure from school, as explained in Mr. Jessop's letter, was that the boy's weak lungs had caused a mild bronchitis to develop into bronchial pneumonia, it might indeed be some time before he was well enough to send away again. But Lily saw no reason to bore the art class with all these trivial details. She was far more interested in Robert Glenford's reaction to her news. As soon as she mentioned that she would have to be leaving London, he had left the shelter of the studio wall and had begun moving purposefully through the crowd of agitated ladies until he reached her side. Lily watched his progress and dropped her long, tear-wet lashes to conceal the gleam of triumph that lit her eyes. Of course he could not bear the thought of being separated from her! She had known he was smitten already, and here was the proof! Now, if only he would admit he'd been fooling about his poverty, she could invite him down to Hayvenhurst and while away the boring hours of Gregor's convalescence with bringing him to the point of a proposal.

Or, if it turned out that he was indeed as poor as she claimed, she could still invite him down and beguile the time with a flirtation. But, Lily thought, it was absolutely necessary that she find out the truth, one way or another, before she made a fatal mistake. Either getting engaged to a poor man or having an *affaire* with a rich one before he proposed would be a fatal error in Lily's world.

"Did you say you're going to be staying at Hayven-hurst?" Robert inquired when he reached Lily's side.

She dimpled slightly, not enough to contradict her general appearance of grief-stricken concern for her stepson. "Indeed I am. Lady Hayvenhurst was my dear Julian's sister, you know, and as she is widowed and childless—and the estate is not entailed—the lands will very likely pass to Gregor. As the heir to Hayvenhurst it's only proper that he should spend his holidays there, getting to know his future tenants and dependents." She'd put this point of view to Lady Hayvenhurst some months earlier, as one way of dealing with the problem of school holidays, and had been summarily rejected with a statement that Lady Hayvenhurst was too old to deal with a small boy bouncing around the estate. When Gregor was older, Lady Hayven-hurst had said, there would be time enough for him to learn the management of the estate; she had no intention of dying in the next ten years, or twenty either for that matter! But now, Lily thought, Lady Hayvenhurst could hardly refuse to accept her poor sick nephew and his concerned stepmama.

"It happens," said Robert, "that I have business in that neighborhood myself. I wonder if it would be possible for me to call on you while I am there?"

Lily bit her lip. The conversation she had planned at this point would require very delicate maneuvering and would be very difficult to manage with all the rest of the art class listening avidly. Fortunately, Augustine Parris was beginning to harrumph and make irritated noises about the need for his students to set up their easels and get to work. Lily made him a pretty apology for disrupting the class, explained that she was much too upset to work that afternoon, and withdrew into a corner of the studio where she and Robert could talk with a little privacy. They stood in the shelter of a vast canvas, stretched, primed, set on an easel, but as yet innocent of the first strokes of paint.

"That may be rather difficult," she said innocently. "Hayvenhurst Hall is so isolated! The nearest train station is *quite* a long drive, and the first village where there's a decent inn is even farther away."

Robert looked every bit as stricken by this news as she had hoped he would be.

"Surely there must be *some*place where visitors can stay?"

"I fear not," Lily said mournfully. "Only the Hall itself. And Dagmar—Lady Hayvenhurst—entertains very little, although if she knew enough about one of my friends perhaps I *could* persuade her—"

"But I happen to know she's having a house party right—" Robert began while Lily was still speaking. The two of them broke off and stared at one another. Then they both spoke again, Robert slightly in the lead this time.

"It's a great imposition, but if I could only join the house party for a few—"

"Dagmar is *so* exclusive, she hardly even likes to let Gregor and me stay—"

Silence again.

"There must be some mistake," Robert said at last.

"I know how much this means to you," Lily ventured. If only the man would get down to specifics instead of beating about the bush with this tale of a nonexistent house party!

Robert's countenance cleared and he smiled at her. Lily had a confused sense of the sun breaking through clouds, and her head whirled until she had to remind herself that she was still in Augustine Parris's dirty studio, not on a grassy hill with flowers bursting into bloom. It was, she thought, quite unfair for a man to be so provokingly handsome and not to give one any idea of his real worth—which helped her concentrate on the subject at hand.

"Nothing," Lily said, almost truthfully, "would give me greater happiness than to have you visit Hayvenhurst while Gregor and I are there. I'll do everything I can to arrange it."

"How did you know what it meant to me?"

Lily gave a little laugh and glanced at Robert sidewise through her lashes. Most provokingly, he didn't seem as impressed by this look as he had been by her half promise to help him visit Hayvenhurst. Good heavens, could it be that the man was really poor and that he was counting on her or Dagmar to help him restore his fortunes? That he wasn't truly smitten by her?

Lily gave this last thought no more consideration than it deserved. Of course he was madly in love with her. How could he fail to be? That question required no more study. But he *could*—just possibly—be as poor as he had claimed on Friday. And that was something she really must clarify before matters went any farther.

"I'm afraid, though, my sister-in-law is a terrible snob," she said sadly. "She's had some very bad experiences with fortune hunters since Lord Hayvenhurst died. It's reached such a point that she won't have anyone to stay unless he provides impeccable references showing that he has an income quite the equal of hers."

"What an amazing thing to require!"

"Dagmar is rather eccentric," Lily agreed, wishing she'd been able to think of a better story on the spur of the moment. Suddenly she remembered a bit of corroborating detail. "But, you see, just now she is terribly nervous that someone will try to steal the Hayvenhurst Emerald. It was the one treasure my darling Julian brought back from his last South American expedition, the one where he caught that fatal fever in the jungle. Dagmar values it above everything, and the fear of losing it makes her rather suspicious of strangers."

"Then why the devil doesn't she put it in a bank vault?"

Lily laughed with unfeigned merriment at this notion. "Really, Mr. Glenford, you Americans have such a quaint sense of humor!" She hadn't meant to get drawn into a discussion of how her sister-in-law should protect the Hayvenhurst Emerald. It was time to remind Robert Glenford of the point of this story. "But you can understand why she's so cautious. If only she could be sure that you have no motive for wanting the emerald, I'm sure she wouldn't mind my inviting you to join us."

"Well, if that's all she wants—" Robert began.

Lily looked up at him, lips slightly parted, eyes glistening. Her delicate little fingers curved and tightened gently on his arm.

"I mean," he said more slowly, "if that's all she cares about, I'm afraid I can't oblige her."

"Can't," Lily said slowly, "or won't?"

Very gently, Robert lifted her fingers from his coat sleeve. "I should be very sorry to think you as suspicious as your sister-in-law. Perhaps we can contrive some other way for me to visit Hayvenhurst."

"You're a damned fool," Peter Farquharson said later that night. They were sitting in comfortable bachelor squalor over a late dinner of cold meat and warm bread, Peter's mother having gone out to a church committee meeting and given the cook the night off. "You had an invitation to Hayvenhurst almost in your pocket, and you had to throw it away because of this Haroun-al-Raschid fantasy about pretending to be an anonymous poor artist. Which fantasy, may I remind you, won't last ten minutes once Mrs. Whitworth gets to Hayvenhurst and chats with your Cressida, to whom you've already revealed all." He made a long arm across the table and refilled his friend's wineglass. Robert was looking tense.

"I know," said Robert, agreeing with his friend. He sipped the dark, rich port and stared into the swirling surface of the wine, imagining Cressida's hair streaming about her face like the rippling liquid. He hadn't actually seen Cressida with her hair down, and if he didn't find a way of getting to Hayvenhurst to patch up their quarrel, he might never do so. But the image was tantalizingly clear to him. Perhaps he had some artistic talent after all. "But you didn't see the lady. I felt like something being delicately invited to walk into a trap."

"I've seen Mrs. Whitworth," Peter told him. His eyelids drooped down and a dreamy smile passed over his face. "She was at the Sloane-Breckinridges' lawn-tennis tournament last year. Played abominably, could hardly serve without a fault, but she won the first set because she was opposite some young fool who couldn't keep his eyes off her. Can't say I blame him. *I'd* walk into the lady's parlor *any* day."

"Better you than me," Robert said. "There must be some other way for me to get to see Cressida." The girl in the wineglass gave him a mocking smile and disappeared in a spiral of dark red drops. Robert swallowed the last of the wine too fast and felt his head swimming. When he *did* see Cressida again, he wouldn't let her get away in a fit of temper. He would hold her and tell her how he felt about her and kiss her until she couldn't argue anymore. She must care for him or she wouldn't have been so jealous about Lily. And if she didn't he would make her care.

But first he had to get to see her again. "Can't I get into Hayvenhurst Hall without using Lily Whitworth?"

Peter lit a cheroot and blew a series of perfect blue smoke rings through the air. "Don't know," he said, puffing away contentedly. "Mrs. Whitworth wasn't funning you about the problems, y'know. That is—first I've heard about Lady H. demanding references of her house guests—but she ain't exactly welcoming to strangers. Not since her young brother died to get the Hayvenhurst Emerald out of the Amazon swamps. I hear she feels she owes it to his memory to display it properly, and thinks everybody who comes to the house is after it. I wouldn't want to lay odds on your chances of getting in to talk to Cressida if you just march up and knock on the front door. She almost canceled the St. Withburga's Church Garden Club tour this year, but my mother went to school with Dagmar and she twisted her arm to let the ladies have their viewing of the grounds. Threatened to tell who organized the betting ring and made the book their last year at St. Withburga's Academy, or something like that."

"Your mother bet on horses?" Robert began to grin, glimpsing a side of the starchy Mrs. Farquharson he'd never imagined before. "When she was a schoolgirl?" He had trouble visualizing Mrs. Farquharson in that role. It was much easier to imagine Cressida as an enchanting, long-legged schoolgirl, all black stockings and flying braids.

"Oh, no, never had anything to do with the gee-gees,"

Peter explained. "Story I heard was that Lady H.—of course, she was Dagmar Whitworth then—made up a book of odds on the headmistress' lectures. How many times she'd quote 'Work for the night is coming' in the daily prayer, who'd get sent up to her study, how long it would take her to notice a note pinned to the back of her dress—schoolgirl nonsense."

Robert's hopes subsided. "It doesn't sound quite strong enough to blackmail Lady Hayvenhurst into taking on an unknown house guest. Doesn't your mother have anything else on her?"

Peter shook his head regretfully. "Too well chaperoned, these girls' boarding schools. But there's something else . . . if I could think of it. . . . Pass the port."

Robert filled his own glass first and drained it while Peter was mulling over the problem. His picture of Cressida as a schoolgirl vanished; in her place was the tired, pale girl he'd found in London, too thin in her shabby brown dress. She hadn't even given him a chance to tell her that the Liberty silks were for her. Robert imagined the brown dress away, replaced by the swathes of lavender-blue silk that picked up the shimmering color of Cressida's wide eyes. The silk was slipping down off her slender shoulders; skin pale and smooth as ivory gleamed under the peacock print. . . . Robert groaned and recaptured the port bottle.

"Got it!" Peter announced, sitting up with a start. The front legs of his chair thudded against the carpet and the enchanting vision of Cressida vanished like a burst bubble.

"Don't go popping up like a Jack-in-the-box again," Robert requested his friend. "Bad for the nerves." Perhaps another glass of port would settle him down. And soothe his aching heart.

"No gratitude," Peter mourned. "Here I've found the solution to your problem, and all you want is the port. Romantic solution, too. Girl like Cressida, from what you've told me of her—she'd love it. Craigie!"

This introduction of a new motif confused Robert's wandering brains. "Not Craigie. Cressida."

"No, my gardener."

106

"Cressida's your gardener?" This sounded rather too improbable. "You're drunk, Peter."

"We're both drunk. Don't interrupt. Complicated train of thought. My gardener's named Craigie."

"Happy for him," Robert said politely.

"Has an uncle. Also named Craigie."

"Runs in the family, does it?"

"Uncle," Peter enunciated with painstaking slowness, "Uncle is Lady H.'s head gardener. Get him to take you on. Undergardener."

Robert frowned. "Gardener? I'd have a better chance to see Cressida if I worked indoors. Don't you have any connections with the butler?"

"Don't look a gift gardener in the mouth," Peter said severely. "Besides, you don't know anything about buttling."

"Don't know much about gardening either," Robert pointed out.

Peter dismissed this objection with an airy wave of the hand. "What's there to know? Pick a few flowers, dig and delve. Healthy outdoor life. Close to nature. Pick it up in no time."

Put that way, it sounded reasonable enough to Robert.

And in his empty glass, Cressida shimmered against the curve of the crystal, with the dregs of the port wine at the bottom of the glass turning into the folds of silk that had now slipped to the floor.

Chapter

6

Cressida lifted a red-hot spoke from the laundry room stove and carefully inserted it into the Italian iron, a hollow tube raised like a flower stem on its slender pedestal. Drops of sweat gathered on her forehead; she brushed them away with the back of one arm, careful to keep her hands white and clean as she picked up a collar from the stack of snowy white linen that had been starched earlier.

It was Thursday afternoon.

Mrs. Simpson looked on from the open door of the laundry room. She had opened the door very quietly, scarcely believing what she would find inside; now shock and horror kept her silent as Cressida smoothed the collar over the shining outer surface of the Italian iron. Under her hands the linen acquired the perfect starched curve of a flower petal. She carried the smooth collar carefully to the wooden stand where the freshly ironed linen cooled. Here she looked up to find a place for the collar, caught Mrs. Simpson's eye, and stood with her hands foolishly upraised, blushing already.

"And may I ask the meaning of this, my girl?"

Mrs. Simpson sailed down the three short steps into the laundry room.

"It's, ah, it's Thursday afternoon," Cressida stammered. "Linen to be soaked on Monday night, boiled on Tuesday, dried on Wednesday, and mangled, starched, and ironed on Thursday and Friday afternoon." She gabbled off the recently learned lesson.

"I am," said Mrs. Simpson with terrible humility, "moderately familiar with the laundry maid's tasks. What I should like to know is *why* I find my newest underhousemaid doing the laundry maid's work when she should be sewing her new uniforms—and where that lazy slut Daisy might be when *she* should be starchin' the footmen's collars!"

"Daisy," Cressida explained, "has a headache. It's very warm in here, you see."

"Of course it's warm. Laundry rooms are always hot. It's a good healthful atmosphere."

"And I finished sewing up my black dress last night. So I thought—"

"Underhousemaids are not required to think. That is not part of your duties. Underhousemaids," Mrs. Simpson said, emphasizing with one finger uplifted, "are to sweep the carpet, light the fires, clean the silver, and *carry the coals upstairs*."

Cressida flushed. "I'm sorry about that. Was James very angry? I didn't understand the rule that the footmen aren't to help us carry coals—and it's a silly rule anyway," she added, forgetting her place, "for James is quite a lot stronger than I, and he *said* he didn't in the least mind—"

"James is a young fool who'd do anything for a smile from a pretty girl," Mrs. Simpson said, "and he has been spoken to by Mr. Flynn. It's you I'm concerned with, Jane. It doesn't matter whether you're letting somebody else do your work or doing somebody else's work for them— you've got to stop. We all have our ordained places, and what d'you think would happen if we all stepped out of them and did whatever work we felt like whenever we wanted?"

"I don't know," said Cressida.

"Anarchy, that's what!" Mrs. Simpson told her. "As

long as Mr. Flynn and me command this household we'll have everybody in their places where they belong, and none of this changing jobs and chopping heads off and throwing bombs and other anarchists' goings-on. Now just you remember your Christian duty like it says in the hymnbook, dear. 'The rich man in his castle, the poor man at his gate, God made them high and lowly, and ordered their estate,' and that goes for the housemaid and the laundry maid just as it does for the rich and mighty. When I come down to the servants' hall of an afternoon I expect to see you, Jane, sitting in your chair and doing some good plain sewing or listening to an improving chapter of the Bible, and I expect to see Daisy working in the laundry like she's supposed to. What'll come next, I wonder? I shouldn't hardly be surprised to find you out-of-doors, staking plants and dead-heading flowers for Craigie!''

Cressida laughed politely at what she recognized as an amazing flight of fancy for Mrs. Simpson.

"I don't know what to do with the girl, and that's a fact, Mr. Flynn," Mrs. Simpson confided to the butler when she returned to the peace of the upper servants' sitting room. She recounted the tale of Cressida's misdemeanors. "It's not that she isn't willing, for a sweeter-natured, more willing worker than Jane I've never had. But she seems to have no understanding at all of her proper place. Asking the footman to carry coals—I know that sounds like laziness, but she swears it only seemed good sense to her, and I'm inclined to believe it, for the other times I've caught her out of place she's been doin' extra work, not evadin' it. Peeled a tub of carrots yesterday because Lizzie the kitchen maid had cut her finger, took Daisy's place in the laundry just now because the lazy girl claimed to have a headache—'' Mrs. Simpson looked up to heaven and sighed.

"You're not goin' to turn her off?'' That was Mrs. Leonard, the cook, who had been napping in the corner armchair.

"Not if she learns her place," Mrs. Simpson replied grimly.

"Oh, good. For I don't know what I'd do without her, and that's a fact." Mrs. Leonard sank back down to enjoy her interrupted nap while both the housekeeper and the butler stared at her in horror.

"*You* couldn't do without her!" Mrs. Simpson repeated in horror.

"Mrs. Leonard," the butler said in measured tones that made the cook open her eyes again, "the doings of the housemaids are, properly speaking, not in your province to approve or disapprove."

"Did I say anythin' about her dustin' and sweepin'?" the cook asked indignantly. "That's for Mrs. Simpson to judge, and well I know it. But the girl's been helping me in her free time by copyin' out the menus for upstairs, and a great relief I do find it not to have all that fancy handwriting and scrollwork taking up my time."

"You—let—a housemaid copy the menus?" Mr. Flynn sounded scandalized.

"An *under*housemaid," Mrs. Simpson amplified, laying one hand upon the crackling black bosom of her dress.

"An' a very nice job she's done of it, too. Look at this if you don't believe me! It's my lady's dinner for tonight. Pottage Mongols, augully o vine, and codebuf."

"*Potage à la Monglas*," Mr. Flynn read aloud, "*Anguille au vin*, and *Côte de boeuf aux oignons glacés*. A very suitable light menu for her ladyship, although I question the choice of the eel in wine sauce; it has been known to give her indigestion."

"Not the way I cooks it," said Mrs. Leonard.

"However, the mushroom soup with Madeira and the beef sirloin with glazed onions are unexceptionable. And . . ." Mr. Flynn glared as Mrs. Simpson, for once forgetting all order and precedence, neatly twitched the menu out of his hand.

"And all," she said, examining the neatly handwritten list, "perfectly spelled, which is *not* one of Mrs. Leonard's strong points."

111

"Dear me," said the butler into the ominous silence that followed. "I was not aware that the Farthingdonshire Christian Orphanage included French in its curriculum."

"They don't," said Mrs. Simpson grimly. "The girl's an imposter. I always suspected as much." She raised her hand to the bell rope that would summon one of the under-servants from their hall.

"Wait! What's the matter?" Mrs. Leonard pleaded.

"Writes French, takes on other people's work, talks la-di-dah, and *reads* in her spare time," said Mrs. Simpson, summing up the new underhousemaid's sins. "That girl's never young Jane Baker as was to be sent from the orphanage. Now I think o't, she told me herself the first day her name was something else, some pagan nonsense. At the time I thought she was just giving herself airs. Now I'll wager she's some young lady playing a joke on us."

"A lady she may be," Mr. Flynn said in his precise way, "but I take leave to doubt very seriously whether this is any joking matter. Allow me to add my supplications to Mrs. Leonard's. Of course, dear Mrs. Simpson, any matter involving the discipline and supervision of the female staff must be entirely up to you. But may I ask whether, barring her voice and manner, you have any complaint to make about—er—'Jane'?"

"Didn't you just hear me say that I've never had a sweeter girl or a more willing worker?"

"Then is it absolutely necessary to turn her off?"

Mrs. Simpson's pudgy face set in a mutinous pout that made her look like a balked toddler. "I'll not be made fun of in my own hall."

"I doubt that such is the girl's intention," Mr. Flynn said gently. "I have myself had occasion to observe the child in the last four days. She is desperately unhappy about something—that much is obvious; what, I cannot guess. But I would judge that, far from intending to play a joke on us, she has come here because she is running away from something."

"I'll lay my month's wages that girl never did anything wrong in her life!" Mrs. Leonard argued.

"I am inclined to agree, madam—nor did I mean to imply otherwise. There are many evils in this world from which an innocent young girl might well flee." Mr. Flynn had himself followed the serial installments of *A Maiden's Blush* with as much interest as Cressida, and with somewhat better understanding of the Wicked Viscount's intentions.

Mrs. Simpson nodded, as one reluctantly convinced, but her hand did not leave the bell rope.

"No doubt we will learn what troubles her in good time," Mr. Flynn continued. "In the meantime, can there be a safer refuge for the child than here at Hayvenhurst Hall? With your excellent cooking to bring the roses back into her cheeks, Mrs. Leonard, and with you to supervise her behavior and protect her from the dangers of the world, Mrs. Simpson, surely she will grow happier, learn to trust us, and confide her troubles in us at last."

"Oh, all right," the housekeeper agreed, dropping her hand from the bell rope without pulling it. "You'd make anything sound reasonable, Mr. Flynn, even a lady masquerading as a housemaid. But as for protectin' her—well, we can only hope Waverley don't pay us a visit."

"If he does," said Mr. Flynn, "I rely on you to keep her belowstairs, Mrs. Simpson."

Having been evicted from the laundry, Cressida retreated to her favorite place in the environs of Hayvenhurst Hall. The Long Walk could not rival the display of brilliant color produced by ranks of bedding-out plants in the more formal parts of the gardens, but the aged brick covered with filmy green vines, with an occasional cluster of sweet-scented pink roses, was much more to Cressida's taste. She wandered happily down the walk, admiring the way the arches separating sections of the garden framed the view of the lake at the end and thinking how much fun it would be to make all the rest of the Hayvenhurst gardens look like this one. The green bushes in the topiary garden could be allowed to return to their native state, the tortured forms of flowering plants crammed together in the Clock Garden could be replaced by tall, graceful native perennials with room to breathe, and Marble Arch. . . .

Cressida shook her head. She couldn't think of a thing to do about Lady Hayvenhurst's collection of statuary. But she was sure that Mr. Craigie would have any number of ideas, if only he could be given a free hand.

This reminded her that he had promised to lend her a copy of Mr. Robinson's second book, and she turned her steps toward the gardener's cottage.

The picturesque old thatched cottage stood in a secluded corner of the grounds behind the greenhouses, surrounded by a grove of ancient oaks that provided shade and shelter to the little house. Cressida had just knocked on the door when an object came flying out of the small casement window just above the door, accompanied by what she assumed were curses in broad Scots. She was already retreating and babbling apologies when Mr. Craigie's white head appeared at the window.

"Oh, it's you, lass. Sorry about the boot—I thought it was her ladyship come with some more ideas for beautifying the grounds. If I can make her think I'm in a foul temper she usually goes away again without telling me what she's thought of this time. Seein' it's you, you may as well come in and sit down. The door's unlocked. Make yourself comfortable and I'll be down in a minute."

Cressida found it impossible to obey this command, as the interior of the cottage was not only dark and musty but also filled with a random assortment of furniture, books, china vases, cooking pots, old mismatched shoes, and all the other impediments of a lifetime's occupancy, scattered as randomly as though a high wind had just picked up the house and given it a good shake to redistribute the contents. She stood in the midst of the clutter, repressing an urge to begin straightening the room, until Mr. Craigie clumped down the stairs with one boot on.

"Sorry about the mess," he apologized briefly. "I'm moving tomorrow. Here's the book you wanted. I'd invite you to have a seat outside on that *rustic bench* her ladyship installed, but I can't seem to find my other boot."

"It's—er—already outside," Cressida told him.

The rustic bench to which Mr. Craigie alluded was a woven stand of wicker and naturally bent tree limbs placed under one of the oaks that shaded the front of the cottage. It was attractive to look at but, Cressida quickly discovered, vilely uncomfortable to sit on. "Like most of her ladyship's grand ideas," Mr. Craigie said sourly, "better in conception than in practice."

Cressida could contain her curiosity no longer. "Mr. Craigie, why are you moving? You haven't given notice, have you? And—" She was not quite sure how to phrase her other question. "When we met the other day you seemed to have rather a strong accent."

"Lady Hayvenhurst expects a Scotch gardener to talk broad Scots," Mr. Craigie explained. "She hired me twenty years ago on the strength of my name and was most disappointed to learn that I grew up on an English estate and was tutored with my employer's son, thereby becoming not only literate but freed of the appalling diction which characterizes most of my compatriots. However, it is a servant's task to conform to the employer's expectations, no matter how peculiar they may be. I made a point of acquiring the appropriate accent for use before her ladyship and any of her guests. When I saw you the other day, I thought you were with that gaggle of ladies from St. Withburga's, so I had to stay in character. However, now that I know you're here to stay, I'll be damned if I'll play the stage Scotsman every time you drop by for a visit—which I hope you'll do quite often, my dear. By the way, you speak rather elegantly yourself for an underhousemaid. Where were you in service before?"

Cressida thought it safest to parry Mr. Craigie's curiosity with her own questions. "Then you haven't given notice?"

"No. I'm being shifted out of the cottage to make room for my new undergardener. Lad my nephew recommended. English, but I'll teach him the accent before Lady H. talks to him. Starts Monday—just in time for me to take a much-needed holiday. I'm away up north to visit my mother's people in Aberdeen. There's not much to do here in summer anyway, and young Robbie—that's the new lad—can pick it up from my notes. And when I come back I'm to have one of the new row cottages. Brick," Mr. Craigie said, sighing luxuriously, "running water right outside the back door, and *no* problem with the drains. An old man like me deserves his comforts. Young Robbie can have this place with my blessing."

"You mean he's being given this lovely cottage? Oh, I'm so sorry!"

"Haven't you been *listening* to me, girl? I'm happy as a grig to be shifting—except for the trouble of packing up. Save your sympathy for the boy," Mr. Craigie recommended. "Place leaks summer and winter, chimney smokes, and I wouldn't want to hazard a guess what lives in the thatch. Her ladyship should have had it torn down years ago, but no, she thinks it's Charming and Picturesque."

"So it is."

"Well, it's time she found some other poor fool to be charming and picturesque in it!" Mr. Craigie said with sudden vehemence. "Bad enough when it was just the cottage, but lately she's wanted whoever sleeps here to get up during the night and check on the Hayvenhurst Emerald. I'm too old for such games, and I'd like to know who's going to steal the bl—the blasted thing anyway. The new lad can have the damp, and the rheumatism, and the guard duty on the emerald and all with my blessing. But it's going to be a struggle shifting all my things over the weekend," he concluded with a sigh.

"I'll help you," Cressida volunteered. "We seem to have plenty of free time at the big house, and Mrs. Simpson doesn't care to have me helping the other servants with their tasks." She blushed, remembering how annoyed the housekeeper had been to discover her in the laundry.

"Many thanks for the offer, Jane, but you'll have enough to do this weekend yourself," Mr. Craigie told her. "What with opening and airing the East Wing for Lily Whitworth and her son, not to mention a room for her brother if he comes too, which most likely he will, not being one to miss a month or two of free meals and . . ."

"Lily Whitworth is coming *here?*" Cressida breathed in horror.

"Yes, lass, but don't fret. I see you've already heard about that ne'er-do-well brother of hers. Don't let it worry you," Mr. Craigie advised her. "There's always the chance Waverley won't trail along with his sister, and even if he does, we're all up to his tricks by now. Mrs. Simpson knows better than to send any of the young and pretty girls upstairs when Waverley's here. And seein' you're so worried, I'll ask her to make sure to keep you out of sight until they leave."

"Oh, thank you—*thank* you!" Cressida breathed. She had barely taken in Craigie's warning about Waverley, being far too absorbed in the fear that Lily Whitworth would not only recognize her and bring her masquerade to an end, but would tell her father exactly where she was and what she had been doing. It would be bad enough, Cressida reflected, to be exposed as an impostor and turned out of Hayvenhurst. It would be ten times more humiliating to have her father come here to fetch her, boring Lady Hayvenhurst with his artistic perorations and criticizing the paintings in the family portrait gallery and trying in various unsubtle ways to get Lady Hayvenhurst to commission a painting from him.

But apparently Craigie and the rest of the servants were prepared to help Cressida stay out of the visitors' path, without even asking why she was so eager to avoid them. It was, Cressida thought, very kind of them.

Beside her, Craigie patted her hand. "There, there," he said. "I knew you were a good girl. You've nothing to worry about, lass."

On the strength of that assurance, Cressida sailed happily through an energetic weekend of airing sheets and making beds and beating the dust out of rugs and draperies in the seldom-used East Wing.

"Why does Lady Hayvenhurst want her sister-in-law to stay here, so far from her own rooms, when there are plenty of unused bedchambers all clean and made up in the

117

West Wing?'' Cressida asked Abby, her roommate and guide through the intricacies of servants' etiquette. "Not that I mind the extra work, you understand," she added quickly lest Abby think she was complaining about having to spend her Sunday afternoon freshening rooms that had slumbered beneath dustcovers for months.

"*You* may not mind," groaned Abby, straightening with one hand on the small of her back, "but *I* could think of better ways to spend a sunny Sunday! Her ladyship ain't overfond of her sister-in-law," Abby explained. "And the brother—Waverley—*nobody* is real fond of him. Like to house him in the duck pond, so I would! *And* her ladyship ain't used to children, and I don't think she knows what to do with her nephew. You did hear that Mrs. Whitworth is bringing the boy down? He got sent home from school for doin' somethin' too awful to speak about," Abby said, repeating the garbled version of Lily's letter that had been reported in the servants' hall. "I reckon Lady H. thinks she'd rather have him playin' his tricks over here, where she won't have to hear about them."

Cressida envisioned a lurching, spotty-faced adolescent with nasty habits involving hatpins and butterflies. "Well, I'm glad I won't be having much to do with them," she said, bending over the bed to straighten the spread.

Abby gave a hollow laugh. "That's what you think. Simpson always promises to keep us girls belowstairs when Waverley's here, but she always forgets once the visitors are here. Can't blame her, really. Everything's so quiet here most of the year, Lady H. not bein' one for entertainin', and Simpson gets set in her ways. Then that Lily Whitworth and her brother start ringing the bells and demanding this and that, and Lady H. gets upset and starts ringing her own bell, and before long Simpson is that flustered she can't remember who's supposed to be where. You'd better learn to use this." She fumbled in the befrilled bosom of her white apron and pulled out a four-inch hatpin.

Chapter
7

Wary though she felt, Cressida was not expecting any immediate problems on the Monday when Lily Whitworth took up residence at Hayvenhurst Hall. Lily's train was not due to arrive until late afternoon. She was to take tea on the terrace overlooking the Clock Garden. After that she was supposed to retire to her room to rest until it was time to dine quietly *en famille* with Lady Hayvenhurst. The garden terraces were not Cressida's responsibility, the rooms allotted to Mrs. Whitworth and her brother and stepson were immaculate, and Mrs. Simpson had arranged for a young girl from the village to assist the cook with serving dinner. There should have been no danger of Cressida's having to come into contact with the family that entire day.

She spent her free hours after the midday meal in the garden, clipping flowers with which to decorate Lily Whitworth's room and wondering idly whether the new undergardener who was coming that day could possibly be as nice as Craigie and whether she ought to take a spray of flowers down to the cottage to brighten it for him. Probably not, she decided regretfully; out-of-doors she was safe enough from incurring Mrs. Simpson's wrath by another violation of servants' hall etiquette, but once she set foot within doors anything could go wrong. For all she knew, cleaning the apprentice gardener's cottage was strictly the province of the kitchen tweeny or the front hall footman, and somebody or other would be deathly offended if she interfered. She had much better stick to putting fresh flowers in Mrs. Whitworth's room; that at least was her responsibility, for Mrs. Simpson had personally requested her to see to it. And once that was done, she would take herself belowstairs and remain in the lowly but safe obscurity of the servants' hall all evening—for the rest of the week if possible—or however long Lily Whitworth meant to stay.

Cressida clipped away, humming happily and filling her basket, in blithe ignorance of the consultations in the butler's rooms that had led to her being given this task.

"Doing the flowers is for the young ladies of the house, not the maidservants," Mrs. Simpson had protested when Mr. Flynn made the suggestion.

"This household is singularly lacking in young ladies," the butler had pointed out, "and Lady Hayvenhurst will be quite happy to be relieved of the chore so that she can spend more time pottering in the greenhouse. If 'Jane' is indeed, as we suspect, a young lady, then she should be able to arrange flowers to perfection. And," he added, convincing the housekeeper with his last and most telling argument, "whatever she does with the flowers, she won't offend anybody."

Both Cressida and Mr. Flynn were, as it turned out, somewhat oversanguine in their expectations. Before Lily Whitworth had even taken off her veiled hat, she sneezed three times, stared with horror at the faintly reddened tip of her nose, and decided that the peonies on her dresser were to blame for the disaster.

"Who put these common flowers in my room?" she demanded, pointing at the vase full of pink and red peonies. "Don't you know I detest peonies above all things? Besides, they clash with my half-mourning. Get that vase out of here at once!"

The tip of her nose was positively red from sneezing.

She glowered at the calm, statuesque housemaid who stood in the doorway with her suitcases; when the servant girl didn't move quickly enough, Lily reinforced her order by throwing the offending vase across the room, peonies and all.

Lily's maid had given her notice that morning, just before her mistress left London. The task of unpacking for young Mrs. Whitworth had been assigned to Martha, a large placid housemaid who usually supervised the younger girls in dusting the china ornaments downstairs. Martha could flirt with two footmen at once and simultaneously give orders to the underhousemaids without ever letting a flustered look cross her freckled face or losing a strand from her intricately plaited crown of butter-yellow braids. But she was not accustomed to having flower vases thrown at her—though, to be fair, Lily had only meant to hit the wall; it was her shocking bad aim that resulted in drenching Martha's starched white apron with wet peonies.

Martha fled.

The kitchen and servants' hall were already in the disarray that Abby had predicted. Mrs. Leonard, faced with the problem of setting her carefully planned dinner back an hour and a half to accommodate Lily's late arrival, was systematically reducing the kitchen maids to tears. Mrs. Simpson was closeted with Mr. Flynn, planning a duty roster for the footmen and maidservants so that nobody should be exposed to Lily's temper or Waverley's gropings more than once a day. Martha reached the servants' hall to find that she was, momentarily, the senior woman present. She glowered at Abby and Cressida, who were sitting peacefully in a large basket chair with their heads bent over the *Illustrated London News*. Cressida was teaching Abby to read via the subject dearest to her roommate's heart, the doings of royalty and their relatives.

"You!" Martha jerked the periodical out of Cressida's hands and tossed it on the floor. "That Mrs. Whitworth ain't satisfied with my 'umble services. One of you lot better go up there and see if you can make her happy."

"Not me," Abby said promptly, "not with that Waverley in the next room to 'ers."

Cressida shrank back in the chair, certain that she was about to be exposed.

"Well, Jane better not go," Martha said as her temper cooled. "She started the trouble by putting them red peonies in the room. Mrs. Whitworth's delicate artistic sensibilities was offended by the color. It'll have to be you, Abby."

Abby slipped from the chair, grumbling under her breath. Cressida breathed more easily for a few minutes—until a boy arrived at the door to say there was measles in the village and the girl who'd been hired to help with dinner couldn't come. Mrs. Simpson came back from the butler's rooms to catch the end of this message, looked around the hall and saw Cressida sitting carefully idle so that she wouldn't offend anybody. "No help for it," she sighed. "Don't worry, Jane. Even that Waverley won't try anything while he's dining with her ladyship—I hope!"

Cressida edged into the dining room, her arms aching with the strain of carrying a heavy soup tureen so high that it obscured her face. She set the soup down and scurried out of the room with her head bent.

"Girl!" Lily Whitworth called. "Come back here!"

Cressida edged back into the dining room, praying that the white lace-trimmed cap pulled low over her forehead would help to disguise her.

"My soup spoon is tarnished," Lily informed her, holding up a spotless and gleaming piece of silverware. "Bring another one." She looked straight through Cressida as she spoke and continued the story she was telling Lady Hayvenhurst as though she had not interrupted herself for a moment. "Really, provoking though it was of Gregor to get himself sent home, I'm not at all sorry to leave London for a few days. There was a young American in my drawing class who was making quite a nuisance of himself—totally besotted, poor boy! He begged me to let him follow me down here, but of course I couldn't let him impose on you, dear Dagmar, especially when I know almost nothing about his circumstances.''

Cressida stood rooted to the carpet, turning Lily's soup spoon over and over in her hands. Even without hearing the name, she had no doubt that Lily was referring to Robert. And, of course, she already knew that he was in love with Lily. So why should it hurt so much to hear it confirmed?

''I really think he was about to do something desperate when it dawned on him he couldn't see me again,'' Lily droned on, studying her reflection in the gleaming soup tureen with satisfaction. ''Don't be taken in by any strangers appearing at your door with sad stories, Dagmar!'' She looked at the soup bowl in front of her, then glanced up at Cressida with no sign of recognition. ''Well, what are you waiting for, girl? Get me a clean spoon, and hurry about it!''

Mrs. Simpson was annoyed, but not surprised, to find Cressida in tears in a corner of the kitchen a few minutes later, while the cook loudly demanded a replacement helper. ''And one with steadier nerves this time, *if* you please, Mrs. Simpson!''

At least, Cressida reflected sadly the next day, she might as well stop worrying about being recognized by Lily Whitworth. Clearly the woman had never really seen a servant in her life; she belonged to that all-too-numerous class that regarded servants as slightly inferior pieces of furniture. For that matter, Cressida recalled, Lily had hardly seen her in London either. She probably wasn't the type to pay much attention to other women, especially thin plain girls who would be no competition at all.

Not that *she* cared if Robert Glenford wanted to make a cake of himself over Mrs. Whitworth! Cressida blew her nose defiantly, wiped her face with the hem of her apron, and told herself that it didn't matter if her nose was shiny and her eyes red from crying in corners all morning. As long as Robert didn't come to Hayvenhurst and she didn't have to see him, she was happy for him to amuse himself in whatever silly manner he chose.

Perfectly happy.

On that defiant note, Cressida marched into the servants' hall, prepared for once to spend a virtuous afternoon reading the *Illustrated London News* to Abby, or helping Mrs. Simpson wind her skeins of knitting yarn, or whatever else the perfect servant girl would do with her free time. She had no intention of attracting notice by any aberrant behavior while Lily Whitworth was staying at Hayvenhurst Hall; invisibility and blending in with the other servants were her best disguise.

She wound yarn and listened to a reading of the second chapter of Isaiah and spelled out the captions under the pictures in the *London News* for Abby and was so bored that she began to think seriously about slipping out into the fine drizzling rain for a walk in the garden. Even if she wasn't supposed to *work* in the garden, she could at least *look* at the flower beds and think about how much better she would have arranged them.

Cressida's need for escape became acute when the rest of the housemaids gathered around the table for a giggling game of fortune-telling with one another's hands. Teasing references to past gentleman followers and coy hints about present ones became broader and broader until Cressida's cheeks were flaming.

"Wot about Jane there—don't she want ter know about 'er future?" Martha loudly demanded.

"Come 'ere, Jane, maybe the tea leaves'll tell us why you talk so pretty," said another girl, seconding the demand.

"I'd rather they'd teach *me* to talk like that," sighed Lizzy, the lowliest of the kitchen maids, "I'd marry a toff fer sure!"

The other girls guffawed, and while Cressida was off guard Martha slipped off her chair and captured Cressida's slender hand— "I can read palms, too," she announced, "and I see a gentleman in yours."

"What, our Jane's got a gentleman in the palm of 'er hand?" squealed one of the others. "Who? Waverley?"

"Tall and black 'aired," Martha announced, "and . . . I think 'e's a foreigner. Talks with a bit of an accent, like. You bin flirtin' with those Eyetalian circus acrobats as come through the village for the fete next week, Jane?"

Blushing furiously, Cressida snatched her hand free and stammered something. The girls fell silent as Mrs. Simpson appeared in her rustling black dress. She announced that the fires in the upstairs dressing rooms were to be lit, as Mrs. Whitworth complained that the rain made her cold.

"I'll go," Cressida volunteered, and fled to the peace of the empty dressing rooms without even thinking about the danger of discovery. Certainly she didn't think about the mysterious Waverley, whom she hadn't even seen since his arrival the previous day.

Going into Lily Whitworth's room did make her a little nervous; even knowing that Lily was downstairs with Lady Hayvenhurst, Cressida felt as if her presence lingered about the room. The clinging scent of some heady perfume, the sensual glide of a silk negligee draped across a chair, the litter of empty chocolate wrappers and half-finished illustrated magazines all seemed to evoke Lily Whitworth's lazy, sensual personality.

"You don't know all that about her," Cressida chided herself, "you're prejudiced." If Robert loved Lily, she must really be a very nice person. All the same, Cressida hurried through the task of lighting Lily's fire without taking care to protect her new black dress from smudges.

The little room next to Lily's had been assigned to Gregor, the erring stepson. Cressida was surprised at how barren and bleak it was. She knew Gregor had been in bed from the time they arrived yesterday until just after luncheon today, and she had rather expected to see the room littered with illustrated books and the bedclothes tossed in a heap. Instead the bed was made up neatly and the boy's clothes were all hanging inside the wardrobe; and there was no sign of any books or any other amusements such as one would expect a doting stepmother to offer an invalid. Perhaps the boy wasn't allowed books; perhaps he had been sent to bed as a punishment for some bit of misbehavior on the journey rather than because he was ill. All the same, the empty tidiness of the room squeezed Cressida's heart, and she spent precious minutes carrying a scuttle of coals up to lay a fire in the boy's empty grate.

She was in a hurry to finish her task by the time she came to Waverley's room, and there were gray smudges on her skirt and black marks on her hands from the dirty job. And the fireplace in Waverley's room was full of the sort of trash Cressida had to clean up after her father's parties: something broken, something sticky, and a smolder-ing cigar butt in the middle. Muttering crossly to herself, she scraped out the trash and began the task of laying a proper fire. She was late; any minute now Lady Hayven-hurst's guests would be coming up to wash and change for dinner. And no matter what she did, Cressida could not dispel the odor of old tobacco smoke that hovered about Waverley's fireplace.

"Filthy habits," she muttered between her teeth. "No wonder none of the servants can stand him!"

"Oh, but some of the girls do like me," corrected a soft voice behind her. Cressida shot to her feet and cracked her head painfully on the underside of the carved mantel. "That old bitch of a housekeeper sends away anybody who's caught being nice to me. That's why you've heard such dreadful stories about me in the servants' hall."

Lily's brother was no taller than Cressida and his skin was as white and smooth as a lady's. He had a silky brown beard and large, moist-looking eyes that reminded Cressida of a spaniel's. She wanted to laugh at her first sight of this dreaded figure. Why had those silly girls downstairs made Waverley out to be some sort of monster? He was nothing but a silly, slightly effeminate boy, like the ones who ruined their eyes and their brains drinking absinthe with Papa's crowd in London.

"You *have* heard dreadful stories, haven't you, little girl?" Waverley murmured. His large eyes were fixed on Cressida's like a hound eyeing a juicy tidbit, and he put

126

out one soft white hand to stop her as she tried to edge past him. He caught her chin in a surprisingly firm grip and turned her face toward the light. "Yes, I can see you're nervous of me. That's a great mistake. I can be very nice to pretty girls, especially if they're nice to me."

"I'm not pretty," Cressida contradicted quickly, "and I'm not scared of you, Mr.—um—"

Waverley's laugh was as soft and smooth as something rotting away under water. "Why, you don't even know my last name, do you? I'll wager the servants only call me 'that brother of Mrs. Lily's.' How disrespectful. I'll start by teaching you some respect—then we can move on to lessons in being properly nice."

His free hand came down on the nape of her neck and he pulled her to him. His lips came down in a punishingly hard kiss that bruised Cressida's mouth. She felt nauseated, half stifled by the silky beard and the stench of cigar smoke and the taint of brandy on his breath. He was backing her into a corner; she felt the softness of long velvet draperies behind her and then a pressure against the backs of her knees. Not a corner. The tall four-poster bed. All at once Cressida believed every dark hint she'd heard and discounted about Waverley, and she was quite thoroughly frightened. Her arms were free; she swung wildly out, forgetting that she still clutched the coal scuttle, and felt its hard metal edge bang into something soft. Waverley released her and swore under his breath. Cressida ran from the room before he could grab her again.

Waverley stood in the open door, thoughtfully rubbing his bruised shin and making no effort to follow Cressida. He watched the housemaid's black dress and white stockings disappear around the bend of the front stairs. A moment later he heard Lily's voice raised indignantly and his sister made her appearance, flushed with anger. "Imagine the impudence," she announced. "I just caught some dirty little maidservant using the front stairs! She nearly knocked me down! If I could tell one of these dreary servant girls from another, I'd have her turned off—I would indeed."

"Oh, I think that can be arranged," said Waverley.

"Ring the bell, and when someone comes, tell them the maid left her coal scuttle upstairs and ask who was laying the fires here today." He handed Lily the forgotten coal scuttle with a courtly bow. "But don't bother to complain about the girl. I have a score to settle with her too, and I can think of *much* more amusing things to do than having her turned off for impudence."

Gregor Whitworth had slipped into his barren little room unnoticed while Waverley held the new servant girl captive. He had been repressing his need to cough and entertaining fantasies about dashing into the next room to rescue the girl from Uncle Waverley. Hopeless, of course; Uncle Waverley was much stronger than he was and wouldn't hesitate to have him whipped for interfering. He hated himself for his cowardice.

Now he clapped both hands over his mouth and listened much more intently as Uncle Waverley outlined his amusing plan for revenge on the impudent housemaid.

Chapter
8

Cressida frowned slightly as she made her way down the Long Walk the next afternoon. It wasn't that she objected to running an occasional errand in the afternoons; goodness knew, she was scarcely overworked at Hayvenhurst Hall! What with the massive body of custom and code that restricted each servant's tasks so severely, and the small army of indoor servants required by this code, Cressida found that she had considerably less work to do now than in the days when she and Betty had been trying to maintain Riversedge with little help and less money. Still, she had been a little surprised by the content of this latest task. After all the fuss there'd been over her peeling vegetables in the kitchen and starching collars in the laundry, she hadn't expected to find that an underhousemaid's duties included cleaning the locked greenhouse at the far end of the Long Walk.

If Mrs. Simpson had been free, Cressida would have consulted her over the puzzling orders that Martha had transmitted—or would she? She turned the massive iron key to the greenhouse over in her hand, frowning down on it. Martha had said the orders came from Mrs. Simpson; it would have been impertinent to question them. And she had given Cressida a key to the greenhouse. It must be all right. Mrs. Simpson, with her insistence on everybody knowing and keeping to their proper places, surely wouldn't have sent Cressida to infringe on the gardeners' territory. Cleaning the greenhouses must be a recognized part of the housemaids' tasks, something Abby had forgotten to mention to her.

Abby hadn't been available for consultation either; she'd been sent off on some other chore.

It *had* to be all right. Probably Lady Hayvenhurst had noticed that the windows of that locked greenhouse were all streaked and dirty, so that she couldn't see out and very little light could filter through to the plants. Probably she didn't trust the gardeners to do the windows properly; what did they understand about cleaning?

Despite the weight of the bucket in her other hand and the mop balanced across her shoulder, Cressida walked briskly, with a little added spring in her steps as she contemplated the task ahead of her. She might not do so well at keeping up a bright party conversation with Papa's artistic friends, she thought. She might not dress so boldly and aesthetically as Isolde. But after all these years of running Riversedge she was an *expert* on housework. When she was done with the greenhouse, the windows should sparkle like the Crystal Palace to show off Lady Hayvenhurst's prized exotic plants. And she herself would have a whole afternoon working among plants, in her comfortable print dress instead of the stiff black uniform she was supposed to don for afternoon wear, in a place where she couldn't possibly get into any trouble or offend anyone.

Two of the three elements in Cressida's notion of the perfect life were available that afternoon—working around growing plants and not being in trouble with anyone. That should be quite enough to make her happy. So why did she keep thinking wistfully of the third part of her dream? She had deliberately made sure that Robert Glenford would make no part of her life. It was too late to be regretting that decision.

Cressida found herself unable to banish regret entirely. Rather than ruin a lovely misty June day, she incorporated Robert into her fantasy. Wouldn't it be perfect, she mused, if she really were a servant girl at Hayvenhurst Hall and Robert were a stalwart manservant? Not a footman—they were too stiff—perhaps a gardener. They would enjoy sweet brief meetings and stolen kisses on days like this; they would go to the village fete hand in hand and join in the villagers' innocent amusements; they would look forward to the day when Robert succeeded to Alexander Craigie's position and took over the lovely old Tudor cottage that Mr. Craigie disliked so. Then they would be married, with Lady Hayvenhurst's blessing, and Cressida would move into the cottage and cook and clean for Robert and never, never have to worry about sophisticated London people making fun of her and whisking Robert away into their world.

The dream was so real, so compelling, that Cressida could almost convince herself the gardener laboring in the distance was Robert. His straight back and broad shoulders and the curling dark hair that just showed under his hat brim could all have belonged to Robert. He turned aside with his wheelbarrow into one of the little side gardens opening off the Long Walk before she was close enough to dispel the illusion.

Her heart beat unaccountably fast as she neared the rose-covered archway where the gardener had turned off the walk. It would be better, Cressida told herself, not to peep in and get a closer look at the young man; chances were he had a Neanderthal brow over a pimply face and her dream would be shattered on the spot. Much, much better simply to go on pretending. . . .

She cast the merest passing glance into the little side garden. The brick arch that framed the entrance was wreathed in the green vines of a rambling rose whose tight pink buds were just about to unfurl. Beyond that frame of green leaves and new pink rosebuds was a little court enclosed by mellow walls of aged brick, with the back wall all but covered by a curtain of lilac-tinted white wisteria.

The sunlight broke through the low clouds for a moment just as Cressida glanced in, bathing the flowering vine and the man before it in a golden light. The gardener stood leaning on his mattock, watching the archway steadily, almost as if he had been waiting for her.

Cressida felt a flutter of incredulous joy deep in her throat. It was impossible that Robert should be here, dressed like a common workingman, just as if her dream had been brought to life.

"Robert?" Her voice was an unromantic croak. Usually she did better than that in her waking dreams; perhaps this was real after all.

"Cressida." He didn't even seem surprised to see her. Perhaps, Cressida thought happily, her soul had been calling to his, and he had followed her—

Or perhaps Isolde had told him where she was.

"What are you doing here?" Wonderful. She sounded as if she were accusing him of some crime. She dropped her mop and bucket and took two steps forward, hands outstretched. "I mean, how lovely to see you, but why—" She couldn't get through the archway. Robert had walked through with no trouble, but Cressida's full skirt and billowing apron were snagged in a dozen places by the unclipped rose canes sprouting on either side of the archway. One thorny vine hung down from the top of the arch and caught her by the collar.

"Don't move," Robert said at once. "You'll tear your dress." The golden sunlight seemed to follow him as he took two quick steps forward and knelt at Cressida's feet, gently untangling her full skirt from the rosebushes. She stood perfectly still, looking down at the dark hair that curled out from under his old blue cap. It was almost like a dream come true: the overgrown private garden, Robert kneeling at her feet.

Except that she had been stopped at the entrance to the garden; and Robert wasn't there for *her*. The pause while he freed her skirt from the thorns had given Cressida time to think—and to remember Lily Whitworth's boasting about her American suitor. "He begged me to let him follow me down here," Lily had said at dinner on Monday night; and here, two days later, was Robert in disguise as a gardener.

"I have to explain, I guess," Robert said as he tugged the last of the thorny canes away from Cressida's skirt.

"No, you don't," Cressida told him. "I already know about it. Lily Whitworth was talking about it at dinner."

"Oh, she told you?" Robert looked dismayed.

Cressida forced herself to laugh. "No, she didn't *tell* me, exactly. She hasn't noticed I'm here—at least, not that I'm somebody she met in London. She was telling Lady Hayvenhurst about you while I served the dinner."

"I'd like to know how she found me out so quickly," Robert muttered. He bent his head over the thorns in Cressida's skirt, plucking them out one by one with steady, skillful fingers. "You must think I'm an idiot, but you see—"

"Not in the least," Cressida said quickly before he could go on. She did not think she could bear to hear Robert confirming Lily's boasts, to hear his voice telling her that he was so enthralled with Lily Whitworth that he would stoop to any subterfuge to see her. "I understand perfectly. You don't have to explain anything—indeed, I wish you wouldn't."

"Oh." Robert glanced up at her, his hands momentarily stilled. He managed to invest the single syllable with a wealth of disappointment, and Cressida felt unreasonably irritated. What did he *want* of her? She'd already given away far too much of her feelings; he couldn't really expect her to be thrilled that he was so besotted with Lily Whitworth as to go through this ridiculous masquerade. Indifference was the best she could offer him. Cressida struggled to achieve that.

"It's none of my business anyway. Why should you care what I think?"

"I care a great deal what you think. I always have."

He kept looking up at her with those pleading eyes, as if he didn't know that any woman would give him whatever he asked when he looked at her like that. Cressida could just imagine what Lily Whitworth would give him for such a look, and she couldn't bear to think of it any longer. "Fine. If you want my blessing on your pursuit of Lily Whitworth, you have it!"

A great light shone on Robert and he began to smile. So Cressida still thought he was besotted with Lily Whitworth? And it still annoyed her? Good. She couldn't be as deeply in love with this Trevor Bayne-Fleetworth as Isolde thought. Probably Isolde had got it all wrong anyway.

But there had been that damning sentence in Cressida's letter. Not even a sentence—just the phrase that he'd half seen before Isolde snatched the pages away. ". . . cannot bear to see him again, so . . ."

"Do any silly thing you want to," Cressida continued, feeling angrier as Robert continued to smile. "Dress up like a servant, climb the wall, serenade her at midnight. *I* don't care!"

"You're not," Robert said gently, "in any position to sneer at dressing up like a servant. At least I've a good reason for my masquerade."

"And I suppose I don't? What do *you* know about it?"

"I saw what you'd written to Isolde."

Cressida's face turned white and she swayed where she stood. *"No."*

"Sit down." Robert put his arm around her waist to support her.

"I can't," Cressida said with a little more spirit, "I'm still caught in this rosebush!"

"Oh. Yes. Yes, I see." Robert gently tugged at the trailing vine that had fastened itself in Cressida's hair. "I'm afraid your cap will have to come off."

"That's all right." Cressida found it difficult to speak; the gentle touch of Robert's fingers was a sweet torment. She was beginning to lose track of all her lies and pretenses. She had to pretend that she didn't care about Robert's pursuit of Lily Whitworth; she had to pretend that she didn't react to his hands brushing her neck as he worked on freeing her from the vine; she had to . . .

No. No more pretense. Isolde had shown him her letter. He knew exactly how she felt about him. And he had no more decency than to tease her about it now. A tide of red swept up Cressida's neck and face.

"Come and sit down," Robert urged when he'd finally worked the vine loose. "You'd better, really. You hair's all loose—well, it's very pretty, but probably not quite correct for a kitchen maid."

"Housemaid," Cressida corrected automatically. She felt very weak, as if she'd just run a long way, or as if she hadn't eaten in days. Her knees were trembling too much to support her. She walked to the stone bench set against the far wall and seated herself, leaning back against the brick wall. She felt very tired, too. It would be pleasant just to go to sleep right here. In a moment she would have to twist her hair back up in a knot and pin her cap on, but right now her hands were shaking.

"Isolde shouldn't have shown you my letter." Had they been laughing together at her? Cressida couldn't believe her sister would be so cruel.

"She didn't. Exactly. I just had a glimpse at what you'd written. But enough to make a pretty good guess at the situation—especially with what Isolde hinted. I saw enough to know that you were running away from some man."

What a strange way to phrase it, Cressida thought.

"You shouldn't have run away," Robert said. "You could have come to me."

"You!" Cressida was shocked out of her apathy. "Are you *mad?* You're the last person I would have gone to! The whole reason I left London—"

"Yes, yes, I know." Robert looked hurt, which Cressida couldn't help thinking very unreasonable of him. "All right—I suppose you *might* have turned to your father first, but it's obvious he wouldn't be much help. But why on earth couldn't you have asked me to intervene? If I'd known Trevor Bayne-Fleetworth was pestering you, I would have been only too happy to knock his teeth down his throat. But I thought it was Isolde he was interested in."

"So did I," said Cressida. She felt utterly bemused by this latest turn in the conversation. What did Trevor have to do with her sudden realization that she couldn't bear to pose with Robert?

"Then he didn't—he wasn't bothering you?" Robert shook his head slowly. "Isolde said as much, but I couldn't believe her. Your letter—you *said* you were leaving London because you couldn't bear to see him again—"

"I didn't say that. . . . Did I?" Robert seemed to be recollecting a completely different letter from the anguished note Cressida had sent to her sister.

"Yes, you did." Robert frowned, trying to remember the exact words he had glimpsed before Isolde snatched the letter away from him. "I saw that one line. You said, '. . . cannot bear to see him again, so—' "

"And that's all you saw? Isolde didn't let you read my letter?"

"That would hardly be proper," Robert pointed out. "But she did explain—about your wanting to get away from Bayne-Fleetworth, that is."

Cressida took a long, shaky breath and mentally blessed her interfering big sister, who had at least stopped short of exposing her foolish weakness. Thanks to Isolde, Robert had gotten it all wrong—and perhaps there was still a chance to save her pride. He thought she was in love with *Trevor*. She half wanted to slap his face for even imagining such a thing. But that would be foolish—then he'd just want to know who she *had* been referring to in the letter. And if he hadn't guessed by now, Cressida had no intention of spelling it out for him.

She felt grateful that Isolde hadn't given away all her secrets after all. What could she tell Robert that would conform to the words he'd seen, yet would keep him from guessing the truth? She would have to pretend that he was right—that she was enamored of Trevor Bayne-Fleetworth. Ugh.

"That's true," she said, dropping her eyes. "I wanted to get away from London because—it's very painful, Robert, loving someone who doesn't care for you—especially if you have to see him all the time—"

Not a word of untruth in that, but her heart was pounding, and if she dared meet Robert's eyes he would see at once who the "someone" was. Cressida felt like the worst liar in the world.

"You feel like that about an ass like Bayne-Fleetworth?"

Cressida felt her cheeks burning. "You don't know Trevor," she said shakily, "or you wouldn't describe him like that." That, too, was perfectly true. Robert would probably find plenty of worse phrases to apply to a man like Bayne-Fleetworth.

"Maybe I don't," Robert conceded, "but if he likes Isolde better than you, he *must* be an idiot. And I don't think much of your taste, either," he added sharply. "I suppose it's being kept isolated so much at Riversedge, never getting to meet any decent young men."

"I don't need to meet any 'decent young men,' " Cressida said. The only one she knew had already broken her heart so much more thoroughly than an idiot like Trevor Bayne-Fleetworth could possibly have done.

"No? Well, it seems to me you need a keeper," Robert growled. "Disguising yourself as a servant girl, for heaven's sake! Of all the idiotic tricks!"

"You're doing the same thing," Cressida pointed out. "And for much the same reason. I don't think you are in a good position to criticize the things we do for love." She rose, slipped carefully through the entangling vines around the arch, and collected her mop and bucket. "Now, if you don't object, I propose to maintain my disguise by doing the work I was sent down here to perform. I advise you to forget about me and do your own work, if you don't want to be sacked before you ever get to see your precious widow!"

Anger at Robert's bullying, wiser-than-thou tone sustained Cressida the rest of the way down the Long Walk. Slowly the mist of rage cleared from her eyes and she found herself wanting to smile at the flowers she passed.

"I'm very unhappy," she said in a low voice.

The clematis vines seemed unconvinced.

"I need to stay away from Robert or he'll guess how

I feel about him, and that would be humiliating beyond words."

The blue bellflowers that bordered the walk nodded up and down in a passing breeze.

"*I came* here to get away from him. It's absolutely terrible that he's accidentally followed me."

Lilies of the valley, gleaming white in a shady corner, released their sweet fragrance in a cloud that bemused Cressida's senses and left her smiling for no good reason at all. If she had any sense at all she would be utterly dismayed by Robert's appearance at Hayvenhurst Hall. She was supposed to be getting over her love for him, not torturing herself with more meetings. It was going to be absolute hell watching him court Lily Whitworth.

But even that was better than not seeing him at all.

The locked greenhouse stood by itself in a corner between the last walls of the Long Walk and the reed-lined shore of the little pond that ended the vistas of the walkway. Beyond it was the grove where Mr. Craigie's Tudor cottage hunched under the oaks.

Robert's cottage now, Cressida thought dreamily. "Robbie," Mr. Craigie had called him, and she'd never guessed.

If he were really a gardener, he'd never be able to marry Lily Whitworth, and perhaps someday he'd get over his infatuation and settle for the new underhousemaid at the Hall, and she would live with him in the little cottage with its thatched roof and its diamond-patterned leaded casement windows, and she'd plant a dear little cottage garden with herbs and flowers in joyful profusion. . . .

Reality destroyed her dream just as she was pretending that the heavy iron key to the greenhouse was really the key to "Robbie's" cottage; while the key was still in her hand, before she'd quite touched the greenhouse door, reality came screeching down the path in the form of a small frail boy with heavy spectacles overshadowing his pinched white face.

"No, miss, don't go in there. Please, you mustn't!"

The little boy skidded between Cressida and the door in his haste, tripped over an empty flowerpot, and almost crashed through the lowest of the filthy glass panes. Cressida caught him by the shoulder and just managed to save him, but they both sat down rather quickly in a tangle of skirts and mop and flowerpots. The little boy stared up at her, white-faced and open-mouthed, wheezing for breath in a way that quite alarmed Cressida.

"Don't be so upset," she said gently, absentmindedly patting his shoulder. "Everything's going to be all right, you know. There's absolutely nothing to be upset about. It's a lovely day. Isn't it nice to be free to play in the garden on such a beautiful day? Look, the mist is rising over the lake. I think it's going to be sunny after all. Do you like to catch frogs around the shores of the lake, or doesn't your mother let you go near the water?"

For a moment her gentle nonsense seemed to be having some effect; the little boy's painful wheezes for breath had been replaced by slower, deep gasps, and there was a hint of color coming back to his cheeks. But at this question he stiffened in her arms.

"*She* doesn't care what I do," he said. "Nobody does."

"Well, that would be a pity if it were true, but I'm sure you're exaggerating," Cressida said briskly. "People often feel like that when they're annoyed with their parents, you know, but it passes and then you remember how much your parents really love you."

But she'd disappeared into Farthingdonshire with much the same feelings about Papa, Cressida remembered. She'd told herself that he cared nothing for her and would only be annoyed that she wasn't there to pose for his picture. Was that *quite* true? Would he be worried about her?

Of course not. Besides, Isolde knew that she was well and happy and hadn't been snatched off the London train by a mad murderer. The two cases were quite different.

"Now, I expect your mother is wondering where you are at this very moment," Cressida said cheerfully as she brushed the boy off. "You need to go back to her, and I need to clean this greenhouse."

"*No*, miss!" The little boy thrust himself before the greenhouse door, arms outspread as though he could forcibly prevent her from going in. "Nobody's supposed to go in there. Didn't Simpson tell you? Aunt Dagmar keeps her very special plants in there and she doesn't let anybody else tend to them. You'll be turned off if you go in, truly you will! *Please* don't, miss!"

Aunt Dagmar? Cressida thought. Then this must be—"Are you Mrs. Whitworth's stepson? Gregor?"

The child nodded.

"Then, Gregor," she said gently, "you mustn't call me 'miss,' because I'm only a servant girl. You call me Jane, and I—I suppose I call you 'Master Gregor.' And right now I don't call you anything, because I'm supposed to be working."

Gregor shook his head and did not move from his position guarding the door. His lips were set in a firm line that gave his little boy's face a disconcerting look of maturity beyond his years.

"I was sent here," Cressida explained. "It must be all right for *me* to go in." But hadn't she herself thought there was something strange about the orders?

"Martha shouldn't have told you to come down here," Gregor insisted. "She was—I shouldn't tell you—" He bit his lip and looked fearfully up the Long Walk. "Please, miss, could we go somewhere else? If *he* catches me—" He began to wheeze for breath again.

All at once Cressida's resistance collapsed. Gregor was truly frightened—she could see that—and it was far more important to reassure the child than to go on with her task. Besides, she thought as she took Gregor's hand and walked around the greenhouse to the lake, wasn't it strange that he knew Martha had been the one to transmit Mrs. Simpson's orders? If he didn't know something was wrong, wouldn't he have assumed Cressida had had her orders directly from the housekeeper?

"There!" Cressida said cheerfully when they had reached one of her own favorite places, a large flat rock under a weeping willow. The rock jutted out into the pond and was surrounded on three sides by tall green reeds. Wild iris speckled the verges of the pond with lavender and orchid hues, and the willow tree that shaded them leaned down to the water's edge to trail its long green branches in the pond, making a little room with three walls of green reeds and branches and a fourth wall of the willow's gnarled trunk. It wasn't quite like being in the water garden at Riversedge, but it was close enough for Cressida's dreams.

"Better let me go first," Gregor suggested, looking doubtfully at the surface of the rock where the lake water lapped at its edges. "It may not be quite stable."

Cressida opened her mouth to assure him that she'd stepped out onto the rock more than once in the last week, then shut her mouth again as Gregor compressed his lips and stepped bravely out onto *terra incognita.*

"You can come on now—it's quite safe," Gregor assured her, and he turned back with his arm crooked like a gentleman inviting her for a stroll. Cressida laid her fingers lightly—oh, so lightly!—on the bony little arm, and stepped through the reeds onto her secret rock with extra care not to overbalance Gregor in his chivalrous moment.

"You see, we can be quite private here," Cressida told Gregor, "so if there was anything you wanted to say to me . . ."

She let the sentence trail off, half afraid that she might be encouraging the child to break a confidence. But now that they were out of sight of anybody who might come down the Long Walk, Gregor's eyes were bright and he launched into his story without hesitating.

"You see, miss, I heard Uncle Waverley talking to Mama about it last night. He said he was going to teach the impudent little chit a good lesson. Then Mama sent for Martha and asked who the housemaid was who'd been lighting their fires, and Martha said, 'Jane,' and Uncle Waverley said, 'Well, Martha, I want you to help me out now. I promised Jane I'd meet her tomorrow afternoon, only we hadn't thought of a place to meet yet. But now I've got the key to the greenhouse by the lake. I want you to give it to her and tell her Simpson wants her to clean the greenhouse tomorrow at two o'clock.' "

"Martha didn't want to do it," Gregor said, wriggling

about between the willow root and the rock until he found a comfortable position with one arm draped over the root and the other trailing in the pond. "She said nobody was supposed to go in the greenhouse except Aunt Dagmar. But Uncle Waverley smiled at her—I guess that's what he did. Anyway, Mama went away and it was real quiet for a while and there were little smacking noises. Uncle Waverley does have a pretty smile," Gregor added reflectively. "At least, it looks nice until people get to know him and find out how many things he can do that *hurt*, like bending your fingers back or pinching you in soft places. But I guess he didn't bend Martha's fingers back, because I didn't hear her crying. Or maybe she's braver than me."

Cressida turned away and pretended to be very interested in the pattern of ripples spreading out over the water where a fish had risen to snap at a fly. She didn't want Gregor to see the angry tears rising to her own eyes.

"Anyway, he told Martha there was a new dress in it for her if she delivered the message just as he said, and he'd see she was turned off for dallying with him if she didn't do it, so I guess she was afraid not to, so you shouldn't be too angry with Martha," Gregor finished uncertainly. "But after she left I heard Uncle Waverley and Mama laughing about it. Mama said, 'You're not really going to meet the girl, are you?' and Uncle Waverley said, 'Not now. I'll let Dagmar catch her sneaking into the greenhouse and turn her off without a character first. She'll be glad enough of the chance to be friendly with a gentleman when she's thrown out of the house and has nowhere else to go.'"

Cressida drew a long shaky breath.

"I . . . I see," she said when she could speak evenly again. "It was very good of you to warn me, Gregor."

"I hate Uncle Waverley," the little boy said flatly. "He is an evil man."

"No, Gregor, you mustn't say such things!" Cressida exclaimed, momentarily shocked. Then she remembered Gregor's artless comments about "the things Uncle Waverley could do to hurt" and thought that perhaps, after all, the man was evil. But it would do Gregor no good for her to agree. He had to get on with his relatives somehow. "It was a very silly joke for him to play, and not very kind, but you see, you did warn me in time, so no harm has been done, has it?"

She smiled sweetly down at Gregor, willing him to accept her view of the matter and quite unaware that three pale pink blossoms from the early roses beside the greenhouse had floated down to nestle in her tangled hair. Gregor looked back up at her and thought that "Jane" was the loveliest girl in the world.

"Will you marry me?" he demanded, and then flushed. Unbecoming scarlet blotches stained his sharp cheekbones. "Not now, I mean—when I'm grown up. I'm to have Hayvenhurst Hall, you know," he added with an anxious sideways glance to see if this inducement compensated Cressida for his own inadequacies. "We could live here forever, and no grownups to spoil things."

"Of course we could," Cressida said instantly, with only the faintest pang at the thought of a boy who'd played with her and seemed to love her before he turned into a "grownup to spoil things."

"And we'll have ponies to ride, and cakes for tea every day, and all the books we want to read," Gregor promised.

"It sounds absolutely marvelous," Cressida agreed. "And shall we keep a boat here at the edge of the lake?"

"What for?" Gregor looked doubtful at the chilly water lapping around their rock.

"To explore the island," Cressida said instantly.

"There isn't an island."

"Well, then, the mysterious farther shore." She waved her hand at the mist-veiled green vista on the far side of the pond.

"What for? I know what's there—one of Aunt Dagmar's experimental turnip fields."

Cressida thought that Gregor had not been properly encouraged to use his imagination. "You only *think* it's a turnip field," she said, dropping her voice to a thrilling low note. "She had to come up with some explanation for why the field was all dug up, didn't she? Really it's where the treasure is buried."

Gregor gave an excited wriggle and nearly impaled himself on a projecting stubby root of the willow tree. "Pirate treasure?"

"I shouldn't doubt it," said Cressida solemnly. "The trouble is, you see, it is quite a big field, and we don't want to dig it all up. I think the first thing we'd better do is look for a map, don't you?"

"Where?"

"Look around the house," Cressida told him. "There are bound to be clues in a secret writing telling you where the map is hidden." At any rate, she resolved, there would be some clues tomorrow. She might not be able to keep the interest of a high-and-mighty grown man like Robert Glenford, but she could certainly bring some amusement into the life of this lonely, neglected little boy while he stayed at Hayvenhurst Hall.

Cressida and Gregor remained on their secret rock until nearly teatime, elaborating her fantasy of the pirate treasure and planning their search for the map. Once they ducked down low, and Gregor held his hand over his mouth to stifle giggles, when they heard somebody coming down the Long Walk and rattling the locked door of the greenhouse.

"Hmmph!" It was unmistakably Lady Hayvenhurst's voice. "Thought so. That silly brother-in-law of mine has it all wrong as usual. What would one of the underhouse-maids be doing down here, I asked him when he came up with his cock-and-bull story about seeing one of them sneaking down this way, and that he couldn't say. Kept asking me whom I'd hired recently who might be after Julian's treasure. I wanted to tell young Waverley that he was a more suspicious character in my book than any of my servants. Couldn't say that, of course. Not ladylike. But I'll be damned if I don't give him a piece of my mind when I get back to the house. All the same, you'd better keep a sharp eye out for the next few days, young Robbie. I don't want any 'accidents' before the Botanical Exposition next month."

"Aye, missus," mumbled Robert. "Aa'll do thon right enow."

Cressida supposed he was trying to emulate a Lowland Scots accent. It was too bad Craigie hadn't had time to coach him better.

Lady Hayvenhurst's steps receded down the garden path, and after a brief interval Cressida and Gregor heard a man moving toward their refuge.

"I've put your mop and bucket around the other side of the greenhouse, Cressida," Robert said, apparently addressing the willow tree. "Lady H. didn't see them. I suggest you study your role better if you want to pass in future; housemaids don't clean the outbuildings."

After an expectant moment of silence he, too, turned away and went back toward the Long Walk. Gregor and Cressida released their pent-up breath and went back to telling pirate stories until the lengthening shadows warned them that evening was approaching. "I shall be late for tea," said Cressida, "not that it really matters."

But Gregor had gone white. "My stepmama specially wanted me to be there at teatime today. She's expecting somebody important."

While Cressida and Gregor had been telling stories down by the lily pond, a much less pleasant meeting was taking place at the Hall. Mr. Ponsonby Tomkyns, the solicitor who handled Julian Whitworth's estate, had been notified by Lady Hayvenhurst that the boy was too ill to stay on at boarding school and was visiting Hayvenhurst Hall while he recuperated. Mr. Tomkyns was more worried than he liked to admit by this news. He immediately dispatched a brusque note to Julian Whitworth's widow announcing his intention of visiting Hayvenhurst Hall to inspect the child's condition personally.

Lily Whitworth was somewhat ruffled by this intrusion. Her temper was not soothed by the fact that Mr. Tomkyns was a dried-up old stick of a lawyer who evinced not the slightest disposition to be charmed by a pretty face, an enchanting laugh, or tossing golden ringlets. And Gregor's unannounced disappearance, just when she had particularly wanted him to appear clean and well cared for before the lawyer, put the last fine edge on her temper.

None of this appeared in her face and manner as she offered Mr. Tomkyns a platter of iced cakes and stirred sugar into his tea. Lily might let herself go with the servant classes, but she was not such a fool as to offend a gentleman. Granted, she was not *quite* sure that a solicitor qualified as a gentleman, but this particular solicitor controlled Julian's trust fund. He was definitely not someone to be offended.

"More sugar, Mr. Tomkyns?" Lily inquired. Perhaps enough sugar would sweeten the old stick's disposition.

"Sugar aggravates my dyspeptic tendency," Mr. Tomkyns informed her. "This is the boy's third illness in the two years since his father's death."

Lily could think of no socially acceptable reply to either of these statements, though she would dearly have loved to point out that Mr. Tomkyns's sour face would make anyone bilious. Maybe he wouldn't have digestive problems if he would smile once in a while.

"Gregor is very frail," Lily said. She rang for a maid to take away the rejected cup of tea and poured out a fresh, unsweetened cup for the solicitor.

Mr. Tomkyns frowned at her over his half-rimmed glasses. "The boy did well enough before young Mr. Whitworth's death, did he not? As I recall, Mr. Whitworth took the child everywhere—even into the depths of the Brazilian jungle. I find it surprising that he should have had enough stamina to survive those years of exploring, yet should appear frail in the environment of an English boarding school."

"The boy's mother was Brazilian," Lily pointed out. "Perhaps he is poorly adapted to this climate. Goodness knows, I tried to persuade Julian to leave—"

She stopped and bit her tongue. There was no need to tell the solicitor all about her arguments in favor of depositing Gregor with his Brazilian relatives. Mr. Tomkyns might just possibly get the feeling that Lily didn't want to care for her stepson. And Lily's income from Julian's estate was dependent on her "acting as a mother to my soon-to-be-orphaned son," as Julian had sentimentally phrased his will.

Mr. Tomkyns's look of disapproval grew even frostier. "Yes, I know, you wanted him to abandon the boy in Brazil."

"I should hardly call it *abandonment* to allow his mother's family the chance of rearing him," Lily replied. "Besides, that wasn't what I was going to say at all; I meant to say that I tried to persuade Julian to leave Gregor at home in my care instead of dragging him on these exploring trips of his. I am very much afraid the hardships of travel may have broken the child's health. I have always been devoted to Gregor's interests."

"Which explains," Mr. Tomkyns said dryly, "why, as soon as young Mr. Whitworth died, you placed the boy in a boarding school, where he has suffered three serious illnesses in two years."

"Nonsense! He has never been seriously ill," Lily responded. "The headmaster of that school just seizes on every opportunity to send the boys home. I think it saves him money."

"But you just agreed that his constitution was frail."

"It *was* frail," Lily said triumphantly, "when he was racketing around the world with his father. I have every hope that a good steady rearing in a Christian school will build him up again. If he were really ill now, don't you think I'd have him in bed? Instead the little brat has run away to explore the park, just when he knew I particularly wanted to let you see him. The boy needs discipline, Mr. Tomkyns, not coddling."

It was perhaps unfortunate that Gregor should have made his appearance just then, disheveled, out of breath, and with two bright red spots standing out on his pinched, sallow face. Sweat matted his hair into hedgehog spikes and his thick spectacles were misted over. Lily looked at her stepson dispassionately and reflected, not for the first time, that he really was a very ugly little boy. Anyone with a soul would understand immediately what an imposition it was for her to be saddled with this unappealing child who wasn't even related to her. But Mr. Tomkyns wasn't even looking at her; he was paying attention only to Gregor, listening to the wheeze that interrupted the boy's stammered apologies for being late.

"Never mind, Gregor." Lily cut him off sharply. "I only wanted you to come to tea so that Mr. Tomkyns could see how well you are doing in the country air. I'm sadly afraid that instead he will only see that you need the good discipline of your school for a few more years. Perhaps your headmaster can teach you some semblance of civilized behavior; *I* quite despair of the task."

Her long speech had given Gregor the chance to recover his breath, so that at least he didn't cough and wheeze all over her and Mr. Tomkyns. But he turned quite white at the mention of school. "Am I going back there?"

"No—not immediately at any rate," Mr. Tomkyns said before Lily could speak. "Do you know who I am, my boy?"

Gregor nodded and extended a limp, sweaty hand. "Yes, Mr. Tomkyns, sir. You control my trust, do you not? And you came to the school last year when I was ill—at least I *think* you did. I'm sorry, I had such queer dreams with the fever that time that I cannot be sure."

"Quite right, my boy," Mr. Tomkyns told him. "The headmaster had been unable to reach your stepmother that time, so he cabled me for instructions and I thought I would just stop in and see how you were getting on. The doctor told me you were too sick to be moved and that in any event he could not authorize your removal from the school without the approval of Mrs. Whitworth, so I was only with you for the one afternoon that I could spare from my business."

"It was very good of you to come all that way to see me," Gregor said.

Lily's hands were clenched into little white fists under the tea table. "You never told me you had been snooping— I mean, visiting Gregor!"

"There seemed no necessity," said Mr. Tomkyns blandly. "By the time you could be found, the boy was out of danger, and Mr. Jessop, the headmaster, advised me that you were strongly against having him removed from the school. Since I was involved in the winding up of a rather complicated estate legacy at the time, I allowed the matter to drop; but I could not reconcile it with my conscience to leave this third illness unexamined. As I was about to tell Gregor, Lady Hayvenhurst has very kindly invited me to stay here for a few days so that I can satisfy myself as to Gregor's progress. Need I remind you that the terms of Julian Whitworth's will specify that I am to be allowed all reasonable access to the boy?"

"Of course not, Mr. Tomkyns. I am simply delighted to know you take your duties as trustee so seriously. Allow me to pour you some more tea." Lily dumped half the contents of the sugar bowl into the solicitor's teacup and stirred so vigorously that most of the tea splashed over the table. "And I do insist that you try some of the iced cakes. They're a specialty of the cook's, and I know Lady Hayvenhurst will be severely disappointed if you don't eat several." *And I hope they give you an ulcer on top of your dyspepsia, you old toad.*

Lily restrained herself until Mr. Ponsonby Tomkyns had departed to dress for dinner. The solicitor had been given a room in the West Wing, on the far side of the Hall, so she felt no need to control herself once she had reached the privacy of her own rooms in the East Wing. After sending Gregor to bed without his supper as punishment for being late to tea, she paced up and down the length of her bedchamber, slamming things down, tossing dresses across the floor, and cursing her brother Waverley when he stuck his sleek head in to ask what had ripped up her composure so dreadfully.

"That old solicitor is staying for another week!" Lily announced. "To satisfy himself as to Gregor's condition, he says. I daren't send the brat back to school until he leaves."

"Shouldn't advise that in any case," Waverley said with

149

provoking calm. He perched against the corner of Lily's dressing table and began playing with her scent bottles. "The kid was really sick, y'know. Still looks like a drowned rat having a bad day."

"I *know* he's homely! What has that to do with anything?"

"Don't want him dying at school, do you? Raise a shocking stink. Questions. No more trust fund. Poverty. No connection with Hayvenhurst. If *you* don't remember what our life was like before you got your hooks into Julian," Waverley advised his sister, "*I* do, and I've no desire to go back to that hand-to-mouth existence. Best guard the brat's health like your own."

Lily looked at him thoughtfully. "Don't be ridiculous! Gregor's in no danger of *dying*, Waverley; he's a provoking little beast and he likes to sham illness to get away from school." All the same, a qualm of uneasiness assailed her. Waverley spoke so casually, as though Gregor were on his death bed already. *Could* he have been really ill? And could anyone think her such a monster that she'd send him back to school before he was quite strong?

Lily frowned over Waverley's shoulder at her white and golden reflection in the dressing-table mirror. What a hideous expression—it made her look an absolute fright, and old too. Quickly she smoothed out her features and rearranged them in a bewitching smile with just a hint of a pout. Much better. The golden girl who smiled back at her from the mirror looked not a day over twenty and far too sweet to be anybody's wicked stepmother.

"I'm really very fond of Gregor," she said uncertainly. "It would be terrible if anything happened to him."

"That it would," Waverley agreed, "since your income would cease with his life."

"You," Lily said, "are a very nasty man. I *am* fond of Gregor. How could I not be, when he's all I have left to remind me of my darling Julian—not that he *looks* much like his father, I must say, for everyone said Julian and I made a very handsome couple . . ."

"That's the ticket," Waverley advised, sliding off his

perch on the dressing table. "Maternal love—stepmaternal, anyway. Just keep acting the loving mother till old Tom-kyns goes back to London. And don't let the kid catch another one of his bad colds." He sauntered to the door, then poked his sleek head back into the room with a teasing smile on his face. "Now I think of it, Lil, you'd better do the thing right—wrap up in a shawl and knit warm socks for your darling lad . . ."

He pulled his head out of the way just before Lily's scent bottle sailed across the room and burst on the doorpost. "Beast! Get out of my room!" Lily shrieked, never caring that Waverley had anticipated the order. "Go away! Leave me alone! *Everybody* let me alone! I can't bear any more!"

Each shrill exclamation was punctuated by a crash as another article flew off the dressing table and hit the opposite wall with a smack. A bottle of lavender water came through the open door and rained its scent down the plastered wall of the hallway. A bunch of flowers followed it, together with the vase in which they had stood. A small bronze statue of a barking terrier did not make it quite so far, being rather heavy. Safely behind the closed door of his own room, Waverley laughed loudly at Lily's fit of temper.

In the narrow little room opening off Lily's bedchamber, Gregor put his head under the pillow and prayed that Step-mama would not remember his existence for a while. He crammed a handful of blankets into his mouth to stifle the cough that always attacked him just when he most wanted to be invisible and inaudible.

Martha, who was supposed to help Lily dress for dinner, hovered irresolutely on the landing, just out of range of the missiles bursting against the wall.

To Cressida, laboring up the stairs with a scuttle of coal to replenish Lily's dressing-room fire, the sounds of strife were all too familiar. She glanced at Martha and sighed to herself. Someone would have to calm Lily down, that was clear; and she could expect no help from Martha.

Cressida was too used to the role of peacemaker to re-flect that she might be safer to stay out of this storm. Be-sides, Martha was obviously terrified of Lily's tantrums;

even Mrs. Simpson, who'd been drawn out of her rooms belowstairs by the noise, looked worried and uncertain what to do next.

Years of dealing with the artistic temperament left Cressida feeling no such uncertainty. Lily had to be stopped before she gave herself a sick headache and made everybody else in the house miserable; and after Papa and Isolde, Cressida was an expert in cutting off displays of temperament. She set her coal scuttle down in the hall and marched into the room during the brief pause that followed the thud of the brass statue on the carpet.

"My wrist hurts!" Lily announced. "I'm sure it is broken."

"I doubt that, but you may have given yourself a bad sprain," Cressida answered, moving to stand behind Lily. The dressing table, she observed thankfully, was already denuded of ornaments. "Shall I have Lady Hayvenhurst send for the village doctor? I'm afraid he is dreadfully old-fashioned; he'll probably insist that you wrap your arm up in vinegar and red flannel," she invented cheerfully, "but of course you won't mind looking ridiculous if it's necessary to heal your injuries, will you?"

Lily gave a delicate shudder at the idea of displaying herself with any part of her person bound up in red flannel. "Odious man! And in this heat. I should find such a treatment quite insupportable."

"Then it's a good thing the sprain does not pain you so *very* much," Cressida suggested. "Here, let me take your hair down and brush it out before dinner. All those hairpins must be making your head ache."

Lily subsided onto the cushioned seat before the dressing table and admired her own reflection while the housemaid deftly brushed out the long curling strands of shimmering gold. The girl's fingers were cool and gentle, passing over Lily's throbbing temples with a soothing touch. While she worked she kept up a monotonous, restful, low-voiced discussion of how tiring Lily must find the demands of her position and how much all this beautiful hair must weigh her poor head down. It seemed so much to balance on such a slender neck! No wonder Miss Lily's eyes were reddened.

"Oh, do you think they are?" Lily exclaimed, peering anxiously at herself in the mirror. She quite forgot to correct the girl for referring to her as "Miss Lily." After all, it was a natural mistake; she surely didn't look old enough to be married, let alone widowed and with a great hulking stepson to care for!

"There's just the slightest hint of irritation," the housemaid replied, "and I'm sure that'll be gone by dinnertime if you care to put your feet up and rest for a little, Miss Lily! I'll slip your shoes off for you, shall I?"

Hardly knowing how it happened, Lily allowed herself to be guided toward the bed, where she lay down under a silk shawl while the strange housemaid brought a cooling compress to place on her temples. As she watched the girl coming toward her, something in her walk and the turn of her slender wrists reminded Lily of where she'd seen her before.

"I know you!" she announced triumphantly, sitting up on the bed and letting the shawl slide to the floor.

The maid stopped midway to the bed, white and still as a statue, with a look of horror on her silly face. "You—you do?"

"Yes," Lily said. "You're the girl my fool of a brother was after yesterday, aren't you? June—Jane—some plain name like that. I can't imagine what he saw in you." A nagging memory teased at her. "He was going to have you turned off, wasn't he? Some nasty trick or other—I forget what; I wasn't really listening when he told me what he meant to do. Well, don't worry, Jane," she said magnanimously, now that she understood why the girl had looked so pale and frightened for a minute. "I shan't let Waverley make trouble for you. I like you. You shall be my personal maid while I'm staying here, and if you do well perhaps I'll take you back to London with me when I get out of this—I mean, when I leave."

The silly girl looked, if possible, even more upset than she had the moment before. Servants were so dull, Lily reflected as she lay back down on the bed and closed her eyes. It would probably take the maid a few minutes to understand her good fortune. "Pick that shawl up, Jane," she directed in a sharp voice without opening her eyes, "and lay it over me again—and do it properly this time, so that it doesn't slide off! One thing you'll have to learn, my girl, is that I will not tolerate slipshod service!"

Chapter

9

*R*obert caught her when she was running through the long grasses around the lake.

"You're upset about something," he said. He prided himself on being a reasonably perceptive chap. Cressida's prim white cap was askew and a lock of wavy brown hair had strayed out of its tight bun to linger on her neck. "What's the matter?"

"Nothing. Everything. I don't know." Cressida blinked and looked around wildly. "I was just—"

"Going to your favorite hiding place," Robert said. "That's all right; I don't mind sitting there with you."

"You must have work to do."

"So must you. It's the middle of the morning. Why aren't you polishing coals, or burning the tea, or whatever housemaids do in the morning?"

"Because," Cressida said, "I'm not an underhousemaid any longer. I'm Lily Whitworth's personal maid. Don't you listen to the gossip in the servants' hall?"

"No," Robert said simply. It had been rather a blow to discover that old Craigie, the gardener whom he was replacing for these weeks, had all his meals served in the cottage beyond the greenhouse—and that Lady Hayvenhurst expected Robert to continue the arrangement. She was ridiculously nervous about the danger of someone breaking into her private greenhouse; Robert thought that she would probably have liked him to sleep there instead of in the cottage. Not that he minded the extra hours of guard duty. But not taking his meals with the other servants was a serious handicap to his plans for Cressida. So far he hadn't even managed to get her to tell him about that ass Bayne-Fleetworth. Not to mention convincing her of his own superior qualities. Maybe he could do that without talking about Bayne-Fleetworth.

He took Cressida's arm and led her through the grass to the flat rock beneath the willow tree. There was not quite room for two adults—especially when one of them was as large as Robert—so they had to sit very close together. Robert sat back against the gnarled roots of the old tree; Cressida leaned on his knee, hands linked in her lap, and stared out at the peaceful surface of the pond. The arrangement was so pleasant that Robert felt momentarily regretful when Cressida began to explain what had sent her in such disarray to the bottom of the garden. As he understood the sense of her story, though, his fists clenched and he quite forgot to enjoy this chance to have Cressy sitting on his knee—or almost on his knee. Apparently he was going to have to join the queue of gentlemen who thought that a pleasant idea.

"I really should be in Lily's—Mrs. Whitworth's—room now," Cressida explained in a halting monotone. "She had left me some of her dresses to mend, and after I finished the mending I was to let out the seams of her lilac evening gown and attach a new lace ruffle around the neckline, and then sew the black beads back on her jet beaded purse, and then before lunch—well, that doesn't matter."

And he didn't think that refurbishing Lily's dresses was what had Cressida trembling like a frightened rabbit. But for lack of anything better to keep the conversation going, Robert commented that it sounded like rather a lot of work to get through in one morning.

"Well . . . I like sewing," Cressida said. "I didn't mind, really. Only I wish she had permitted me to take the work down to the servants' hall. You see, her brother came upstairs. He said he was looking for Gregor, to take him for a ride. . . ."

And Cressida had known quite well where Gregor was: in his room, wrapped in a blanket and reading *The Cloister and the Hearth* for the third time. They had discussed the possibility of acting out the scene where Gerard and Denys got trapped by a bear, only there was all this mending to get through, and Cressida hadn't liked the sound of Gregor's cough, so she'd persuaded him to spend the morning resting on his bed.

When Waverley appeared, making bluff and hearty noises about taking the brat out for some fresh air and teaching him to get over his fear of horses, Cressida hadn't had any intention of letting him bother Gregor. She moved her chair between Waverley and the connecting door to Gregor's room, spread out Lily's lilac evening gown between them, and said as calmly as she could that Gregor had already gone outside.

"I think he said something about looking at the topiary garden," she suggested. "Would you care to look for him there?"

"Rather look for you," Waverley suggested with a sickly grin.

"But I'm not in the garden," Cressida pointed out. "And I have a lot of work to do for your sister, sir, so perhaps you'd just leave me to get on with it."

Waverley shook his head sadly. "Impertinence, Jane? Dear me, I thought you'd been warned about taking such a familiar tone to your masters. We'll have to repeat the lesson."

"Careful," Cressida gasped, "you'll crumple Lily's—I mean, *Miss* Lily's evening gown."

"Then you'll get in trouble, won't you, pretty Jane? Better fold up your work now—"

Cressida plunged her flashing needle into Waverley's

hand. He gave a yelp of surprise and put his hand to his mouth.

"I'm ever so sorry, sir, I'm sure," Cressida said demurely.

"You'll be sorrier, you little scratching cat!"

This time he caught her wrist and gave a sharp, vicious twist. "Drop the needle. That's right. *Drop* it. You don't want me to bleed on Miss Lily's silk gown, do you, Jane? Why don't you kiss the spot and make it better? Quick, now. It's starting to bleed again—and you know what Miss Lily will say about you ruining her gown. This time you *will* be turned off."

"There are worse things than being turned off," Cressida spat at him, "and you're one of them!"

A ponderous footstep sounded outside Lily's room. Cressida and Waverley froze in their places. The door creaked open and Mr. Flynn's rubicund face beamed in. "Ah, there you are, Jane. Could you leave that mending for a moment and come along with me? Mrs. Simpson wants to see you."

"Jane is my sister's personal maid now," Waverley said. "She doesn't answer to the housekeeper." He had moved so that his body was between the butler and Cressida; Mr. Flynn could not see his fingers locked tight around Cressida's wrist.

"All the servants in this house report to Mrs. Simpson and me." Mr. Flynn moved lightly around Waverley, surprisingly quick for a man of his bulk, and lifted the lilac evening gown from Cressida's lap. He laid it on the bed, dextrous as any lady's maid, and somehow Cressida found that Waverley had backed away and Mr. Flynn had taken her cold fingers in his own. "Come along now, my dear. You can finish the mending after."

Once they were safely downstairs and on the servants' side of the green baize door, Cressida dared to look Mr. Flynn in the face. Had he thought that she was flirting with Waverley? It must have looked like that.

"I know exactly what was going on, young Jane," the butler said, "and you're not to worry about a thing. Mrs. Simpson told me to keep an eye on you when that Mrs.

Whitworth said she wanted you for her maid. As long as you have to work abovestairs, and that Waverley's in the house, there'll always be one of the manservants within call. It's a terrible pity he's cast his eye upon you, but we know you're a good girl and we'll not see you ruined like poor Kat from the scullery was last time Waverley came. Mrs. Simpson still feels that bad about Kat. She's sworn never to leave another of her girls alone where Waverley can get at her."

"Mrs. Simpson can stop worrying about Waverley," Robert said when Cressida reached that point in her story.

"Why?"

"Because," Robert explained simply, "I'm going to find him and—"

"Robert, no!" Cressida had seen that light in Robert's eyes just once before, on a summer day when they'd come upon a tradesman beating his broken-down horse with a heavy whip. The bully had been a grown man, taller and heavier than the schoolboy Robert, who leapt into the road and ordered him to stop; but Robert had taken the man's whip away from him and broken it over his knee, then attacked him in a white-faced fury of desperate, unscientific blows that had the tradesman begging for mercy while Cressida tried to haul Robert away.

"You mustn't kill Waverley," she said now, hanging on to his arm with both hands as if she could ward off his intentions before he ever saw Waverley.

"Even," Robert inquired, "when it's such an obvious service to society? Let go my arm, Cressy. Don't worry, I haven't lost my temper. Yet."

Cressida did not find this quite as reassuring as it might have been. Robert's face had gone quite white and his eyes were glittering like chips of blue grass. She should have thought before she spilled out her tale of woe so heedlessly, should have remembered how much Robert loathed any kind of bullying or violence exerted by the strong against the weak.

She confronted her own heart and wondered if she had actually *wanted* this, or something like it, to happen. She was close to hating Waverley herself, not so much for the way he teased her as for the pleasure he took in tormenting his nephew. It would give her great personal satisfaction to see him go down under Robert's fists.

What a terrible person she must be, actually wanting to see another human being hurt! But Cressida had no time to examine this alarming revelation of the depths to which she could sink. She now realized that she could have had an even lowlier motive for wanting Robert to fight with Waverley.

"Robert, you *mustn't*," she pleaded. "I ought never to have told you. Truly, truly, there is nothing I can't take care of on my own. I *told* you, Mr. Flynn promised there'd always be one of the manservants within call from now on." Not that his promise would do Gregor much good; nor that Cressida put much stock in it for herself. The first time Mrs. Simpson got flustered by too many conflicting demands, the protective net of watching servants would fray to nothingness. But she didn't have to tell Robert all that. The important thing was to get him calmed down. He was about to ruin his life by losing Lily, and it would be all her fault; and Cressida found that even more unbearable than the prospect of watching him stay at Hayvenhurst to court Lily.

"Don't worry, Cressy," Robert told her. He detached his arm from her hands with a careful, controlled gentleness that frightened Cressida a great deal more than any show of anger would have done. "I have no intention of killing Waverley."

"You . . . don't?" Cressida quavered. Robert's lips were set in a thin line and his eyes blazed with the passionate anger she'd seen only once before. "Robert, you mustn't *half* kill him either. That will be just as bad."

"No," Robert contradicted her with an involuntary twitch of his lips, "only half as good. No fear. I'm just going to find the man—alone, for preference—and—er—persuade him that he finds the air of Hayvenhurst Hall unhealthy."

Somehow Cressida didn't believe that Robert's methods of persuasion would be of the subtlest.

"Robert, *no*," she repeated. "Please! Have you thought what it'll mean if you fight with Waverley? You're only an undergardener. You'll be sacked immediately—and then how will you meet Lily and court her? And she might never forgive you for beating her brother to a pulp."

The light of battle died out of Robert's eyes almost at once, to be replaced by a puzzled, almost hurt expression. "Oh—Lily. Yes. Yes, I see what you mean. Does it really matter that much to you then?"

Cressida felt a gray misery creeping over her. How quickly he had changed! It only took one mention of Lily Whitworth to make him realize the folly of getting into a fight over little Cressida Parris. Which was, of course, what she had intended—to make him realize the cost to himself; only she hadn't expected him to be *quite* so easy to persuade. What a hypocrite she was! All this time, while she pretended to herself that she was trying to talk Robert out of an act of violence that would endanger his future, in her secret heart she had been hoping for quite another outcome. The Robert of her dreams would have exclaimed, "To the devil with Lily Whitworth, you are the one true love of my life," or some such words—Cressida hadn't quite allowed herself to be conscious of this fantasy, so it wasn't worked out in as much detail as it might have been.

The Robert Glenford of reality, the young man who was passionately in love with Lily Whitworth and had disguised himself as a gardener just to see her, did no such thing. Naturally. He just stood there looking as if her words of warning had immediately robbed him of the desire to go on with his project. Probably, Cressida thought, he was embarrassed—wondering how to back down.

She couldn't bear to see Robert embarrassed or hurt or at a loss for words. And it was all her fault anyway.

"It's quite all right," she said, too rapidly to choose her words carefully. "I understand. *Perfectly*. You mustn't do anything to jeopardize your chances with Lily—that's the most important thing to think about."

"Is it really?" Robert asked. He looked like a man who'd been badly hurt and didn't yet understand what had hit him. Cressida's heart sank. This was no mere infatuation; he must be truly in love with Lily. Nothing else could account for his dazed, almost despairing expression. Up to now Cressida had allowed herself to imagine that Robert would recover from his infatuation with Lily and see her as the spoiled, selfish young woman she really was. Now she knew that would never happen—and if it did, it would break his heart. For right this minute, upon the mere hint of a threat to his courtship of Lily, he looked like a man who had been wounded to the heart.

"Of course it is," Cressida said, trying to control the unruly quaver in her voice. "You love Lily and nothing must come between you. I completely understand that." And after she had been alone with the knowledge for some time—say, a quarter of a century or so—she would also be able to completely accept it. For now, she would have to lie valiantly. How fortunate it was that Robert thought her to be in love with Trevor Bayne-Fleetworth! At least she would come out of this miserable summer with her pride, if nothing else, intact.

And Robert would come out of it with the woman he loved, and at least *he* would be happy.

"I hadn't . . . expected you . . . to devote yourself so thoroughly to furthering my relationship with Lily," Robert said slowly.

Cressida blinked away the tears that threatened to spill out and smiled at Robert so brilliantly that he would have to think her eyes were sparkling with pure unselfish happiness for him. "Dear Robert. What else could I do? I could not love you more dearly if you were my own brother. Naturally I want you to win the woman you love."

"No," Robert said. "No, I don't think you do. But have it your way. Waverley can live. What do *I* care? If you'll excuse me, Cressy, I'd better get back to work. As you so generously pointed out, we don't want me to be turned off."

He turned on his heel and strode back up the green slope

to the Long Walk, while Cressida sank down on her rock behind the willow tree and stared out across the water with dry, burning, tearless eyes. Now, when tears would have been a relief, she could not cry. She could only clasp her hands together very tightly to try to stop the shaking. She could only look across the rippling silver surface of the lake and count the ripples to try to keep herself from looking ahead into the desert of a long life without Robert. What a fool she was, and what a liar—even to herself! Until now, she realized, she had not truly given up hope that Robert would come to care for her. She had teased herself with dreams of a fantasy world where somehow, by some miraculous intervention of kind fates or fairy godmothers, everything came out all right in the end.

Hands clenched in her lap, Cressida stared down at her wavering reflection among the reeds and faced reality squarely. She was pale and thin and painfully shy, and no objective observer could possibly have fallen into the trap of imagining that Robert could ever for one minute notice a girl like her. She had created that dream for herself, and now she was paying the price of dreaming. This new proof of Robert's devotion to Lily wouldn't have hurt so much if she hadn't wished away everything else he said about the woman and pretended that she was his true love instead.

Very well; from now on she would be sober and practical and realistic. No more flights of fancy. No more castles in the air. And absolutely no more wild imaginings about winning the love of a man like Robert Glenford.

"I'll never dream again," Cressida whispered to herself. "Dreams are all lies!" She would allow herself nothing but strict reality, unadorned by any rainbow fantasies or comforting dreams. It would be miserably dull, but at least her heart would not be broken again. She would have to settle for what she was—whatever that might be.

"A dull little mouse of a girl." Her father's voice came back to haunt her.

"Too shy to be real!" Trevor Bayne-Fleetworth laughed.

"A good girl, my Cressy," old Betty said firmly somewhere in the back of her mind.

It wasn't much to build a life and a personality on, Cressida reflected, but it was the best anybody had ever said about her. She would have to settle for being Good. She would conceal her sorrow with a saintly smile; she would do her duty uncomplainingly and lovingly, she would stay in the background and be good and useful and she would never, never let anybody touch her heart again! By the time she died she would be known and loved by a wide family circle—always assuming Isolde managed to marry and have children, Cressida added in a mental footnote—and all her nephews and nieces and grand-nephews and grand-nieces would cry for Aunt Cressy at her funeral.

"She was so good, and so quiet," they would say.

"She never thought of herself at all."

"She was so sweet, and everybody loved her. I wonder why she never married?"

"Maybe," one of the more romantic grand-nieces would whisper, "maybe her heart was broken when she was a young girl."

But so well would Cressida have guarded her secret that no one would know the truth of that supposition; no one, that is, except the handsome white-haired man, a stranger to the family, who came once a year to lay a white rose on Cressida's lonely grave. "I never guessed in time," he would say. "Cressida, forgive me!"

Cressida frowned slightly and pleated her skirt between her fingers. No, that wasn't quite right. She tried to imagine Robert's voice, to hear with her mind just what words he would use to confess his blindness and his subsequent remorse. Perhaps he would say something like—

"Beg pardon, ma'am, but I canna' understand ye."

Cressida nearly slid off the rock in her surprise and chagrin. That was Robert's voice, all right, but the words were all wrong—and so was the irritated tone. And he sounded as though he was standing right over her!

She peeped around the gnarled trunk of the old willow tree and saw Robert at the top of the green slope. His back was to her; he was holding a spade in one hand and backing slowly down from the Long Walk. Beyond him, she saw a slender figure attired in a poisonous green gown, haloed with a cloud of golden curls.

Lily Whitworth! Cressida ducked back into the shelter of the reeds around the willow tree. Should she make herself known? She had not the courage. Lily would want to know what her personal maid was doing down at the lake when she was supposed to be mending Lily's gown. She would be furious. And Robert would be furious, too, if Cressida interrupted the tête-à-tête that he must have been longing for since he came to work at Hayvenhurst Hall.

"I'm but the puir undergardener body whae's tae replace Craigie while he tak's his wee bit vacation, ma'am," Robert drawled in an imitation Scots accent even more execrable than Craigie's.

While Cressida crouched behind the reeds, Lily spoke, and revealing herself became ten times more impossible.

"Robert, you silly boy, you needn't pretend *now!* There's nobody here but us. Why did you not *tell* me you were here? Oh, well, I suppose it is not so easy for the outdoor servants to communicate with the gentry in the house, is it? You were right to be discreet and wait for a good chance—but now you don't have to wait. Isn't it fortunate that I happened to stroll this way and recognized you?"

"Amazing coincidence," Robert agreed in a strangled voice.

"Well, you needn't look as if you were stunned by it," Lily exclaimed. "Oh, are you afraid I'll be angry with you for following me here? You naughty man! I *should* be angry with you, I know. I should be very, very angry. But instead—" She laughed prettily. "Do you know, I am rather touched. I had no idea you would go to such lengths to be with me. Why, you're just a rash, impetuous boy at heart, aren't you?"

Silence. Cressida could imagine Robert taking Lily in his arms, showering her with kisses, demonstrating just how rash and impetuous he could be given the right incentive. She peeped around the willow tree again and was rewarded by the sight of Robert standing a good three feet from Lily, hands behind his back. She could almost feel the tension implicit in his pose, the taut muscles of neck and shoulder, the hands locked tight together. She could just imagine how he must be feeling, longing to embrace Lily and pour out his words of love.

What she couldn't imagine was why he didn't do just that.

"I'd better get on with my work now," Robert was saying. "You—we—wouldn't want me to be sacked for negligence, would we?"

"Noooo," Lily agreed with a long-drawn-out, pouting sound. "But how vexing, for I don't know when we shall be able to meet again! It's that interfering old stick of a solicitor. Heaven only knows how long he means to spy on me, and I shall have to be quite *rigidly* respectable until he's gone.

"But never mind," Lily concluded brightly, "now that you've shown how much you love me, I can bear anything!"

It was almost the exact reverse of Cressida's feelings. She risked another glance around the willow tree and saw Lily standing much, much closer to Robert, her face uplifted for his kiss. She shut her eyes quickly and crouched down against the rough bark of the tree, a huddled bundle of misery, until the lengthening silence assured her that she was alone at last.

Chapter
10

The village of Lesser-Gantley-sur-Marsh, five miles from Hayvenhurst Hall, was prepared to make the most of the sunny day that greeted its annual festival. More years than not, rain or the threat of rain forced the fete into the narrow confines of the church and vestry. On this brilliant Saturday afternoon, the absence of clouds inspired the villagers to spread themselves.

After so many years of hastily moving dripping stalls and games into shelter they had almost forgotten how to hold an open-air fete, so the final arrangement was cheerful but rather confusing. Morris dancers gamboled in the open square before the railway terminal. A coconut shy and an Aunt Sally were set up in the grassy field behind the church. The flower show became part of the decoration, with vases of flower arrangements set out on doorsteps and windowsills all the way down the one broad street that ran from the railway station to the old arched bridge over the river. Knots of ribbons and paper flowers covered the bridge itself. And at the far end of the bridge, a group of wriggling children imaginatively costumed as nursery-rhyme characters demanded a penny for the church restoration fund as a toll from anyone who wanted to pass by them and investigate the jumble sale booths. In repayment for the penny, they recited the nursery rhymes on which their costumes were based.

"But I *don't* want to look at the jumble sale," Robert Glenford protested to an implacable Cressida. "And we've already been past the nursery brats three times."

"Robert," Cressida said severely, "I'm ashamed of you. Don't you want the church roof repaired? We can give the children another penny each, and then you can look at the jumble sale stalls for presents to send back to your aunt and six cousins in America."

"I don't *have* an aunt and six cousins in America," Robert said.

"Oh, yes. I forgot. That was one of your lies, wasn't it? Like being poor. Like being a gardener, for that matter." Cressida sighed ostentatiously. "Poor Mrs. Whitworth! I only hope she isn't taken in by all your Banbury tales." She was rather enjoying bullying Robert, especially since it was in a good cause. Hadn't she claimed that her only love for him was a sisterly affection? Cressida didn't know how to make that assertion true, but at least she knew how to act as if it were true. Isolde had given her plenty of examples of a patronizing, ever-so-superior elder sister instructing a younger sibling.

And if the bullying made Robert uncomfortable, all the better, Cressida thought in a reckless mood. *She* didn't need to watch her tongue around him; he would never love her anyway, so what matter if she annoyed him a little today? And it would doubtless do him good to learn that there was one female in the world who wasn't reduced to swooning and prattling gibberish by the sight of his blue eyes and manly profile and. . . .

Cressida bit her lower lip and told herself to stop thinking along those lines. Contemplation of Robert's profile was not conducive to her treating him like an erring younger brother. She would do better to contemplate his many failings. Unfortunately, at the moment she was finding it hard to remember just what they were. Except for his unaccountable refusal to run the gauntlet of the costumed school-children again. . . .

"Really, Robert, I should never have thought it of you," Cressida declared, "but then I've heard often enough that the very rich are that way."

"What way?" Robert eyed her warily, sure that she meant something stinging, but not yet quite certain which way the attack would come.

"Mean," Cressida explained. "Penny-pinching—literally! Surely you can afford another penny or two for the church building fund? It's not as if it were coming out of your wages as an undergardener, after all."

"It's not the pennies," Robert muttered, "and you know that. If you want, I'll write out a check to cover the whole cost of restoring the church roof. Right now. But I'll be da—dashed if I'll listen to that brat in the blue tailcoat reciting 'Little Boy Blue' again at any price! I never knew there were so many blasted verses!"

"There weren't," Cressida told him. "Mrs. Lambert, the vicar's wife, wrote some more especially for the occasion. She wrote extra verses for all the nursery rhymes. She tried very hard to make them appropriate and to put in local references."

Robert looked at her suspiciously. "You're pulling my leg. No thinking human being could have produced those awful verses. I was assuming that they came from some long-lost and thoroughly corrupted folk version that some overenthusiastic folklorist had restored from oral tradition."

Cressida bit her lip to restrain a smile. She agreed with Robert about the awfulness of the vicar's wife's poetry, but she had no intention of being in sympathy with him today. About anything. It was bad enough that she was spending this holiday with him. How on earth had it happened? She'd resolved to avoid Robert like the plague, but once again he'd made it impossible for her to refuse his invitation.

Only two days ago Mrs. Simpson had announced at dinner that the entire staff was to have Saturday afternoon free to attend the village fete. Cressida gathered from the resigned smiles and restrained gratitude of those around her that this was not quite such a treat as it sounded; she understood a little better when the vicar's wife came in on Mrs. Simpson's heels and began briskly signing up volunteers for the various stalls and charity booths at the fete. Apparently it was a Hayvenhurst Hall tradition to lend out the servants for the setup and cleanup work at the fete. By the time Mrs. Lambert got through assigning the servants to their work teams most of them had seen their holiday vanish into a maze of tasks from setting out flower vases to scrubbing the roundabout.

Robert, thanks to the requirement that he spend his days and take his meals at the gardener's cottage, had managed to miss Mrs. Lambert's importunities. But as soon as he heard about the fete, he was at Cressida's side. "I'm taking you," he announced.

"There's no need," Cressida told him. "We're all going together. And I expect to be much too busy to see any of the fete on my own account." She gave a little sigh, thinking of the list of chores for which Mrs. Lambert had "volunteered" her.

"I'll help you," Robert said when Cressida explained her assignments. "You'll be through in half the time, and then we can enjoy the fete."

"I'm sure you can think of better things to do with your holiday than to squire me around a village festival. Shouldn't Mrs. Whitworth have first claim on your free time?"

Robert's grimace might have been described as a smile; if one could smile with teeth gritted, that is. "Come off it, Cressida. Gentry don't mix with the servant class. The village fete is no place for me to try a clandestine meeting with Lily."

"Oh," Cressida said lamely. Robert had looked almost as if he were in pain when she mentioned Lily Whitworth's name. Did it hurt him so much to know he couldn't meet her on Saturday? "I'm sorry."

"Don't waste your sympathy on me," Robert said. "After all, I have every other day of the week to meet

Lily, and Hayvenhurst's gardens provide some appropriately inspiring spots. Doesn't it make you happy to think that I can spend quiet hours murmuring sweet nothings into Lily's little ears in the romantic setting of a rose garden or a topiary hedge?''

What made Cressida, if not exactly happy, at least able to bear this image was the knowledge that so far Lily had not managed a single clandestine meeting with Robert. As Lily's personal maid, she had ample opportunity to hear Lily grumbling about the continued visit of Mr. Ponsonby Tomkyns and the difficulties his presence caused her. Cressida didn't mind hearing Lily on that subject. What she did mind was hearing Lily express her sublime confidence that Robert was madly in love with her—for Lily had been quite unable to keep her tale of secret love from her maid.

"For those who like that sort of thing," she said, quoting a reviewer of her father's more avant-garde paintings, "I suppose it is the sort of thing they like. But you still needn't waste your time escorting me around the fete."

"I guess I can bear it," Robert said. "Anyway, someone's got to keep you safe from Waverley. He'd think the village fete a perfect opportunity to pounce on you."

"You said yourself that servants and gentry don't mix," Cressida pointed out.

"Waverley," said Robert, "is no gentleman. I'll be waiting at the back door Saturday morning. We can ride in together and I'll help you with your chores at the setting-up."

And that, however unsatisfying, had been that. Cressida congratulated herself on her new realistic view of life. The silly girl of just a week ago would probably have turned this village festival into another romantic daydream, pretending to herself that Robert stuck to her side out of love and not out of brotherly concern, reading a totally imaginary devotion in the way his eyes rested on her wherever she went.

Fortunately, two days of hard rain before the fete kept Cressida inside, out of Robert's way and able to practice her new role as a severe elder sister to him without the distraction of his physical presence. And for the first part of this afternoon, the rain-wet, puddled, muddy village street had made their setting-up chores onerous enough to keep her from indulging in any more disastrous flights of fancy. Robert had worked like three men, manhandling tables, moving trestles, hammering in nails to stabilize shaky stalls and even helping Cressida to pin the tucks in the voluminous spotted petticoats that transformed a life-size straw doll into "Aunt Sally" with a clay pipe in her painted mouth.

As a result, Cressida and the other maidservants had found themselves free to enjoy the fete far earlier than they'd expected. Transformed from workers into spectators, they wandered from one end of High Street to the other, chattering about the vicar's roses and Lady Hayvenhurst's lilies and the other entries in the flower show, tossing sticks at the clay pipe in Aunt Sally's mouth, cheering the grinning farm boy who managed to break the first pipe. And somehow, by the second promenade up and down the street, Robert and Cressida had become separated from the other Hayvenhurst servants.

The sun sparkled down on a rain-washed street, slightly battered floral displays, laughing girls, and portly village wives in their best starched Sunday dresses. Robert bought Cressida a knot of violently colored cerise ribbons and a paper cone of gilt gingerbread nuts. When Cressida mentioned that it was a pity Gregor hadn't been allowed to come to the fete, Robert immediately bought a crudely carved wooden horse, a tinsel pinwheel, and a second cone of gingerbread nuts.

"You're too nice," Cressida exclaimed. "When you don't even know him!"

"You like the boy," Robert said. "That's enough for me. Anyway, it sounds as if he has a wretched life of it between being sick all the time and having a st—"

He stopped short and turned red.

"And what?" Cressida asked.

"Um. Nothing. Forgot what I was going to say," Robert mumbled.

Between being sick all the time and having a stepmother who doesn't love him. The words sounded as clearly in Cressida's ears as if Robert had spoken them aloud. Could it be that Robert was at last beginning to see through Lily?

If he was, he would be too loyal to discuss her failings with another girl—even one who was like a sister to him. Cressida munched on a gingerbread nut and reflected that it was very hard to preserve a mood of sober realism when the sun was so bright and everybody around her was laughing and singing and Robert was being so *nice*. If only it could be like this forever!

"Tell your fortune, pretty miss?"

They had reached the slightly muddy field at the end of the street where the gypsies were camped. Not officially part of the fair, they had nevertheless managed to set up a meat-pie stall and a fortune-telling booth. To attract passers-by, a handsome boy with a fiddle stood at the verge of the field, playing cheerful tunes in a lugubrious rhythm.

Cressida had heard all about the gypsies from Abby. They set up their stalls at the fete every year, and every year the vicar complained that the money spent on them was lost to the church building fund. The village policeman solemnly threatened the gypsies, a few pieces of silver crossed hands, and it was found to be impossible, for one reason or another, to bar their stalls from the fringes of the fair.

The old woman who had spoken, a withered brown husk wrapped in layers of brilliant petticoats, caught Cressida's hand and pulled her toward the tent where she told fortunes. "A pretty girl, a hardworking hand, a pretty voice," she mumbled. "Maidservant's hands and lady's voice. What's the riddle here, missy?"

"No riddle." Robert saved her, tossing a coin into the air so that the old gypsy let go Cressida's hand to snatch at the bright sparkle of silver. He was between Cressida and the fortune-teller in the next step. "We're here to dance, mother, not to have our hands read," he declared, smiling down on the old gypsy woman. "Can you persuade your husband to play a waltz tune for us?"

"Husband!" The fortune-teller cackled and grinned. "Grandson, he is, and well the *gorgio* gentleman knows it." She called out something in Romany, evidently repeating Robert's weak jest, and the darkly handsome boy with the fiddle showed them a flash of white teeth before he tucked the instrument under his chin and began a lilting, melancholy version of something just barely recognizable as a waltz.

"There's drier ground in the center of the field," Robert murmured in Cressida's ear. "Shall we?"

He slipped one arm about her waist in preparation for the waltz and Cressida thought she would faint from sheer happiness. Or fly. She felt as if she were flying already. For once in her life she was graceful and unselfconscious. The sliding melody of the fiddle told her to dance today and forget tomorrow; the sweet intoxication of Robert's touch told her that a moment of love was worth a lifetime of repentance. Her feet moved of their own volition in the dizzying turns commanded by the gypsy music. Her limbs tingled and she turned up her face to Robert's, lost in his tender smile, forgetting all her good resolutions between one measure of music and the next. She saw herself reflected in his eyes and knew herself beautiful and worthy. Their steps matched perfectly and they moved in the same dream for three measures of waltz time.

Then a high, confident, imperious voice cut through the melody like a saw through soft wood. "Robbie! Come here, I want your help!"

It was Lily Whitworth. She stood at the edge of the gypsy camp, posed like a fine lady who wouldn't dream of muddying her slippers, an exquisite vision in white lace and *broderie Anglaise* clinging to the arm of her brother Waverley. As Robert turned his head to look at her, she beckoned him to her with one imperious gesture. The music stopped with a grating jerk while the gypsy boy watched warily to learn what the *gorgios* intended now.

Cressida's feet found their proper place in solid damp earth, the same earth that had already draggled the hem of her calico dress. She saw the scene through Lily Whit-

worth's scornful eyes. Suddenly the enchanted field with
the fairy musician became a muddy patch of ground where
a few poverty-stricken tinkers camped, getting a penny or
two from foolish servants who knew no better. And she
herself was firmly set in the middle of that scene, Lily's
thin plain maidservant who had to be taught a lesson—
taught that she wasn't to enjoy herself with the new undergardener, because he was Lily Whitworth's property.

Robert started across the field to hear Lily's commands.
Like her dog, he comes to her whistle! Cressida thought
scornfully. Perhaps that was unfair; Robert *was* supposed
to be a servant at Hayvenhurst—he had to obey orders.
But today was supposed to be his holiday—and hers. *That*
was unfair. But it didn't matter. Nothing mattered, except
that she had briefly forgotten her true place in the scheme
of things and that Lily Whitworth had reappeared to remind
her before it was too late. She turned away from Robert,
wishing there were someplace she could hide. Maybe she
could go into the fortune-teller's tent and have her palm
read.

"Fancy seeing you here, Robbie." Lily Whitworth laughed
up into Robert's impassive face. "You won't mind helping
me for a few minutes, will you?" She invested the question
with such arch flirtatiousness that everybody within earshot
smiled.

Everybody but Cressida.

"Well, ma'am—" Robert hesitated, half turning back
toward Cressida.

She must look like a poor, bedraggled, forlorn thing beside Lily Whitworth. Robert had been so angry that he
wouldn't have a chance to be with Lily at the fete. He
must be over the moon now that she'd made up an excuse
to spend time with him. Well, Cressida certainly wasn't
going to stand in his way. She didn't want Robert's company because he felt sorry for her or thought it would be
rude to abandon her! "Of course you must do as Miss Lily
asks, Robbie," Cressida said at once. "Please don't mind
me. I was just going to—going to—"

"We can finish the dance you had started, pretty Jane,"

Waverley said softly, holding out his arms as if to encircle her.

Cressida gasped and stepped back, remembering at the last minute to bend her knee and duck her head so that it looked as if she were only curtsying. "Oh, no, Master Waverley. 'Twouldn't be proper for me to dance with the gentry. 'Sides, I was just going to—"

She glanced about and saw the gypsy woman's gaudy tent with its tatters of bright rags over the doorway. "To have my fortune told," she finished breathlessly, and slipped into the scented darkness beyond the rags before Waverley could catch her. A dark form just outside the curtained opening blotted out the faint light that filtered into the tent, and for a heart-stopping moment Cressida thought that Waverley was going to follow her. Then she heard the low rumble of a strange voice. It was the gypsy man who'd been tending the meat-pie stall, solemnly warning Waverley that his people believed it was very bad luck to interrupt Mama-Loula while she looked into the future.

"*Very* bad luck," he repeated solemnly, "especially for the *gorgio.*"

And Waverley, who was so brave when threatening a small boy or teasing a girl, apparently retreated in the face of that veiled threat, for Cressida heard no response from him. When the rags across the opening parted once again, it was the old gypsy woman who slipped into the tent.

"I—I'm sorry," Cressida apologized. "I don't really want my fortune told. I just wanted to get away from *him.*"

"From the fair *gorgio?*" Mama-Loula asked. "I think not. It is the dark one you flee, and it is the dark one who'll be your fate."

Cressida squeezed her eyes shut and swallowed the lump in her throat. At least, in this darkness, Mama-Loula could not see her face. "I think you misunderstand the situation," she said. "Things are not—it's not the way it looks."

"I see that," Mama-Loula said unexpectedly. "Gentlefolk playing as servants, and servants dressed as gentry. Your people play strange games, little one, and you are not very clever at seeing through your own lies. But do not

176

worry." With a quick darting movement, she seized Cressida's hand, and Cressida felt a rough finger tracing the lines of her palm. Before she had gathered courage to protest, the gypsy woman released her hand and sat back with a satisfied sigh. "Yes. The fair woman is not for your friend, and it will all come right in the end, little one. But you should not be so proud."

Cressida could feel her cheeks burning in the darkness. "I think I had better go now," she said stiffly. "I apologize if my taking shelter here has caused any problems for your people. Waverley—the fair man—could make trouble for you."

Mama-Loula chuckled. "Oh, I think not so much trouble, little one. We are not much loved by your people, but he is hated in this village. Even the man in black who always tries to send us away would not do so to please *that* one. You stay awhile, until he grows bored and goes away. My grandson will tell you when it is safe to go. And while you wait, I will teach you how to make the dark man look upon you as he should."

"Isolde already tried to teach me about flirting and stuff," Cressida said sadly. "I'm afraid I am not a very quick learner." She fumbled in her purse and drew out a shilling. "Thank you for telling my fortune—and—for trying to make Waverley go away."

The soft, bright rags over the entranceway brushed against her cheeks and twined over her arms like a lover's parting caress. Outside, the afternoon sun was bright enough to make her blink. Waverley was nowhere to be seen.

Neither was Robert. Doubtless he was off somewhere with Lily. Well, that was what she had wanted, wasn't it? For the two of them to go away together—since it was what *he* so obviously wanted—and to leave her alone?

Cressida blinked furiously against the sunlight. It must be the shock of this light after the darkness of the tent that was making her eyes water so. After all, there was no reason for her to feel tearful. She was where she'd wanted to be, in the country; she'd finally gotten away from Robert;

she had a whole half holiday left to enjoy the village fete without anyone pestering her. Why, she didn't have a care in the world!

Cressida set off to enjoy the fete with her head high and a song on her lips. If her vision blurred a little every now and then, and if the gay song she was humming rapidly degenerated into a melancholy memory of a waltz, those minor details were of no interest to anybody except herself.

She wandered along the street where the flower show had been set out until she glimpsed Robert, obediently lifting and moving plants under Lily's direction. Every command Lily gave was accompanied by a peal of laughter and a languishing look up into Robert's eyes, and she seemed to find it necessary to put her hand on his arm whenever she was indicating where a pot should go.

Cressida's vision blurred and she turned aside, down a narrow lane between two houses.

Midway down the lane Waverley stood waiting for her with open arms.

"I thought you'd be coming this way," he said with a smirk. "Don't like to see m'sister flirting with your rustic swain, do you? Let me give you a word of advice, Jane. It don't do to get in Miss Lily's way. If she wants to amuse herself with Robbie, she will. You'd do better to see the fair with a man who appreciates your charms."

The last word was accompanied by a knowing grin that made Cressida feel ready to sink. "Thank you," she said, "I'm perfectly happy as I am. Let me pass, please."

Waverley leaned one arm against the wall of the nearest house and smiled at her. "Now, why would I do that? By the way, you might want to know that old Tomkyns took the morning train back to town. So now there's no reason why Lily shouldn't do anything she wants with that country yokel."

That, Cressida thought dully, explained a great deal—Lily's almost feverish gaiety and her willingness to take risks like openly flirting with Robert in the middle of the village fete. The week of self-control must have been very hard for her.

Unfortunately, it didn't explain how she was to get past Waverley.

"Come now, pretty Jane," Waverley teased. His knowing eyes lingered over her flushed cheeks and the bodice of her old, tight dress. Cressida felt hot and breathless, like a cornered fox facing the hounds. "Pay my toll and I'll let you pass—this time. One kiss—is that so much? I'll wager you wouldn't begrudge a kiss to your mucky undergardener. At least I'm clean, and—"

A loud and slightly tipsy chorus of "The maiden in the hay" drowned out whatever Waverley had meant to say next. Cressida turned and saw with relief a group of maidservants from Hayvenhurst Hall crowding down the narrow lane. A moment later their bright skirts and beribboned bonnets surrounded her.

"Jane, where's 'ee been?" scolded Lizzie.

"Lady H. give us all a half crown to try the coconut shy and the Aunt Sally," Abby announced. " 'Ere's yours. Come along of us, now!"

Like a wave of white aprons and printed calico, they surged around Cressida and retreated with her to the safe ground of High Street. Only one girl remained behind, smiling up at Waverley with brazen pleasure.

"Why, Master Waverley," Cressida heard Martha say, "fancy meetin' you 'ere!"

"You shouldn't go off by yourself like that, Jane, and you knowin' that Waverley's got his eye on you," Lizzie scolded mildly. "Lucky for you our Martha's cat jealous. She saw you and Waverley down the lane and complained so much we thought we'd better rescue you."

"But it's true about the half crown," Abby put in. "Ever so generous, Lady H. is."

There was a slight smell of ale about the group of girls, as though they'd been doing a little unofficial celebrating on the steps of the Star and Anchor, where the menservants were drinking up their own holiday half crowns. Certainly they were all very merry. Lizzie slipped on a muddy patch in the road and managed to fall with more shrieks and more display of stockinged leg than Cressida would have thought possible. Abby displayed a talent for singing old country songs in an innocent little voice that somehow invested the words with all sorts of hidden meanings. And the other three girls were frankly and loudly determined to find a sweetheart apiece before the evening dancing began.

"I thought the wagon to take us back to Hayvenhurst was leaving at dusk?" Cressida asked upon hearing this plan.

"Gentry leaves at dusk," Abby told her, slipping an arm about Cressida's waist. "Lady H. likes us to do the same, 'cause she thinks the fair's not safe for young girls like us after dark. Somebody might Take Advantage."

"That's right!" Lizzie agreed with more enthusiasm than discretion. "That's why you want to miss the wagon, Jane, love. Fair's no real fun till after then. Us just has to stay out of Lady H.'s way for another hour."

They didn't quite make it. Just as the sun was dipping behind the seventeenth-century tower of the village church, Lady Hayvenhurst swept through the village collecting potted plants and servant girls as she went. The other girls complained under their breath, but Cressida was happy enough to see the wagon that was to carry them back to Hayvenhurst. Lady Hayvenhurst gave her one glance and apparently decided that this one servant girl, at least, could be trusted to come along without nagging. She concentrated on herding the other girls before her like a gaggle of brightly dressed geese. Cressida followed at her own pace, too dispirited to keep up with the others. She was almost at the edge of the village when something moved beside her, coming sleek and whispering out of the shadows between the houses.

"Not so fast, pretty Jane." Waverley caught her by the arm and drew her into the narrow space between the last two houses on this side of the village. "You don't want to miss the dancing, do you?" A smile flashed across his face. "I've been waiting all day to sport with you on the village green. It's all right, you needn't thank me now for saving you from that dreary ride back to the Hall; I know how grateful you must be."

"Let me *go*," Cressida said between her teeth. "Lady Hayvenhurst will miss me."

"Dear Dagmar has more to do than count servant girls on the wagon," Waverley said. "Listen! They're leaving already."

With a sense of unreality Cressida heard the creak of the wagon wheels and the clank of harness. "Your little friends won't say anything," Waverley told her with satisfaction. "They'll think you slipped away so you could dance with your gardener boy."

Cressida tried to get free, but Waverley's slender fingers gripped her arm with surprising strength. Perhaps she should scream? That seemed ridiculous—and she would make herself look ridiculous as well, screaming for help as though she couldn't take care of herself in a village full of people. Any minute now someone would see them in the lane and rescue her.

Waverley meant to kiss her; his cruel smiling face was coming closer.

"Don't," Cressida said. "You'll be sorry."

"Oh, I don't think so. It's the girls who weep after an indiscretion, Jane, not the men. You may weep afterward, if you like," Waverley said with an air of great generosity. "I don't mind."

Cressida felt hot and cold with fear. This was some nightmare, going on while everybody in the street laughed and drank and danced. It couldn't be real. Surely someone would interrupt them soon.

"I shan't cry," she said in a tight hard voice that she hardly recognized as her own. "I only meant to warn you. You make me sick. If you don't let me go, I shall probably *be* sick all over you. That won't do your fine suit much good."

Waverley only laughed and bent closer. "I'll take my chances."

There was a shadow behind them. Cressida relaxed in relief; then Waverley's soft mouth closed over hers and she heard a low laugh from the end of the lane. The heavy steps moved on, and she could not cry out in time.

"You see?" Waverley murmured. "Perhaps your little friends should have warned you. This Midsummer's Eve fete gets rather—wild—at dusk. The vicar goes in to his tea at sunset, and he goes to bed after that so he won't have to see his flock behaving in ways he'd have to reprove. We'll just be one courting couple among many, and nobody'll see us if they think we don't want to be seen."

She should have screamed while he was talking. Now his mouth came down over hers again, and she could feel his tongue probing her tightly closed lips while he pushed her hard against the wall. His whole body was against hers now, and the rough whitewashed stones of the wall jabbed into her back, and she felt faint with disgust at the soft feel of his mouth and the taste of smoke and ale.

"Beg pardon, good sir, but I've come to fetch my lass for t'dancing."

Waverley's head came up in surprise and Cressida opened her eyes wide on Robert's face. Shadows hid his expression from her, but as Waverley half turned she saw Robert's closed fist come up from below his waist, faster than thought, into Waverley's silky pointed beard. There was a crunching noise; Waverley's head snapped backward and he sat down in the muddy lane, looking surprised and sleepy.

"And Miss Lily's waiting for you to drive her home," Robert added, still in that deceptively mild tone. "Not feeling well, are you, sir?"

He picked Waverley up by the shoulders and dusted the back of his jacket with solicitous pounding slaps, each of which made Waverley's head rock back and forth on his neck. "Here he is, Miss Lily," Robert called toward the street. "I'm thinking your brother's had a drop too much of our rough ale. Gentry shouldn't drink with us in the lower classes, should they, miss? I'll just set him in the carriage for you."

He half carried Waverley into the street and lifted him bodily into the groom's side of the shiny black tilbury. "You'd best drive him home now, miss."

Cressida sagged against the cottage wall and breathed

deeply. She was very near making good on her threat to Waverley. In the street she heard singing and laughter and Lily's voice saying something to Robert in an undertone. She couldn't catch the words of their interchange, but Lily sounded peevish and Robert very calm.

A moment later, the tilbury moved off and Robert came back to her, smiling broadly. "All's well that ends well," he said.

"How can you say that!" Cressida was suddenly close to tears, and fiercely, irrationally angry with Robert for his calmness. "You'll be turned off now for certain."

"I think not," Robert disagreed. "Waverley won't argue with my story. There's no shame to a gentleman in taking a drop too much of the village's strong ale, but he'd be a laughingstock if it was known he'd taken a blow from a servant and done nothing about it."

"Oh, he'll do something about it," Cressida predicted, remembering Waverley's vengeful pursuit of her. "He's not the sort to forget an injury."

"Just now," Robert said happily, "his brains are that muddled, I'd be surprised if he doesn't forget his own name." He slipped an arm around her waist. "Well, now. We've both missed the servants' wagon, haven't we? We'll have to walk home. So we might as well stay and enjoy the dancing first, don't you think?"

He hadn't explained why he had missed the wagon. Probably, Cressida thought, he had planned to stay and dance with Lily. What a scandal that would have been! Worse by far than his scuffle with Waverley. Robert seemed to have no sense of class distinctions whatever. And as for Lily, she had no sense period when it came to Robert.

And that was something for which Cressida couldn't altogether blame her. Even now, after all her resolves to stay away from Robert and quit building castles in the air, she felt lighthearted and half intoxicated at the prospect of an evening's dancing with him.

The knowledge that Lily was on her way out of the village didn't hurt, either.

Chapter

11

*L*anterns sparkled around the great oak at the edge of the village green. A boy with a wooden flute joined a smart young man with waxed mustaches and a mandolin to make music for the dancers. Cressida repressed a smile at the sight of the ill-assorted pair, but when the music started she caught her breath in amazement. Jigs and old morris tunes and sparkling country dance measures poured out as if on a single long breath, bright cascades of tinkling notes weaving in and around the soft breathy tones of the wooden flute. Cressida's toes twitched and her heels complained about the weight of her sensible shoes.

"Slip 'em off," Robert suggested. "All the other girls are."

And indeed, there was a line of discarded shoes tossed drunkenly heel-to-toe under the bench outside the inn. Cressida's good black walking shoes joined the throng; Robert politely averted his eyes and two girls she didn't even know made a wall of outspread skirts while she dealt with her stockings. The girls disappeared, the music called to her, and there were lines forming for something called "Black Nag." Or was it "Shepherd's Hey" or "Lark in the Morning"? The dapper young man with the mandolin shouted out the names of the dances so fast that Cressida's head spun, trying to keep up.

Childhood memories guided her through the country dances. She hadn't been allowed to dance with the cottagers since she put her hair up and let her dresses down, but now her feet were cleverer than her head, remembering the steps and turns, the weaving in and out between the lines, the clapping of hands and the little jumps at the end. She held hands with Robert and parted with him again to spin around in the sweaty embrace of a boy from the butcher's shop, paraded in and out through a long line of farm-workers, and found Robert again at the end of the line. They raised their arms to make an arch through which laughing couples ran, pair by pair, until at last it was their turn and the arch turned inside out. She advanced and retreated, dipped and swayed, crossed arms with the village girls in a circle that shut out all the men, whirled and spun in a froth of calico skirts to meet her love once again.

"Ale and Bread!" the mandolin player called out, and the music stopped on a dazzling display of double and triple runs. Robert looked about, puzzled. He hadn't managed the country dances so well as Cressida, but nobody minded having to push and pull the new gardener through his paces.

"It's not a dance, dear heart," Cressida teased. "He's announcing that it's time to feed the musicians." She leaned on his arm quite unselfconsciously, panting from the exertion of the last quick dance, and Robert looked down at her laughing face. She was intolerably, heartbreakingly lovely tonight, with her brown ringlets tumbling about her face and her bright print skirts swirling about her bare legs. And for once there were none of the idiots from Hayven-hurst Hall about to interrupt them. It was his evening—his night—midsummer eve, a night of magic and a full moon. Robert exulted.

"Ale?" A hand proffered a foaming tankard. Startled, Robert reached for the tankard; it moved right by him. Cressida took the offered drink and smiled up at the hulking clodhopper who'd brought it.

"Thought you might be thirsty, missy," the brute said. "I'm all in a muckle sweat myself after that last 'un. Don't think us've seen you here before?"

Robert tightened his arm about Cressida's waist. "No. We're from Hayvenhurst Hall," he said dismissively.

Cressida drained the ale mug and handed it back to the farmer who'd brought it. "Thank you so much," she said. "I was indeed thirsty."

"Come and sit down." Robert drew Cressida away from the crowd gathering at the inn door to a grassy spot under the oak tree.

"It'll stain my new skirt," she protested.

"Sit on my knee, then," he suggested without much hope. To his amazement, she took the offered seat, perching as lightly as a bird about to take flight. A precious, excited, slightly tipsy little bird. "Didn't anybody ever tell you not to drink so fast?" he muttered. "Or not to flirt with the locals?"

"I wasn't flirting," Cressida protested. "I was only being polite."

"Well, then, be rude next time. You're my girl tonight."

Tonight. The single word pierced Cressida's bubble of happiness. Of course. When Lily Whitworth was unavailable, Robert was perfectly willing to while away an evening dancing with her. But tomorrow they'd be back at Hayvenhurst, and he'd be making eyes at Lily and Lily would be telling her all about it and she would have to stand behind Lily and listen politely and comb out the golden ringlets without pulling a single hair on Lily's precious head.

Maybe she should have stayed in London.

Maybe she should go home now.

To pose half naked as Diana, with any muscular young man Papa could cajole into posing as Actaeon. Probably Trevor Bayne-Fleetworth. Cressida half closed her eyes and shuddered.

"Here, now," Robert said, misunderstanding her gesture of negation, "it's not so bad, being my girl. I only lure damsels into the woods and murder them during the dark of the moon. There's a full moon rising tonight, so you're perfectly safe with me."

Cressida glanced through her lashes at Robert, afraid to look straight at him for fear he would read what was in her heart. *Safe? I've never been safe with you—least of all on midsummer's eve under a rising moon!*

"Safe?" she repeated aloud. "Am I really?"

Her voice trembled a little on the last word. Robert looked at the swirl of smoky lashes on Cressida's pale cheek and wondered if she knew just how damnably provocative she sounded. He saw a moving shadow on the other side of the oak tree, a flash of white teeth, and a fiddle tucked under a dark chin. It was the distraction he needed.

"The gypsy fiddler's come to play a last tune for us, now that the others are tired out," he said. The upsurge of desire he felt for Cressida roughened his voice. "Let's dance again." *Because if I sit here with you on my knee much longer, my love, I won't answer for the consequences!*

He was expecting another merry jig-time mix of reels and country dances, music to keep them both moving and breathless until they were far too tired for passion. Instead the fiddling boy looked at him, winked, and began the slow, lilting waltz that had been interrupted earlier by Lily Whitworth's untimely appearance. Robert slipped his arm about Cressida's waist, took her hand in his, and spun her out onto the smooth close-cropped grass of the village green.

A few of the country folk had learned to waltz, on holidays at Bournemouth or at barn dances where a cousin from the city taught sweating boys the steps. But these stumbling couples were unable to keep up with the smooth gliding and magical turns of the pair from Hayvenhurst Hall. Two by two, they dropped back to stand along the edge of the green and watch this unexpected end to their evening's gaiety.

Cressida was hardly aware of their audience. She was under the double spell of the music and of Robert's arms about her. Gliding, flying, with the soft grass under her bare feet as luxurious as any carpet, she neither knew nor cared what was to come next. If a vagrant thought of the morrow did trouble her for a moment, she banished it between one turn and the next. Why worry about the future— or the past? The past was work and service and loneliness, the future was more of the same. She had only this one glimmering hour under the rising moon, and she would not spoil it by worrying about what couldn't be changed.

The gypsy music turned a simple waltz into a lament for lost love and a promise of new hope. The languid measures were a stairway of golden steps right up into the sky. Cressida spun in Robert's arms and could have sworn that her head brushed the topmost leaves of the ancient oak and that every leaf was edged with gold, glowing with mystical life against the night sky. The soft night air caressed her skin with sensual promise; a naughty breeze whispered under her skirt and cooled her bare legs. Robert's arm about her waist was strong and steady; her hand on his shoulder was all she needed to guide her through a night full of magic and mystery. A pulse throbbed in her throat, and each breath she drew seemed too sweet to be followed by another.

Slowly, almost reluctantly, the waltzing notes spiraled down to a close, and with the last slowing turns Cressida felt herself sinking back to solid ground. The oak leaves above her head were a dull green, glimmering gold where the light from the lantern struck them. The gypsy boy had put his fiddle away. A spattering of applause came from the edge of the green. Robert took her hand and bowed like a performing artist. Still half caught up in the magic of the dance, Cressida lifted up the hem of her full skirt with her free hand and sank almost to the ground in a deep, formal curtsy.

When she raised her head, the villagers were drifting away in twos and threes.

"It's late," Robert said. "The fete's over—and I'm afraid we've a long walk home."

The last lantern under the tree was extinguished with one quick puff; gold and green changed to moonlight silver and midnight blue.

"Not too far," Cressida said, "not for me." The evening

was not truly over until they reached Hayvenhurst Hall. She could hold on to the magic for that much longer.

The winding country lane gleamed white under the moon, and on either side the white flowers of crabapple trees and wild rambling roses echoed the silver tones of moonlight. Two inky black shadows moved ahead of Cressida and Robert, elongated shapes joined at the hands. Cressida looked at the shadows and pretended they belonged to two other people—a maidservant and an undergardener from Hayvenhurst Hall, returning tired and very much in love from the midsummer fete at the village.

They could be those two other people for a while yet. As long as they walked this moonlit path, she didn't have to go back to being plain Cressy Parris, who should know better than to imagine she could capture a man like Robert. And *he* didn't have to go back to being the foolish rich American whom Lily Whitworth could wind around her little finger. He could be her Robert—the playfellow of her memories, the love of her dreams—the Robert who chose to dance with her on midsummer eve.

If only there were a way to capture this moment and make it last! Cressida sighed involuntarily for all the fairy tales that were never true, all the fairy hills that were only grassy mounds to mortals.

"Tired?" Robert asked. He slipped his hand under her elbow to give a little more support.

"Not in the least," Cressida said truthfully. "I could walk another twenty miles tonight."

"I know what you mean," Robert agreed. "There's magic in the air, isn't there? I almost feel as if I could drink the moonlight. What would it taste like, do you suppose? Sparkling like champagne? Sweet?"

Cressida considered the question seriously. "No, not bubbly like champagne; that's rainbow light, or the light of a spring morning. I think moonlight tastes very cool and bittersweet, and it's gone before you quite know you've drunk it." *As this hour will be gone, too soon, my love.*

A low-hanging branch of a flowering crabapple tree

brushed Robert's head. He reached up and broke off a spray of flowers, white turned to glowing silver in the moonlight, and tucked them inside the frill on the front of Cressida's print dress. Honeysuckle teased him with its sweet, evanescent fragrance; he robbed the hedgerows and twined a crown of green vines and soft, sensuous yellow-white blossoms for Cressida's head.

"Stop," Cressida protested when he reached for a white rose from the next bush. "I've no place to put any more flowers!"

"You *are* the flowers," Robert told her. "Remember the story of Blodeuwedd?"

"The girl made out of flowers? But she was cruel," Cressida protested mildly.

And you're cruel to me—pushing me into Lily Whitworth's arms, pretending you don't know or care how I feel. But he didn't dare say that; so he took her hand again and they walked in silence down the lane.

But the troubling thought, once raised, wouldn't go away. How could Cressida be so insensible to the magic of this moonlit summer night? Didn't she feel the attraction between them? He wasn't imagining it all; he *couldn't* be imagining it. Her hand trembled in his, her lashes were so dark against the paleness of her cheek, her voice shook when she answered him. She must feel it too. They belonged together. They had always belonged together. She was his. This man she'd run away from in London—he didn't matter. Surely she must see that now. Bayne-Fleetworth wasn't with her now; *he* was. He loved her. Damn it, he deserved her, and any minute now he'd stop walking and tell her so—kiss her and shake her and love her until she forgot all about that ass Bayne-Fleetworth!

But from moment to moment, he delayed. It was so sweet to be wandering through this lane with Cressida, to feel her long cool fingers in his hand and see her profile crowned by his slightly tipsy wreath of honeysuckle flowers. The silence that was on them was composed of silver and pearl and moonlight, something too fragile and perfect to break.

Gradually, as they walked and as he stole glances at Cressida, Robert began to worry. She didn't look like a girl returning tired and happy from a dance with the only man she should ever consider loving. She looked sad. The moonlight turned everything into silver and shadow, he couldn't be sure what he was seeing, but he thought there was a tear trembling on her lashes.

And the closer they came to Hayvenhurst Hall, the sadder she looked. Her long graceful back and neck drooped, the corners of her mouth turned down—she looked like a child abandoned on the steps of an orphanage.

Maybe she was just tired.

Or maybe she was wishing she'd spent the evening with Bayne-Fleetworth.

Robert couldn't refrain from rubbing salt into his own wounds; he had to test his theory.

"Do you ever think of going back to London?"

"I suppose I shall have to, someday." Cressida was looking away from him, gazing with great intensity at a muddy cow pasture and a barred gate.

"Yes, but do you *want* to? Do you miss . . . um, people . . . there? Still?" Robert cursed himself for a coward, but he couldn't bring himself to mention Bayne-Fleetworth's name aloud. Besides, what would he do if she started crying?

Cressida blinked away tears and stared at the cow pasture until she felt quite sure she had control over her voice. It was just as she'd predicted. While they danced in the village Robert had amused himself by flirting with her and making pretty speeches, but now that they were almost back at Hayvenhurst Hall he was beginning to remember Lily. And once he remembered Lily, he was probably embarrassed to think of how he'd been carrying on with Cressida, and he was beginning to think that it would be convenient if he persuaded himself that it was her own idea to leave!

How could she ever, even in daydreams, have considered loving such a man? He was fickle and shallow and probably not capable of any deep emotion whatsoever and he thoroughly deserved Lily. In fact, they deserved one another, that precious pair, and she hoped they would be very happy together!

And he was still waiting for an answer.

"I have no intention of returning to London in the near future," Cressida said. The effort to keep her voice from wobbling made her sound harsh and loud. "But don't worry. I understand perfectly." She slipped her fingers out of Robert's hand and walked quickly ahead of him down the lane. Just a few more steps and they would see the gates of Hayvenhurst Hall before them. Just a few more steps and this whole mistake of an evening would be over.

"Just *what* do you understand?" Robert demanded, catching up with her.

She would not look at him.

"Oh . . . that tonight is best forgotten. That tomorrow you'll be wanting to dance attendance on Mrs. Whitworth again, and that it would be embarrassing to you to be reminded that you spent a summer's night dancing with her maid. So," Cressida said, each syllable light and crisp and final as she could make it, "I won't remind you. That's what I understand."

And on the last word, she rounded a bend in the lane and saw the wrought-iron gates of the Hall before them, black iron tracery changed to silver lace in the moonlight, a glimmering web of lace strung between two sentinel gateposts. It was right for it to look like an enchanted gateway tonight; this was where good fortune changed to ill, Cressida thought, love to coldness, friendship to forgetfulness. . . .

"*Do* you, by God!" Robert's curse was all of this earth, and so were the strong hands that closed on her shoulders to swing her around until, startled, her magical mood of resignation broken, she looked up into the real and living and furiously angry face she loved best in all the world.

"Well, I don't see what you're so angry about!" Cressida exclaimed in shock. "Aren't I trying and *trying* to see that you have what you want? Nobody could be more understanding—"

"You," Robert said in conversational tones that belied

the angry, steely grip on her shoulders, "you don't understand a damned thing, Cressida, and you never have!"

"But—"

His mouth on hers stopped the question. Cressida flinched momentarily, expecting a bruising kiss to match the anger in Robert's hands and eyes. But there was nothing hurtful in the lips that descended over her own, warm, questioning, loving. He held her still and he would not let her go, but he forced nothing on her beyond that first touch of lip to lip.

He did not need to. Sweetness and joy beyond her imaginings swirled through Cressida. She answered that first tentative touch with her own, moving closer to Robert, putting up her hands to rest on his own shoulders. With a tremor of assent he wrapped his arms about her then, holding her so close that she could feel his heart pounding against her breasts. For a long, perfect moment they were as close as they could be without melting into one another entirely.

Clothing, Cressida thought, was a nuisance. So was standing up. And her ribs hurt. . . .

As soon as she wriggled in protest, Robert let her go—but not very far. She stood within the circle of his arms and smiled up at him. Some dim, faraway corner of her mind suggested that this wasn't an entirely proper reaction. Girls were supposed to slap men who stole kisses, not to grin up at them as if they'd never had so much fun in their entire lives.

But I never have *had so much fun,* Cressida argued silently with that outraged portion of her thoughts. *Why should I slap him for doing something I liked so much?*

You're not supposed *to like it,* her proper self responded. *You would have slapped anybody else who kissed you, wouldn't you?* And, of course, she would. Except that not very many people had tried—only Waverley, and before him. . . .

"What are you thinking of *now?*" Robert demanded, thoroughly bemused by the rapid play of expressions across Cressida's face: first joy, then doubt, bewilderment, defiance, and finally, intense concentration.

"Trevor Bayne-Fleetworth," Cressida responded, with a giggle at the sheer incongruity of the thought. "You see . . ."

Robert said several words that she did not quite catch, very rapidly, under his breath. "Bayne-Fleetworth! I'll be damned if I don't make you forget *him!*"

And he did.

When she slipped into the kitchen of Hayvenhurst Hall, quite half an hour later, Cressida was exhausted and disheveled and too happy to think straight. Not that there was much to *think* about, exactly; she and Robert had hardly talked at all after her mention of Trevor Bayne-Fleetworth. But then, there were other ways to communicate besides talking. In the morning they would get it all straight. For now, Cressida was happy enough to float up to bed without breaking the spell of the evening.

Someone had been kind enough to leave the back door unlocked for her; Abby, probably. Humming a waltz tune under her breath, Cressida bolted the kitchen door behind her, thought about nice things she could do for Abby to show her gratitude in the morning, patted her hair and the front of her dress straight by feel, tiptoed through the dark kitchen for the backstairs, and tripped over a basket of fire irons that had been set out for polishing.

"My goodness," she said to herself, gathering her skirts about her, "I wonder if I am rather tipsy after all." It had been a long time since she had drunk that tumbler of ale in the village; one would have thought the dancing and the walk back would be enough to sober her.

It would be a dreadful nuisance to be turned off for drunkenness just when she was so happy and wanted nothing more than to be where Robert was every minute of every day—not that they couldn't meet perfectly well in London, of course—but Cressida felt a superstitious fear of going back to the flat where her father and sister held artistic sway. Somehow, without meaning to, Papa and Isolde would spoil everything!

Besides, how embarrassing to be turned off as the servant girl who'd come back from the village fete too drunk to walk across the kitchen! Imagine what Isolde would say if she ever found out that her mousy little sister had been even more outrageous than she ever was!

Giggling quietly at the thought of Isolde's annoyance, Cressida crept toward the stairs with more circumspection this time. She had almost reached them when the green baize door swung open and the light of a candle blinded her.

"I might have known it," said Lily Whitworth. Behind the golden flame of the candle, her high-piled golden hair was a halo around a face that looked too sour to belong to an angel in white lace. "Isn't it bad enough that *I* should have to sit up half the night waiting for my *maid* without your also making enough noise to wake the rest of the household when you finally do come in? Come upstairs and brush out my hair. You're lucky I don't turn you off without a reference."

There had been times, Cressida thought, when nothing would have suited her better. But not now. Not with the glorious prospect of seeing Robert tomorrow, of saying out loud in the light of day the words of love that had been implicit in their sweet intoxicating kisses tonight.

So, although it was a shatteringly disappointing end to a midsummer night's dream, she followed Lily Whitworth up the front stairs as meekly as any mousy little abigail, followed her into the overscented bedroom, and took down the perfect coils of golden hair while Lily preened before the mirror and talked without stopping.

"What a marvelous evening it's been!" Lily exclaimed while Cressida deftly removed hairpins and dropped them in a marble holder shaped like an open hand. "Gracious, Jane, don't tug so. Why are you so clumsy? It's bad enough that Waverley had to overindulge so that I was forced to take him home so early—at least I thought it was bad at the time. But it turned out quite well in the end. Dagmar had the most *fascinating* caller tonight. A Mr. Sheridan. Fairfax Sheridan. And he's quite taken with me, of course." Lily blew a dreamy kiss at the mirror. "Lily Sheridan—sounds pretty, doesn't it? But I couldn't give up my darling Robert for a total stranger; besides, although Mr. Sheridan talks of his estates in Ireland, his coat is last year's cut. I'm afraid those Irish estates don't bring him in a very great income. I couldn't marry a man who would find it a burden to dress me properly, could I? It wouldn't be kind."

All the same, it was clear that Mr. Sheridan had quite engaged Lily's attention; she prattled on about him for some time. Cressida gathered that he had come to warn Lady Hayvenhurst about a gang of thieves who might be plotting to steal the Hayvenhurst Emerald.

"He was quite *deliciously* mysterious about how he came by this information," Lily said with a delighted shudder. "All he would say was that he was a gentleman of private means who occasionally assists the police with their inquiries. Oh, and he thinks the local police may have been bribed to turn a blind eye to this gang's activities. Doesn't it sound absolutely *chilling?* And everybody knows Constable Yaring takes a bribe from the gypsies to let them camp outside the fete every year, so why shouldn't he be paid off by the thieves too? And besides," Lily added with an air of clinching her own arguments, "as Mr. Sheridan pointed out, Lady Hayvenhurst saw Constable Yaring at the fete this afternoon and he didn't say *one word* to her about this gang of thieves, so that practically *proves* he's in with them!"

Lady Hayvenhurst had been much distressed by these revelations. Somehow, during the course of the evening's visit, she had decided that it might be well to invite Mr. Sheridan to stay at Hayvenhurst for a few days. At least he would recognize the thieves if he saw them. He had, in fact, offered to look over the security arrangements for the emerald, but Lady Hayvenhurst had put him off for the present.

"I suppose," Lily said thoughtfully, "she feels it will show to more advantage in a few days."

Cressida agreed without really wondering why an emerald should look better at one season than at another. She was half asleep and bored to tears by Lily's long-winded recitation of all the charming naughty things Mr. Sheridan had said to her and all the brilliant rejoinders she had made. A mention of Robert's name, though, woke her up at once.

"So you see, I really didn't mind having to leave early with Waverley," said Lily, finishing her recital. "But I'm sure darling Robert was quite devastated." She tilted her head and smiled coyly at the mirror. *"You* can't have been much consolation for him, can you, Jane, with your missish ways, so prim and proper! Maybe he found some village girls to dance with. Did he?"

Cressida pretended to be concentrating on a nonexistent tangle in one of Lily's gilt ringlets.

"Well, *did* he?" Lily repeated sharply. "Don't fall asleep on your feet, Jane. After all, I'm the one who had to wait up! Did Robert console himself with you or did he go off with some of the village lasses? I'm sure there were plenty there who'd be willing enough."

"I really couldn't say, Miss Lily," Cressida replied in her dullest tone. Lily relaxed slightly in her chair.

"Well, it's plain to see you didn't spend the evening with him, or you'd not be so dull and sleepy now. I'm sure a girl who'd been kissing our Robbie in the garden would look more alive than you do."

Cressida's hands closed convulsively about the lock of hair she was combing, and Lily gave a cry of pain. "You clumsy girl! What is it *now?* Are you shocked because I don't act as miminy-piminy as you, pretending I don't know what it's like to kiss a man? Listen, Jane, that interfering old snoop of a solicitor left this morning, and I'm in no mood to have his place taken by my own maid. You dare— *dare*—criticize my words or actions, and I *will* turn you off, so be warned! I'd do it for the way you pulled my hair just now," Lily added in a calmer tone, "except that it would please Waverley, and I'm in no mood to do him a favor. Besides, no one else in this godforsaken spot can dress my hair the way you do. I think I'll take you with me when Robert and I are married—*ow!*" Lily half turned in her chair and slapped Cressida's face with all her strength. "You careless girl—that's twice in five minutes you've all but yanked the hair out of my scalp!"

Cressida drew in her breath sharply. *Ladies don't hit back.* Her mother's voice echoed a long-ago fight with the boy who delivered the milk and teased the painter's daughters.

"Sorry, miss," she said tonelessly when she had recovered her calm. She went on combing the clinging golden ringlets and twisting them around her fingers. Her face burned with the slap, but she hardly felt it. Could Lily be serious about marrying Robert? Had he been courting them both simultaneously? The question burned her mind while Lily settled back and talked at her mirror.

"I'm almost sure he has money, you know, Jane. And of course he's madly in love with me. If I could just be certain about his fortune, I'd accept him in a minute. Couldn't *you* find out something for me? You servants all gossip about your betters—I know that. It would be easy enough for you to find out the truth."

"I really couldn't say, miss," Cressida repeated. "Besides, everybody in the servants' hall thinks Robbie's just the undergardener—remember?"

"Oh. Oh, yes, I forgot." Lily frowned at her reflection, then put the tips of her fingers to her forehead and smoothed out the lines that showed. "His true identity is just our little secret, isn't it, Jane? You wouldn't tell anyone, would you? Here—I'll tell you what. You can have this silk garland," Lily said with an air of great generosity, picking up a soiled white wreath of limp imitation lilies.

"Thanks ever so, miss." Cressida made no move to take the flowers, and Lily looked up at her maid's reflected face.

"Now don't sulk, Jane," she said. "You know I wasn't really angry when I slapped you. And it may have been dull waiting on me here, but you'll like it better when Robert and I are married. I shall make him take me to Paris, and if you're good and don't breathe a *word* about him until it's all settled, you shall come too! And after Paris we'll go to Italy—Rome and Naples and the Isle of Capri . . ."

"It's not a very good life for a child, being dragged all

around the world like that," Cressida said without thinking, out of her own memories of Papa's grief-stricken dash for Italy with daughters and painting gear trailing behind him.

"A child?" For a moment Lily seemed genuinely puzzled, then her face cleared and she laughed. "Oh—Julian's brat! No fear. I don't mean to take *him!* Were you afraid I'd make you work as a nursery maid, poor Jane? No, now that old Tomkyns is out of the way, the boy can go back to school on Monday—and *stay* there. It's for the best, really," she added defensively at Cressida's expression. *"I* haven't the least idea how to take care of a child, and as you say, traveling all over Europe wouldn't be good for him. He'll be much better off staying at his school until he's grown up. Robert can easily afford to make some sort of arrangement to pay for his taking holidays there too, so there'll be no need for us to be continually interrupting our life to look after him."

In the dark, narrow little room that opened off Lily's bedroom, Gregor slipped back to bed with suppressed sobs shaking his thin shoulders. There was no reason, he told himself, to be so upset now. He'd only heard what he had been expecting and dreading ever since Mr. Tomkyns departed that morning.

All the same, it was bad to hear it made definite—worse than he had imagined it would be. His stepmother's light, cold voice, so self-assured, offered no hope of a reprieve. He thought briefly of appealing to her, then dismissed the thought. Stepmama Lily was cruel. She had slapped his darling Jane just now. She wouldn't inconvenience herself for his sake.

It was time for desperate measures.

Chapter

12

Cressida woke at dawn from a light sleep in which dreams of Robert mingled with Abby's snoring and the twittering of birds outside the window. Once she was fully awake, the sound of snoring tended to overwhelm everything else.

It was Sunday morning. Lily Whitworth didn't go to church. It would be hours before she woke and rang for her maid to dress her. Cressida slipped on her clothes quickly and quietly and tiptoed down the back stairs. She wasn't going to go back to sleep; rather than trying to think about Robert in a narrow little room where somebody was sleeping off the effects of the village ale, she might as well sit among the roses in the Long Walk and think about Robert there.

It was a perfect June morning. The sky was lavender blue with streaks of gold at the eastern edge; tiny beads of dew sparkled along the edges of rose petals and turned spiderwebs into a delicate tracery of crystal and diamonds; the damp grass sank silently under Cressida's feet and gave her the momentary illusion that she was the only living being in a silent world. She went down the Long Walk until she could see the mist rising from the lake.

The small enclosed rose garden where she'd first seen Robert was quiet and empty. Cressida sat on the damp stone bench and drifted off into a happy daydream in which the intoxicating memory of Robert's kisses mingled with a vision of the two of them back at Riversedge, the garden and the river and the high-ceilinged rooms of the shabby old house theirs forever, to fill with love and laughter and a dozen children.

She knew that part of the dream was not likely to come true. For all she knew, Papa might have sold Riversedge by now; certainly he was determined to sell it. But she was in no mood to let reality disturb her imaginings. Robert's love was real enough; she could still feel the warmth of his hands. Just remembering how he had held and kissed her last night made her shiver with anticipation of the day when they could be truly together, with no rules and conventions and disapproving people to come between them.

As for Lily Whitworth, with her sublime confidence that she had only to raise her finger to have Robert by her side—Cressida was in no mood to consider that either. Lily was wrong. She'd been imagining things. Maybe Robert had *thought* himself in love with her at one time—but that was all over now. Wasn't it? He couldn't be in love with one woman and at the same time kiss another and hold her so tenderly—could he?

A small frown creased Cressida's white forehead. Her dream world was refusing to cooperate. Last night she'd felt no need of words between herself and Robert; they had been one soul, one heart, entwined in perfect love. But all that had taken place on the far side of the gates of Hayvenhurst Hall—those wrought-iron gates that she had fancied as the passageway between love and loneliness. And almost as soon as they passed through the gates, everything changed; doubt returned, magic was banished.

With her first words Lily Whitworth had begun filling Cressida's ears with her plans to marry Robert—and now Cressida wished that Robert had seen fit to say *something* last night. "Will you marry me?" would have been the right thing. At the time she'd thought it went without saying. Now the memory of some actual words would have helped her to maintain the dream.

Or, Cressida thought, she could have helped him to say the right thing. For instance, when he was kissing her for the fourth or fifth time and his hands had replaced the sprig of flowering crabapple in her bodice, she could have said, "But what about Lily?"

Then Robert could have said, "Lily who?" and *that* would have been most satisfactory.

If she pretended hard enough, she could almost make herself remember his saying something like that. But not quite. Some underlying honesty wouldn't let Cressida "remember" things that hadn't actually happened.

And it was getting harder and harder to recapture the gentle moonlit dream world of last night. For one thing, the Long Walk was no longer the silent, empty world it had been when she stole out of the house a few minutes ago. The sun was rising, two birds were fighting over a particularly succulent worm, and somebody was making loud, disgusting choking and splashing noises at the edge of the lake.

Cressida jumped up, her heart pounding as the meaning of the sounds penetrated her dream-drugged mind. Was someone drowning in the shallow waters of the lake? Splashing, coughing—and now an ominous silence. Dreams forgotten, Cressida picked up her skirts and ran to the end of the Long Walk.

The early-morning mists still swirled about the far shores of the lake. For a moment she thought she had imagined it all; then she saw a small dark head breaking the surface of the lake, right under the willow tree where she and Gregor liked to sit and tell stories.

Her legs were shaking and there was an ache in her side by the time she reached the rock. There he was again—just out of her reach. Cressida jumped into the water. It was no more than knee deep where she stood, but with her first step out toward Gregor she went down to her waist, and with her next step she was up to her armpits. Weeds and wet skirts swirled around her knees and tugged at her legs. Wading out to where Gregor flailed was like moving in the dreadful slowness of a nightmare—three steps, the longest in her life, and the water was up to her chin when she flung herself forward and grabbed wet cloth in both hands.

It was Gregor's shirt collar. Cressida tugged with all her strength and drew the boy to her. There were wet slimy weeds around his legs. His eyes were half closed and he didn't seem to see her, but he gasped for air whenever she could get his head above water.

"Hush, hush, it's all right," Cressida murmured as if she were soothing a baby. "I've got you now. It's all right." But was it? The lake was more treacherous than she'd ever suspected. She couldn't swim and it would not be easy to wade back to shore with Gregor in her arms and the weeds trying to trip her and pull them both down.

"Help!" she called out, rather faintly.

Gregor had relaxed in her arms with absolute trust, but at her cry his limbs flailed spasmodically and he doubled up, almost overturning them both with his panic-stricken floundering.

"It's all right," Cressida murmured soothingly. "Don't worry. We can get back to shore on our own, and then you can tell me how you came to fall in, a great boy like you, and isn't it strange that the lake is so deep in spots? I thought it was just a shallow fish pond." As she spoke she kept her eyes on Gregor's and moved with infinite caution toward the shore, praying that she wouldn't stumble or step into an especially deep hole. There really was no danger as long as Gregor didn't panic again, but she wanted to get him on land and dry as soon as possible. His pinched little face was almost green and he wheezed with each breath in a way that alarmed her. And whenever she paused in her meaningless prattle he began to stiffen again. "See, we're ever so much closer now—it's just that it is rather tricky going because the bottom of the lake is so uneven. I wonder why that is? Maybe we're walking over an ancient ruin, or—"

Cressida's foot slipped down an endless slope of slimy

weeds and her speculations came to an abrupt end as she got a mouthful of greenish-tasting lake water. Gregor's arms and legs flailed wildly and he hit her in the eye, quite hard, as she started to get back on her feet. She lost her grip on him and struck out herself, half blinded by the spraying water and terrified that the little boy would somehow manage to drown in four feet of water. More than that where the underwater holes were. Where *was* he? Water cascaded down her dripping hair and over her face and she threw her hands out, feeling for Gregor.

Two strong, large, warm hands took hers and lifted her unceremoniously above the water.

"Stop thrashing about like a frightened cow," said Robert. "I heard you calling for help. If you'd only had the sense to stand still and wait for me none of this need have happened."

With that supremely unromantic speech he deposited her, squelching slightly, on the lake shore. Gregor was already there, scrabbling about on the large flat rock as if looking for something. Cressida wiped the loose ringlets out of her eyes with the back of one wet hand and tried to say several incompatible things at once. How was she supposed to know Robert was coming? And was it her fault Gregor had fallen in the lake? And who asked his opinion, anyway?

She was still spluttering with the effort of deciding what to say first when Gregor cried, "There they are!" and dived almost under her feet to retrieve something shiny, with brown tortoiseshell rims.

His glasses.

Cressida looked at Gregor. There was something very strange about this, but she couldn't quite make her mind work.

"Come to my cottage," Robert suggested. "I'll get you both into some dry clothes, and then I want to hear all about it."

"No!" Gregor cried, panic-stricken again for no reason that Cressida could see. "I won't have my clothes taken away—I won't, I won't!"

"More fool you, then," Robert said. "Do you want to

have pneumonia again? And wet or dry, you'd better explain to me why you were messing about in the lake. You're old enough to know better, young man."

"Anybody can fall in by accident," Cressida said. It seemed to her that Robert was being unnecessarily harsh.

"Yes, but most people who fall into a lake don't carefully fold their glasses up and put them on a rock before they have the accident," Robert pointed out. He looked sternly at Gregor. "And you can't swim. What were you up to?"

Gregor's eyes seemed to grow very large behind the thick glasses, and his mouth quivered slightly. "I—I think I'm going to be sick," he said, and a moment later he was very sick indeed all over the lake shore and the boulder where he'd left his glasses.

Cressida looked at her favorite rock sadly. A couple of buckets of lake water and a scrubbing brush would clean it up again, but somehow she didn't think she was ever going to feel the same about sitting in that spot under the willow.

Robert looked at Cressida and smiled slightly. "One of these days," he said in an undertone, too low for Gregor to hear over his own retchings and gurglings, "one of these days you'd better tell me *why* you're so fond of the boy. His charm is not exactly evident at first sight."

Ten minutes later, Robert had a roaring fire going in the dark downstairs room of his cottage. Cressida's thin calico dress was drying rapidly, but her thick, curly hair still dripped from time to time. She hoped she would have a chance to slip back to the big house and repair the damage before anybody saw her; it was still early, she might get away with it. Gregor had accepted a blanket to wrap around himself but had stubbornly refused to take off his wet clothes. She was anxious to get him back to the house, too, and into some of his own dry things.

"Now," said Robert, taking up a magisterial position before the fireplace. He looked sternly at Gregor. "You didn't get yourself that far out in the lake by accident."

Gregor shook his head. "No. But I wasn't trying to drown myself. Truly I wasn't."

"Well, *that's* a relief!" Robert said with a laugh.

"I wasn't going to drown myself until I was actually back at school," Gregor explained further, and Robert's laugh stopped on a harsh indrawn breath.

Gregor looked at Cressida. "You're not angry with me, are you, Jane? You know what Stepmama is like—I heard her with you last night. I thought that if I could get wet and stay outside in my wet clothes maybe I'd be ill again and then she wouldn't be able to send me back to school."

"That," Robert said with feeling, "is one of the silliest damn notions I ever heard! You may not like your school much—I didn't care for mine at times—but it's a damn sight better than being sick in bed. Especially for somebody with a weak chest like you. People *die* of pneumonia."

"I know," Gregor said with a dead, defeated calmness that made Cressida shudder. "That's all right. I'd rather *be* dead than go back. You don't know what it's like there. They—"

He stopped and clamped his wide mouth shut. With his hair still wet from the pond, his thick glasses enlarging his eyes, he looked more like a frog than ever.

"I suppose you've been bullied," Robert said with slightly more sympathy than before. "It happens to boys who are different—yes, in America too!" he said as Gregor looked up in surprise. *"I* came in for a bit of teasing, my first term at school, because I was fool enough to admit I liked reading poetry. And writing it. Lord, I thought I never *would* live that down!" He grinned at Cressida over Gregor's head. "But it will make your life a lot easier if you learn to fit in, Gregor. And you might as well start now."

"You don't believe me," Gregor said. "Nobody does. It's not just teasing. It's—"

Abruptly he was sick again, this time all over the blanket and his wet clothes.

"Now those things will *have* to come off!" Cressida exclaimed, "and high time too!" She'd been worried about letting Gregor shiver in his wet clothes. Now she ignored his protests and pulled his malodorous shirt over his head. "Stop fussing, dear, but everything had better come off. I'll run up to the Hall and get some fresh clothes out of your room in a minute. . . ."

Her voice trailed away foolishly as she took in what she was seeing. Gregor's thin ribs were covered with the yellowish marks of half healed bruises.

"Who did that to you?"

"I *told* you," Gregor mumbled into his hands. He was shivering worse than ever, and when he bent over Cressida saw a pattern of small round burns on his back.

"I apologize," Robert said. He looked at Cressida. "Do you think you could bring those clothes now? Gregor and I need to talk. And," he added in an undertone meant only for her, "I think he'll do better with me alone for a few minutes."

When Cressida got back with Gregor's clean clothes, herself in a fresh print dress with only a faint gleam of dampness along her parted hair, Gregor was sitting at the kitchen table drinking a mug of hot tea and talking animatedly to Robert about his father's orchid-gathering expeditions in South America. Every third word was in Portuguese, and he sprinkled four-syllable Latin scientific names into the story as freely as an ordinary boy would throw in a few cricket statistics—and he looked quite happy. As soon as he could get a word in edgewise, Robert sent the boy upstairs to dress.

"I don't know what that blasted woman was thinking of!" he burst out as soon as Gregor was out of earshot.

"Lily?" Cressida tried not to look too happy; it wasn't appropriate. But, like Gregor, she had every confidence in Robert's ability to deal with the situation—and meanwhile, his tone of annoyance verging on contempt was like music to her ears. How could she have imagined him in love with Lily?

"Who else?" Robert scrubbed one hand through his hair till it stuck up like the fur of a damp and angry cat. "Gregor was telling the truth—I don't doubt him, now, and I was absolutely wrong to belittle his fears the way I did. He says he tried to tell Lily, but she didn't want to hear about it, said he'd been having bad dreams when he was ill. But—well, you saw what he looks like; and I wouldn't want you to hear the stories the kid told me. The bullying at that school has gone beyond all normal bounds of decency."

"I didn't think there *was* such a thing as decent bullying," Cressida said without thinking.

Robert shot her an irritated glance. "You're a woman. You wouldn't understand. A certain amount goes on—look, I don't say I approve, but one has to learn to put up with some things. But that school is seriously out of control. Sounds like a modern Dotheboys Hall," he said with feeling, "a place where expatriate parents and those too lazy to look after their own children farm the boys out just to be rid of them, and ask no questions thereafter. And Gregor's not the only victim by a long shot. A boy nearly died last year when the bullies held his head under water too long. That's why they were so quick to send Gregor home when he developed pneumonia; they can't afford more questions asked. By God, I'm going to ask some questions, though," Robert said with passion. "I'm going to bloody well put them out of business!"

"And what about Gregor?"

"He's not going back there," Robert said grimly. "I guarantee it. And Madame Lily is going to know just what she's done to the child, if I have to drag her here by the scruff of the neck!"

"I suppose," Cressida said sadly, "that means I'd better tell her you want to see her." Even in such a worthy cause, she hated to arrange a meeting in the gardens for Robert and Lily.

Of course, she trusted him absolutely. He was the love of her life; he had been so tender and kind last night. He was somehow going to rescue Gregor from that aawful school.

It was just that it would have been nice if they'd had even a few moments alone to talk about last night, a chance for Robert to *say* something to support the evidence of his loving kisses.

And it would have been even nicer if they could think of some way to rescue Gregor without sending Lily down into the rose garden to meet Robert. Cressida toyed with the ideas of burning down the school, kidnapping Gregor, and murdering Lily. None of them seemed to be quite what was required. Regretfully, she accepted that Robert was going to have to talk to Lily himself. She might not listen to Gregor, but she would have to listen to Robert, and once she understood the situation, surely even Lily wouldn't send a little boy back to a place where he was bullied and tortured.

Robert spend a wholly frustrating day waiting in various enclosed gardens opening off the Long Walk for Lily Whitworth to show her blond head. Once he glimpsed Lily on the terrace, but she was talking and laughing animatedly with a man whose fair hair outshone her own golden locks, and she never glanced at the hedge where Robert lurked. Twice Lady Hayvenhurst sailed by to inspect her pet tropical plants; the second time she spoke sharply to him about neglecting his duties by spending so much time out of sight of the greenhouse, and Robert had to go back to deadheading the flowers that grew around the glass walls.

By dusk he'd given up hope and was considering the possibility of marching up to the front door of Hayvenhurst Hall, using his own name and wearing an impeccably tailored suit, and simply demanding to see Mrs. Whitworth. It didn't seem like a very good idea. Given Lady Hayvenhurst's near hysteria about allowing strangers within the gates, she would probably have him escorted off the premises before he could explain his business. If she recognized that for the last two weeks he'd been masquerading as her new undergardener, she would *certainly* have him escorted off the premises, and he would be lucky if he didn't end up in a jail cell.

And he didn't have an impeccably tailored suit. All he owned were American-made suits of a rather decent cut for America, but distinctly inferior to English tailoring; and even those were safely stored away in Berkeley Square for the duration of his job at Hayvenhurst Hall.

Berkeley Square. Peter. His mother was a friend of Lady Hayvenhurst's; that was how Peter had known about this position. Robert leaned on a handy spade, revolving plans for getting Peter's mother to introduce him to her old school friend Dagmar so that he could bully Dagmar's sister-in-law into treating her stepson better.

It was impossible. Every plan he invented took him another step away from the ultimate objective—the protection of one sickly, frightened little boy who currently thought that Robert could work a miracle for him.

Like Cressida, Robert began thinking about kidnapping, murder, and arson; like Cressida, he regretfully discarded all these notions of direct action as impracticable.

And then Lily came around the corner of the greenhouse in a rustle of white shiny stuff and floating gilt ringlets, smelling like the essence of a hundred summer gardens, and Robert's face lit up in a most misleading way.

"Oh, my dear," Lily crooned, "you *are* glad to see me, aren't you? Poor darling, was it a terribly long wait? I'm sorry, Dagmar has a guest and I couldn't get away from him—well, it was really my duty to entertain the man, you understand."

"I saw you doing your duty," Robert told her. "On the West Terrace. You—er—looked quite dedicated to the task."

His voice was grim; Lily not unnaturally leapt to the conclusion that he was jealous. And well he might be! Fairfax Sheridan made pretty speeches; she couldn't quite remember the last time Robert had compared her eyes to bluebells or her lips to a freshly opened rose, though of course his love-struck looks said it all for him, dear, sweet inarticulate Robert. Fairfax Sheridan had kissed her hand; Lily couldn't remember feeling such a thrill from Robert's touch.

Come to think of it, she couldn't remember Robert ever having kissed her—that is, she corrected herself quickly, she could not recall that she had ever permitted him the

liberty. Of course he had *wanted* to—how could he not?
And tonight, Lily thought, feeling herself very daring indeed—tonight she might just grant him the privilege. She
was eager to compare the touch of his lips with Fairfax
Sheridan's. Of course Robert was rich—she was *almost*
sure he was rich—and Fairfax Sheridan only had those estates in Ireland. Still, she owed it to herself to *know* that
Robert would suit her before she acceded to his courtship.

"Don't be jealous, my dear," Lily murmured, leaning
toward Robert. "It wouldn't be very polite of me to look
sour and hateful toward the poor man, would it now?"

Robert was speechless for a moment. Jealousy had not
occurred to him; he was simply annoyed that Lily had made
him wait all day to talk to her, when Gregor must be suffering agonies of suspense!

But then, she couldn't know how unhappy Gregor was,
could she?

"Er—did Cressida tell you what I wanted to talk to you
about?"

Lily's pretty little face looked quite blank. "Who?"

Too late Robert remembered that Cressida had been summarily rechristened by the housekeeper. The trouble was,
he couldn't remember just what she was called now. "Jo-
anna? Janet? Joan," he concluded with relief. One syllable.
About what his brain was good for these days. "You know.
Your new maid."

"Oh—Jane!" Lily's pretty laugh had never tinkled more
brightly. "Poor girl, I think she is quite enamored of you."

"She is? What makes you think that?" Robert asked
hopefully. Not that he really needed confirmation, after
Cressida had been so sweet last night. But if she'd been
confessing her love to Lily, he wouldn't mind hearing about
it. She hadn't actually *said* anything last night.

"Not that it matters, of course." Lily dismissed her maid
and Robert's burgeoning hopes in one breath. "Why, you
can't even remember her name! The girl would be quite
crushed if she knew that. No, she didn't say why you
wanted me to come to you. But then, she hardly needed
to, did she?" Lily gave Robert the enchanting smile that

had won Julian, not to mention a legion of younger admirers, and glanced coyly away. A moment later she glanced back and was annoyed to see him looking as grim as if he'd just been invited to make war rather than love.

"It's about Gregor," Robert announced.

"Tiresome brat!" Now Lily understood. Robert wasn't eager to become stepfather to that ugly little boy. Who could blame him? "Don't worry, darling. He goes back to school tomorrow. He should have gone today, only the little beast disappeared this morning until the whole household was in an uproar looking for him and he'd managed to miss the last train north. It's an excellent school," Lily improvised. "Keeps the boys year-round if you want them to stay." That was the only thing she really knew about the school, and the only thing she wanted to know. "So you needn't worry about Gregor's being in the way."

"I hadn't found him a nuisance," Robert said gently. He found it necessary to speak very slowly and carefully and to keep his hands locked behind him. Otherwise he just might strangle this silly, cold-hearted woman. How had he ever thought her charming? No wonder her first husband had spent all his time hunting rare orchids in Brazil. "In fact, I should like to see more of him. Why don't you let him stay with you for a while?"

Lily pouted prettily. "Dagmar won't have him here once I go back to London; she says she's too old to take on the care of a child. And I can't afford a flat large enough for both of us."

"Oh, well, if that's the only problem," Robert said with relief. He hadn't really wanted to think Lily as black as Gregor painted her; stepmothers were always assumed to be cruel, and at least some of the time the assumption had to be unfair. Perhaps Lily really wanted to keep Gregor by her and simply hadn't been able to afford it.

"I think we can work something out about a flat," he said without thinking of the consequences. "I own several buildings in London. One of them's a block of flats in Mayfair. Maybe not suitable for a child—I've never looked it over . . ."

Lily's smile was so dazzling that for a moment Robert thought Gregor had seriously misjudged his stepmother. Could it really make her that happy to have the boy with her?

"Darling," Lily exclaimed rapturously, "I knew you'd solve everything! I've always *longed* to live in Mayfair." And so much for that taradiddle about his having lost all his money. Her gamble had paid off; she'd always known Robert was rich. It only remained to accept his proposal. "And it doesn't matter about the flat being suitable for a child; Gregor will be at his school most of the time." Robert frowned at that. What ailed the man? "You don't really want him to stay with us all the time?" Lily thought a year-round school the greatest invention since the steel-fronted corset. "Surely you'll want to be alone with me once we're married."

"Married!"

Robert looked as if he were choking on something. Poor boy, the joy of knowing his suit had succeeded must be too much for him. "Yes, darling," Lily murmured reassuringly. "I cannot resist you any longer. We shall be married whenever you choose." She swayed forward until Robert put out his arms to catch her. Leaning back against his shoulder, Lily lifted her face to be kissed. Neither of them noticed the sound of a stiff ruffled skirt rustling down the Long Walk.

"Robbie! Is this how you guard my greenhouse? Pay attention to your duties, young man!"

Something prodded Robert in the small of the back. He jumped and let go of Lily, who promptly slid to the ground with her eyes closed.

It was Lady Hayvenhurst holding the spade he'd put down when Lily appeared.

"And what," Lady Hayvenhurst demanded for good measure, "have you been doing to my sister-in-law? Not but what she probably asked for it, the little slut."

At this, Lily's eyes popped open and she sat bolt upright, recovering from her faint with commendable rapidity. "It's all right, Dagmar!" she cried. "You don't understand."

Lady Hayvenhurst gave vent to a most unladylike snort. "Understand what? Why you have to trifle with the servants? For pity's sake, Lily, try to restrain your flirting to the guests. I haven't time to go and hire a new gardener now."

"But he's not a gardener!" Lily wailed, scrambling to her feet. "He's been in disguise, Dagmar, and it's *very romantic*."

"In disguise?" Lady Hayvenhurst all but shrieked. "I knew it! He's not really Craigie's nephew—it's a vile plot to steal the emerald! Thieves!" Now she really was shrieking. Robert watched, appalled, as she threw her head back and screamed for help. "Murder! Housebreakers! Robbery!"

It was really amazing how many servants Hayvenhurst Hall employed, and how fast they could move given the incentive of some excitement going on at the bottom of the garden. Before Robert could get a word in edgewise, the Long Walk was filled with chattering housemaids and footmen, tweenies and knife boys, and other people Robert had never seen in his time as undergardener. Lady Hayvenhurst's new house guest, the fair-haired Irishman, was edging cautiously up toward him on one side; on the other side, the portly butler Flynn took slow and reluctant steps and brandished the spade that Lady Hayvenhurst had released to him. Somewhere in the background, behind the tweenies and housemaids and cook, Robert thought he could see Cressida's white face and violet-shadowed eyes watching him.

"Arrest that man!" Lady Hayvenhurst cried, flinging her arm out dramatically and pointing at Robert. "He's an imposter! He's after the emerald!"

Flynn on one side, Sheridan on the other looked at Robert's six feet of height and the broad shoulders revealed by his workshirt. They performed two or three steps of a complicated ballet calculated to express great desire to rush at Robert while actually allowing the other fellow to get there first.

Robert stood and waited. He could have begun to enjoy

the situation were it not for Cressida's worried eyes in the background. Whatever happened next, it couldn't be worse than having Lily Whitworth throw herself into his arms.

"Mr. Sheridan, do you recognize this man? Does he belong to that gang of thieves you warned me of?" Lady Hayvenhurst demanded.

Fairfax Sheridan squinted at Robert from a safe distance. "He might be—and then again he might not," he added swiftly as Robert clenched his fists. "I've not seen all the gang, you'll understand, your ladyship."

Lady Hayvenhurst snorted again. "Only reason I'm letting you stay at the Hall is so you can identify the rascals for me. Now make up your mind, Sheridan—is he or isn't he!"

"Of course he isn't," squealed Lily, who had been rather surprised to find Robert rather than herself the center of attention all this while. "He's a gentleman, and he disguised himself as an undergardener so he could see me, and we're to be married, and he's far too rich to have any interest in stealing from you, Dagmar, so there!"

"Is this true?" Lady Hayvenhurst demanded of Robert.

"Er—which of it, ma'am?"

"An *American* gentleman," Lily added quickly, to explain Robert's failure to address her sister-in-law appropriately.

Robert's overstressed brain was whirling like a squirrel in a cage. What was all this talk about marriage? He might have paid a little too much attention to Lily Whitworth the day he met her, before he found Cressida again—but he *knew* he'd never asked the blasted woman to marry him! It wouldn't be polite to call her a liar in front of her sister-in-law. On the other hand, he couldn't stand there in front of Cressida and everybody and agree that he and Lily were engaged to be married. It might have been amusing to fan Cressida's jealousy of Lily earlier, just to reassure himself that she really did care for him, but the time for that was past. On the *other* hand. . . . He stole a glance at Lady Hayvenhurst, standing like a narrow implacable pillar as she waited for his answer.

"Well, young man?" she prodded him. "It shouldn't take so much time for you to decide who you really are."

"Oh, but it does," Robert said fervently. What could he say? What *should* he say?

If he wasn't engaged to Lily Whitworth, he was an imposter and she would throw him out; Fairfax Sheridan might not be able to do it, but Robert had no illusions about his ability to stand up to the small army of domestics gathering in the Long Walk. Could he explain the truth—that he'd disguised himself for love, yes, but for love of the girl known at Hayvenhurst as "Jane"? Then Cressida's imposture, too, would be discovered, and Lady Hayvenhurst would likely decide they were working together to steal the Hayvenhurst Emerald and have them both locked up. Robert didn't think Cressida would be likely to forgive him for getting her incarcerated in the village jail, even temporarily. She wouldn't be in a hurry to forgive him for getting engaged to Lily Whitworth, either, but that was all a mistake and he'd be able to explain it to her as soon as all these people cleared off.

Besides, any turn of events that ended with his expulsion from Hayvenhurst Hall would also end his chance of helping young Gregor. Robert had given his promise to the boy; he did not intend to disappoint him.

As Lily Whitworth's fiancé, he would have some say in the boy's future. He would *insist* on it, by God! And once Gregor was taken care of—he didn't yet know exactly how—he would get out of this fraudulent engagement. And he didn't know exactly how he would accomplish *that,* either, given that no gentleman would jilt a lady; but he'd figure something out. Later. When he had time to think it out properly. When all these people went away, and he could sit by the lake with Cressida and watch the evening mists over the water—then the two of them would work something out.

"Yes," he said, avoiding Cressida's eyes. "Your friend Mrs. Farquharson can vouch for me. Her son Peter—er—arranged for this job when he heard that I needed to be at Hayvenhurst for a while."

That, Robert thought, had been suitably vague, establishing his credentials while saying nothing about his relations with Lily Whitworth. Unfortunately, Lily was not disposed to leave matters this vague. Somehow, while Lady Hayvenhurst conducted her own searching inquiry into Robert's background, two disconcerting things happened.

His engagement to Lily became an established—and very public—fact.

And Cressida slipped away without giving him a chance to explain.

Very late that night, Gregor woke and saw a slender figure wandering among the marble statues on the front lawn. He slipped through Lily's bedroom like a shadow and tiptoed downstairs. The great oak door was standing open, and among the moonlit statues his mother's new maid was standing with her head bowed.

"What's the matter, Jane, dear?" he asked.

Cressida lifted her head and wiped away a tear. "Nothing, really. It's—I—if you *truly* love somebody," she said with a kind of fierce desperation, "you must be happy for them to have what they want, mustn't you?"

Gregor nodded slowly. "But, you know, I don't think Robbie—Mr. Glenford, I mean—will be happy with Stepmama. He is so nice, and—well, I just don't think it is best for him. I wish he would marry *you* and we could all live together. That would be nice, wouldn't it?"

Cressida swallowed a sob. Gregor looked so frail and so worried; how could she trouble him with her sorrows? "It would indeed," she said as cheerfully as she could manage, "but as that's not going to happen, why don't you and I plan to set up house together when you grow up and can do what you want? Maybe by that time Papa will be successful again and we'll buy back Riversedge—or maybe he won't sell it. Anyway, we'll fix it up and live there together. Did I ever tell you about the island in the river where the water pirates live?"

She sat down on the stone plinth of one of the statues and patted the space beside her. Gregor crawled up beside

217

her and she put her arm around him. The warmth of his little body, the trust implicit in the way he relaxed against her, gave her some comfort—not much, but enough to steady her voice. "Someday," Cressida began brightly, "someday at Riversedge. . . ." She rambled on through long stories about a vague, golden future when they would live together at Riversedge and make the gardens beautiful again and explore by the side of the river and it would always be summer. Her dreams weren't much comfort either, but they were all she had left now.

Chapter
13

Over the next few days, while Cressida mourned the final loss of her love and Gregor waited on tenterhooks for his fate to be decided, the gentry abovestairs tried to sort out their own tangled emotions. Nothing seemed to be quite settled yet. Lily had so far acceded to Robert's wishes to keep Gregor back from school for another week.

"But after all, they're not actually *married* yet," Gregor said sadly to Cressida, "and anything might happen."

"So it might," Cressida agreed. For once, though, her imagination did not leap to encompass the possibilities of that "anything." Her ability to dream seemed to have died on the moonlit night when she spun tales of Riversedge to soothe a troubled little boy. Since then she felt that she had been little more than an automaton, going about her duties efficiently and properly, feeling little and imagining less. Life was safer that way. Dull, but safer.

In time, she supposed, she might as well return to Papa's flat in London. There would certainly be no danger, now, of being forced to model with Robert. In time . . . in time. . . .

"Anything might happen yet," whispered her traitorous

heart, and Cressida was just weak enough to stay on at Hayvenhurst Hall a little longer. After all, there was Gregor to think of. If Lily decided to send him back to that horrid school, Cressida decided, she would run away with him! They might not be able to go to Riversedge, but she would find them some safe haven in this world—someplace where they need never see Lily again . . . or Robert.

For her part, Lily was having trouble deciding anything at all. A week earlier she would have thought that confirming Robert's wealth and becoming formally engaged to marry him would be all she needed for perfect happiness. Having achieved both these aims in one evening, she was conscious, from time to time, of a creeping discontent that she couldn't quite put into words. True, Robert was handsome, wealthy, and well mannered. He was unfailingly courteous to her and she had no doubt that he would be appropriately generous once they were married.

And if he wasn't quite as forward, quite as passionate as she had expected him to be—well, so much the better! She'd grown heartily tired of Julian Whitworth's excessive delight in her body. That was the way men were—one had to put up with it if one wanted anything from them—but if she had any sense at all she'd be quite pleased to have found one who *didn't* keep trying to kiss and fondle her.

Instead she felt—what? Piqued? Annoyed? Lily smashed a few ornaments, spoke crossly to her quiet maid, gave Jane a torn ruffle of nearly clean lace to make up for her fit of temper, and still didn't know what she felt. She only knew that she was enjoying Fairfax Sheridan's company far more than that of her fiancé. Which was ridiculous. Sheridan was hardly courteous; one day he showered her with extravagant compliments, another day he treated her with an offhand disdain that had her trying all her wiles to get some response out of the man. He took appalling liberties with her—the man's hands traveled more than any explorer in the Royal Geographical Society—and then, just when she was ready to give in to whatever he wanted, he withdrew into that moody silence again.

He was driving her mad!

And Robert was no help at all. He looked half distracted and hardly there, seldom spoke to her, and had developed a disconcerting habit of diving around corners or disappearing in the general direction of the servants' quarters. Lily couldn't imagine what ailed the man—but despite his undoubted wealth, she was beginning to wonder if she hadn't made a mistake after all. Perhaps she should have accepted Fairfax Sheridan.

Who had not actually asked her to marry him in so many words.

But then, neither had Robert, and she had not the least doubt of his feelings.

It was all very confusing.

Robert himself was not confused at all. He was quite simply miserable. Since that disastrous evening when Lady Hayvenhurst had surprised him with Lily, he had not had a single chance to speak with Cressida. That very evening Lady Hayvenhurst had directed him to move into one of the guest bedrooms abovestairs. Telegrams sent to London and Scotland produced, in short order, Robert's wardrobe of upper-class clothes and a very disgruntled Craigie, who was loudly unhappy about having his Scottish vacation interrupted.

And Robert, dressed as a gentleman and installed in a bedroom two doors down from Lady Hayvenhurst, found that he was as thoroughly cut off from life belowstairs as if a river in flood, rather than a swinging door covered with green baize, separated the two halves of the house. As Lily's maid, Cressida spent very little time in the public part of the house. She flitted in and out of Lily's bedroom in attendance on her mistress and then disappeared down the back stairs to the servants' quarters.

The one time Robert had tried to follow her through the green baize door, he had been stopped on the far side by the butler, a discreet and portly gentleman who somehow ushered Robert back into the gentry's proper place without giving him any chance to say what he'd come for. At the same time, without actually being impertinent, Mr. Flynn had let Robert know that he disapproved of young gentle-

Catherine Lyndell

men bothering the servant girls in this household and that he had the darkest suspicions of any engaged gentleman who had to follow his fiancée's maid into the servants' hall.

And Cressida had stopped walking in the gardens during her free time. Absolutely and completely stopped. Robert skulked in the Long Walk for the better part of three rainy days and got nothing for his efforts but a summer cold and Lily's annoyance.

It was intolerable. He hadn't had a chance to explain why he was complying with this mockery of an engagement. If Cressida had an atom of sense she'd *understand* why he was doing it—for Gregor's sake, and for hers too, come to that—but no, obviously she thought the worst of him, which was why she was avoiding him so. Robert remembered, guiltily, the ambiguous phrases with which he'd teased Cressida into thinking he might care for Lily. For God's sake, he'd only done it to get some reaction out of her. Anybody with any intelligence would have seen through him. Cressida must have the brains of a peahen to think he could ever, for one minute, take Lily seriously. And what did he want with a birdbrained girl like that?

Only to share my life with her, his heart replied. And so, for lack of anything better to do, he continued sneezing and watching the gardens until at last—five miserably long days after he'd been turned into a gentleman—his patience was rewarded.

"Would you move, please? You're blocking the path." Cressida brandished a wickedly sharp pair of garden shears in Robert's general direction and he backed away hurriedly.

"Cressida, I have to talk to you. I've been waiting for *days* to catch you alone."

"Oh?"

The single monosyllable was anything but encouraging, but Robert plowed doggedly on. "You have to understand why I—why Lily thinks—well, I had to let her think— achoo!" This damned cold he'd caught wasn't helping matters any.

"I think I understand perfectly well," Cressida said.

"Would you move, please? I want to cut some roses to fill this basket."

"I'll help you," Robert suggested.

"Thank you, I can complete the task more quickly on my own—and all I want," Cressida announced, looking *through* Robert rather than *at* him, "all I want is to finish cutting the fresh flowers for your fiancée's room. Anything but peonies, Miss Lily said, and I aim to give satisfaction." She beheaded two red Lady Wycherly roses with vicious snaps of her heavy gardening shears. "As you should know." A handful of buds too tightly furled to use in any flower arrangement fell with a light pitter-patter into the basket. *"Sir."* Two salmon-pink Reine Pedauque roses and a cream-tinted Gruss an Aachen joined the shrieking medley of colors.

"Cressy, it's not like that," Robert protested, dodging between rosebushes at some risk to his gray worsted suit. "You know better. I thought we understood one another. That night of the fair—"

"Maybe," Cressida interrupted him, "we were all wrong about your masquerade."

"What?" Robert sneezed again.

"I think you really are an undergardener," Cressida announced. "If you were a *gentleman,* you wouldn't mention that night to me—especially now that you're about to be a married man!"

"It's not like that! I—achoo!" An uncontrollable sneeze interrupted Robert's attempt to declare his love.

"Oh, I think I know exactly what it's like. You haven't changed a bit, have you, Robert Glenford? You can only remember a girl as long as she's actually in your arms— the next day it's on with the new love, off with the old!"

Cressida snatched a cut rose from the basket and advanced on Robert, waving the thorny branch menacingly. "Here! A bridegroom-to-be should have something to decorate his suit!"

She jammed the largest and thorniest of the red Lady Wycherly roses into the top buttonhole of Robert's gray vest, pushed him backward into the rosebush with the same motion, turned, and marched up the path with her basket of clashing roses while he was still swearing under his breath and struggling to extricate himself.

In the neighboring alcove, Waverley put his finger to the housemaid Martha's lips and leaned forward to hear the conclusion of the quarrel. What luck! He'd thought this visit would be all but wasted; Lily's maid Jane was impossible to get at, and he'd had to content himself with quick trysts like this one with the willing Martha. Willing, eager girls were such a bore!

Now it seemed that he might have another chance with the virtuous Jane—not so virtuous after all, Waverley laughed to himself as he watched Jane hurrying up the path and laughed again at the sound of Glenford's *sotto voce* curses.

"Get along up to the house, Martha." He slapped her familiarly on the buttocks when she bent over to straighten her stockings, just to hurry her along. He was bored with Martha—and he wanted to think out his plan of attack. So! Glenford had been getting what he wanted from Jane—and on the very night of the fair, too—but now that he'd been recognized as a gentleman and had become engaged to Lily, he must be ending the affair. Waverley hadn't heard the beginning of the conversation, but he could reconstruct it well enough. Glenford must have summoned Jane to tell her that their affair was over. That made sense to Waverley. Naturally he wouldn't want to be caught with the maid, now that he was courting the mistress. And Jane had been furious with him for dropping her—Waverley had heard that part, just the last blazing end of the quarrel. Jane sounded miserable underneath the fury. Well, it served her right—little Miss Purity, pretending outraged innocence when Waverley stole a kiss or two, when all the while she was having it off with the undergardener! He'd see her paid back for that.

As for Glenford, Waverley thought magnanimously that he bore the man no grudge. After all, by toying with Jane and jilting her so unceremoniously he had probably done Waverley a good turn, all unknowing. The little chit would be looking for someone to comfort her now; she wouldn't turn him away so pertly as she'd done before. And if by any chance she did resist his advances, he would simply point out that he now knew how far from virtuous she was. What right did a girl who'd been sleeping with the gardener have to refuse a real gentleman? And—perhaps more to the point—what did Jane think would happen to her if Dagmar and Lily knew what she'd been doing with Lily's fiancé?

One way or another, little Jane would be his. Waverley chuckled quietly to himself. His high good humor was enhanced by the sight of Robert, his hair ruffled and his good gray suit ripped by thorns, starting up the garden path far too late to catch up with Jane.

Waverley fell into step beside Robert and walked back toward the house with him. Glenford looked startled to see him but kept silence. Waverley had no intention of following suit. It would be fun to tease the man a little, and practically risk free now; Glenford would hardly lay violent hands on his fiancée's brother.

"A little annoyed, are we?" Waverley inquired archly. "What's the matter? Afraid that pretty housemaid will tell your fiancée you've been having it off with her?"

"You misunderstand the situation," Robert told him.

"*Do* I," Waverley said in tones of deep interest. "Explain it to me?"

"There is nothing to explain."

"All over, is it? Good."

Glenford scowled so ferociously that Waverley thought it wise to drop back a few paces, leaving the man to go his way alone. In any event, he had confirmed his suspicions—for Waverley took this denial to mean simply that Glenford's affair with the maid was past history and that the shy Jane was now fair game for him. If Glenford were the right sort, he could have simply passed Jane on to Waverley once he was through with her, saving all this trouble. But one couldn't expect an American to have the right instincts. And in any case, it might be more fun to surprise Jane with the news that she had acquired a new lover to replace the fickle Glenford. Waverley began thinking in good earnest. The first requirement was to get Jane alone, somewhere away from the house—someplace where the butler and footmen couldn't interrupt them. But a place enclosed, where they could have privacy—and where she couldn't get away before he explained her situation to her.

He had a place in mind. And given how upset Jane had been at the ending of her affair with Glenford, he could also think of the perfect way to lure her there.

The only tricky bit would be seeing that she got the message at the right time. Waverley smiled at Robert's broad back. There was no hurry about it. It might even be better to let Jane simmer for a few days.

Chapter

14

Robert stormed back to the house with his face set and his fists clenched by his sides. The shreds of composure left him after Cressida's attack had all but disintegrated under Waverley's teasing.

An imaginative observer watching Robert's progress back to the house might have pictured small puffs of steam coming out of his ears. To Cressida, peeping through the curtains of Lily Whitworth's room, the steam was all but visible. She told herself that he was fickle and unreasonable and that he had *no right* to be this angry. Who had jilted whom, anyway? Or—not jilted, she corrected herself with scrupulous fairness. He had made her no promises.

But he had kissed her until her senses reeled, he had declared that she was not to flirt with anybody else, he had told her how beautiful she was in the moonlight, he had *acted* like a man in love, and Cressida had returned that imagined love with all her heart.

And the very next day, he had engaged himself to marry Lily Whitworth.

She was definitely the wronged party, and Robert had no right to look so annoyed just because she'd pushed him into a rosebush; it was no more than he deserved.

All the same, she felt that she would very much prefer not to meet him just now. Cressida pointed out a crumpled sleeve on Lily's favorite day dress, got permission to leave, and escaped down the back stairs to the goffering irons in the laundry room.

Her darkest suspicions as to Robert's character would have been substantiated if she had known that he wasn't even looking for her at that moment. He was looking for his fiancée.

"A man can only take so much rejection," Robert muttered. "Not to mention being laughed at, teased, used as a stand-in for Trevor Bayne-Fleetworth, and finally, pushed into a rosebush—and in front of that worm Waverley to boot!" Cressida had only been toying with him all along. Probably she'd wanted to practice her kissing techniques so that she could impress Bayne-Fleetworth when she finally deigned to return to London. Probably she'd been delighted when Lily maneuvered him into this engagement; it gave her the perfect out. Not only could she look at Robert with parted lips, all roses and moonlight and sweet intoxication, and then go back to London to moon over that ass Bayne-Fleetworth; she could do so with a delightful sense of being absolutely in the right. *Of course* she wasn't about to let him explain!

"I'll show *her!*" Robert vowed under his breath, taking the front stairs two at a time. "I'll go ahead and *marry* Lily Whitworth, that's what I'll do! At least *she* appreciates me! And then Cressida will be sorry!"

No doubt she would discover, once Robert was well and truly Wedded to Another, that she had mistaken her heart all along. She would cast off Bayne-Fleetworth like a worn-out glove and hasten back to the little village church where, that very morning Robert was to wed his sweet, adoring Lily. But alas, it would be too late. She would spring from her hired carriage only to hear the joyous sound of the wedding bells ringing out their peal over the newly joined couple; as Robert and Lily exited the church, she would fall in a faint before them. But Robert would not even notice the pathetically thin, haggard ghost of a woman he had once loved, for his eyes would be bent on his new-made bride and his lips would be touching Cressida's—

Robert paused on the landing and swore under his breath. This fantasy was getting out of hand. *Lily's* lips, not Cressida's! He would be bending his head to kiss . . .

Try as he might, he could not conjure up the image of Lily as his life's partner. Cressida kept stepping into the picture most inopportunely, just when he thought he had banished her to a lifetime of sorrow and remorse.

Oh, well. It was high time he learned to control his over-active imagination. Look at all the trouble this ridiculous masquerade had gotten him into—well, not trouble exactly. He was engaged to marry a beautiful woman who loved him to distraction, and he'd learned just in time that Cressida was as heartless and fickle as ever. Who'd call that trouble? He was a very lucky man.

Pausing again before Lily's door, Robert straightened his shirt collar, wondered briefly why he didn't *feel* more lucky, and raised his hand to bang on the door.

Mrs. Simpson stepped between him and the door just in time.

"I'm sure I wouldn't know how these things are done in America, sir," she informed him with a sniff, "but in England it is not at all the thing for a gentleman to be visiting a young lady's bedchamber."

Robert lowered his hand. "Even a gentleman who happens to be engaged to marry the young lady in question?"

Mrs. Simpson rolled her eyes heavenward. Lord, but this young American was besotted! He might have been able to talk his way out of that kiss in the Long Walk without getting engaged to Mrs. Whitworth. But no, he had to agree like a mooncalf to everything she said. He might still be able to work himself out of the engagement before a date was set. But no, he seemed bent on compromising himself and Mrs. Whitworth even further. Anybody would think he really wanted to marry her.

Maybe he did. As the housekeeper, Mrs. Simpson knew better than to step out of her assigned place by asking such a question of one of Lady Hayvenhurst's guests. But she did wonder how well this American gentleman really knew Mrs. Whitworth. And she did think it was no more than her Christian duty to keep him from compromising himself further before he'd had a chance to assess Lily's character.

"I will convey a message to Mrs. Whitworth," the housekeeper said firmly, "indicating that you wish to meet her . . . *downstairs*."

Robert slunk away, feeling like a little boy who'd been caught in the pantry. By the time Lily had received the message, shrieked in annoyance that Jane wasn't there to dress her hair, slipped into something filmy and clinging, doused herself with scent, and made her grand entrance, most of Robert's first impulsive fury had worn off. Why had he wanted to see Lily, anyway? He'd had some notion of announcing that he wanted to be married immediately. What a harebrained notion! Robert still supposed he might as well marry Lily, since the only woman he could ever love had turned out to be a heartless flirt who could toy with a man's heart and then cast the bleeding remnants away; but he felt perfectly capable of waiting a good long time for the wedding. Months, certainly. Years would be better.

There was, however, one other subject they needed to discuss, one that Lily had been evading for the five days since they became officially engaged; and today, when Robert was no longer in a mood to put up with evasions, was an excellent time to get the matter settled for once and all.

"I need to talk to you about Gregor," he announced before Lily had wafted her delicate way to a seat on the green brocade sofa.

Lily drew the trailing skirts of her dress about her ankles. "Always Gregor," she said, pouting. "Why do you never want to talk about *us,* Robert darling? We have so much to discuss—the wedding, and our honeymoon trip, and my dress allowance . . . ."

"But you see, Lily," Robert explained, "I can't possibly concentrate on any of these important things while I'm still worried about Gregor. I'm going to be his stepfather now, you see, and I mean to be a good one." It was, he thought bleakly, the only real satisfaction he was likely to get out of this marriage.

"Of course, darling," Lily said, acquiescing with a smile and a shrug. "I'm sure you'd be good at anything you tried to do, my love. Now tell me, what do you think of this shade of green? Doesn't it make me look positively *ancient?*"

She lifted one full sleeve and draped the clinging fabric against her cheek, tilted her head, and smiled up at Robert.

Robert glanced briefly at Lily. She was sitting in a most awkward position, where the light filtered through her transparent green sleeve and cast blotchy green-tinged shadows across her face. Perhaps it was the effect of the shadows, throwing the contours of her face into relief, or perhaps it was his mood; but he did notice for the first time that there was a network of fine lines at the corners of her eyes and that her chin protruded slightly beyond the line of a perfect profile. What had she asked? Whether the color made her look old? Well, it did, but he couldn't say that, of course—one had to be tactful with women.

"Well, it's certainly not your most becoming dress," he temporized. "Perhaps you're right—it might be the color that's the problem."

"What problem?" Lily dropped her sideways-leaning, tilted pose and clenched both hands in her lap. "For your information, Mr. Sheridan said I looked like a mermaid in that dress!"

"Could be," Robert agreed. "Can't say I'm acquainted with any mermaids myself." He certainly hadn't visualized them as tense creatures with predatory little hands and hard eyes. A mermaid should be gentle and romantic, a creature to love and cherish and protect—a girl with soft brown ringlets and great, beseeching, loving lavender-shadowed eyes that encompassed a world of joys and sorrows and . . .

"Stop!" Robert shouted at his wayward fantasy.

The mermaid with Cressida's eyes swayed, trembled, and vanished. He was back in the Green Parlor at Hayvenhurst, with a fiancée who looked scared out of her wits at being closeted with this shouting madman.

"Sorry, Lily," Robert apologized. "My mind wandered for a moment. Now. About Gregor."

Men's minds *didn't* wander when they were looking at Lily Whitworth; she didn't believe Robert's explanation for a minute. He must be angry about something. What had she done to upset him? Who could tell? Men were so irrational and emotional; all a girl could do was smile prettily and agree with everything they said until they calmed down again.

When Lily smiled, it usually didn't take long for men to forget their anger.

She smoothed her skirts and looked up at Robert with a flashing smile that made him forget all about the tense lines at her eyes and mouth.

"He's not to go back to that school."

Agree with everything, Lily told herself. At least until Robert was himself again. She was halfway to regretting her bargain—she thought that she might at least have waited until her inquiries into Fairfax Sheridan's family and fortune were answered—but she had no intention of being jilted. It would be too humiliating. "Of course not, Robert, dear," she agreed in her caressing voice. "I suppose you'd like to choose a school for him yourself?"

"Eventually, perhaps. I don't intend that he should go anywhere for the time being," Robert told her, and Lily could not repress a squeak of dismay. "That last school was a serious mistake. Did you know—" He broke off. "No, of course not. You couldn't know how bad it was."

Lily shrugged. "I knew Gregor complained from time to time. Children will do that, you know. It's a mistake to take them too seriously—"

Robert was looming over her, suddenly looking much larger than before. Lily shrank away from him. "No," he said with deceptive mildness. "The mistake is in *not* listening. I made that error myself, at first. Now I know exactly what they did to Gregor at that school—what happens there to any little boy who's too odd or too weak."

He told her then, in unsparing detail, and before he had half finished Lily's eyes filled with tears.

"I didn't know," she whispered. "Please believe me, Robert, I had no idea. He told me he didn't like school, that was all. I *didn't* know," she repeated vehemently. "I thought—it seemed like such a good solution, a place where he could stay over the holidays, and the fees weren't too outrageous. I didn't want to hear that there was anything wrong." She sniffled once without even trying to disguise the inelegant action, and Robert found himself liking Lily better than he ever had before.

"Of course you didn't," he said. "I told you—I made the same mistake myself at first, pooh-poohing his fears, telling him that he had to learn to stand up for himself. But you can see, can't you, why I won't have him sent back there?"

Lily nodded. The prospect of taking charge of Gregor herself was so horrible that her imagination failed to encompass it, but at that moment she felt guilty enough to take it on. "We'll keep him with us," she said, "and I'll stop going out in the daytime. I'll teach him his ABC's—"

"I think Gregor is rather beyond that," Robert interposed gently. Lily, in the full floodtide of her remorse, did not even hear him.

"And wipe his nose," she went on, "and darn his little socks, and I'll even stay home two nights a week to read him a bedtime story!"

Robert, most unfeelingly, burst out laughing. How long had it been since Lily even *looked* at her stepson? "You needn't sacrifice yourself to that extent," he told her. "What Gregor needs, I think, is a good tutor—someone to give him the fundamentals of Greek and Latin and algebra. And he needs some outdoor sports to build him up and help him get on with other boys. I'll take him on cross-country hikes," Robert said, "and teach him baseball—no, that won't do over here, will it? Cricket. Only somebody will have to teach me first."

The future began to look somewhat more bearable to Lily. With a large enough flat, and full-time tutor, she need not actually devote her life to Gregor—she could, in fact, go on just as she liked. Even better, in fact, because now there would be none of those niggling little worries about bills and dunning tradesmen that had hampered her since Julian's death. Instead, there would be all the new dresses and hats she wanted, and dinner and dancing with Robert at the smartest restaurants, and parties where everybody would envy her handsome American husband and admire her for making the sacrifice of keeping her sickly little stepson home instead of sending him to school.

"Do you know, Robert," Lily said, "I believe I shall quite like being married to you after all!"

But Robert scarcely heard her. It had occurred to him that Cressida really ought to be told that Gregor's problem was solved, and he was trying to figure out how to get away from Lily and get a private interview with her elusive maid.

In the end he took the simple and direct approach. He waited until Fairfax Sheridan took Lily out for a carriage ride and then asked the first manservant he saw to request Jane to wait upon him in the small drawing room.

If Cressida had been alone, she would have treated Robert's request with the contempt she felt he deserved. But young James, the footman who brought the message, had—like the rest of the servants' hall—been following the three-cornered romance with great interest, and he wasn't about to lose his moment of drama by conveying Robert's message discreetly and secretly. He announced his mission in a loud clear voice, at a time when the servant's hall was full of people. The housekeeper and butler looked up from opposite corners of the room; their eyes met over Cressida's head, and she knew from their pleased looks that she was doomed.

Robert couldn't know that his impulsive summons would have been sidetracked or lost outright if the staff of Hayvenhurst Hall had thought him another of Waverley's stripe. But both Mrs. Simpson, the housekeeper, and Mr. Flynn, the butler, had approved of Robbie the undergardener, the quiet, well-spoken boy who'd turned out to be a rich American in disguise—and they approved, too, of his romance with Jane. In fact, they had been watching the story unfold with bated breath. It was as good as the serial stories in the papers! Every evening in the housekeeper's rooms they traded theories. Mrs. Simpson had been of the belief that Jane was an heiress running away from a forced marriage to her wicked cousin; Mr. Flynn thought she was a lady's maid evading a seducer like Waverley. Robert's elevation to the status of a visiting gentleman and his engagement to Lily had brought Mr. Flynn's theory into prominence. If Jane were really Robert's social equal, wouldn't he marry her instead of Lily Whitworth? He must have suffered a brief attack of class consciousness. Give him a few days to experience Mrs. Whitworth's temper and self-centered vanity, and he'd realize that his true love was Jane, be she never so humble in her origins.

"Not a lady's maid," Mrs. Simpson had insisted, "a lady. There must be some other reason he didn't ask her to marry him."

"Such as?" Mr. Flynn probed.

Mrs. Simpson grasped at straws. "Maybe she's married already. To that there wicked cousin who wants her fortune."

Mr. Flynn's sniff was eloquent. "I don't like that theory."

"Why not?" Mrs. Simpson demanded.

"Because," Mr. Flynn said, "it reduces the chance of a happy ending for our dear Jane."

So when Robert tried to arrange a meeting with Cressida, the housekeeper and the butler scented a happy ending and joined forces to persuade Cressida that she must respond to the gentleman's request. In vain did she remind them that they'd promised to see she wasn't harassed by gentlemen intent on causing her to lose her virtue.

"That Waverley, he's a different matter," Mrs. Simpson puffed. "Young Mr. Glenford is a proper gentleman. He doesn't mean to harm you."

"That's all you know about it," Cressida muttered darkly, but after a few more pro forma complaints she smoothed her curls, set her cap primly in place, and went off to the drawing room. Clearly she wouldn't have any peace belowstairs until she convinced her fellow servants that there was nothing between herself and Robert.

And besides, she was ready—almost—to show Robert just how little she cared what he did or said. Why, she didn't give a snap of her fingers for a man who'd court two girls at once the way he'd done! She was lucky—*lucky* to be rid of him!

She would have danced into the drawing room singing a gay aria from one of Verdi's operas, but for some reason she couldn't recall any of the happy songs right now—only the sad ones about parted lovers and eternal heartbreak. Besides, maidservants didn't dance and sing. Cressida retreated into her assumed character and entered the room as a proper servant, meek and quiet, hands at her sides, keeping a respectful distance from the young gentleman who'd sent for her.

"You sent for me—sir?" She managed to pack a wealth of insult into that single syllable. Robert, reeling under the scorn in those wonderful lavender-brown eyes, wondered briefly how that lecher Waverley had been able to keep coming after Cressida. He felt about two inches high, and she'd only looked at him once. Waverley must be a braver man than he'd given him credit for being.

"I did." Robert ran a finger around the inside of his collar. His throat seemed to be closing up again. Perhaps he wasn't quite over his cold yet. "I—need to talk to you."

"Yes, sir. Of course, sir. I await your orders, sir."

"About Gregor," Robert clarified. Damn it all, why did women always assume he wanted to talk about love? "I thought you might want to know that Lily has agreed to my plan. He's not going back to that school."

"I see," Cressida said. "Thank you. I know he'll be very happy to hear it."

"I—thought you might like to tell him yourself," Robert said, "since you're fond of him."

"Yes, thank you. I would."

She was no more responsive than a marble statue. Robert

longed to see some flicker of life in her pale, composed face. How had she managed to turn off all her feelings like that? It must be a gift women were born with. She had probably done this before—when he had returned to America. She had probably looked at his letters like this, unmoved, disinterested.

"You can tell him," he said, "that he's not to go to any school at present. Lily agrees with me that he needs some time at home. He's to stay here for a little longer. After we're—"

He could barely make himself say it; for some reason the words sounded so much like a prison sentence. "After Lily and I are married," Robert forced himself to go on, "Gregor will, of course, live with us."

He had the reaction he'd been probing for—but not in words. Cressida looked up at him for a moment, and in her wide violet-tinged eyes he saw a lifetime of anguish and regret. Her pain met his own, and for that moment the world reeled around him; then she looked down at her hands again, and Robert's grasp on reality steadied.

Only it seemed to him that all the color had gone out of the summer's day, and that he was doomed to live in this bleak grayness forever.

"I see," Cressida repeated in a voice so low he could hardly hear her. "Of course, that would be—the logical thing. Excuse me, please. I must go."

She was gone before he could find the words to keep her. What would he have said, anyway? It was a fact that he was engaged to marry Lily. It was a fact that Gregor's future peace of mind depended on that marriage. It was a fact that Cressida had shown him nothing but scorn and contempt when he tried to explain why he'd acceded to the engagement.

It was, in fact, all her fault that he'd slowly been drawn into treating this mockery of an engagement like the real thing. He would never have contemplated actually marrying Lily Whitworth if Cressida hadn't rejected him.

Now, each day that passed saw him more firmly enmeshed. He might have been able to work something out if he'd spoken up immediately after that disastrous evening when he was caught with Lily in his arms. If only Cressida hadn't disappeared—together they might have found a solution that would save Gregor and extract Robert with honor.

Now it was too late. To break off the engagement now would be the act of a perfect cad. Lily loved and trusted him. Gregor needed him.

And Cressida had no business to look at him as if he were cutting the soul out of her just because he happened to mention some plain facts in a perfectly natural way.

Robert swore under his breath and smashed his fist into the white plaster relief work surrounding the fireplace.

A few chips of plaster flaked off, revealing the Tudor carved wood concealed behind the eighteenth-century plaster. Apart from that minor damage, the wall was unharmed.

Robert's knuckles were badly bruised, but not badly enough to distract him from the ache in his heart.

When Cressida found Gregor and told him the news, her heartache was soothed for a moment by the blaze of joy in his face. A moment later, when the full impact of Lily's decision sank in, his face fell again.

"Living with Stepmama," he repeated. "I didn't think— that is, if she wants to—Jane, darling, does Stepmama *want* me with her?"

"Of course she does," Cressida lied stoutly. She would have wagered all she possessed that Robert had forced Lily to this decision, but one couldn't tell a little boy that the woman in charge of his life didn't like or want him. "I'm sure she's been longing to have you with her all along, only her flat in London is so very small, you know."

"You think so?" Gregor sounded puzzled, uncertain, and for the first time, younger than his age. Cressida gave in to her impulses and drew him onto her lap as if he were the little child he sounded like.

"I'm certain of it," she told him. "Any mother would want you with her. If you were my boy, I wouldn't like you to go away to school where I wouldn't ever see you."

And there was enough unforced honesty in that statement

to reassure Gregor. "No," he agreed, leaning his head against her shoulder. "No, we would live together in—that house you told me about, with the garden growing right down to the water, and the pirate island—"

"Riversedge." Cressida supplied the name he'd forgotten and tried not to feel the pang of homesickness and heartsickness that struck through her.

"Yes. I wish you *were* my mother," Gregor said, "and we could live there. That would be ever so much nicer than staying in London with Stepmama."

"I would like that too," Cressida said, "but remember, Robert will be there too—and you do like Robert, don't you?"

Gregor nodded firmly. "Yes. But—he might not like Stepmama so well. After he's lived with her for a while. People quite often think they want to be friends with Stepmama, you see," he explained seriously, "because she is so beautiful, like a fairy princess. But then after they've known her for a little while they stop being friends, and she's unhappy and angry until she finds some new people. That might happen with Robert, and then she will be angry and won't want me there. . . ."

Cressida began to have just a faint sense of sympathy with Lily Whitworth's desire to send Gregor away to school. It could not be easy to live with a child who was so perceptive—and so tactless about expressing his perceptions.

Not easy, no; but Gregor was worth it, she thought. She hugged his thin shoulders closer to her and kissed the top of his head where his black hair spurted forth in an unruly spiral. "Well, that's *not* going to happen with Robert," she told him, "because he has promised to marry your stepmother, and Robert always keeps his promises."

She couldn't help reflecting that he had made no promises to her—not in words, anyway. She was proud of the fact that her voice quivered only a little.

"He really does love Lily, too," she went on at random, "and when people are loved, it's very good for them. Your stepmother might have been quick-tempered sometimes, but perhaps that was because she was missing your father and needed someone to love her. Now that she has Robert—"

Cressida had to swallow a lump in her throat before she could go on.

"Now that she has Robert," she resumed with determination, "she'll be happier, and she'll want to make him happy. She'll want to be more like him—patient and good-tempered and kind. I've known Robert a long time. He likes everybody. He loves life. He is the best person to be with I've ever known. . . ."

This time she absolutely *couldn't* go on. After a long silence, Gregor twisted around in Cressida's arms and looked at her face. The tracks of tears were plain to see.

"I suppose it'll be all right," he said. "But, oh, I wish you could be my stepmama and marry Robert instead of her!"

"So do I, Gregor," Cressida admitted at last. "So do I."

Waverley had decided that the abandoned summerhouse on the far side of the lake would be an ideal place for his seduction of Lily's pretty little maid. The lake shore on that side was damp, almost marshy in wet weather, so there was little danger that anyone would be strolling around the lake for pleasure. The rambling roses that had grown up over one wall and the roof of the summerhouse, unchecked and unpruned, gave its dilapidation a romantic air that would be sure to appeal to a silly girl. And most important of all, the summerhouse was far enough from Hayvenhurst Hall and its outlying buildings that nobody would hear Jane if she did think of calling for help.

Waverley did not anticipate screams or struggles; he rather thought that little Jane had been softened up by her disappointment when the clod of an undergardener turned out to be a gentleman who preferred the mistress to the maid. Everyone knew that once a girl fell from virtue, she was likely to become a slave to her own sensuality. After a week or two without Glenford's lovemaking to keep her happy, Jane should be quite ready to appreciate the em-

braces of a gentleman who made no pretense of being other
than what he was and offered no false promises of love and
marriage.

And if she wasn't quite ready, well, he had a few home
truths to deliver concerning her position at Hayvenhurst
Hall and the rapidity with which Lily would send her packing if her affair with Lily's fiancé were to come to light.

No, Jane shouldn't trouble him with too much resistance.
All the same, Waverley believed in being well prepared for
any eventuality. So he chose this secluded place for their
next meeting, and he even went to some trouble to make
it comfortable. At various times when he could hope to be
unobserved he pilfered small furnishings from the unused
rooms at Hayvenhurst Hall: a rug from this room, three
satin-covered pillows from that, a pink curtain to drape
artistically over the place where dry-rot and termites had
all but wrecked one wall of the summerhouse.

Once Jane had been brought to see reason, they might
be using this retreat rather frequently; it was worth his
while to make it pleasant.

But he hadn't anticipated the amount of trouble he'd
have sneaking the pillows and other comforts out of
Hayvenhurst Hall. No one ever went into the closed-off
rooms of the West Wing; but on Waverley's first raiding
trip, when he was carrying the small carpet in a roll under
one arm, he bumped into that blasted Irishman who'd
wormed his way into the Hall on the pretext of a threat to
the Hayvenhurst Emerald.

"Er—little something for m'sister's room," Waverley
said awkwardly. "She suffers from cold feet, y'know."

To his relief, Fairfax Sheridan didn't ask why Lily would
need another carpet on top of the one already in her room;
he nodded abstractedly and edged past Waverley without
speaking.

But the next day, Waverley had to wait half an hour to
carry off the pink satin cushions he'd set his heart on,
because Sheridan was pacing up and down the hall just
outside his door and knocking on the paneling; and the day
after that, when Waverley visited the lumber room in the

attic, he found Sheridan down on his knees with his eye to the keyhole of a closet door.

As before, Sheridan seemed as embarrassed as Waverley at their unexpected meeting. He scrambled to his feet and rapidly dusted off his grimy trousers. "Er—just keeping an eye on things for Lady Hayvenhurst, y'know," he explained. "Have to keep my eye out for those dastardly thieves who're after the emerald."

"Well, you won't find them in the attic," Waverley snapped. "They're hardly such fools as to look for it there."

Fairfax Sheridan smiled and spread his hands. Against his will, Waverley felt the man's undeniable charm working on him. "Ah, it's a poor fool I am, and no mistake, sir, but what am I to do? Lady Hayvenhurst is so nervous of thieves that she won't tell even me exactly how she is protecting the emerald. She won't even tell me which room she keeps it in."

Waverley looked the Irishman up and down disbelievingly. "You mean you really think it's in the *house?* Why—" He broke off with a suppressed laugh. "Oh, never mind. If you don't know, why should I enlighten you?"

Fairfax Sheridan left the attic, blushing bright red up to his ears, and Waverley happily poked among discarded furniture until he found the plaster statue of a bathing girl that he'd come for. It would, he considered, set just the right tone for his little retreat.

On the way downstairs he remembered the Irishman's ludicrous mistake and chuckled quietly to himself. There was something very suspicious about a man who claimed to be helping the police protect the emerald and yet knew so little about it. If Sheridan gave him any more trouble, Waverley thought, he just might mention this conversation to Lady Hayvenhurst and see if he couldn't get the man thrown out of the Hall.

He probably ought to do that anyway—but it was too much work, and he had better things to do. Whistling under his breath, Waverley strolled down to the summerhouse and set his latest acquisition on the fall of pink drapery.

MIDSUMMER ROSE

The plaster girl's curves glimmered pearly white against the rich pink velveteen of the curtains. Waverley felt his blood simmering with anticipation. Yes, the statue was the perfect final touch, a little sensual reminder to get Jane aroused and eager for his caresses.

His little retreat was ready. It was time to arrange the final act—or, no, Waverley thought happily, not final at all. Rather it was to be the beginning of a long-running play. He did not think he would tire of Jane for quite some time.

After being discovered by Waverley in the attic, Fairfax Sheridan decided not to spend any more time worrying about the emerald that day. Waverley's hints had suggested that he was looking in the wrong place anyway. No use trying to get sense out of that little worm—he was clearly the type who enjoyed teasing and annoying better men. But perhaps Waverley's sister Lily would be some help.

When he found Lily in the green drawing room, she was pale and obviously distressed, with the traces of tears on her lovely face. Without thinking, Sheridan took out his handkerchief and gently dabbed away the marks of tears. He was a true connoisseur of beauty, and he hated to see a lovely thing marred.

"What's troubling you, princess of my heart?"

Lily turned brimming eyes up to meet his concerned glance. "Oh, everything! Nothing! I—I'm a heartless, wicked woman, Mr. Sheridan, and I hate myself!"

"Ridiculous," Sheridan said on the spot. "You're too lovely to be anything but an angel herself, sent down on earth to dazzle us poor mortals into a better way of life."

Since this description accorded rather well with Lily's customary view of herself, she brightened up quickly—but not too quickly. She managed to tease Fairfax Sheridan into repeating himself, with variations, until her good opinion of herself was quite restored and she had almost forgotten that painful scene with Robert.

"It does seem strange," she said at last, "that I felt so sad when I was with my fiancé, and now I'm happy again with you, Mr. Sheridan! Doesn't it seem to you that it ought to be the other way around?''

She put two fingers to her lips and widened her eyes slightly, and Fairfax Sheridan responded most gallantly and appropriately. They discussed how amazingly well they got along, and how sad it was that twin souls must be parted by the foolish regulations of society, and Lily was all but ready to throw Robert over for Sheridan when some unlucky imp prompted her to mention her late husband.

"Another twin soul to yours, this Julian, was he?" Sheridan glowered as if he could actually feel jealous of a dead man.

"Hardly," Lily answered with a sad, quavering little laugh. "Dear Julian! At first, of course, I loved him to distraction, but you know, Mr. Sheridan, he did not *trust* me, and nothing can be so fatal to true love as a lack of trust—don't you think so?"

"I do indeed," Fairfax Sheridan agreed fervently, thinking at the same time that if he were married to this pretty charmer he wouldn't trust her out of the house—no, he wouldn't trust her one step outside of their own bedroom—and by God, he'd make her happy enough to stay there, too!

"Of course I didn't know the worst of it until after his death," Lily went on. Her bosom heaved with indignation and her eyes sparkled brilliantly. "But he didn't even leave me an income of my own! All I have comes through an allowance for Gregor's maintenance!"

Fairfax Sheridan did not drop the little hand he had been holding, but he chilled imperceptibly and seemed to retreat a fraction of an inch.

"Nothing at all of your own? But I thought the Whitworth estates were quite extensive!"

"They are," Lily agreed. "Gregor will be wealthy."

"That's atrocious!"

"Yes, I thought so too."

"Surely such a will wouldn't stand up in court!"

Lily's eyes brimmed over with new tears. "Oh, please. I could never be so crass as to challenge my dear Julian's will, even though his lack of trust in me cut me to the quick." Besides, old Tomkyns had informed her that in view of her indiscretions during Mr. Whitworth's last visit to the Amazon, indiscretions recorded by some slimy private detective, she would be most ill-advised to attempt any legal challenge.

"No—no, of course not," Fairfax Sheridan agreed. Without seeming to retreat, he managed to let go Lily's hand and get to his feet. "After all, I'm sure your allowance through the estate is quite generous."

Lily laughed bitterly. "Hardly! It's barely enough to pay for a poky little flat and a few rags to put on my back."

"Then," said Fairfax Sheridan in a polite but distant tone, "isn't it fortunate that you are engaged to a wealthy man?"

Chapter
15

Gregor swung his thin legs back and forth, drummed his heels on the bed frame, and finally wound both legs around the straight-backed chair in front of him, where Jane's roommate Abby sat.

"Ow!" Abby complained. "Don't *do* that, Master Gregor. You kicked me."

"Sorry, Abby." Gregor carefully unwound his legs and sat as straight and quiet as he could.

"And you shouldn't be up here anyway," Abby went on. "Lord only knows what'll happen should Mrs. Simpson hear of it. And I *told* you—I don't *know* where Jane's gone. It's her free afternoon and I'll not have you spoiling it."

"You do know," Gregor said. "And I'll go away if you'll tell me."

Abby made a stern face, then relented. "Oh, all right, but you must keep it a secret, mind you—and especially don't tell your stepmother. It's the most romantic thing," she sighed. "One last meeting with his lost love before the cruel barriers of Class and Fate divided them forever—just like Jane was reading to me last night in *Lord Lynworth's Love.*"

Finally Abby explained that Jane had had a touching letter from Robert Glenford. "He said that he loved her and only her for all time and that he dreamed of her all night and that he had to see her once more to explain why a Cruel Fate forced him to Wed Another."

Gregor thumped the bed frame with his heels, swinging his legs back and forth, back and forth, while Abby watched him anxiously.

"You *said* you'd go now."

"It doesn't sound like Robert," Gregor said finally. He put his thumb in his mouth and nibbled on the ragged edge of the nail.

"That's what Jane said was in the letter," Abby insisted. "I can't read it myself. All them spikes and curlicues, the way gentlemen write, and fancy ways of sayin' the same thing over and over. Plain print and short words is hard enough without goin' to all that extra trouble, if you ask me."

"It doesn't sound *at all* like Robert," Gregor repeated.

"Well, 'twas signed with his name, and she's gone to meet him in the old summerhouse just now, so I reckon she'll be able to ask him if he writes like himself, mister smartypants!"

Gregor turned white. Abby put her hand to her mouth. "Oh, I'm that sorry, Master Gregor. I spoke without thinkin', just like you was my little brother. I didn't mean nothin' by it—"

"That's all right, Abby," Gregor said absently. His white, pinched face seemed too old for his little-boy body. "But . . . she can't have gone to meet Robert just now. He's in the drawing room. My stepmother is playing music for him and Mr. Sheridan."

"Then who—" Abby began. She and Gregor looked at each other.

"Waverley," they said together.

Waverley scowled and sucked his right wrist. A few drops of blood oozed out where Jane had clawed at him. He wondered if it would get infected. These servant girls were often as dirty as little animals. The thought made him feel rather sick, but not sick enough to let Jane go. The door to the summerhouse was locked and the key was in his pocket, and as soon as he recovered from her vicious attack he meant to teach her a lesson she'd remember.

"You shouldn't have done that," Waverley said in his slow, silky voice. "Oh, pretty Jane, you really shouldn't have done that."

Cressida shrank back among the satin pillows and made no answer. She watched Waverley's every move with desperate attention. He was between her and the door. He meant to stay there. And the door was locked, anyway.

She took a deep, calming breath and moved her right hand unobtrusively until it rested on the base of the plaster statuette.

"Be reasonable," Waverley said. His voice quavered slightly. Why was Jane looking at him like that? Her steady gaze unnerved him. The lovely violet eyes were narrowed, and her head moved slightly whenever he moved. She reminded him of a cat at a mousehole. He reminded himself of the mouse. The comparison wilted what had remained of his lust after Jane clawed him.

What they both needed, Waverley thought, was a little reminder of where the real power lay in this relationship.

"Be reasonable, pretty Jane," he repeated more firmly. "You're forgetting who you are—and who I am. *And*," he added on a note of silken menace, "what I know about you."

He was gratified to see Jane's sudden pallor. "How—how did you find out? Do you know Papa?"

"Papa? I thought you were from the orphanage!" Confusion momentarily checked Waverley and he felt a wave of irritation. What a stupid girl! Couldn't she recognize a threat when she heard one? Did he have to spell it out for her?

His poise recovered, he proceeded to do just that.

"I mean," he said, drawing the words out to savor the delicious taste of anticipated revenge, "I know about you and Robbie, the undergardener. You weren't so happy when he turned out to be a gentleman, were you? Because he's too good for you now. He threw you over for m'sister.''

Jane's taut, watchful pose slackened slightly; her shoulders drooped. Waverley, watching her face closely, thought she was close to tears. Good. She would weep on his shoulder, he would murmur a few words of comfort, and then all would proceed as planned—if not better. Initially he'd thought a little resistance on her part would be stimulating, but that was before she'd flown at him with her claws out, drawing blood and startling him into a momentary retreat before she got at his eyes. Resistance was only amusing when one could be sure of overcoming it easily; a girl like this Jane, so deadly serious and so perfectly willing to hurt him, was no fun at all.

"You see," he said to drive the point home, "there's no point in making such a show of defending your virtue for my benefit. We both know you've got no virtue left to speak of. And you do know what would happen to you if my dear sister knew about you and Robbie, don't you? She wouldn't like that at all—oh, no. You'd find yourself out in the street without a reference before you had time to pack your bags.''

"I—don't see—what any of this has to do with *you*,'' the girl told him. Stifled sobs were interrupting her words. Waverley felt a moment's reluctant admiration. She was very near to breaking, but she was still putting up a gallant resistance. By God, this verbal battle was almost as good as the token fight he'd expected to go through as he pushed her down among the cushions! He could feel his manhood rising again as he beat down her protests, showed her just what her true situation was, showed her who was master here.

"It means, Jane, that all roads lead to me," he explained almost kindly. "You came here from the orphanage, didn't you? You're too old—they won't take you back in now. And without a reference, you've small hope of finding another position in this county. You'll have to go on the streets—or find some gentleman who'll protect you." He smiled sweetly. "Luckily for you, I happen to know of one not a hundred miles from this very room. So if you want to do it that way, it's all right with me. I tell m'sister, she sacks you, I pick you up outside the lodge gates. But why not skip all that unpleasantness? Be nice to me now, here, and nobody has to know about you and Robbie."

The girl's lip curled. "I'd sooner be 'nice' to that spider scuttling across the floor!"

Waverley jumped. "Where? Oh, *ugh*. Horrid things!" He shivered with revulsion; he really did have a horror of crawling insects. But he managed to skitter away from the spider in a way that brought him to Jane's side. As soon as the insect disappeared into a crack in the wall, he relaxed and slipped an arm round her waist.

"All right, Jane," he said, kindly but firmly, "a token fight is one thing, but you're overdoing it. You know you've got to come to me sooner or later, my girl, so make it now and spare yourself some unpleasant scenes." He jerked her up against his body, holding her with both hands about the waist and pressing her against his enlarged manhood. God, that felt good. He could almost spend himself right now, before he even had her skirts lifted. What a waste that would be! Breathing quickly, Waverley reached down and got a handful of Jane's full calico skirt. He had to tip her backward and push her skirts up, now—right now. The need in his groin was becoming a painful ache. He'd soothe it and then they could talk again—

The pain suddenly transferred itself to his head. Waverley yelped, let go of Jane, and sat down. He put both hands tenderly up to his head, hardly caring that she backed away. The sharp explosion in his skull echoed for a moment, making his vision of the world waver around the edges; then his sight cleared and he saw the broken end of the plaster statuette in Jane's hand. She was raising it to hit him again!

"Don't do it, girl," he croaked. He rose to his knees and lunged forward, grabbing the front of her dress as she swung again. He pulled her forward, off balance; the strained calico fabric gave way with a long tearing sound.

Jane's blow went awry, only clipping him over one ear, and she fell against him and they both wound up on the floor. Before Waverley could consolidate his advantage Jane was up again, looking like an avenging Fury with her dress hanging down off her white shoulders and her brown curls falling about her face. The jagged end of the broken statuette came down again, going right at Waverley's face, and he rolled frantically out of the way, and while he was still looking at the descending statuette a thunderous darkness crashed over him from behind and the world temporarily ended.

When he regained consciousness it seemed that only a second or two had passed, for Jane was still standing there in the ruins of her dress with the white plaster statuette in her hand.

"You didn't need to do that," she said in reproachful tones. "I was taking care of myself perfectly well."

Somehow Waverley didn't think she was talking to him. He moved his head cautiously, opened one eye, and got a clearer view of the brown thing beside him. It was a man's shoe.

"Didn't look like it to me," said a voice that Waverley thought he ought to recognize, but the pounding echoes of surf inside his head distorted everything. He opened his other eye and continued taking stock of the situation.

There was another shoe beside the first one.

And a pair of gray trouser legs. Peculiar-looking trousers—excellent cloth, but rather badly cut.

And behind the trousers, an irregular jagged rectangle of light where the summerhouse door had been burst off its hinges.

Waverley closed his eyes again and groaned. That damned American! Why did *he* have to turn up just now?

"He's awake," said the American's voice. The toe of one shoe poked into Waverley's ribs. "Get up, you."

Waverley squinted up at Glenford's tall figure. "Why?"

"Because," Glenford said in a tone suggesting that it was

the most reasonable thing in the world, "I want to hit you again."

"Ummmph." Waverley closed his eyes. "Not worth the effort."

"No, you're not," Robert agreed pleasantly, "but I've been wanting to do this for a long time."

A hand fastened in Waverley's collar, jerking his head backward as Robert lifted him bodily to his feet. Nausea assailed him at the sudden movement; the light from the open door wobbled about and set off trains of sparks inside his head.

"I think I'm dying," he moaned.

"Oh, not from one little knock on the head," Robert said cheerfully. "I'm *going* to beat you nearly to death, but I haven't really started yet."

"She hit me on the head first," Waverley got out between clenched teeth, fighting the nausea that threatened to overpower him. He jerked his head toward Jane, then wished he hadn't.

"She did? Good for her," Robert said.

"I wish I'd *killed* you!" Jane said to Waverley.

"No mercy. Unwomanly," Waverley croaked. "Disappointed in you, pretty Jane. Girl with eyes like yours ought to be more forgiving. Carried away by love of you." He cocked an anxious eye at Robert to see how this apology was working. The American still looked thunderously angry. "Won't happen again."

"Damned right it won't," Glenford told him. "Cressy's going to be long out of your reach before you get out of hospital."

"Would you hit a sick man?"

Glenford's grin looked to Waverley like the essence of everything he'd always feared. "Watch closely."

He shoved Waverley back against the wall. Waverley winced in anticipation and screwed his eyes shut, waiting for a blow that never came. Instead, something soft and ruffled and strongly scented landed against his chest.

"Robert, don't! How can you be such a brute! Poor Waverley is too delicate for your great bruising games."

Waverley drew in a breath of air heavy with jasmine and warm woman-scent, and sighed with relief. Good old Lily. Always came through in a pinch. Always would. Wouldn't let her fiancé beat up on her brother. Bad form.

The strangling grip on his collar had been released. Waverley let himself sag gently downward until he was sitting on the floor, all but hidden behind Lily's full flowing skirt. Everybody seemed to be talking at once; he couldn't follow the conversation at all. Neither, he suspected, could they.

"You idiot, Cressy," Glenford was saying to the little maidservant. "Didn't you know better than to meet him in a place like this?" The American was not a very clever man, Waverley thought muzzily. Here he'd been having an affair with the girl and he couldn't even get her name right.

"You've half killed my poor brother!" Lily wailed at Glenford. "Whatever possessed you to be so brutal?"

"I wasn't meeting him!" Jane cried indignantly as she tried to gather up the remnants of her bodice. "I was meeting you! And you were late!"

"Call *me* a brute?" Glenford shouted. He was going rather red in the face. "Look what your precious brother did to Cressida!"

"Jane," Waverley croaked from the floor, "you mean Jane, don't you?"

"Waverley, darling," Lily crooned, "we've talked about this before, haven't we, dear? Mustn't chase the maids at Hayvenhurst. Dagmar doesn't approve. Naughty, naughty." She turned and shook one white finger down at Waverley's semirecumbent form.

Glenford had turned back to Jane. "What do you mean, late? I had no idea you were here until Gregor dragged me out of the drawing room and told me Waverley had you down here at the summerhouse."

"She's only a servant girl," Waverley defended himself to Lily, "and not even a virtuous one at that."

"And a shabbier excuse for attempted rape I never heard," Glenford told him. "I suppose you'd never have done it if I'd told you that Cressida's father was a famous artist with a country house and a flat in London."

Waverley tried to laugh, but his aches and pains kept getting in the way. "A girl like *that?* The little serving maid from the orphanage who used to clean out my fireplace until Lily decided to turn her into a lady's maid? You've been reading those romantic novels the servant girls pass around among themselves, Glenford."

"How romantic do you feel about being slowly strangled?" Glenford asked him.

Waverley propped himself up on one elbow. "Come off it, Glenford. I know you Americans like to pretend class doesn't matter, but you can't really think a little skivvy like Jane cares who tumbles her next, can you? You're just jealous because I wanted to enjoy some of what you were getting." He was beginning to enjoy himself, now that Lily's presence protected him from this crazy American's violent fits. "Oh, yes," he said, grinning, "I heard you two going at it in the shrubbery the other day, remember? How long have you been having her, anyway? Did it start on the night of the fair, or were you already—"

Robert's fist came out of nowhere, a minor explosion at the side of his jaw that knocked him back against the wall and made him bite his tongue so hard he tasted blood.

"You're a bad influence," Robert told Waverley. "I never hit a man when he was down before." He grabbed Jane's wrist. "Come with me, Cressida. We don't have to stay and listen to any more of this. And I need to talk to you. What do you mean, you were meeting me?"

"Your *letter*," Cressida said, indignant and breathless, as Robert hurried her out of the summerhouse.

Waverley half expected that Lily would follow them, but she remained where she was, looking down at the recumbent form of her brother with a queer little smile that didn't reach her eyes.

"They're lovers?" she said.

Waverley nodded.

"It started before Robert asked me to marry him?"

Waverley nodded again.

"And it's still going on? While he was engaged to me?"

Waverley had his breath back now, and a cautious test

suggested that his jaw was not broken. "I didn't want you to find out, dear sister," he said mournfully, "but yes, that's what was happening. I tried to give Glenford a friendly hint, but he paid me no heed. So I thought I would try to distract Jane from the man—it was the least I could do for you, after all. But you see what came of it."

Lily regarded him for a long moment. Her eyes were quite hard and cold, like chips of glass; Waverley couldn't imagine what she was thinking behind those bright hard eyes. "I think," she said eventually, "you had better tell me all about it. It's too late, you see, to spare me anything."

And too late, Waverley thought with regret, for him to have any chance at all with little Jane. Who'd have thought that Glenford would be such a hypocrite, trying to keep the girl after he'd gotten himself engaged to her mistress? These Americans had no sense of decency!

All that was left to him was the bittersweet pleasure of a double revenge. "I didn't want you to know," he repeated. "They've been meeting regularly in the garden, laughing at how easily you were fooled and planning how they would continue the affair after Robert married you. . . ."

His fertile imagination continued to supply details with which to embroider the story. And Lily listened to every word.

"I need to *talk* to you," Robert repeated, pulling Cressida after him by the hand.

"Well, *I* don't need to talk to *you!*" Cressida pulled back with absolutely no effect.

Robert paid no more attention to her words than to her attempts at resistance. "Where can we go that Lily won't bother us for a while? Ha! I know—my old cottage. Craigie will see to it that we aren't interrupted."

"No, he won't," Cressida said rather desperately. "I want to be interrupted. I want to go back to work. *I don't want to talk to you!*" She leaned back, digging both heels into the gravel of the path. Robert stopped and looked at her for a moment and let go of her hand.

"You see," Cressida said, fighting the sinking feeling in her heart, "we really don't have anything to say to one another. You're going to marry Lily, and I—*no*, Robert! I said *no!*"

His big hands almost closed about her waist. Apparently without effort, he swept her up to his shoulder and carried her along the garden path. When Cressida tried to push his hands away, her bodice fell down and left her indecently exposed.

"Ah, Craigie," Robert said at the door to the cottage. The old gardener hobbled out and looked up at Robert's burden with an amused glint in his eye. "We want a few minutes of privacy. Could you see that no one interrupts us?"

"Craigie, he's abducting me!" Cressida cried. "Do something!"

"Aye, mistress." Craigie took off his cap. "Thought all along you were a proper lady and not one of the servant girls, so I did." He opened the door of his cottage wide. "Right this way, Master Robert. I'll turn aside anybody who comes looking for you."

"Craigie, I thought you were my friend!" Cressida all but shrieked as Robert stooped to carry her through the cottage door.

"I am that," Craigie chuckled. "Time you young things settled your differences."

The door closed behind him and they were alone in the dim, crowded front room. Robert stood before the door, arms folded, clearly not intending to move. Cressida glowered at him and felt her way to a prickly horsehair sofa. The need to hold her ruined dress up around her shoulders was a distinct handicap to expressing all she was feeling. Not that she had much practice in the matter, but just now she would rather have liked to imitate Isolde, who swore and threw small domestic articles when she was in a temper.

Cressida didn't know any swear words. And she couldn't throw things and hold her dress together at the same time.

She was, she recognized ruefully, very poorly equipped for scenes of passion.

And here she was, being abducted and locked in a cottage for the second time in as many hours! Why couldn't things like this happen to Isolde, who would have known what to do about them?

A small rueful giggle escaped her lips.

"Well, if that isn't the outside of enough!" Robert said. "Cry if you must, throw things, scream, push me into rosebushes. Go ahead. I'm strong—I can take it. But I didn't expect you to *laugh* at me."

Cressida thought this over for a moment. It was very strange, but she couldn't feel indignant at Robert any longer. True, he had just been excessively high-handed with her—but then, he'd also just saved her from a fate worse than death, or tried to. It wasn't his fault that she'd hit Waverley with the statue first.

"What did you expect?" she asked at last.

This room was dark, with the one small window almost totally obscured by three layers of dingy curtains; and crowded, not that Craigie had unpacked his furniture again; and very small. Robert's head brushed the heavy oak beams of the ceiling, and his shoulders were almost broader than the door behind him, and there was hardly room for the two of them to move without touching one another. Cressida swallowed in the silence that followed her question. She could hear Robert's breathing, heavy and quick; he could surely hear hers. He could probably hear the pulse that throbbed in her throat. A sense of urgent expectancy rushed through Cressida, and with it there came an unexpected and improbable joy. She felt unreasonably certain that something wonderful was about to happen.

"To begin with," Robert said at last, "you could explain why on earth you thought you were meeting me in the summerhouse."

Cressida stared. "Because you asked me to!"

Robert shook his head. "I *would* have asked you, if I'd known the place was there, and if I'd had any hope you would come. But I didn't even know the summerhouse existed until Gregor came haring into the drawing room with some story about how Waverley had lured you there to do you no good.''

"But you did," Cressida cried indignantly. She held up her bodice with one hand and felt in the pocket underneath her skirt with the other. By some miracle, Robert's letter had survived all the vicissitudes of the past two hours. It was a little crumpled, but she smoothed it out again. There were a few stains on the sheet of paper, but those could readily be explained by the rough time she'd been having recently; there was no reason to confess that she'd shed a few happy tears over the letter before she stuffed it into her pocket and ran down to the summerhouse to meet Robert.

"What's that?"

Perhaps Robert had gone mad. Come to think of it, that might explain his engagement to Lily.

"The. Letter. You. Wrote. To. Me." Cressida spaced the words out carefully, watching for some sign of comprehension. "Asking me to meet you—"

She got no farther before Robert snatched the crumpled, tear-stained sheet from her hand. "Hmm. Signed 'Robert Glenfordd.' Did you think I couldn't spell my own name?"

"Under the stress of strong emotion—" Cressida began to excuse him.

"And there's plenty of that here, isn't there? 'I love you and only you'—well, that's true enough," Robert said casually.

Cressida thought it was quite unfair that her heart should turn over at those words. It was, after all, no more than he'd said in the letter.

But he went on, reading phrases from her precious letter as though he'd never seen it before. "I 'dream of you all night'? Well, yes, but I expect to get over it in time. And a 'Cruel Fate forces me to Wed Another'?" Robert snorted and crumpled the precious page in his fist. "I see I don't explain exactly what the Cruel Fate is. Sheer fustian, my girl! I ought to be insulted that you think I wrote such romantic trash. And in any case, how could you take it for my handwriting?"

"If you're trying to tell me you didn't write that letter," Cressida said, "just say so. You don't have to go on about—romantic rubbish—and all that. I know, now, I was an idiot to think you'd—that you meant—oh, never mind!" Never in a million years would she let him guess how she'd wept for joy over the words he sneered at. She wished she could look pale and proud like Isolde in a fit of Artistic Temperament—but that was beyond her. She was a small, tear-stained, bedraggled thing, and Robert had only dragged her in here to laugh at her foolishness in believing that he'd write her a love letter after all that had gone wrong between them, and any minute now he would walk out the door to his Lily—and good riddance! Cressida told herself with a small defiant sniffle.

It was the sniffle that undid Robert. Cressida looked so vulnerable, perched on the sofa with her hair falling about her shoulders and her dress in rags, that he'd hardly been able to keep his hands off her this long. When she lifted her head and sniffled and he saw the tears she was trying to blink away, he couldn't keep his distance or remember how terribly she'd snubbed him every time he showed how he loved her. She was just his Cressy, his darling girl, whose eyes held enough love and sorrow for the whole world, and he had to kiss that look of misery off her face or die trying.

"Don't," he said. He knelt in front of the sofa and put his arms around her and pulled her head down to his shoulder. "Don't cry, Cressy, darling girl, we can make it all right—I don't know how, but we can—you did come," he said in a dazed happiness. And then he kissed her, and she was returning his kisses; her arms were so tight around his neck that she might strangle him. Not that it mattered; he'd die happy. Somehow, in all the excitement of the last hour, the crucial point about Cressida's presence in the summerhouse had escaped him until now. "You did come to meet me," he repeated. "I mean, even if it wasn't me that wrote the letter, you thought it was. If I'd really asked, would you have come to me?"

"Oh, *blast* it all," Cressida said crossly. At least one of

Isolde's words had come to mind in time to be of some use.

She sat up and pushed her tangled hair back from her face. Her lips burned where Robert had been kissing her with such abandon. It was too late now, she thought—too late for pride, too late for pretense. "Yes," she told him. "I may as well admit it—it's too late to do anything else anyway, isn't it? Of course I came."

"Why?"

"Because I'm an idiot!" Cressida snapped. "Because I'm a romantic fool who believes all the romantic rubbish she hears. Because I love you, God help me, and no matter how many times you forget all about me and go chasing after some other woman I don't seem to learn my lesson. *Now* have you heard what you wanted?"

"Yes," said Robert with deep satisfaction. He wrapped his arms around her again. This time he drew her down onto the carpet with him. She tasted like honey and flowers and summer rain. He couldn't imagine anything sweeter. Well, yes, he could, but this was neither the time nor the place.

After a long, drugged interval he thought of something he needed to point out. "But I never have forgotten you," he murmured in between kisses. "It's you who forgets all about me."

Cressida shook her head.

"But you never even bothered to answer my letters." How that had hurt at the time! It shouldn't matter now—not now that he had the grown-up Cressida in his arms and had heard her confession of love—but somehow that old betrayal still pained him. Cressida had been the one fixed star in his firmament, and when he'd lost her, the sky had been black for a long time.

"Robert Glenford, I think you really have lost your mind," Cressida said. She kissed the corner of his mouth, then his cheekbone, and then the tip of his left ear. Robert felt as if he were floating away on a sea of bliss. Who'd have guessed that the tip of the ear was so sensitive? "You know perfectly well that *this*"—she held up Waverley's crumpled forgery between two fingers—"was the first letter you ever sent me. And you didn't even send it, come to think!"

"Here now!" Robert sat up straight and stared Cressida in the eyes. "What about all those letters I wrote you from America?"

"What letters?"

"The ones you never answered, damn it!"

"You mean the ones you never *wrote!*" Cressida snapped back. "Damn it," she added for good measure. At least by the end of this fight she would have a satisfactory, Isolde-like vocabulary. "I never heard one word of you after. . . ."

Some thought about dates and times was forcing it on herself. She had been so desperately unhappy that year; for a long while she'd refused to think about it. Even now the memories were blurred. "Wait a minute," Cressida said. Her fine righteous rage was deserting her again as she tried to think. "When did you write to me? Not right after you got to America?"

"No," Robert confessed. "I was too busy at first. Business—my guardian had cheated—oh, it doesn't matter. There were bankers and lawyers buzzing around me all the time; I hardly had a minute to myself. Things didn't settle down until October or thereabouts. I remember now—" His laugh was strained. "The very end of October, it was. I wrote you the first long letter on All Saints' Eve. I remember thinking it might be a bad omen; but I was so lonely and miserable that night."

"I too," Cressida whispered. "Mama died the last week in October." The crowded front room of Craigie's cottage was stuffy and warm, but she wrapped her arms around herself and shivered. "Poor Mama, she hated the cold so— she was made for summer and flowers. She said she didn't think she could face another winter. And after she was dead," she went on drearily, staring into the shadows as she relived that dark time, "when it was too late, Papa took us to Italy where it was warm and sunny and he could be with his artist friends. We stayed in Italy almost a year—

261

and—I don't think anybody ever forwarded our letters from home."

"But they would have been waiting when you came back."

"I don't know," Cressida said. "I suppose so. I don't remember anything. Papa would have gone to see Mrs. Jasper—she's the postmistress, remember? And keeps the general store? So if we had any mail come while we were gone—"

"You most certainly did," said Robert.

Cressida frowned as disconnected scenes came back to her. "He did. And he was in a towering bad temper when he came back. He stamped all over the house and shouted about dunning tradesmen and miserable money-grubbing shopkeepers. And. . . ." She drew a long shaking breath and her eyes sparkled. "Do you know, I think he threw all the letters in the river without looking through them? Because he didn't have any envelopes in his hands when he came into the house. I remember now. He was waving his hands in the air. I asked if there were any letters for me and he said no, of course not, who'd write to a child?"

"And you believed him?"

"Now I think he must have thrown all the mail away in a fit of temper and didn't want to admit it," Cressida said, "but at the time—yes, I thought he was right." She gulped. "After all, why *should* you remember me? But I thought maybe you knew we'd been abroad—maybe the vicar had written you with the news of Mama's death and you were waiting until we came home again and a Decent Interval had passed. So I kept hoping. I looked at the mail when it was delivered every day for—oh, for quite a long time," she finished desolately.

Robert grabbed her and kissed her soundly. Cressida felt an amazed delight blooming within her where, just for a moment, she had remembered that cold empty time when she'd lost those she loved best.

"I *won't have* you looking like that," Robert said with suppressed violence. "You're not to be sad ever again, do you hear? Because I *love* you—and I have *always* loved you—and I *did* write to you, time and again, until I thought you would never answer and I should stop pestering you—and you're never going to disappear like that again. Because," he said between kisses, "I intend to go everywhere you go from now on."

A high screech, like the call of an agitated peacock, sounded faintly through the room. Cressida stiffened in Robert's arms.

"That might not—be a very—good idea," she said breathlessly.

"Why not?"

"Because that's Lily Whitworth screaming for me. She must want me to help her dress for dinner—and I *don't* think you want to be in the same room with the two of us just now, even if it were proper for you to be in her bedroom!"

"No more I do," said Robert, still holding her firmly, "but why should you jump to attend that screaming harridan? You don't care if she sacks you—you're giving notice anyway. Stay here with me."

Cressida shook her head. "As far as she knows, I'm still her maid," she pointed out. "And dear Mr. Craigie will try to keep her away from here—and he *does* care about *his* job—and he's in enough trouble already for pretending you were his nephew from Lanarckshire."

Reluctantly, Robert released her. "I can see some sense in what you say," he admitted, "but it bodes ill for our married life, don't you think, that you start by disobeying my first command?"

Married life. Cressida thought she had never heard two more delightful words. "I think it bodes very well indeed," she said with a smile, "that *you* start by recognizing my superior good sense!"

"Jaaaane!" The screech was nearer now. Cressida picked up her skirts. "I *must* go," she said breathlessly. "It's not fair to let her have a temper tantrum at Mr. Craigie instead of me."

"You'll give notice immediately!" Robert called after her.

Chapter

16

Lily was rather proud of herself. Any woman who had just discovered that her fiancé was having an affair with her maid might be excused for having a tantrum on the spot. Lily felt that she in particular, with her delicate sensibilities, might have been allowed to faint or burst into hysterics.

Instead she listened to Waverley's revelations with no outward show of emotion. Indeed, while he talked, she was already planning how to salvage the situation. Nor did she feel the slightest inclination to have hysterics. An icy numbness had enveloped her from the moment she saw Jane in Robert Glenford's arms. This could not be true—it could not be happening. Her Robert embracing a servant girl in front of her? Men strayed, of course, Lily understood that; but they didn't take pride in their indiscretions. They didn't flaunt them before decent women. As soon as he saw Lily, Robert should have been on his knees, beseeching her to forgive him, promising total faithfulness from now on.

Instead, he had acted as though he cared for nothing but that little maid's feelings—as though it didn't even matter to him what Lily thought about this disgraceful affair—as though he had completely forgotten her.

That was not true, of course. It *could* not be true! Lily glanced around the summerhouse distractedly. What was she searching for? Of course—a mirror! If she could only glance at her own reflection for a moment, if she could just *see* the perfection of her white skin and carefully dressed golden locks and her tender blue eyes, she would stop having these terrible doubts of Robert's love.

She would just have to take it on faith that Robert hadn't *really* forgotten his love for her. He was temporarily mad, that was all—and it was that little maidservant's fault! Lily couldn't see how such a shabbily dressed, slight little thing could attract men the way she did, but there was no denying that Jane had a sadly deleterious effect on the men of her acquaintance—not just Robert, but Waverley too! It must be that men, with their grosser, more sensual natures, could sense an underlying wantonness in Jane that Lily herself was altogether too pure and spiritual to perceive.

Clearly, the thing to do was to get rid of Jane and the wanton, sensual promise that she held out to these poor deluded men. Then everything would return to normal. Waverley would behave himself—or, at least, he would misbehave himself with some girl who would have better sense than to make such a fuss about it—and Robert would remember how much he loved her, and Lily herself would not feel so cold and frightened any longer.

How long had Waverley been going on with his lubricious descriptions of Robert's depraved actions? Too long. It would be dark soon. It was time to act.

Lily walked out of the summerhouse, leaving Waverley behind talking to the air. She couldn't waste time comforting her brother now, and she had heard quite enough of what he'd seen Robert and Jane doing in the shrubbery.

Jane was not waiting for Lily in her room.

An impatient ring of the bell produced a frightened-looking little tweeny who stammered that Jane wasn't in the servants' hall either, ma'am, that she hadn't seen her since dinner, beg pardon, ma'am.

"That will be enough." Lily dismissed the chit with a wave of her hand.

Was it possible that Jane had run away? That would be convenient, but Lily was in no mood to count on luck to solve her problems. She went in search of her errant maid.

The outside servants were curiously unhelpful—impossible, Lily thought, these country types! Someday she would really have to speak to Dagmar about improving the class of servants she kept; these yokels didn't even seem to know the way about their own grounds. They kept misdirecting Lily, affecting confusion about which maidservant she was looking for and which way the bewildering array of garden paths led. Finally, after making the tour of the Long Walk twice from different approaches, Lily took matters into her own hands.

Jane appeared on the second call, looking breathless and disheveled—as well she might! The little slut hadn't even bothered to go back to the house and change her dress before she went off with her lover—with *Robert*. Lily's lips pressed together at that thought, and if she had had any momentary impulse of pity for the girl, with her dress torn and her white shoulders bruised by Waverley's hands, the impulse died in that moment. Jane didn't look like an abused servant girl. She looked like a sensual slut who'd been well and truly kissed, with rosy lips and cheeks and stars in her eyes and her brown hair falling loose about her face.

No man's embraces had ever left Lily in such a state of sensual exaltation. She felt vaguely jealous for a moment, not just that Jane had been with her Robert, but that Jane had known some pleasure that had always escaped her.

But then, decent women *didn't* feel such things.

"I wish you to attend me, Jane," Lily snapped. "I am going to drive out into the country."

"Yes, ma'am," Jane said. "But I—"

"I feel the need of solitude after today's distressing experiences," Lily interrupted her. "I have told my groom to bring the gig around but not to go with me. For propriety's sake, I must have some companion, and you will do as well as another."

"Yes, but—" Jane began to raise some foolish objection, which Lily had not the patience to hear. Did she think that her affair with Robert entitled her to talk back to her mistress? She'd soon learn better!

"Put on a decent dress and be at the front steps in five minutes," Lily instructed her, and then thought better of it. "No, I'll come with you." No telling what would happen if she let the girl out of her sight.

Lily discouraged all Jane's attempts to speak to her until they were some miles from Hayvenhurst Hall. She was rather vexed to realize that she herself did not know exactly where they were. She had been lost in her own thoughts, driving rather mechanically, and it was not until the horses protested the steady pace at which she'd forced them that she paused to look about her. They had just passed over a hump-backed bridge remarkably like the one at Lesser-Gantley-sur-Marsh. The village before them, for all Lily knew or cared, could have been an exact copy of Lesser Gantley: there were the same thatched cottages lining the narrow way into the village, the same oak towering over the village green, and the same dilapidated Norman church.

And the same total absence of any signposts to guide the traveler.

"You'd think they could at least put up the name of the village somewhere!" Lily exclaimed.

"Middleham-on-Trent," Jane told her. "We are about twelve miles from Hayvenhurst Hall, and the horses are tired. Do you think it might be a good idea to turn back now? It will be dark before we're back at the Hall—and I think there's a storm brewing."

Lily glanced around the village. She supposed Jane must have read a signpost before they reached the place, something she herself had missed while she brooded over the day's events.

There was a train station. Good. This place would do as well as any other. And this open square before the church gave her room to turn. Lily flicked her whip at the horses and pulled on the reins until they had managed to turn the gig in a tight circle.

"Yes," she said deliberately. "*I* shall return now—but without you, Jane."

"But—"

Lily raised the thonged carriage whip she carried in her left hand.

"Not one word out of you!" she said. "I've had enough of your sly ways and wanton immorality, Jane. I was shocked by my brother's revelations. I cannot have a girl of your character in my service. You may consider yourself dismissed as of this moment. Without a character."

"But I was hired by Mrs. Simpson," Jane said.

"Who will be as shocked as I was to learn of your depravity. Get down."

"Yes, but I—"

"*Down!*" Lily raised the carriage whip and was gratified to see that Jane hastily scrambled down from her seat on the gig. When the girl was standing in the road, Lily took a small purse from her reticule and tossed it in the dust at her feet.

"I am not completely heartless," she informed her erstwhile maid. "In that purse you will find enough money to pay your fare to London and to keep you for a week there. By the end of that time," she sneered, "I am sure a girl of your *talents* will have found a much easier way to earn a living than posing as a respectable lady's maid!"

Jane's face was quite white. With a graceful movement that Lily could not help envying, she stooped, picked up the purse, and threw it squarely back into the gig. "I don't need your money!"

Lily shrugged. "Have it as you will. As you pointed out, there's a storm coming up. It's no night to be left out without shelter. But then, I suppose your sort can always find somebody to take you in for the night."

She drove on before Jane could start pleading and imploring to be taken back into service.

On the way back to Hayvenhurst Hall, Lily could not keep from noticing the menacing storm clouds Jane had pointed out. She gave a mental shrug. It was the girl's own fault if she was left stranded in a strange village. Lily *had* offered to pay her fare to London, and she did wish with all her heart the girl had taken the money; she would not feel truly safe until Jane had vanished into the streets of the city.

The girl had left her no alternative. Since Fairfax Sheridan had inexplicably cooled in his attentions, Robert was Lily's best chance at an advantageous marriage. She could not be expected to suffer interference from her own maid. Now that Jane was gone, Robert would doubtless forget his infatuation in short order, and all would be as it should be again.

The first step in mending matters was to find Robert. He had temporarily forgotten how much he loved her; very well, Lily told herself, she would just have to find the man and *remind* him of his great and overmastering devotion to her. It shouldn't be hard. Look at what he'd gone through already, just to be at Hayvenhurst Hall with her!

The search for Robert was an annoying repetition of the one she'd gone through earlier for Jane. He wasn't in the house; the servants were stupid and unobservant and spoke in a broad country dialect she could barely understand. Lily wound up circling the house and grounds with a frustrated frown marring the perfection of her smooth white forehead.

A disquieting whisper inside her suggested that it might be wiser to wait until the morning, when tempers had cooled, to find her fiancé; it was just possible he was in no mood to be found now. Lily ignored that prompting from her cowardly nature. The cold fear that had possessed her in the summerhouse was still driving her on. While there was even the remotest shred of possibility that Robert did not love her—that a man she'd set her heart on *could* ignore her beauty—Lily could not rest happy. If one man could be immune to her charms, what about others? And without her beauty and its effect on men, what did she have?

She *had* to find Robert and mend matters with him. Even—Lily frowned in distaste at the thought—even at the cost of submitting to those carnal embraces she really found boring and pointless. Flirtation was pleasant—having a handsome man kiss her hand gave Lily a delicious *frisson*—but what came after was just an annoyance she could well do without—hot and sweaty and indelicate. And they always mussed one's hair.

Jane hadn't seemed to mind having her hair mussed by Robert.

The storm clouds were still piling up in the sky, a black and menacing mass. The golden sunlight of late afternoon had become a green-tinged, sourceless, shadowless illumination. The whole world seemed to be trembling on the brink of some revelation. Lily felt her mind working with unnatural clarity, even while her limbs were sluggish and unresponsive. She wished the storm would break. She wished she could forget how Jane had looked, the wanton little thing, with her lips all red from a man's kisses. She wished it did not matter so much to her that Jane had seemed to enjoy the sort of tussle Lily had always found pointless and degrading. There was some secret she did not know. Nobody would ever tell her.

Lily clenched her smooth white hands. She could have howled in frustration, but there was nobody about to howl *at;* she'd wandered far from the house in her search for Robert, and all the outdoor servants had prudently taken shelter from the coming rainstorm.

At the far end of the Long Walk Lily glanced again at the clouds. The first fat raindrops spattered against her skirt and she said several unladylike things under her breath. She would never be able to get back to the house before the storm broke and soaked her. She would be a figure of fun, drenched and dripping and miserable. Lily hated being ridiculous above anything. Wasn't there someplace where she could take shelter until the rain had modulated? There was that greenhouse—but Dagmar always kept it locked. Silly Dagmar with her silly suspicions. If Lily could just get into the greenhouse, she could wait out the storm there, and perhaps Robert would become worried that she was missing and would come looking for her, and they could have their reconciliation at once, and . . .

Lily drew in a sharp breath and her eyes narrowed. There was someone going into the greenhouse. She caught just a glimpse of a gray suit and hat. It must be Robert; who else would bother to traipse all the way out here among all these boring plants? Perhaps he had already begun to search for her. Yes, that must be it. Wonderful! They would be trapped together in the rainstorm, and by the time it ended they would be more thoroughly engaged than ever.

Lily's agile mind skirted over the distasteful and indelicate maneuvers she would probably have to go through to satisfy Robert's sensual needs. It was *necessary*, that was all, and she should have seen that before. Men were like that—they couldn't control their animal natures. If she'd understood Robert's needs he wouldn't have had to sully himself with that little servant girl.

Two more fat raindrops splashed down. One landed on the very tip of Lily's perfect nose. She picked up her skirts and ran for the greenhouse, laughing with exhilaration that everything had worked out so perfectly.

She was already at the greenhouse door before it occurred to her to wonder how Robert had gotten a key; her hand was on the knob when she saw that one pane in the side of the greenhouse had been gently removed. Trust her Robert not to let a locked door stand in his way! But he should have realized, if the greenhouse was locked, she couldn't possibly be inside! She swung the door open, a laughing reprimand on her lips, and froze in the open doorway.

The man standing in the center of the greenhouse, over a pile of broken pots, was Fairfax Sheridan.

As Lily watched, he up-ended another pot, dumped the contents on a potting bench, ran his fingers through the mold, and cursed under his breath. He reached over his head for another of the clay pots lining the top shelf. This one housed a large spiny plant with protruding globular sections that almost speared Sheridan's jacket as they swung free. Lily watched dispassionately as Sheridan evicted the cactus from its home and searched the potting soil. Like many of Dagmar's rare plants, the cactus had been an extraordinarily ugly object. Lily did not mourn it in the slightest.

Still, Dagmar would definitely be testy if Sheridan worked his way along the potting bench until he reached her prized orchid collection at the far end of the greenhouse.

It did not occur to Lily to be afraid. Moving closer, she rested delicate fingertips on the potting bench and cleared her throat lightly. "I think," she said, "you had better tell me exactly what all this is about."

Fairfax Sheridan was lifting down another outsize cactus when Lily spoke. He sprang into the air like a frightened cat. The heavy clay pot fell out of his hands and burst on the floor between them like a bombshell. Lily squeaked in annoyance and stepped back. "Clumsy man! You've got dirt all over my new carriage costume."

"A little dirt could be the least of your worries," Sheridan told her. He was breathing quickly; there was a black smear of potting soil across his forehead, where he'd put up a dirty hand to wipe away the sweat of his exertions, and his eyes gleamed alarmingly under sweat-dampened yellow hair. "Who sent you here?"

"No one." Lily took another step back. "I came alone."

"Good." Somehow, moving cat quick, Sheridan stepped behind the potting bench and came out on the other side, between Lily and the door. "Be a good girl, and you'll go back that way."

He was standing so close to her that Lily could see the pulse beating in his neck and could feel the animal heat of his body. He could have kissed her without any trouble at all. But there was nothing of the romantic suppliant in his manner now. He was angry, impatient, on the verge of doing something appalling—and Lily found this new Fairfax Sheridan too exciting for words.

She laughed gaily. "Oh, but I think I'd rather go back *with* you! And then you can explain to Dagmar why you've been throwing her cactus collection on the floor."

"You're playing with fire," Sheridan growled.

Lily knew it, and she was intoxicated. This perfect statue of a man, this controlled courtier, had finally come to life—and *she* had done it!

"Tell *me* what you're doing here, and let me be the judge of that," she suggested.

"You know damned well what I'm doing," Sheridan said. "And since you're here, you can damned well help me out. I've been talking to the servants. This greenhouse is always locked and it's supposed to be guarded. Nothing's locked up at the Hall, and a kid with a bent pin could open the old lady's jewel box—plenty of pretties there, too, but *it's* not there. It has to be somewhere in this greenhouse."

"What does?"

"The Hayvenhurst Emerald, of course. And since you walked in on me, you can show me where it is, or—" Sheridan paused menacingly.

"The gang of thieves," Lily said slowly, "the gang you warned us about. They never existed, did they?"

"Sure they did. I'm them," Sheridan said ungrammatically.

"And there aren't any Irish estates either, are there? You're as poor as I am. No wonder you lost interest when you found out I didn't control Julian's fortune!"

"Quick mind," Sheridan said admiringly. "I admire that in a woman. Not often you get brains and beauty too. I want you to know, Lily, if you'd had money, I *would* have married you."

"You'd probably marry your own grandmother if she had enough money!"

Sheridan thought it over briefly. "Couldn't. Against the law."

"And what makes you think I would have married *you?*"

"Oh, you would," he said with maddening confidence. "I can tell. But now you're going to tell me where the emerald is hidden, if you want to keep your pretty head on your shoulders."

It was too much for Lily. Robert didn't want her. Fairfax had only been looking for a rich wife. And he thought the Hayvenhurst Emerald was going to solve all his problems. It would all be tragic if it weren't so absurd, or funny if it weren't tragic—she couldn't decide which. She let out a whoop of laughter that changed to a sob in midbreath, choked, laughed, felt tears streaming down her face and did nothing to stop them.

"Damn it, Lily, don't get hysterical!" Sheridan snatched up a watering can from the floor and held it ready to dash the scummy water into her face. The horror of that prospect inspired Lily to draw a long shaky breath and at least try to calm down. But the sight of Sheridan's grubby hands set her off again.

"You poor idiot," she gasped between giggles, "you mean you went to all this trouble, you made up that story about a gang of thieves so you could . . ." She spluttered and gasped and started again. ". . . so you could worm your way into the Hall and steal a *flower?*"

"No." There was a dangerous edge to Sheridan's voice. He put down the watering can and raised his hands to the level of Lily's neck. "Not a flower. The Hayvenhurst Emerald. And now you're going to stop giggling and tell me—where—it—is!" On the last words he put his hands around her neck, squeezing just lightly enough to punctuate his threat. Lily thought she should have been afraid now, but she was still caught up in her hysterical laughter.

"I am—I did!" she managed to say between sobs and laughs. "It's there—and there—and there!" She pointed at the spectacularly ugly greenish-white orchid that bloomed all over the greenhouse. The limp stems hung from the ceiling, sprouted from banks of moss, trailed across windowpanes, bearing their bloated green-tinted flowers like globs of pale unhealthy flesh.

"You're mad," Sheridan said, but without conviction. His hands dropped limply away from her throat. They rested, heavy and lifeless, on Lily's slender shoulders.

"No. That really is the Hayvenhurst Emerald. I *am* sorry, Fairfax," Lily said. "You've had a lot of work for nothing. This is it. My dear Julian was a fanatical plant collector—you knew that, didn't you? And it seems a green orchid is a rarity that will be highly prized in the plant world—though I can't imagine why," she said with a shuddering glance at the pallid, bulbous growths. "Poor Julian brought the parent plant back from his last expedition in Brazil. It cost him his life; he never recovered from that last attack of malarial fever. *I* wanted to burn the hideous thing," she said, "but Dagmar said it would be a—a memorial to his life's work. She said it was more precious than any jewel."

"*Is* it?" Sheridan asked eagerly.

Lily shrugged. "Well, when Dagmar unveils it at the next meeting of the Royal Horticultural Society, I'm sure all those old botanical professors will be most excited. But as for getting *money* for it—no, Fairfax," she told him gently. "Oh, Dagmar has a bee in her bonnet about some other horticulturalist stealing an example before she can get the plant recognized as Julian's discovery. But I don't think even a professor of botany would pay much for a cutting. And it's worth—just precisely nothing—to anybody else!" Hysterical laughs began to interrupt her speech again. "Like me—just for show—not worth much to anybody!"

She laughed until the tears streamed down her face and her head buzzed. Fairfax Sheridan tightened his grip on her shoulders until she cried out with the pain.

"Stop that!" he said thickly. "Stop it, you idiot woman—you'll have everybody in the Hall coming to find out how a screaming hyena got into the greenhouse!"

"I don't care!" Lily threw back her head and laughed through the shaking Sheridan was giving her.

"*But I do,*" Sheridan said through his teeth, and his mouth descended on hers, heavy, bruising, demanding. What had begun in anger turned to passion; Lily knew the moment of the change in Sheridan. It happened to her in the same moment. A feverish, sensual excitement overwhelmed her. This mad Irishman was from a different world than the polite gentlemen who'd courted Lily, roused unsatisfied longings with their diffident kisses, then left her bored and unhappy after a few strenuous moments in bed.

He was pushing her down among the dirt and the broken pots now, and Lily let him; her hands clawed on his back and drew him down to her, on the rich earth-scented jungle of the greenhouse floor. Green vines and greenish white flowers trailed down from the benches and curtained their bodies. An animal heat rose through Lily, something quite unlike anything she had experienced before. She was shamelessly greedy for Fairfax Sheridan's stocky body, and she took what she wanted and gave him all he desired without thinking once of what this might be worth to her when they rose up from their improvised bed.

"I can't afford to marry you, Lily, my dear," Fairfax Sheridan said tenderly some time later. "Hold still—I've found a wee darling bit of greenery behind your sweet little ear."

"Mmm," Lily sighed when Fairfax kissed the place where the errant bit of broken vine had lodged in her hair. They were lounging in her bedroom, most improperly, but after that first explosion of passion Lily had realized that the greenhouse was a most uncomfortable place for a meeting and that they shouldn't risk being caught amid the destruction Fairfax had wreaked on the plants and pots. Giggling like children, they'd run hand in hand through the pelting rain to the massive lowering bulk of Hayvenhurst Hall, sneaked, dripping, up the stairs to Lily's bedroom, and shut themselves in for a leisurely evening. Fairfax had hidden behind the bed curtains while Lily rang for a servant and sent a message that she was too indisposed to come down for dinner.

"I can't afford to marry you, either," Lily told Fairfax serenely, "but I mean to anyway."

"What will we live on?"

"I have that little income for taking care of Gregor," Lily reminded him. "We'll elope tonight and take him with us. That stodgy old Tomkyns might fuss if we told him our plans. He might even check up on your past, and I have a feeling that would not do, would it, Fairfax, darling?"

"Not in the least," Sheridan admitted cheerfully. "It was quite true what I told the old battleaxe—er—I mean, your respected sister-in-law. I have indeed assisted the police with their inquiries. But I've done it by way of answering a great many impertinent questions by a great hulking brute of a police sergeant with the bad habit of shining a bright light on me while we talked. I've no desire at all to repeat the experience."

"And if old Tomkyns found out, he'd probably trump up some legal excuse for taking Gregor away from us. Not that I'd really mind," Lily admitted. "I haven't done at all well by the poor little brat."

"Nonsense," Sheridan said, nuzzling his face against Lily's half-uncovered breasts. "A darling, sweet, tender-hearted girl like you? He's been lucky to have you."

"The trouble is," Lily mused aloud, "if we lose Gregor, we lose the income. So I think we'd better leave before morning. With him. We can write from the Continent and tell old Tomkyns to send the money to Paris—or maybe Nice . . ."

"You think he won't kick up much fuss if we present him with a fait accompli?"

"A what?"

"Once we're settled abroad," Fairfax said, "I shall read to you every night, darling girl. A knowledge of the classics and a smattering of foreign tongues is a great advantage to people in our line of work. Now, just how are we going to get away from this godforsaken country hole without anybody noticing?"

Lily explained her plan while Fairfax Sheridan lounged on the bed and played with the strings of her negligee and did his best to distract her.

"One thing, though," he said when she'd finished. "Your plan sounds like a bit of a nuisance. Solicitors always kick up a dust. And we'd have to leave a forwarding address."

"Yes, but we must have *something* to live on!" Lily cried in exasperation.

"And so we shall, darling blue eyes, so we shall." Sheridan reached down to the floor for his discarded coat, felt in the breast pocket, drew out a small object, and waggled it before Lily's face. "Remember what I was telling you in the greenhouse?"

When Lily understood Sheridan's meaning, she burst into laughter and agreed that his plan was better than hers. And when they'd gone over the details to her satisfaction, she lay back on the bed and they worked out another kind of collaboration that gave mutual satisfaction until a thundering on the door interrupted them.

Lady Hayvenhurst was saying something about propriety. Robert brushed past her and repeated his thunderous pounding on Lily's bedroom door. "To the devil with your conventions!" he snapped over his shoulder. "The woman I love is in there, and I want her—now!"

Lady Hayvenhurst shrugged her shoulders. "Oh, very well. My sister-in-law has no more use for decent manners than a cat would have, and if you feel the same way, who am I to disturb love's young dream? You'll be sorry later, though."

Robert shook his head and banged on the door for the third time. Why on earth was the woman maundering on about Lily? And why was Lily taking so long to open her door?

At last the bedroom door swung open and Lily stood silhouetted in the light from her lamp, a vision of delight swathed in something flowing and half transparent, with her hair for once not carefully coiffed but tumbling in a damp stream down over her shoulders. Her eyes were bright and her lips looked fuller than Robert remembered.

She looked, in fact, like a woman who expected to be made love to. Robert quailed, remembering that he had not yet formally broken his engagement to Lily. And there was Gregor to think of, too. But, dash it, there was also Cressida, and she'd been with Lily for *hours* now. Hadn't she broken the news?

"Oh—it's you," Lily said, and Robert felt a tide of relief

washing over him. Whatever she did or did not expect of him, at least Lily wasn't in a mood for declarations of passion. "Whatever is it, Robert? And can't it wait until morning? I sent a message that I was feeling ill—"

"Won't trouble you for more than a moment," Robert said. "It's Cressida."

Lily stared. "Who?"

"Er—Jane. Your maid. I must speak with her," Robert said, feeling rather desperate as Lily still blocked the doorway. "Look, Lily. Things aren't what they seem. I'll explain later. But Jane has been with you all afternoon and evening—"

Lily shook her pretty head and all the yellow curls bounced around her face. "No. Oh, dear!" she cried softly, and Robert felt sure her air of dismay was assumed. "Didn't she tell you? That was too bad of her, seeing what you two have been to one another. Jane gave notice immediately after we returned to the house, Robert, and I haven't seen her since. She said that she wanted to get away from all the gentlemen like you and Waverley who only wanted one thing from her."

A day earlier Robert might have believed that Cressida could reject him like that. Now he knew that Lily was lying. "I don't believe you," he told her with a pleasant smile. "Nobody has seen her since you called her to wait on you. I think you've got her in here and you're trying to keep us apart."

Lily tightened her grip on the door frame. "You're mad," she said. "Go away. I *may* speak with you in the morning—if you're ready to be reasonable by then."

"If she's not there, you'll have no objection to letting me look around," Robert said. He smiled again. "Move aside, Lily. I don't want to hurt you—unless, of course, you've done something to hurt or frighten Cressida. In that case I just may forget that I'm a gentleman."

"Dagmar!" Lily appealed. "Will you let him behave like this in your house?"

"Yes, I think so," Lady Hayvenhurst said while Robert gently lifted Lily out of his way and went on into her room.

He thrust a curtain back from the arched window and raised his eyebrows in surprise at what he found there.

"So that's why she didn't want to let me in!" He had little hope now that he would find Cressida here, but he threw open the wardrobe doors and looked under the bed anyway. Then he returned to the hall, dragging his one discovery along by the arm.

"I found this on your window seat behind the curtains," Robert told Lily very politely, nodding at Fairfax Sheridan. "Under the circumstances—"

"I don't want to marry you anyway!" Lily exclaimed before Robert could finish his sentence. "I love Fairfax and we're going to be married—and you shan't stop us, Dagmar!"

"Why on earth would I wish to stop you?" Lady Hayvenhurst asked with genuine bewilderment.

Robert wondered what Lily and her new fiancé meant to do about Gregor. Somehow he had the feeling that Lily's brief attack of guilt was already forgotten. Probably they'd try to shove him back into that school or some other place just as bad. Poor boy! Maybe he could talk Lily into letting the kid live with him and Cressida instead.

Tonight, though, didn't seem the best time to raise the subject. Everyone was overwrought. Lily in particular seemed to be extremely excited. Perhaps tomorrow they could discuss the subject like rational beings.

Robert bowed and withdrew down the curving front stairs, closely followed by Lady Hayvenhurst. When they reached the ground floor he stopped and bowed again to her and began to make his apologies for leaving Hayvenhurst Hall so abruptly.

"Sit down, young man," Lady Hayvenhurst told him. She raised one shapely hand and motioned toward the small drawing room. "You're not going anywhere tonight."

"I *must*," Robert explained. "I must find Cressida—Jane. Who knows where she has gone?"

"Doubtless she has returned to her father's flat in London, and not before time, too," Lady Hayvenhurst said. "I have grown quite fond of your Cressida, and I quite understand her desire to get away from Augustine Parris's ramshackle way of life for a while. But it really will be more suitable for her to be married from her father's home, don't you think? And you would have had to go there anyway to get his permission."

Robert's jaw dropped and he stared at Lady Hayvenhurst until she told him briskly to stop imitating a bovine animal and to use his hypothetical intelligence on the matter at hand. "Of course I know who Cressy really is," she told him, "I've known all along. The child is the living image of her grandmother. If she wanted to be anonymous, she should have taken service at some place a little farther from her home village."

Lady Hayvenhurst explained that she had been discreetly keeping an eye on Cressida during the weeks she had been "in service" at Hayvenhurst Hall. Robert thought that Lady Hayvenhurst hadn't done so well at this as she seemed to imagine. But there was no point in quarreling over past errors, and he began to accept Lady Hayvenhurst's view of Cressida's disappearance.

"I expect Lily was atrociously rude to your Cressida," Lady Hayvenhurst said calmly when Robert told her a little about the distressing scene in the summerhouse. "She probably sacked her on the spot. And Cressida hates tantrums and loud voices and quarreling. The last train to London leaves at six-thirty, and Cressida had more than enough money for the fare. Go on up to Parris's Chelsea flat in the morning and you'll find her there."

"She wouldn't have left without saying good-bye to me," Robert insisted.

Lady Hayvenhurst fixed him with a sardonic eye that made him feel about ten years old. "No? Your Cressida *does* tend to run away from situations."

"That," Robert said, "was before she had me to protect her." But under Lady Hayvenhurst's withering glance he did not feel like much of a protector. Perhaps, after all, Cressida had simply returned to London, assuming he would be bright enough to follow. He couldn't think where else she might have gone.

Catherine Lyndell

"You're sure the six-thirty was the last train to London?"

Lady Hayvenhurst nodded. "And before you ask—no, I'll not lend you a carriage so that you can go chasing after her! What sort of impression do you think you'd make, arriving after midnight? You can take the morning train, call at a decent hour, and speak to her father. That's how these things are properly arranged."

In all the confusion of that evening, nobody noticed Gregor. The adults of the household were not entirely to blame for this; one thing Gregor had learned at his horrible school was the art of being inconspicuous. That had saved him some painful moments. So had his bad habit of listening at doors to other people's conversations; and since nobody had ever told him this was wrong, he could not really be blamed for continuing this habit when he was sent home from school.

In fact, what happened to Gregor that evening was nobody's fault, least of all his own.

He had been in his room, reading quietly and hoping nobody would remember his existence, when Lily came into the adjoining room with Fairfax Sheridan. The damp giggles and wet smacking kisses interested him not at all, but the desultory conversation that came between kisses captured his attention with the first mention of his name. Thereafter he listened avidly, standing by the door with his ear pressed to the crack, while his skinny body slowly grew cold and stiff in the draft from the window.

He did not understand all of what Lily and Fairfax said—there was some giggling about bent hatpins, for instance, which completely passed over his head—but he took in enough to frighten him badly, especially when Robert burst into the room.

His darling Jane, whom Robert for some reason called Cressida, had disappeared. And Robert wasn't going to marry his stepmother. Instead, Lily was going to marry that Irishman who pinched his cheek and laughed at everything he said, and he was going to be taken to Europe to live in hotels with them. No Robert—no Jane—no countryside to explore and play and dream in!

It wasn't fair!

Gregor sat up late that night and came to the conclusion that there was only one thing to do. Robert might think Jane—Cressida—had gone to London, but Gregor was sure she wouldn't do that. She hated cities. No, Cressida—he really would have to learn to call her that—*Cressida* was unhappy about something, or she wouldn't have run away. And she would have gone to the place she always talked about when she was sad, the garden by the river with flowers growing down to the water's edge, the place where the two of them were going to live together when he grew up.

It had been thoughtless of Cressida to leave without him, but he could forgive her—she was probably upset at the time, and she didn't know he would have to run away too. She was only a girl; he should be able to catch up with her quite easily. All he had to do was to follow the river.

It didn't occur to Gregor that there was more than one river in England, or that the old house called Riversedge could be farther away than a small boy might be able to walk. At nine he was capable of constructing long tortuous chains of logical reasoning, but he still left a few facts out from time to time. That night it seemed quite simple to him. The lake at the bottom of the Hayvenhurst gardens flowed into a stream that joined a river. Cressida's house was on the edge of a river. He would simply walk along the bank until he found her.

In the middle of the night, with the thunderstorm still rumbling intermittently overhead, and with his stepmother and Fairfax Sheridan snoring together in the next room, this reasoning seemed to make perfect sense. Gregor dressed in darkness, opened his window to the light of distant lightning flashes, and knotted his sheets together in the best tradition of heroic escapes. He burned his palms sliding to the ground, and the sheets stopped several feet too soon so that he landed hard and almost twisted his ankle, but he didn't cry out at either of these minor mishaps. Cressida, he thought as he licked one stinging hand, would have been proud of him. She *would* be proud of him, when she heard what he'd gone through to join her. All he had to do now was to find her. . . .

The Long Walk, so peaceful and friendly by day, turned into an arcade of slimy monsters of inchoate shape under the rain and the occasional flashes of lightning. Gregor was almost relieved when the rain streaked his pebble lenses so thickly that he could no longer see through them. He tucked the spectacles in his shirt pocket and crept on through a vague, blurry world illuminated in bits and pieces by the momentary crackle of electricity. Fortunately he knew the lake shore quite well, right down to the little creek that drained into the River Marsh. The only thing was, he wasn't quite sure how far the little creek went before he reached the riverbank. And his shoes squelched in the soft mud of the banks and made this part of the journey quite unpleasant. Gregor set his teeth and stumbled on, trying not to think of the rain on his face and the way the mud sucked at his shoes.

He was still carefully not thinking of these things when the mud under his feet turned into a rain-drenched slope and he tried to put his free foot down upon the air. His other foot shot out from under him and he went rolling and tumbling down the bank of the rain-swollen River Marsh. His fingers brushed something and he clutched at it—a branch; for a moment his fall was stayed, then he was in the river and the broken branch was in his hands, and the black, invisible current was sweeping him downstream far faster than he had planned to go.

Chapter

17

*L*ady Hayvenhurst and Robert Glenford entered the oak-paneled dining room of Hayvenhurst Hall from different directions. Both looked agitated.

"I'm glad I finally found you," Robert announced. He waved an ink-smeared bit of paper in the air. "Have you seen this? We'll have to go after him at once!"

" 'Them,' not 'him,' " Lady Hayvenhurst corrected. "How did you know they'd broken into my jewel box?"

"Gregor wouldn't do something like that!"

"Gregor? Are you mad? I'm talking about my sister-in-law and that stage Irishman she's decided to espouse. They even had the impudence to leave a note!" Lady Hayvenhurst waved her own bit of paper in front of Robert.

Eventually they both calmed down enough to compare notes.

Lady Hayvenhurst had awakened to find her jewel box standing open and most of the best pieces gone. In their place was a slightly cheeky note from Lily, explaining that she and Fairfax Sheridan would need the money far more than Lady Hayvenhurst and pointing out that she had left the opals and turquoises, "which she says," Lady Hayvenhurst repeated with indignation, "are more suitable for a woman of my age than precious gemstones!" Abruptly she sat down and began to laugh. "Lily was always a greedy little thing, and this time she's overreached herself. I wonder what she'll say when she learns that the diamonds and rubies were paste copies."

"Paste?" Robert repeated.

"You don't think I'm such a fool as to keep my good pieces in that trumpery lacquer-ware box, do you? They're on deposit at the bank." Lady Hayvenhurst began to laugh again. "Well, the settings are real enough. She's welcome to melt them down for what she can get. And I've changed my mind. Why go after that precious pair? We're all better off without her."

Months later, Robert heard rumors of the beautiful blond woman in Switzerland who posed as "Lady Hayvenhurst" and enticed young men into card games with her husband by wagering her jewels with an air of desperation. By that time, however, he had learned a little discretion, so he never told Lady Hayvenhurst what use Lily had made of the stolen replicas.

Now, though, thoughts of Lily were far from his mind. "I didn't mean to go after her," Robert said quietly. "It's Gregor I'm worried about."

The ink-stained note had been left under Robert's door sometime during the night. Gregor wrote that he knew his stepmother was planning to take him away with her new husband and that he didn't intend to go. He was going somewhere else first, and he didn't want Robert to worry, but would he please, *please* not tell Lily where Gregor had gone?

"Idiot," said Robert, scowling over the barely legible note. "How the devil can I tell anybody where he is if he doesn't say where he's going? And to take off in a storm like that, without a word to anyone—"

"He must have assumed you would know where he meant to go."

Robert threw up his hands. "*I?* I barely know the boy! He must have taken shelter with one of his friends."

"Gregor doesn't *have* any friends in the neighborhood," Lady Hayvenhurst pointed out. "He was always traveling with my brother, and then Lily put him in that school. In any case, he doesn't get on well with boys of his own age. The only person he spent much time with here was . . ."

They looked at one another.

"Cressida?" Robert and Lady Hayvenhurst said simultaneously.

"She used to talk to him about Riversedge," Robert said. "Made it sound like heaven on earth. I don't suppose— He couldn't have made it that far, of course—it's ten or twelve miles from here to Middleham by road."

Far less, of course, if you followed the straight course of the River Marsh to its junction with the Trent. But Gregor wouldn't have known about that route. Would he? As they were waiting for the gig to be brought around, Robert listened to the faraway roar of the rain-swollen river and shuddered. If they *didn't* find a footsore and repentant Gregor trudging along the winding country lanes that led to Middleham-on-Trent—if they *did* have to drag the river—

Robert firmly thrust that picture from his mind and concentrated on a much more attractive one: the image of himself thrashing that brat within an inch of his life for giving them all such a fright!

And the gig never did come around. Instead, well after Robert had fretted himself into a frenzy by carefully *not* thinking about Gregor and the river, there was the stately Sunday carriage, with four horses harnessed, and a sweating groom who wanted to explain that it was none of his fault if young Mrs. Whitworth had taken a notion to harness up the gig and take it out at first light, and that long ride she'd gone on yesterday was none of his fault either, and if you asked him—

"We didn't," said Robert. He handed Lady Hayvenhurst up into the carriage and jumped up beside her. "Never mind. Tell us later. I'll drive," he said all in one breath.

Robert was sick with apprehension by the time they reached Middleham-on-Trent. All the way along the rain-washed country lanes he had been looking for a small boy curled up in the shelter of a hedgerow, a tired boy trudging along the lanes on blistered feet. None of the farmers or carters they passed could remember seeing a child on the road; and the image of the tumbling, sleepy, powerful river was very strong in Robert's mind.

"Should we stop and ask the people in the village?" Lady Hayvenhurst suggested as they pulled into Middleham.

"What's the use? If he came this far—*I* don't know, maybe he got a lift with a carter or something—he'll be at Riversedge." Robert whipped up the horses and they passed through the village at a brisk trot.

The old house stood under the trees where it had always been, between the village and the River Trent. As he maneuvered the carriage up the rutted drive, Robert saw the signs of neglect: peeling paint, shutters hung awry, brown paper plastered across a cracked window.

None of these things mattered beside the one glorious fact that the front door stood open.

"He's here!"

"There may have been a housekeeper left to take care of the place while the family is away," Lady Hayvenhurst cautioned him. Her hands were clasped tightly together and her face showed the lines of encroaching age in the pitiless sunlight. All the way to Middleham she had said nothing but "I should have paid more heed to the child. *Julian's* child."

"He's here." Robert jumped down from the carriage, went to the horses' head, and gentled them until they stood still in this curious place of deep ruts underfoot and swaying, whispering shadows overhead. "A housekeeper wouldn't leave the door hanging open like that—or—" He sniffed the damp morning air. "Or toast sausages in the parlor. He's here," Robert repeated for the third time, "and I am going to half *kill* that boy for the fright he's given us!"

He went into the house like a storm wind, shouting for Gregor at the top of his voice; and subsided abruptly when he found two damp people huddled under blankets in the parlor, drinking cocoa and letting their sausages drip burning fat into the fire.

"Cressida?"

Her brown hair was drenched and hanging about her face in wet elf locks, and she was white with strain; but her smile dazzled him in the morning light, and he thought that he had never seen her so lovely.

"How did you get here?"

Cressida looked up from her kneeling position before the sputtering fire. Robert's tempestuous entrance seemed to have swept a gust of fresh morning air and sunlight into the damp parlor. She let out a deep sigh of relief and happiness and felt the enormous weight of Gregor's need and Lily's temper and everything else slip from her shoulders, quite simply, leaving nothing but herself and Robert in a room that seemed to be filled with morning glories bursting into bloom. Later she was to look at the parlor in some bemusement, observing that the cracked windows were closed and that the threadbare curtains were still drawn; but just now she rose to her feet in a cloud of white butterflies and moved toward a Robert who had brought the glory of the garden inside with him.

"I knew you'd come for me," she said happily.

He put his arms around her, warm and solid and real. Not the knight in shining armor of her dreams, but a real man whose tense embrace told Cressida just how desperately worried he had been.

"Yes, but—I thought you had gone to *London!*"

"Is that what Lily said?" Cressida realized that although she'd been right to trust Robert's love for her, she might have overrated his intelligence. Imagine him believing anything Lily Whitworth told him!

"More or less. We came here looking for Gregor."

Gregor looked terrible that morning. There was a long ugly scratch across his forehead, and he seemed to be naked under his blanket. But the thick pebble-lensed glasses were safe enough, and the beam he directed at Robert was blinding in its perfect certainty and joy.

"Jane—*Cressida,*" Gregor corrected himself painstakingly, "saved me. She jumped into the river and nearly drowned. It was flooded and so deep the water was over both our heads!" He dropped his toasting fork quite into the fire while he waved both hands to show Robert how high the water had risen.

Robert's face paled and his arms clutched Cressida so tightly she could barely breathe. "Nonsense, Gregor!" she said cheerfully before Robert could let his imagination run away with him and upset him. Men! They were so fragile and emotional. "You were quite safe on the island, and as soon as the water fell you could have waded across. I just didn't want to wait that long to be with you."

Robert put both hands on Cressida's shoulders and studied her face gravely. Cressida kept a bright smile on her face. Not for her life would she have confessed to Robert how frightened she had been when she waded into the roaring river, when her feet slipped while she brought Gregor back, that one very bad moment when the water had almost closed over her and Gregor.

She didn't need to tell him all that. She realized, meeting his grave look, that he knew it already. He knew just how cold and wet and frightened she had been.

"You will *never* do something like that again," he said in a low voice.

He was angry because he loved her, and because he had been frightened for her. Cressida leaned her forehead against his shoulder for a moment, feeling the strong play of muscles in his arm, the steady beat of his heart. How had she come to know so much without a word being said? A few days ago she would have shrunk from Robert's anger, would have convinced herself that it meant he didn't care for her, and then would have fled into a golden daydream in which nobody was ever angry and flowers never faded and winter never came.

Now she knew better. In every way. She had fought the river for Gregor and for her own life, and won, and the real world this morning was too bright and dear and precious to be traded for a misty daydream. This summer would pass, autumn would wither the flowers and winter would blow the dried seed heads into the air. And she would go into this cold turn of the year with Robert by her side, and that was better than any number of imagined eternal summers with some imaginary companion who never lost his temper or got tired or dirty or disheveled.

"And even if this summer ends, there will be another spring next year," she said softly. And maybe a new soul to greet that spring with them—if they were married *immediately*. . . .

"You," Robert said without conviction, "are quite mad, Cressida. Babbling. Making no sense at all. I suspect the dip in the river has turned your brains. It's a good thing you're marrying me—you need a keeper."

"I expect that's it," Cressida agreed. "I shall go completely mad soon, and drift around the house in my tattered wedding gown, talking to shadows. You'll have to lock me in the attic and pretend to everybody that your wife has gone away on an extended visit."

"Only if I get to come up to the attic at night."

"After the servants are asleep?"

"Of course. Nobody must know . . ."

"I think you're both mad!" Lady Hayvenhurst interrupted them.

"*And* letting the sausages burn!" Betty pushed into the room and rescued Gregor's toasting fork with the charred sausage on the end. "Knew it would end badly, letting you two camp out in the parlor like Gypsies when I was ready and willing to air out the best bedroom and cook you a proper meal." She handed the toasting fork back to Gregor and looked Robert up and down, hands on her hips. "And who might *you* be, young man, with your arm around my Cressy? No need to tell me—you haven't changed a bit, young Rob."

"I haven't?" Robert said with some dismay.

"Not in anything that counts," Cressida said. She snuggled closer into the bend of his arm. "Taller, maybe. Bigger shoulders. Even handsomer. Nothing important."

"I should like to know," said Lady Hayvenhurst in an

unaccustomedly plaintive tone, "I *should* like to know just how you two waifs of the storm came to be here."

In a slightly confusing chorus, Cressida and Gregor explained how they'd both come to be at Riversedge that morning.

"—left me here, and she must have thought I'd no recourse but to take the train to London—"

"—fell into the river, but I kept my glasses on—"

"—Lily wouldn't know I'd always lived in this county, of course. So I just walked through the village and knocked until Betty heard me—"

"—swam for *miles* and *miles* before the river washed me up on this island—"

"—thought I heard somebody crying in the middle of the night—"

"I wasn't crying. I was just calling for help!"

"To be sure you were," agreed Cressida at once, "and a very sensible thing to do, when you find yourself on an island in the middle of a river and it's pitch dark and you don't quite know how to get to the shore." She dropped her toasting fork again and hugged Gregor fiercely. "Only, next time take the *road*, won't you? When I think how near we came to losing you—" Her chin trembled and her eyes filled with tears.

"Nobody's lost," Robert said. He knelt on the carpet and put his arms around both Cressida and Gregor. "Nobody's *going* to be lost. Gregor won't have to run away again, because he's going to live with us." He looked over his shoulder at Lady Hayvenhurst. "Surely Lily can't claim him now? After abandoning him like this?"

"Am I really *abandoned?*" Gregor beamed at them.

It took a little while for Robert and Lady Hayvenhurst to explain their side of the story, and they were still talking when a tall, bearded man strode into the parlor.

"Cressida!" he boomed. "What, may I ask, is the meaning of this?"

Cressida jumped to her feet. The color that had been returning to her face drained out of it again, and she seemed smaller and slighter than she had been while she was holding Gregor. "P-Papa?" she stammered.

"I'm glad to see you still recognize your father's countenance," said Augustine Parris with heavy irony. He glanced around the room. "Ah, Glenford. What are *you* doing here? Isolde gave me to understand that Cressida ran away because she couldn't bear the sight of you. Now it looks as if you've compromised her thoroughly. Oh, well, as long as you're here, you can help me carry the canvases I came for."

"Canvases?" Cressida echoed.

"Some examples of my early work," Augustine Parris explained. "For my agent to show that American collector who bought *Girl with a Basket of Violets*. He hasn't bought any of my new sketches. Need something to get him interested again."

Robert cleared his throat. "Ah—sir? *I* bought *Girl with a Basket of Violets*." He put his arm around Cressida. "And now I want the original."

"You bought it?" Parris blinked. He ignored the rest of Robert's announcement. "Thought you were as poor as the rest of us. Oh, well, another thing those girls of mine got wrong, I suppose. Well, then! Come along with me. Since you can afford it, I've some prime examples of early Parrisiana to show you."

"Augustine Parris," Lady Hayvenhurst interrupted in her most majestic tones, "leave that boy alone! He doesn't want your paintings—it's your daughter he's after."

Parris blinked again. "And who the devil—saving your presence—but who *are* you, madame, and why are you interfering in a private sale of art?"

"I am Dagmar, Lady Hayvenhurst, and your dissipated life must be affecting either your eyesight or your mind if you don't recognize me when we've lived in the same county these thirty years. And I'm interfering, as you so graciously put it, because the rest of you don't have enough sense to cook a sausage without burning it, let alone manage your own lives." She plucked Gregor's toasting fork out of the fire and inspected the charred remnants of the sausage through her lorgnette. "I have been considering this aspect of the problem ever since dear Cressida took refuge in my house, being shocked—as well she might be—by your disgraceful carryings-on in London." Handing the toasting fork to Betty, Lady Hayvenhurst looked Augustine Parris over with a small, satisfied smile on her lips. Cressida had the distinct feeling that she liked what she saw. But why should that matter?

After a prolonged and disconcerting inspection, Lady Hayvenhurst gave a sharp nod. "Always thought the man had possibilities. And now we're both free—I'll do it," she said as if to herself. And then, to Augustine: "It's high time somebody took charge of you, Augustine. You were a conceited, self-centered little boy, and you haven't improved with the years. But you *are* talented, or were, and I suppose it's my duty to protect your talent."

"It is?" Parris seemed stunned by this turn of events.

"Certainly," Lady Hayvenhurst told him. "Do you think I should consider marrying again if it were not my clear duty? True, I have at times been lonely in my widowhood, but I should continue to cherish the memory of my dear Hayvenhurst were it not that other and higher considerations now supervene. You, Augustine Parris, have been on the road to ruin since your good wife's death. Not only are you a disgraceful father and a terrible manager of your own affairs, but you are wasting your God-given talent. You will undoubtedly drink yourself to death if you remain in London much longer. What you need is a quiet life on a country estate and someone to see to the mundane necessities of life for you while you devote yourself to your art."

"Marrying! But—but—"

"You will find Hayvenhurst Hall admirably suited to your artistic pursuits." Stopping Lady Hayvenhurst was rather like trying to stop a ship under full sail with a favoring wind. "Now that my sister-in-law has so obligingly removed herself—permanently, one hopes—I shall have that wing redecorated to give you a studio with a north-facing light. A quiet country life, far from your decadent friends and their self-destructive habits, will do much to restore the steadiness of your hand and the clarity of your eye."

"My hands do *not* shake!" Parris protested. He held up one hand, fingers outspread, to prove his point. All five fingers trembled slightly. "At least, not when I'm not dealing with madwomen—like—did you say a studio of my own?"

"Certainly," Lady Hayvenhurst affirmed.

"With a north light?"

"Nothing else would be suitable for this century's master of light and color."

"And of course you wouldn't let me be troubled by dunning tradesmen."

"Such persons never enter the grounds of Hayvenhurst Hall."

Parris subsided and Lady Hayvenhurst turned her attention to Cressida. "I shall write to Ponsonby Tomkyns at once, instructing him to begin proceedings to see that my sister-in-law is legally removed from her guardianship of Gregor. Since her flight to the Continent with my jewels and an Irishman of dubious respectability clearly shows her lack of interest in that guardianship, I do not expect the legal proceedings to cause any undue difficulty. In her place I wish to name you, Cressida."

"Me! But—"

"The boy is attached to you," Lady Hayvenhurst stated. "For myself, I find the care of the young excessively wearying; besides, having failed to observe how unhappy Gregor was, I do not consider myself qualified to act as his guardian." She descended from the magisterial pose for a moment and held out her hands in appeal to Cressida. "My dear, I'm too old to start raising a boy. Many more escapades like this one would kill me. Whereas you are young and energetic and think nothing of plunging into a flooded river to keep the child company. I ask you, who is better suited to take charge of him?"

With that rhetorical question she returned to her full speech-making mode. "In any event I must preserve the peace and quiet of my household so that my new husband can practice his art undisturbed. I think Gregor should live with you and Robert. You should be his legal guardian. And I will, of course, see that the income from Julian's estate for Gregor's upkeep passes to you.''

"Of course we want Gregor," Robert spoke for Cressida, "but we don't need the money.''

"I was not addressing you," Lady Hayvenhurst told him. "A woman should always have a little money of her own. Now, if everything's settled, I think we can find room in the carriage for all of us.''

"Three of you," Robert corrected. "Parris, we came without a groom. Will you drive Lady Hayvenhurst and Gregor back?''

"Er—yes. Certainly. Whatever you wish.''

Cressida wondered how long her father would remain stunned and passive. Not too long, was her guess. But Lady Hayvenhurst was right. He needed someone to take care of him. And already he was overcoming his regret for the fashionable dissipations of London, thinking about a studio and a north light and someone to serve him regular meals on time.

They would be good for each other.

"But what about you?" Parris asked Robert.

Cressida felt her prognostications about the future already coming true. She couldn't remember the last time Papa had troubled himself about anybody else. Already Lady Hayvenhurst was improving his character—and she hadn't really started yet.

"Oh, I think we'll stay here for a while." Robert's arm tightened round Cressida. "You can send a groom back with the carriage later. No hurry. As long as we're here," he said blandly, "I wish to inspect the house.''

Cressida gasped.

"I understand it's for sale," Robert said to the air, "and my bride and I will need somewhere to live.''

He kept his arm around Cressida and they stood in the doorway and watched while the other three got into the carriage and drove away. There were morning glories in bloom all around the open door, long tangled neglected vines covering the front of the house with blue and purple bells like an arch of flowers at a wedding, and Cressida felt as if they were already married.

So, judging from the kiss Robert gave her as soon as the carriage disappeared, did he.

"Betty said something about borrowing a cup of milk from the neighbors," he murmured in her ear.

"Mmm. The nearest neighbor is a quarter of a mile away." Cressida put her arms around Robert's neck and kissed him back with enthusiasm.

"The situation," Robert said, "verges on the improper." He unwound Cressida's arms from his neck and held her wrists in one hand. "And if you go on kissing me like that, Cressida, with a deserted house behind us and your face looking like that, I shall probably forget . . ."

He didn't get a chance to say what he might forget; Cressida kissed him again and he started drawing her back into the house. Cressida thought that if they went on this way there certainly would be a baby in the spring, and they probably should stop some time and get married. Only not now—she didn't want to interrupt what Robert was doing, and anyway the vicar would be busy lending Betty a cup of milk, and the house was *quite* empty just at the moment, and . . .

"Isolde," she murmured, "would be proud of me."

"Quite, quite mad," Robert said. "Making no sense at all. I'd better carry you up to the attic right this minute."

They didn't get quite that far.